PURGATORY MOUNT

Adam Roberts

This paperback first published in Great Britain in 2021 by Gollancz

First published in Great Britain in 2021 by Gollancz
an imprint of The Orion Publishing Group Ltd
Carmelite House, 50 Victoria Embankment
London EC4Y 0DZ

An Hachette UK Company

1 3 5 7 9 10 8 6 4 2

A CIP catalogue record for this book is
available from the British Library.

ISBN (Mass Market Paperback) 978 1 473 23095 8

Typeset at The Spartan Press Ltd,
Lymington, Hants

Printed and bound in Great Britain by Clays Ltd,
Elcograf S.p.A.

MIX
Paper from
responsible sources
FSC® C104740

www.gollancz.co.uk

Then there appeared a mountain, dark in the distance, and I,
Ulysses, tell you now: it was the tallest I had ever seen.

[*Inferno*, 26: 133–135]

Dante said: O Stephen will apologise. O, if not,
the eagles will come and pull out his eyes.—

> *Pull out his eyes,*
> *Apologise,*
> *Apologise,*
> *Pull out his eyes.*
>
> *Apologise,*
> *Pull out his eyes,*
> *Pull out his eyes,*
> *Apologise.*

[Joyce, *Portrait*]

Contents

One

The *Forward*

The *Forward*, interstellar exploration craft. Here, present, correct: its crew of five. To assist these brave explorers, the ship has been equipped with a great quantity of advanced technology and an even larger quantity of supplies, dry store as well as livestock – animals from pygs and sheep all the way down to chickens, mice and microbes. The ship was shaped like a kilometre-long church spire, a comparison that dates from the period when churches were architecture with common cultural currency. But only pygs go to church these days. So say, rather: the ship was shaped like a gigantic bullet, crafted of ice many hundreds of metres thick – shield, fuel and a reservoir all at once. Inside this titanic sheath was a structure made of metallic plastic, eighty major compartments and many smaller spaces and corridors, ship's supplies and life-support. The drive shaft extended fourteen hundred metres to the rear.

Now the *Forward* was entering the system of V538 Aurigae. The eagles are coming! The eagles are here!

The ship was shaped like a bullet to streamline it, because interstellar space is not a vacuum. It is, rather, an extremely attenuated gas: ions, atoms and molecules spread so thinly that one might encounter only a single atom in each cubic kilometre (or, of course, one might encounter areas considerably more

3

dense with particles). At the speeds needful for interstellar travel, even flying into the path of one molecule releases significant energy, and flying for centuries at very high speeds is, in effect, to fly through an atmosphere. Moreover, at such speeds, evasive action is sluggish and limited, and however good one's forward sensors, there is always the chance that your craft will encounter a damaging, perhaps even a catastrophic collision event on your travels. It all adds to the spice of the journey. But the *Forward* made it to V538 Aurigae without such disaster. Indeed, if one believed in Providence, one might find fortuity in the fact that our natal star, the Sun, happens to exist in what is called 'the Local Bubble', a relative cavity in the interstellar medium some 300 light-years in breadth and height, in which the density of space is markedly lower than the surroundings. The unusually sparse gaseous and molecular matter in this cavity is the result of a supernova explosion fifteen million years ago, the force of which cleared much of this space. This works to facilitate travel between stars in our local group. And so human beings pour into this space, flying in all directions, because, like Mallory with Everest, space in every direction *is there*. Dark, dark, dark – oh, we all go into the dark. It's almost as if Providence *wants* humanity to spread out from its natal star! Eagles leaving the nest.

Of course, you don't believe in Providence. No matter!

The five human beings crewing the *Forward* had travelled to V538 Aurigae to see for themselves. To check it out. They were coming to observe at first-hand a strange feature spotted on the third planet of this system, V538 Aurigae γ. This feature had been noted by a passing probe – an unmanned device which had been moving at a significant fraction of light speed and had come no closer to the Aurigaean system than half a light-year. At such distances and velocities no very detailed or precise data could be collected, although enough information returned (eventually) to Earth to suggest some unusual terrain on Aurigae γ. It was probably nothing. Certainly, nobody suspected that it might be an alien megastructure, or anything of that sort. No intelligent alien life had yet been encountered, and neither had any human being yet visited any archaeological remnant of vanished intelligent alien civilisations. Still, it gave the owners, which is to say the crew, of the *Forward* somewhere to go, something to look into.

They did not realise as they set off from Earth that they would strike gold.

As the *Forward* approached closer and closer to the Aurigaean system and was able to analyse better data from γ, the lineaments of the artefact became clearer. A pillar on a conical base, or perhaps it would be better described as a continuous hyperbolic tower. It stretched 142 kilometres above the surface of the planet, far above the atmosphere and into space. Presumably, therefore, the artefact represented an alien space elevator, or at least the remnants of one. As the *Forward* approached closer still, the data became more accurate and informative. The structure stood on a roughly circular island, two hundred kilometres across, and grew, as a mountain might, smoothly from the bedrock. It manifestly was not a naturally occurring element in the landscape: therefore, it had been constructed. But it had been constructed so as to resemble a massively elongated mountain, with its peak outside the air. There were many terraces running around the circumference, but twelve main ones. In all this it resembled the mountain of Purgatory, as described in Dante's medieval Italian epic, and so the crew began referring to it with that name. To be precise: Dante's fictional mount had possessed nine terraces, with one extra, a magic garden, at the very top; but this alien structure was close enough in broader resemblance for the name to stick.

5

There were no signs of contemporary industry, technology or life anywhere on γ.

The Captain (we can call them that, although it's not how they or their fellow crew members thought of them) walked the *Forward*'s corridors. The ship's infrastructure was a smart-shell which could reconfigure itself in various ways. When the mission settled into orbit around γ it would heat its skin to free itself from its giant ice-sheath, shake itself out slowly into a new config and start spinning to simulate gravity. As it was, still being inside its ice-hide, it was configged to be a varied and meaningful arrangement of different-sized chambers and linking corridors that, on the flight to γ, utilised the slow .2g acceleration to give the crew somewhere to walk on. And now that it was approaching its destination, the structure had recon-figged to turn former ceilings into new floors.

The deceleration pulled a rather more testing fraction of *g* than had the acceleration. But the Captain's body was quite strong enough to cope with that.

The Captain walked the corridors as they had done throughout the voyage. Each light-year of the forty traversed lasted them a week – which meant that this passage had entailed almost a whole year on duty, sleeping little, checking and monitoring much, personally patrolling their ship. The Captain could easily have watched their ship eat up the light-years more rapidly – that was, after all, what the other four crew members had done (one had watched the entire voyage pass in a month) – but the Captain did not judge such rapid passage compatible with their manifold shipboard duties. As it was, at a week per light-year, many circumstances and problems hurtled around them: the pygs and other animals on board raced hither and thither so rapidly they were blurred lines, more contrail than living creature. The ship's hal was able to sync its input-output to the Captain's, or at least it was able to do so *most* of the time.

6

In the event of a sudden and unexpected emergency, it naturally took the Cap time to gearshift up to the one-to-one of clock-time on board. Indeed, in many cases, the Captain preferred to overshoot, to in effect slow down clock-time relative to themself, one-to-one-point-five or even a higher ratio, to give them more time to consider and react – and that, of course, took them even longer to orchestrate. But emergencies were rare, and for most of the voyage the Captain was content to wander their ship, light-year markers passing weekly. They got a *sense* of how things were going that way: they could feel, intuit how the ship was operating, the temporal disparity notwithstanding.

As targeted deceleration ate into the *Forward*'s speed, the other four crew members slowly phased down their perceptual time-consciousnesses to something closer in ratio to shipboard clock-time. No reason to be abrupt about this. Don't bolt down your changes in temporal perception, or you'll get temporal indigestion, figuratively speaking. A complex of psychological impairments was associated with the 'bends' of enforced sudden-ness of perceptual temporal reorientation.

Do you do 'time'? Is that something in which you believe?

Well, all right then!

Let's talk names. The five crew members each had many different names, depending on which in-group, relation or specifics were concerned. For the purposes of the voyage, and within the interactions of their time together, they had adopted on-ship monikers, and although it is a little tricky to translate these, we can start with the crew member who was responsible for the animal life on board. They took their responsibilities seriously, and many times during the voyage this individual dialled down to actual clock-time in order to check on the biomes, to ponder the data assembled by the agribots, to run specific tests on livestock health and so on. They did this regardless of whether the ship's hal notified them of a specific issue – as for example

7

when, around the twenty-light-year mark, a glitch in agribot code meant that too many chickens and sheep were culled and butchered at once, such that these two animal populations almost died out, and new storage units had to be excavated from the ice in which to store the meat (it took six months for the stable populations of these animals to be re-established). When that happened, hal called on this person's expertise, you can be sure! But the longer the voyage continued, and even when there was no specific reason to dial down, this individual did so. It seemed they actually liked getting their hands in the soil, examining the animals and all suchlike labour.

For this reason, their fellow crew members called them Pan. To be clear (and at the risk of mere pedantry), the name 'Pan' was not the one they actually used. The name they actually used referenced a figure from a different culture-text altogether, one whose mere composition is hundreds of years in the future as I write this. Pan is an approximation, although a reasonable one. They were a figure gifted with magic (in the Clarkean sense of the word) and given responsibility over beasts, birds and plants, but who pursued that responsibility with a zeal that tipped them over into, as the others saw it, eccentricity.

If this crew member was Pan, then let's call the Captain Zeus. The analogy is weaker here but will serve. With the other three individuals – Apollo, Dionysus and Hades – the cultural translation is less and less helpful, more and more imprecise. But let's go with it. Why not?

Zeus, Apollo and Hades had worked together previously, many decades before – on a voyage to 61 Cygni and back again to Earth. All three liked the challenge, liked satisfying their outward urge and their curiosity. And the mission had been profitable! All three were meat-eaters, and Dionysus had a particular taste for pyg-meat, although, since they'd dialled themselves into a very steep perceptual–temporal gradient, they didn't eat very often. Their bodies subsisted on infed nutrients and hydration, and their consciousnesses, habituated to a accelerated perceptual rhythm, were rarely moved to enjoy food as a somatic delicacy. This meant that the pyg population increased significantly over the course of the voyage. But that was all right.

And now, all five of the crew adjusted themselves increment-ally towards a closer perceptual approximation of clock-time. There was no hurry. Deceleration took a while, and the closer they got the more data they received. Of course, they wouldn't start getting really tasty info on the artefact – this strange pillar, this alien Purgatory Mount – until they were actually in orbit, and exploring it in person.

Captain Zeus stalked the corridors and chambers of their ship. The pygs and chickens and deer streaking past them moved, day by day, slower and slower. From their point of view, of course, the Captain, having marched with almost impercept-ible slowness for decades – for their whole lives, and the lives of their parents and parents' parents – having, indeed, been wor-shipped as an actual god in pyg societies – was now, for reasons that went beyond what they could ever understand, *speeding up*. It was no wonder that the pygs grew too terrified to approach the Captain as they made their way about the craft.

Daft little critters.

'If,' says Apollo, using their actual voice now that they and Zeus were within easy perceiving distance of one another, 'it's a space elevator, or the remains of one, then we would surely expect to see other artefacts – space stations, perhaps abandoned; structures on other planets, perhaps abandoned.'

Apollo sounded like Apollo to Apollo, but to Captain Zeus their voice sounded low and rumbling and rather splendidly menacing.

'Agreed,' Zeus said. 'And yet nothing is showing up on any scan or scope.'

9

Zeus sounded like Zeus to Zeus, but their voice was high and piping and pleasantly comical to Apollo.

Apollo basso-profundo'd: 'Unless we're looking for the wrong sort of thing.'

'Or,' squeaked Zeus, 'unless it was never a space elevator in the first place. Unless it served some other purpose.'

'Political dominance,' low-groaned Apollo, Paul Robeson style. 'Religious observation – perhaps it's a gigantic cathedral. For all we know, it is hollow. It could be positively riddled with chambers. And who knows what might be inside such interior spaces?'

'For all we know,' squealed Zeus, 'it contains alien technological wonders. Faster than light drives. Time machines. We can't be sure until we actually go there – step out upon that alien world, walk through those alien chambers!'

'A structure of such dimensions, such sheer *height*,' boomed Apollo, 'were it made of mere rock, would long since have collapsed back into an entropic heap of rubble. Therefore it must be, either, constructed wholly of some super-strong material, or else reinforced within with ribs and spars of such a kind of stuff. And that in itself would be a discovery of history-altering dimensions. We could return to Earth with the wherewithal, finally, to build a Dyson sphere!'

In this fashion they dreamed, wide awake, of what the consequences of their voyage of discovery might be. And as they chatted, their voices slowly converging, from below and above, on a common timbre, Pan was silently going about their work, testing the soil in the various ship's biomes, collating data on the various animals, wandering the faux-forests and communing with the beasts. An artificial balance was maintained in the ship's artificial environment. Most of the animals were herbivores and insectivores, to keep the vegetation and insects in check, and the lack of carnivores – apart, of course, from the pygs, and a few flying raptors – meant that these creatures were prone to unexpected population booms that had to be controlled by the ship's systems directly. When the chickens, the goats or the sheep began to overbreed, agribots would cull the populations, and the meat would be stored for the crew to consume later. Pan did not like this. That is to say, they didn't like the final destination of the meat (being vegetarian themselves, they barely tolerated their crew mates eating flesh) but, worse, they disliked the *inelegance* of it. In their mind, the perfect ship's mission would be built around a *self-sustaining* string of biomes. Pan yearned for natural harmony, and in their downtime they studied how large a craft would have to be to manage such a thing. Very large, it seemed. Very much larger than the *Forward*.

And so these five decelerated towards γ, and towards Purgatory Mount.

:2:

The mysteries associated with this mountain were not dispelled by closer inspection. The *Forward* settled into a comfortable orbit around γ – unofficially named Dante by Zeus, and subversively referred to variously as Dantette and Aligbarely and Planet Comedy by Hades – and sent down a glitter cloud of drones and probes. The orbit rolled the ship leisurely around the dayside and nightside in forty minutes, which meant crew members could sit at the observation blister and stare at the landscape-seascape below. It was hypnotic. Hades extrapolated from the first deep-dive data that the planet had once enjoyed a hundred thousand pascals of pressure at sea level. This had dropped, now, to a quarter of its former level, and the sea levels were in retreat, with associated dieback of even the hardy, rudimentary vegetation that characterised this world's only life form.

'We've arrived, by remarkable good luck, while this process is ongoing,' Hades told the others, over supper (chicken casserole and fresh vegetables for all, save only Pan, who watched the others with a pained expression on their face and picked at a salad). 'In another, let's say, fifty thousand years the atmosphere will have leaked almost entirely away – the surface sea will finally evaporate and the surface atmosphere will reduce to a number of hundreds of pascals. Like Mars, before we started reforming it. It will become a desert and dead world.'

'It's already dead,' grumbled Apollo.

Pan, uncharacteristically, was moved to conversational inter-action.

'It has vegetation,' they pointed out.

'I'm talking about the sort of life I can hunt and eat,' said Apollo, with a menacing smile.

'You can eat vegetables,' Pan observed mildly.

'I can,' said Apollo, spearing a gobbet of spice-fried chicken on one chopstick and holding it up, 'but I prefer meat.'

'At any rate, I challenge your prognosis,' said Zeus, haughtily. 'Dante is much closer to its star than Mars is to the sun, which means considerably more energy is being pumped into its global system. I suggest the atmosphere will *entirely* boil away in much fewer than fifty thousand years.'

'If it had the mass of Mars,' said Hades, looking contemptuous in the face of this challenge to their authority (it being not offensive enough to merit calling the Captain out in a duel, but enough to incommode Hades in the enjoyment of their meal), 'then you would be correct. But the earth-like mass of this planet –' not giving Zeus the satisfaction of using their naming for it – 'means that it will be millions, not mere thousands, of years before atmospheric gases finally absent themselves altogether.'

They shunted a rack of calculations and equations into the crew's shared Social and watched as Zeus pointedly ignored the data.

'I'm more interested,' the Captain said, 'in the past than the future. Once upon a time, as the Brothers Grimm might have said, intelligent beings lived here. They assembled, or sculpted, or somehow created this structure. Why? More to the point – how? Our job, comrades mine, is to master the technologies involved. We're forty light-years from Earth – once the images from our data arrive home it will poke a stick deep in the beehive. It will excite a lot of interest. I'd say we have a century or so before the next wave of excited tourists and speculators and maniacs come buzzing round our discovery. Will a century be long enough?'

'To unlock all these mysteries?' Dionysus said. 'I say – yes.'

'I, on the other hand,' said the more cautious Apollo, 'believe we must triage the specific questions we wish to address.' When a person lives tens of thousands of years, a mere century comes, of course, to seem a blip. 'I propose – the structural ones are the most lucrative. If we can replicate whatever it was that enabled our long-gone builders to combine this kind of scale with this kind of rigidity and durability, then we will have the most valuable intellectual property in the history of humanity. It will unlock the ability to build any and every megastructure humanity could conceive!'

'Agreed,' said Zeus.

'One might wonder,' Pan said quietly, 'why the original builders didn't go on to do precisely that?'

The others ignored this intervention.

'If nobody else is going to say it,' put in Hades, 'then I will.

13

We could dial down. We could, if we choose, turn this brief century of research into a thousand years.'

The other four only looked at them.

'I think I'll maintain my sanity, if you *don't* mind,' said Dionysus. They added: 'This chicken lacks flavour. Chicken always does. I suggest we have some roast pyg tomorrow. At least wrap this chicken in a bit of bacon, why not?'

'All right,' agreed Hades, speaking to the proposal to dial down, not to the question of bacon. 'A thousand years might be overambitious. But we can surely dial down a little, and so give ourselves more time?'

'Let's see how the first few clock-time years go,' suggested Zeus, in a conciliatory voice. 'And then we'll make a judgment, shall we?'

The problem, in a word, was *friction*. Not material friction, such as is experienced by these conker-sized probes raining down on Planet Dante, the air heating them cherry-red. Not that. Rather perceptual, cognitive and memorial friction. The mind rubs against the medium of life. That's the definition of living. Which is to say – ablation is the idiom of existence, and what is ablated over time eventually rubs away entirely. Take these five human beings. It is not physical or bodily decay that limits their lifespan to a few tens of thousands of years. Their bodies are capable of, more or less, unlimited self-repair and restoration. Short of a complete firestorm atomisation of their corporeal selves, these are bodies that will last and last. But the consciousnesses housed in those bodies, their carbon strands of mental tissue, howsoever augmented by silicon data processing capacity – well, that's a different matter. Mind grates against the medium in which it moves, or else it isn't thinking at all. Such friction eventually wears mind down. Memory goes first, overloaded by the sheer accumulation of lived experience and information. But memory is also the easiest to prop up with artificial prostheses. Humankind's first forays into technological enhancement was, after all, precisely the restoration and propping up of functioning memory. The earliest computers were talented at remembering things, storing immense quantities of data and retrieving it briskly and accurately; and it soon followed that the first somatic adaptions to incorporate this tech plugged and resolved memory issues. But memory is only one element of consciousness, and even with unlimited artificial memory and flawless recall, the *will* to recall eventually fails. Cognitive capacity can, likewise, be bolstered, but it too eventually wears down to a mere stub. The last two things to go are mere perception – but who would want to live, if living meant merely sitting in a chair thoughtlessly aware of one's surroundings? – and the most stubbornly persistent of all the components of human consciousness, will itself. Some people do subsist on mere will, it is true, all other strands of their minds evacuated and empty and yet still, stubbornly, living on. It is a remarkable thing to see. One might even call it heroic, after the Pyrrhic mode of heroism. But it is not eternal. Even *will*, sooner or later, wears down. And then the individual dies.

So as these five humans stared down the lengthy boulevard of – a conservative estimate – another twenty thousand years of existence, it was *mental* existence they were contemplating. And mental existence, defined by friction, is the same whether you are dialled up to one perceptual minute to one clock-time day, or, on the contrary, are experiencing a whole day while the clock ticks through sixty seconds. Indeed, human beings had come to learn that the latter, the artificial *intensification* of perception (measured with respect to the vibration of caesium atoms in the outer universe) tended to increase perceptual friction to the point where sanity, and life itself, became perilously eroded. Sometimes people indulged, of course, for any number of reasons. But it was smoother to ski fluidly downslope, to watch the universe as a whole flow by in fast-forward – to abbreviate what would otherwise be tediously drawn-out voyages from star to star, for example – than to do the other thing.

But humans are humans, and ever keen to compete with one another. The structural secrets of Purgatory Mount, if these five could uncover them, would make the team vastly wealthy – in terms of status and power (they were already vastly wealthy in terms of material goods and possibilities, of course) – and accordingly they wanted it. If the price of obtaining that knowledge was dialling down to extend the time available to them to unlock the mystery – before the hordes of other humans arrived, having been alerted to this tempting destination, shooting across the long, vacant light-years all the way to V538 Aurigae γ – then that is what they would do.

But maybe the mystery would be more tractable, and such desperate measures would not prove necessary.

'I suggest,' said Apollo, 'establishing a base at the foot of the mountain and spending a little while actually there.'

'What,' agreed Zeus, 'an excellent notion.'

Dessert was a St-Emilion au chocolat torte, followed by cognac laced with psychedelics, and a long and deliciously complicated series of nested trips for all the crew. Then: a refreshing sleep.

:3:

For the first twenty years of B's life the gods embodied the mystery of timelessness. You could sit in front of one for as long as you liked, fidgeting and restless as you inevitably were, and never see them move. Then you would run off, and spend a couple of weeks in some other part of the ship, and when you returned to the god you would discover that he was a yard further down the corridor. They never moved when you looked at them, but *still they moved*. It was one of the core and holy mysteries of religious faith, and B found in it an endless source of wonder and fascination.

He was not the most religious person in his family, or ingroup, but then again neither was he the least religious. He went to church on Saturday, like his friends and family. He believed some of what was preached, and with respect to other parts he had doubts. But it was part of his life, and he tried to get on with living as best he could.

There were plenty of folk who regarded the gods as false idols. Some of these people worshipped a god 'outside the ship', a vague and abstract quantity so far as B could understand it, like admiring strands of dissipating steam instead of drinking the actual coffee. This 'outsider' god had many names – *The Us, A-Lá, Old Jar of Hova* among others – most of which had been winkled out of the shipboard data systems. Hal was supposed to keep a tight rein on what people could access, since its job was maintaining the smooth functioning of the ship, and if people and animals obtained too detailed a sense of how the ship worked, they might (original sin, original sin in every breast) try to break it. But it was possible to sneak past hal's blocks and guidewires, and people on board generally knew more than hal realised they did – and much more than the crew, in their Olympian detachment, could ever have imagined. Folk knew, for instance, that the gods called them 'pygmies', and had discovered also what the word meant: *people of a diminutive stature*. In fact, B's people were none of them *that* much smaller than gods themselves. A few feet, maybe. But the meaning was not one of physical but of *temporal* dwarfism. Ordinary folk were born, grew, aged and died. The gods didn't, or if they did it was on timescales unimaginable to ordinary people. That was good enough for B. Why worship a god you couldn't see when the actual gods, in their sublime immobility, were *right here*?

See God the Grower, poised in a bizarre, impossible to imitate posture, reaching down – reaching past his centre of gravity and prevented from falling over only by the restraint and strength of his bodily servos. He was reaching down towards a stalk of wheat! Try, as a devotional exercise, to see things from God the Grower's point of view – as he reached down, in a single smooth gesture, the stalk of wheat would sprout and elongate, flowing up to meet his hand. Marvellous! Or dart past the terrifying carapace of God the Judger, offering up prayers of propitiation. To touch a god was to invite zaps from the shipbots, burning dabs at first, increasing in intensity to killing blasts for repeated offences. But some people reached out and touched God the Judger nonetheless and wore the resulting scars with pride. To win His favour was to enjoy, the superstition said, a blessed and felicitous life. B doubted this, but he respected the strength of faith that led some people to brush their fingers sacrilegiously, devotionally, against the shiny flank of the god.

Otherwise life was subsistence, and labour, and play, and (after the age of maturation) flirtation and courtship and sex. Religion was an important part, but only a part, of B's life, and that is as religion should be. Or so he thought.

Then things changed. The change happened in three phases.

First, a little after B's twentieth birthday, the gods began, visibly, walking around the world of the ship. And with that the great alteration began.

Ten was the age of maturation for B's people, and there was a celebration to mark the passage. B could see that the age was, in effect, arbitrarily chosen – ten years of age was 40,000 lived hours, and it was said (B was never quite sure from where the information had come – not from hal, at any rate, who guarded the personal secrets of the gods closely) that 40,000 *years* was how long a god lived, so this was the fitting time to mark maturation for the pygmies. B's family and friends gathered in church and songs were sung and beer was drunk and dances were danced. Afterwards B and Dufé ran away together. They had been planning this tryst for months, and although some couples consummated their relationship before the actual marriage-date, both B and Dufé were observant enough not to want to anger the gods by cheating on the vow that maturation entailed. They chased one another down the ship's corridors and through a vacant chamber whose walls were a pattern of hexagons glowing with different intensities of light, and then, laughing, down another corridor and into the biome they had selected for their first time. They chose it because God the Grower was there, and although he was heading now for the exit, he was still on site. Sex in proximity to the gods was thought to increase the chance of fertility. Afterwards, lying together on the moss, in among the orchard trees, laughing and panting, they observed the back of God the Grower.

'Forty thousand years!' Dufé said, in wonder.

'I don't believe it,' said B. 'It's not scripture. It's just a kind of rumour. I think the gods never die, that they never *can* die. How could they be a god, and die?'

Forty thousand years for a god was not, of course, the same scale as it would be for a human. Human measurements were set by hal and cleaved to a computer's sense of neatness: twenty hours a day, ten days a week, twenty weeks a year. But the gods came from another place, and to them a year was 8,766 hours – it had in some opaque way to do with *planetary orbital mechanics*, though B had never quite got to the bottom of what that all meant – so forty thousand god-years was more like a *hundred thousand* people-years. Dufé reminded B of this fact, but he insisted even a lifespan of one hundred thousand years was insufficient to manifest true godhead-ness.

'I prefer to be mortal,' said Dufé, flicking playfully at his ear. 'It means we live in the moment with greater intensity. Maybe the gods should envy *us*?'

At ten B agreed. But by the age of twenty he was starting to think: why do people have to die so young? Most of the people he knew were gone by forty, and only a few ancient gaspers lived to forty-five. The oldest person B had ever seen, a woman who lived in a treetop house in Biome 7a, was forty-nine. It was a matter of intense if disinterested curiosity among the other pygmies whether she would make it to fifty.

'We'll throw a party if she does,' said Lare. 'A super party.'

But where the others were looking forward, B was brooding on what had already gone: how quickly his twenty years of life had slipped past him, and how precipitously his own death was approaching. If the gods could live to be a hundred thousand, or perhaps live forever, couldn't they gift a devout believer like B a *little* more life? And indeed there was a sect that believed the right incantations and prayers would induce the gods to gift pygmy humanity a magic elixir that would extend life, but they were extremists – dyeing their hair white, poking out their eyes and chanting the phrase *I want more lifefuckerlife lifefuckerlife* over and over – and B was repelled by oddball cults like that. Such groups came and went. True religion endured.

Was there not a simpler solution to this mystery?

'We're planning the fiftieth,' said Case, one morning. So it seemed the old woman in 7a was still breathing. 'We want you to go hunt some chickens.'

'Oh, man, what?' said B – since that meant a long trek.

He could, of course, simply hunt the neighbourhood chickens. No doubt their flesh was as tasty as the taste of foreign chickens.

But the neighbourhood chickens were regarded as tabu, so hunters were obliged to trek far distances from home.

'Can't somebody else go get the chickens?' he said. 'Ask Jerí. She's an experienced hunter. I'm not.'

Case smacked him, hard, in the face – it hurt, and the skin there was red for hours afterwards.

'You're in your twenties, aren't you?'

'Yes,' conceded B sullenly, sat on his arse on the ground and holding a hand to his stinging face.

'When was your twentieth?'

'A week ago.'

'So you're a hunter now. Go bring some chickens. Jerí's going too, don't worry. We need lots of food – it's going to be a feast the like of which the ship has never seen before!'

There was nothing for it, but B didn't go straight away. For one thing his face hurt, so he went into Biome 4, a smaller dome through which a sedge-clogged river ran, slowly. Here he found cool mud to slap on his reddened cheek, and then he took a long draught of water and sat under a tree and thought for a bit. He had no idea how to go about hunting, but if he asked Case, or anybody else, he would only get scolded, or beaten, or worse. He wondered about finding a console and asking hal. That, though, ran the risk of alerting hal to the fact that some of the ship's pygmies were culling chickens, and that was risky – it might be in violation of ship's quota or something or anything. Such things were imposed from time to time, for reasons that were baffling to ordinary folk. They were as arbitrarily withdrawn. Better keep hal out of it.

In the end he asked some of the neighbourhood chickens what to do. It felt a little weird, since he was quite specifically asking their help in killing their kind, but they didn't seem to mind.

'We're not as clever as you,' said the first chicken he asked.

'We have simple implants. Eat bugs! Eat the bad bugs, leave the good bugs, clean up the rubbish, cluck and strut!'

'Assume I wanted to hunt and catch one of you,' B asked. 'What would you suggest?'

But counterfactuals were beyond a chicken's ken.

'What?' it asked, putting its head back. 'Whaaaat wha'-wha'-wha'-?' It pivoted and pecked at something in among the grass. When it rotated back upright again, it looked puzzled. 'You? Who are you?'

'We were just talking.'

'Yes! Yaaaas ye'ye'ye'yeh. B?'

'That's right.'

'Hello!'

'What do you fear from a hunter?'

'The hood! The *hood*! B'KAA!' wailed the chicken.

It jumped in the air and ran a zigzag sprint in a widening arc. Then it got distracted by an inchworm arching making its slow way along a branch, from omega to hyphen, and back again. Peck, and miss. Peck and snack.

By then B was on his way. *The hood*.

He stopped off at home, fashioned a flap of cloth into a hood on a stick, and came back out again. Trying this on the local chickens proved its efficacy. Then it was just a matter of supplies. You couldn't always trust the water in far distant corridors, which might be stale, or worse. So he filled a plastic pouch with a couple of litres and grabbed some waybread and took his chicken-catching stick and headed off.

That was where the problems started. B passed through two rooms, a minor biome and finally down the corridor of God the Trickster. For all of B's two decades of life, God the Trickster had stood at the far end of this corridor. If there had been any motion in this god's body, it was not evident to B. Sometimes people would argue, in the spirit of earnest religious disputation, that God the Trickster's left foot, or perhaps his right hand, had shifted by some infinitesimal. But B never saw it. For all his life this holy corridor had been a sacred space, guarded by its motionless god.

Very good. Very good. So now B took this path through to the distant lands – not a shortcut, exactly; more the opportunity to pay homage, in passing, to the god B figured was appropriate to his quest. For who better for blessing a hunter than a trickster god?

But as soon as he entered the corridor B could see something was wrong. For twenty years God the Trickster, his legs greaved in blue-shimmering metal, his breastplate magnificent, his face ageless and beautiful and smooth-skinned, had stood at the far end of the corridor.

Now he was halfway along it.

Worse: after B had overcome his shock, and approached the divine figure, he could see – he could actually *see* – the god's arm in motion. Swinging, millimetrically, inexorably, forward. And... was that the god's foot? Moving forward?

B fled.

It was several corridors and rooms before he could calm his breathing.

:4:

His first thought was: somebody had moved the body of the god – although as this idea occurred to him he realised how crazy it was. Even to touch the god's corporeality was tabu, and to touch it more than once was death. Then there was the question of weight. The gods were only a few feet taller than the average human, true, but their torsos were wrapped about with clothes of metal and plastic, their limbs augmented with solid servos

23

and embedded motor-enhancers of remarkable density. It would take a dozen people even to lift one.

So then he wondered if hal, or the shipbots, had for some reason brought in techgear to move the god's corpus. But that was crazy. It was perfectly crazy, he knew it was, as his heart rate started to settle, because B already *knew* that gods moved. Of their own volition, they moved. Everybody knew it. God the Grower moved slowly but surely, and God the Usher moved the barest fraction of one finger over several lifetimes, but all the gods moved. So faced with the brute fact of a god who had moved, what else to conclude but – the god moved himself.

But – *so rapidly*?

B recovered as much of his poise as he could and found his way to foreign chambers and unfamiliar biomes. Here he fooled three chickens with the hood, wringing their necks and tying the corpses into one floppy package with cord at their throats, which he tied to a pole to carry over his shoulder. He was on the outskirts of a different group's territory, but that didn't bother him – they'd be coming into his space to fetch their own chickens at some point, since they, no more than B's people, could eat their own chickens. There was nothing so formal as a treaty between these different populations of humans – call it a broader understanding. B was more anxious about setting off the shipbots, but he didn't see any until he was on his way home again, and then he encountered one, a tubby device, half the height of a person and moving on a dozen tentacular legs. It simply wandered past him and went on its way. Clearly it didn't mind about the chickens, so that was a relief.

B's path back home took him through the sacred corridor in which – who knows? – God the Trickster might have moved even further. B was scared to enter this space for fear of discovering whereabouts the god now was in it, and even more scared that the god might not be there at all, might have walked clean out of it. The detour was long and tedious, but B took it anyway: down a service corridor, through a swamp biome where tiny biting insects swarmed around his head as though his skull was a gigantic proton and they were the electrons of one of the heavier elements – then all the way down a looping circular corridor in which the floor (the ceiling in his great-great-grandparents' day) was sticky and smelt unpleasantly. Eventually he found himself in more familiar territory, and he crossed a biome in which twelve cows lived – gigantic beasts, bigger than any other animal on board the ship, and precious enough to mean they were continually shepherded and guarded by three dedicated shipbots. B bowed to each of these ship-servant machines in turn and held up his hands in the traditional gesture to show passivity and law-abidance. But then, when he was almost out the other side of the biome, a thought came to him. The gods were bigger than regular humans, but these cows were bigger even than the gods. Of course they were beasts, being grown and maintained like all the beasts on board, primarily for the crew to eat, and only secondarily to port diversity to the stars, maintain a functioning ecosystem and all the other stuff. Nonetheless, B had the sudden inspiration that these cows might be able to help. I mean – their size! I mean: *look* at them.

'Friend cow,' he said, to the one who was nearest.

She was head down – so vast a head, as big as the tin tub in which Gramma A took her weekly baths. She grazed: scrunching great fasces of grass into mouthfuls with a wrenching noise. Chewing, chewing, chewing. At his question, though, she lifted her head and looked at him. For a long time she didn't answer, because she was chewing. But finally she swallowed and said, basso profundo: 'Yes, pyg?'

'Have you heard,' B asked her, feeling abruptly self-conscious and awkward, 'that the gods have started moving.'

'The gods,' boomed the cow, in a low and mellifluous voice, 'have always moved.'

'But slowly,' urged B. 'And now they are moving quickly.'

'The gods,' said the cow, 'have their reasons.' She lowered her head and took another vast, rending gobful of grass.

'But why now? In all my lifetime, and that of my parents, and their parents – in all that time the gods have moved with a mystic slowness. Why speed up now?'

It took longer, this time, for the cow to finish her mouthful. When she had, she twitched a muscle in her shoulder – as if a guitar string had been twanged beneath the skin – and turned her head to the side to get a better look at B.

Then she said: 'Pyg, you understand that we are on a ship?'

'Of course!' said B.

'And that a ship is built to undertake voyages?'

This was a hazier conceptual territory for B, but he'd seen enough on hal's screens to have a general sense of what this meant. Imagine a pond so big that it filled not just an entire biome, but a megabiome ten times the size of the biggest chamber on board. How to cross it? It would take too long to swim; you'd exhaust yourself and drown. So instead you made a tub big enough to carry a person, or (hal's images suggested) big enough to carry many people – perhaps as many as a hundred. That was a *ship*. Their ship, their home, followed the same principle, but on a vastly bigger scale, and crossing not a pond but … well, who knew? Something.

'A voyage,' said the cow, slowly, 'is *from* somewhere *to* somewhere. For generations now we have been in between the *from* and *to*. If the gods are waking from their slowness, I suppose we are finally approaching our destination.'

This was so crushing, so strange and destabilising a notion it took B long minutes to process it. As he stood there, mouth open, dead chickens slung over his shoulder, the cow returned to her graminivorous mastication.

'But—' asked B eventually. 'Where? Destination. What does that *mean*?'

The cow did not raise her head again, so it seemed she had had enough conversation with humans for the time being. B stumbled away, his head full of startlement and his posture hunched. If the ship was its voyage, and that voyage's destination was now accomplished, did that mean that the world was coming to an end?

It was alarming. Not that he was worried for himself, so much: he was in his twenties now, after all, and so sliding down the latter portion of his life. But he had children! What of their futures?

As he slouched back home, his head full of gloom, a distinct and entirely new thought occurred to him, one so revolutionary and awe-striking in its newness that it made his heart race. He talked to his fellow people, and to the chickens and cows – so why, if they began walking around like regular folk, might he not *talk to the gods*? This idea was so terrifying that it made him breathless. Heresy and sin, crime and the breaking of tabu. Wasn't it? Too terrible to contemplate. Unless it wasn't?

But here was Dufé, and the kids scampering at her heels, and for a while being greeted as the conquering hero, returning with three fat chickens, was enough to drive such religious unconventionality from B's mind.

:5:

As a concession to Dionysus, the crew were served bacon for breakfast at the weekend. Captain Zeus approved of this. Now that they were all on clock-time, and by way of structuring their days, the old system of five days of work and two of relaxation seemed to them a good one, and the bacon breakfasts made a pleasant change from the weekday meals of roast chicken and lamb goulash – not to mention the blander vegetable soups and salads and whatnot with which they varied their diet.

'It may only seem a small thing,' they told their comrades. 'But it is important to motivate ourselves. A hundred years is a drop in the bucket, after all! We need to crack on!'

He grinned. His aquiline nose, his sharp bite, and o the stretch of his wingspan! The eagles have come.

They spent longer than they liked reorganising the *Forward*. Orbit meant zero-*g*, which upset and in some cases killed the beasts on board. The process of extricating themselves from their sheath of ice took longer than it should have, for various trivial reasons to do with glitches in the hardware accumulated over the course of their long journey. And there were glitches in the reconfig software too. Those resulted in a couple of weird, unspinnable shapes.

'What the bloody hell?' Apollo boomed at hal – but however apologetic hal was, it was unable to explain what had happened.

'Some cosmic ray or wave or series of quantum anomalies encountered on the way,' hazarded Hades. 'It could be a snark inside hal's programming.'

They ran a purge on hal, which, given the complexity of the system (being complex to begin with, and having evolved both reactively and proactively over many decades of shipboard life to become more arcane and complex still) took a while. It all delayed things, which was irksome, but it threw up a number of interesting results as well. It seemed that some of the beasts on board had been fiddling, in odd little ways, with hal's input-output. Some of the pygs had even poked a virtual limb inside it – the equivalent of mice chewing the wiring, or something like that. The fix grew organically around the glitch, but that also took time, and when, eventually, they were able to get the ship into a spinnable config and return a semblance of gravity to the beasts, they'd lost several weeks of valuable Purgatory research time.

But now, at any rate, they were ready to go.

Two

The United States of Amnesia

1750

the United States Of America

CHAPTER I

It was a barricade. Block, blocko, blockage, right across the street like something out of *Les Miz*. The automatic trash truck wasn't programmed to deal with it. The dumb beast, it trundled up to the barricade and stopped. Big cow of a truck, except a cow would be smarter.

What is blocked here is flowing there. What is fluent there is inarticulate here. Stoppage, flow, stoppage: that's about the shape of it. The shape of Time and Punishment. Of War and Purgatory. Setting up the narrative by bookending it with stasis.

The trash truck waited. Engine humming.

The barricade was a reef of old chairs and sofas, of discarded bicycles stubbled with rust, the bulk of a broken washing machine like an AllSpark Cube and, in the middest of it, an abandoned automobile, all higgled. The obstruction was heaped between the windowless SYKES facility on one side of the road and the shuttered-up Dollar Tree on the right. Ottoline hadn't had anything to do with erecting it, and hadn't the least idea who had. It was the sort of thing that had been happening a lot lately: not just the barricades, like some hazy memory of the French Revolution or something, but their almost immediate abandonment. The trash truck must have sent a notification back to the base. In a while a big-beaked plow-truck would come and clear the blockage and the trash truck would go on its bleeping way.

Ottoline figured she had ten minutes. So she checked the street, sent a little prayer up, please God let there be no crazies in sniper position overlooking the scene. Darted out. Mouse, or squirrel, one of those tiny, timid furry creatures who survived when all the dinos were asteroid-blasted, bye-bye. Survived by lurking, and rushing, and snatching food where they could.

And here was the dino itself, rumbling, rumbling. The back of the truck was lid-down, locked, but any one-dollar app gave you the hack-key to open it. It wasn't secure, and it certainly wasn't *secure* secure.

She wasn't looking for food, of course. She was looking for copper wire. There was a tentacle of it poking from the back of the trash truck. And how much more inside? Maybe just a foot or two, maybe yards and yards and yards of the stuff. Otty wriggled her shoulders out of her backpack, put on gloves (you couldn't be too careful) and began pulling. A yard came free, and then another yard, and just as she was growing excited, it snagged.

And then *all the hell* broke free and her adrenaline levels skied.

All

Hell

There was a yell; glance over her shoulder and three men in fatigues at the end of the street. They could have been anybody—U.S. military, state troopers, local militia, three gun-nuts out on walkabout. It hardly mattered.

"Looters to be shot on sight!" yelled one and raised his rifle.

Otty should have run straight off. Should have, probably. But something tangled in her fight-flight and she didn't. She needed the wire. She pulled at the three yards of copper wire she had thus far liberated, and when it didn't budge any further she flicked a cutter from her pocket and snipped off what had.

The stranger let off a shot. Otty flinched, but either he was firing a warning shot, or else his aim was blooey, because he missed her. The trash truck rang like a gong, and lights on its roof started flashing. Its engine powered up. His (her? Hard to know when they were all swaddled up in scarfs and shellhats) comrades all raised their rifles too.

"Stop where you *are!*" yelled the militia guy. High-pitched voice for a guy, low-pitched for a girl, one of the two.

Otty grabbed the wire and her satchel and ran. She sprinted her sixteen-year-old sprint, a gazelle-y bolt of speed, and had made it to the side alley, the entrance just past the SYKES building, when she encountered a human obstacle. It was a fourth militia dude, waiting at the top of the alley, waiting for her. Waiting to kill her. Oh my Lord. Her heart stuttered. He raised his handgun—a old Florida .65 Pounder with scratches down the side—and aimed.

And she thought: *I'm dead.*

And her heart was beating inside her chest like Animal from *The Muppets* playing the drums. She skidded to a halt, and opened her mouth to say something, and couldn't think of anything to say, and winced with how lame *that* was. You only get to say your famous last words once, after all.

She really ought to have prepared something, to have it ready.

The man's pistol discharged with a resonant thwack. OK. OK: he wasn't shooting *at her*. This new stranger was shooting at the guys behind her. There was the sound of two hands clapping, and again, and again, and then the trash truck sounded its backing-up *bing! bing! bing!* siren and revved its engine.

Otty looked around and saw that the first militia guy was now spread-eagled on the road, on his back. His two comrades were scattering for cover.

"You're Ottoline Barragão," said the stranger, in a voice she was *sure* she'd never heard before and looking at her with eyes she was *sure* she'd never seen before. So how did he know her *name*?

"Uh..." she said.

"We'd better run," said the stranger, "or we'll be sluicing our innards all over the road through *big* gunshot holes. *Big* ones."

Otty found her voice at last. "You shot him."

"He's body-armored like a beetle," the stranger said.

And, looking back a second time, Otty saw that the downed guy was not dead, but was, on the contrary, sitting up.

"But we need—" the stranger began.

Then there was a horizontal hailstorm of projectiles, and the stranger didn't get to finish his statement. The other two militia guys had opened a volley. It sounded like Jamaican percussionists Otty had once seen at a church make-and-bake one time: the Kingston Ringers, they'd been called, and they had spent simply *ages* thrashing their dangling metal sheets with metal poles. Everybody had been too polite to tell them to stop, and they'd certainly seemed to be enjoying themselves, so it had gone on and on.

Otty ducked, scurried and made to squeeze down the alley past the new guy. The gunshots were massive, appalling, like the sky cracking open, pure rage materialized, and she ducked even lower. Lurched into a run, one step, another step, and then, before she'd really gotten going, she stepped hard in a puddle. She knew she'd stepped in a puddle because she splashed herself. She felt it on her hands and a little on her neck. But there was no puddle: the alley was dry and dusty, and the splashing was something else.

Beside her, the stranger's handgun went off with *whumpf* and *whumpf*, and because Otty was doubled over like a ninety-year-old, and therefore because her face was close to the ground,

36

she saw his iPhone hit the dirt. She scooped it up and ran. She didn't even think about it. She just picked it up, instinctual, and rushed.

She ran and then, suddenly, she stopped, the toes of her shoes throwing up two dinky little bow waves of dirt.

The stranger wasn't following.

She looked back up the alley and saw that he had sat down in the dirt, right in full view of the main road, and big divots of plaster were leaping from the wall over his head. The militia dudes were *hammering* fire at him. It was amazing he hadn't been hit.

Or ... *had* he been shot? Maybe he had. But he had definitely dropped his phone, and then he'd sat down, and that meant it was obvious to Otty what his problem was.

Otty could have carried on running, and then things would have worked out one way. But she went back for the stranger, and things worked out another. And who's to say which was the better path? Later she had another choice: to give a thirsty man a glass of water, or not to give him the water, and again paths of possible futurity branched at her decision. But what would *you* do? Leave a man to be shot dead when you could save him? Give a man dying of thirst a glass of water, when there's a faucet right by you? No-brainer. No need for brain, nuh.

He had dropped his phone.

The fusillade from across the street stopped, perhaps because the militia guys were changing their clips. Otty scrabbled back to the solitary fellow, sat in the dirt.

"Come on," she urged, pulling at his arm. "Get up. Come on. On your feet and come with me."

He looked up at her and said: "Who are you?" and it was *super*-obvious then what the problem was.

"Come on."

She knew from dealing with her nanna that you had to be

37

persistent, and not be afraid to heave-ho. Applying this wisdom, she somehow got the stranger up and stumbling confusedly down the alley as the gunfire started up again, and bullets made the dirt boil and sprayed lumps from the wall at the end of the alleyway.

He fell into quite a brisk trot when they were actually going, because he wasn't actually *that* old, not the way Nanna had been. Like any bucklehead, when he started doing something, he tended to keep on doing it until he was actively stopped. So he followed her dutifully as she jinked, cut through the backyard of a deserted house, out on to another street. She didn't like being in the open after what she had just experienced, so she pulled the man through the overgrown hedge, and through to where the James Grabill Memorial School stood in its lonely grounds, overgrown and deserted.

The boards on the school hall window growled as she pulled them back, hefty and resistant. She opened up a chink, and somehow she got the guy inside.

Finally: a safe place to stop and catch her breath. The smell of pigeon crap. The lullaby cooing of the birds in the rafters was like a welcome. A shaft of sunlight coming down through the hole in the roof, illuminating all the dust motes, like a pillar made of pure spirit. The shuffling noises behind the walls were probably rats, but it was best not to think about that.

"What's going on?" the man asked. "Who *are* you?"

"You dropped this," Otty said, holding up the phone. "Yeah?"

He looked with complete bemusement at the phone, so she started searching him for his dockette. Clearly not wealthy, or he'd have one of those elegant miniports on his neck, or else one of the new surgical implants under the skin. He looked at her.

"Wait a moment," he said, in a puzzled voice. "That's ... I know what *that* is. I know what that is."

"It's a phone," she said. "Look, I can't stay, I can't loiter, I have to get home."

Her heart was singing; her head had never felt so clear. This was like in that drama she watched where people played Russian roulette and afterwards talked about the transcendent clarity and joy of having avoided death. It was probably a bit blasphemous to think that way, but then again: she had prayed, before going for the copper wire, and God had—look!—preserved her. She was grateful to God and that reminded her to be grateful more widely.

"But," she said to the stranger, "thank you, yeah?"

"Thank me," said the man, as if testing the phrase out. "All that shooting. Did I help you?"

"Yeah, but you need to … Need to reconnect this, yeah?"

There was, she saw, a rip in his combat jacket. She wanted to get away now (she really needed to be home) but it wouldn't be fair to leave this guy wandering around without any memory. He could die—people did, all the time, just sat on a park bench or something until thirst gummed up their heart and they straight died. So she took a breath and unbuttoned his jacket. He made no objection. Underneath was an overshirt made of some stiffly flexible material, and this garment was half-zipped-down. She saw the dockette: he had a small cradle mounted under his Adam's apple, above his sternum, where a medal might be worn on parade day. He was lucky, though, or perhaps fantastically unlucky—a stray shot had clearly passed through his coat, maybe bounced off his flak-shirt and dislodged the phone. Pinged it right out the top of his overclothes.

"This goes in here, yeah?"

"That sounds right," he said warily.

But he made no move to reinsert the phone, so she did it for him. There was no click, but she got it back in its cradle.

"OK?" she asked.

"OK?" he said. "I mean—OK?"

"*I'm* OK," she said. "But I have to absolutely *go*—yeah? Thanks again."

"You're welcome!" he said, as brightly as a child.

She snuck away. She was already late, and her mom was going to be severe with her. She was still holding the three yards of copper wire in her left hand, but she stowed that in her satchel—better than nothing, she guessed—and climbed back out of the window and ran all the way home.

:2:

There was a gate to Sweetwater, but she never went that way, because it was shaggy with surveillance tech like a pier with mussels. It was easy enough to slip in and out without being seen, and she preferred not to be seen. It wasn't Carl and his pistol, in his little booth, that kept the suburb of Sweetwater safe, you see. It was the fact that it was affluent, and every house was inhabited, and more to the point that every house was dense with cameras and plugged in to police drones. It was money that had as-it-were dug the invisible trench separating this suburb from the decaying once-on-a-time ruins of tumbledown houses and bramble-choked gardens to the west and south.

Somebody, somewhere around a corner, swung a garage door up and open—one of the old-school, non-motorized doors that have to be hauled open by hand. A sheerly metallic noise, like a sword being unsheathed.

A four-hundred-foot-tall eSpire, in red and black, tapering like the Eiffel Tower, loomed over the edge of the bad neighborhood. But she was on her way out of *there*.

So she went around the pool, through the gap in Mr. Wichita's hedge and out on to Bushy Drive. The world around her still thrummed with brightness and wonder—a half-hour earlier she had been shot at, like for-real gunfire really flying in her direction, and she had lived to tell the tale. Then, as she slunk down the side of her house, a new anxiety: her Mom would be furious.

But she wasn't—she hadn't realized that Otty had been away at all.

"How are the bees?" she called from the kitchen, and Otty yelled "super-duper!" reflexly and then thundered upstairs, three steps at a time. But that only postponed the problem, because she really *did* need to check on the bees, and if she went out it would reveal to Mom that she hadn't been in the garden with her hives at all, but had instead been out scouring disreputable parts of the city for copper wire. It was a poser, and no mistake. Otty threw herself across her bed and sprawled. Alive, though! Alive!

She wondered: Who was that guy, who had intervened in a firefight in broad daylight to save a nameless girl?

Then she thought: *But that's not right, he knew my name.*

Or he had done, until his phone popped out of his dockette.

She really-really needed to check on her bees. But first she opened group Closure and winked at her friends. They were all there, of course—whatever else they were doing, they were always there for one another.

~ I got wire, she said.

~ How much? returned Gomery, straight off.

Other affinity groups at school or church might waste time with small talk and phatic nonsense. They were closer than that.

~ A couple yards, only, said Otty.

Gomery was called Montgomery, but he hated the *mont* of his name. Really: He freaked out if any of the friends used it. He wouldn't say why. He was odd that way, Gomery. A little on the spectrum, to be honest, with a number of bizarre and utterly

41

inflexible rules about things. Not calling him *Montgomery* was one of these. Kath's theory was that he thought it sounded like *mong*. Otty thought it more likely Gomery sounded like nobody's name, and so was a blank slate upon which he could build any kind of identity he liked, where Montgomery sounded like an elderly Scottish dude or something, and that was plain insulting for a netwise black hacker kid and master coder. Not that she would describe Gomery as a hacker, exactly. But she could see his point.

~ How *many* yards? asked Allie. Allie liked to be precise about measurements.

~ Better than nothing, I guess, Kathry said, with sarcastic emphasis.

~ Hey, I got shot at, said Otty excitedly. ~ I almost got *killed* over those few yards.

~ No way, said the others, pretty much in unison. ~ For real, shot at?

She told the story. The barricade. The stopped trash truck. Otty darting to pull what she could from the rear.

~ The trucks in Chicago have legs now, said Gomery.

This provoked general ridicule.

~ Get out!

~ Oh yeah, oh no!

~ Imperial walkers, right.

(But they were all sidegoogling to check, and it turned out to be true—not articulated robot-like legs the way police quadpods had, but plasmetal tentacles that hoisted the truck wobblingly up, and enabled it to climb like an octopus over most block-ages, until they got to flat road again and could go back to their wheels.)

~ Anyway anyway anyway, said Otty. ~ These militia dudes rocked up, or maybe they were actual military, or maybe they were actually just nuts, and they started shooting at me, legit and for real shooting at me, live rounds, and this old guy came out and called to me by *name*.

~ This dude knew your name? Cess asked, incredulous.

~ These guys, said Otty, concerned that she hadn't made this part of her narrative crystal, ~ were *firing live rounds*. This was no fireworks show.

~ How did the dude know your name? asked Allie.

~ I have literally no idea and I have *laterally* no idea, said Otty. ~ I have absolute zero, which is nothing kelvin degrees, idea how he knew.

~ Was he police?

They were concerned about keeping their private network private, of course. They didn't want the authorities tangling with their Closure, of course. This was understandable.

~ This guy wasn't police, said Otty. ~ He was pretty shambolic-looking. Thrift-store body armor, all the pieces different brands. He didn't look like he had a ton of money.

~ But he knew your name, said Allie.

~ That's all he knew, I think, said Otty. ~ And anyway he was a bucklehead. His phone fell out and then he didn't know *my* name or *his* name or *any* name no more.

~ I got a whole roll, said Kathry, abruptly putting the conversation through a knight's move. ~ Twenty yards, and small change.

This was news, and bigger news even than Otty getting shot at with real live rounds. There were expressions of amazement. Even Cess, who liked to keep her own counsel, came out of her shell at that.

They made arrangements to meet in person to spool out the new wire: Gomery had one idea how to make best use of it—and Otty's paltry few yards, too—and Cess had another. The group agreed to vote on it, but only after they'd done some homework on them both. Tomorrow was soon enough for a meet.

~ Bees! yelled Otty. ~ I gotta check my *bees*.

~ You *tend* those bees, beebitch, said Allie.

~ Buzz buzz, said Kathry.

And then they were all saying it: Buzz buzz, and Allie said *when roe-seus was an ac-tor in Ro-ome* in this really British-style voice, all deep and r-rolling, which was pretty random.

~ Ho ho, assholes, said Otty.

She signed out.

Downstairs she bumped into her dad, just back from the drone shop.

"And how is your hive doing today, Ottoline?"

"Funny you should say that, Pops-my-Dad," Otty said, making her two forefingers pistol barrels and firing first the left and then the right at his chest. "I'm just going to check on them *now*."

"Did Mom told you she cleared seven dollars on the honey soap she and Frida made?"

"Seven *whole* dollars?" said Otty, already at the back door. "Wows. Time to retire to the *Harm*ptons."

Dad pretended to look crestfallen. "I thought that was pretty good, for something we grow in our garden."

"Think of the garden we'll have in the *Haaarm*ptons," she said, as she pulled the door open, "with such riches. Laters!"

Their backyard sloped sharply down to a fence at the bottom, beyond which was the polygonic symmetry of the Salmeds' roof and, beyond that, the Ravillions' place. The family who used to live in the next house down (the family before the Salmeds moved in) had not liked Otty's bees—those potentially stabby little motes, lazing through the air, coming in through open windows in summertime, humming in and out of their trash. They'd complained, told her parents to remove the hives or they'd sue.

44

Otty, with some shame (although, you know, what could you do?) had acted the kid, been all wide-eyed and innocent and *my bees? fo sho?* and it had devolved into a low-level online legal dispute, of the sort that you get basic legal AI-algorithms to bat back and forth for $15 a pop rather than hiring a human attorney who would charge thousands. They were called the … What were they called? Otty couldn't recall. The McGraths, or the McGarrys, and Otty couldn't even *remember* any more. And then the family had suddenly moved down to Florida, or some-where, and the Salmeds had moved in, and they didn't mind the bees. Otty sometimes gave them honey scent, or soaps, as peace offerings, and they were exaggeratedly, rather embarrassingly, grateful.

And here were the hives. Otty kept her tunic, gloves and hood in a box with a lid by the back door, and now she slipped into them for, whatever it was—the thousandth time, or some-thing. Her first hive had been a hollow log packed with tubes, like scrolls of magic parchment rolled together and stored in a gigantic scroll. Dad had worked for a time at the Ulanov Nursery and got the chance to buy defective or unused stock cheap. He had no use for most of the garden center stuff, since, obviously, they didn't really have much of a garden; but he had picked up the log hive, and Otty had set it up on a stand, and did all the things Online told her to do to attract bees, and soon enough the bees came. It was only when Mom and Dad began noticing her arms and neck stung, archipelagos of tiny ginger-colored volcanos across her skin, that they bought her the protective gear. They couldn't really afford it, and Otty didn't really mind the stings, which really didn't hurt her, much. But she liked having the clothes. It made her feel like a real beekeeper.

The bees sourced their equivalent of pollen from trash, mostly, often industrial waste sugar, sucratine and the sweetened plastics manufactured down past 80th and Park, which meant their honey was not edible. Otty figured it probably *was*, in the sense that it probably wouldn't *actively* poison you. But just a dab of it on the tongue and it tasted weird: artificial and aspartaminatory with a weird tartness somehow folded into the over-sweet rush of it. The color varied, too: sometimes bright yellow like citron-concentrate, sometimes an orange so sharp it was almost scarlet, occasionally a weird liquorice black.

But it certainly smelled strongly of honey, so it made good toiletries and the like. And Mom and Dad liked to see her have a hobby that didn't involve hanging out with her gang and stealing copper wire. And she could always use the pin money. Mom sold soaps to people at church. Dad, who now had a different job, at the drone shop, sometimes moved candles and soap to coworkers who needed dinky little gifts for anniversaries or whatever. It wasn't much, but it was something.

And for Otty, though, it was something more. After the success of that one cheap-ass log, she had chased up everything she could find online about keeping bees. And then she had built up her colony.

It was a decade or more after the antique model of desktop computer had been superseded—the kind with the whirring fans to cool actual no-shit-sherlock *circuit* boards, all slotted neatly inside a huge metal box. Nowadays nobody wanted those, not even Retro Chic geeks. Today's machines were all mini and solidpact except where they were cleverly distributed, and most everyone had the latter sort. But Otty found a use for the old machines. She pulled them from landfill, and out of abandoned old office blocks, and hauled them home on her back, like a peasant from the medieval age or something. Then she took out about half the slotted internal boards, leaving the rest for her bees to build comb on. Then she tied the blocks together into metal hives, and the bees loved the spaces she created. And it was easy to pull the remaining boards out of the mainframe and scrape off honey.

She checked her hives, and the bees murmured through the air about her head. There were rather more dead bees in Hive 2 than she liked, but she cleared them out, and the rest seemed happy enough. It was a small worry, sure. The bees usually cleared out their own dead. It might mean something was up with the harmony of the hive, and it might mean nothing. She would keep an eye on it. And otherwise there was lots of activity, and the honey was forming nicely, and a bee landed on her visor so she got to look at it up close—so intricate, and so wonderful, its fuzzed body, the liquorice-curls of its antennae, eyelash legs, wings slender ovals of frost. Then, a drummer launching a drum roll, the bee trilled its wings, jumped into the pure air and was gone.

A couple of bees got under the weighted rim of her hood and one stuck a jab in her shoulder, through her shirt, but though she felt the nip she didn't care.

Gomery sometimes said: *You, girl, are high on bee venom, girl. It's more addictive than heroin. I saw a vid about it.*

Bee drugs, Otty had said. Metho*drone. Hive-high.*

And now it was time for supper.

And now it was time for family prayers, and Frida was prevailed upon to unplug for a half-hour and she did so without making *too* much of a fuss. Otty said grace and they all amened. Then Mom said a prayer for peace and healing for the whole country, and Frida muttered good luck with *that* under her breath, and Dad rebuked her.

And now the family watched the latest episode of *Smite with Hammer, Smite with Sword*, which was a big-budget historical drama about the Crusades, which they were all watching together as a family. There was a big plot twist in this week's episode, and afterward Mom and Dad discussed it earnestly and the girls slunk away to their own business.

Soon enough it was time to go to bed, and Otty didn't think she would be able to sleep, but perhaps the whole experience of the day had worn her out more than she realized, because...

:3:

She woke before the alarm pinged and, since she was up before anybody else, took the opportunity to check the house feed. A stealthy track into the collective family inbox revealed a message from the school saying that, for budgetary as much as health/ safety blah-blah, in the light of recent attacks by the Bethesda Apocalypse Militia blah-blah-blah, today was designated by the principal a home-study day, worksheets were attached and all students required to complete them, apologies for the short notice and so forth and so forth. No need for anybody else to see *that*, Otty decided, and deleted it, and retraced her track, erasing it as she went. All before she even got out of her bed.

It meant she could get to go out all day, and Mom and Dad would assume she was at school, and she didn't even need to lie about it. She would just go, and M & D would make that assumption. Which would mean the untruth would kind-of be *their* responsibility, when you came to think of it.

It was one of Frida's work days, and Mom and Dad would both be off to *their* work as soon as they had gobbled breakfast, so Otty got up and showered, and grabbed a beakybar and, as the rest of the family were zombie-shuffling about the house, she went out back to check her hives.

All seemed to be humming along. She retreated to her spot, a place behind the hives where an upturned PC monitor with a blanket over it served as a stool and sat where the sun could find her. She went into the private Closure and gave Allie a call.

~ Hi, friend, said Allie.

~ You busy, homebody?

~ What is this *busy* of which you speak, earthling?

~ Just that I got a free day, it's home school but my family don't know, so I'm free. You?

~ Just a regular day for me, Otty.

~ Allie, can I ask your advice?

~ Sure.

~ Can I ask your advice on, like, an affair of the *heart*?

Allie's laughter was an easy, high-pitched vibrato.

~ Otty, you're asking *me*? You think I have any wisdom where straights are concerned?

~ That's the whole thing, said Otty, feeling a spread of warm embarrassment across her neck and chest. ~ You have an *object-ive* view on all the boy-girl stuff, yeah?

~ Not sure objective is how I'd put it, laughed Allie. ~ C'mon, girlfriend—this is Gomery, isn't it?

~ I really *dis*like him, a lot of the time, Otty said, and then stopped.

~ And? Allie prompted.

~ And sometimes I really like him. I mean, really. And that's just—contradictory? Yes?

~ Love is a contradictory business.

~ Hey, said Otty, quickly. ~ Let's not get carried away. Let's not lock, load and fire the L-word.

~ Retracted!

~ I'm only talking about . . . Isn't that moderately paradoxical? And you know how Gomery is. He's all straight lines and logical consistency, and his mashed potatoes not touching his heap of peas, and a clear line between peas-mash and his steak.

~ I'm not grokking the paradox-ness, said Allie.

That was part of her charm; she liked to resurrect antique slang. She had the most amazing appetite for trivia, and general knowledge, of any person Otty had ever met. Otty had to side-google *grok*, but she saw how well it fitted in context.

~ No grokking here, Otty confirmed. ~ No whit of a grok.

~ Not *understanding* why it's wrong, is what I meant. The heart knows what it knows, right? The heart grasps what it grasps.

~ Except that what my heart knows is that I find him really annoying a lot of the time. But that's not my point. He's my *friend*, yeah? You don't date your friends.

~ It's literally part of the word *boyfriend*.

~ But that's just not… Look, you pick a boyfriend or girl-friend, and you *hope* they get on with your friends. You don't date your actual friends. That's like some kind of incest, or something.

~ I don't agree.

~ It would be like me dating *you*.

That high-pitched gurgly laugh again. ~ Oh, how you toy with my heart, fair maiden.

~ Don't come the queer-crush with me, Allie.

Otty's mom was at the kitchen window, peering out into the yard, probably looking for her.

~ I got to go, all right? *Don't* tell Gomery what I said—OK?

~ I promise.

~ Regally promise.

~ Utopianly promise. Cross my atomic heart and hope to die in an atomic explosion.

Otty ran back inside, and thundered up to her room, and grabbed the wire she had scavenged the day before. Then she stuffed this booty into her school bag and called "bye!" to the house in general and then she ran out the front.

One moment, near perfect moment, as she was heading up

to town. The whole day free before her, to do what she wanted to do. Suburbs full of neat houses, and well-patched roofs, and all the herbs, flowers and trees still moist with dew. Beams of sunlight visible through the morning haze, like ligaments linking Earth to Heaven. Otty's heart thrilled.

Nothing lasts, though.

Cess called as Otty was jogging down the street—a public call, which the group generally tried to avoid, since such things were so easily eavesdropped upon, so it must have been important.

Cess was calling all of them.

There are police in my house.

Woh.

What?—and the others were all chiming in: *Right now? Why? What?*

Then Kathry emojid an uh-oh. *They're here too.*

Regular police? Gomery wanted to know? *FBI?*

Interstate.

This was the new force: local police but with powers across state lines. They were mainly concerned with chasing online trails. That meant—probably—they were after the group for their Closure, their personally wired-in and mirrored invitation-only private mini-internet. It wasn't illegal. But above a certain size, such networks gave the government cause for concern. There had been some high-profile cases of encysted internet networks in Japan and Malaysia being shut down by the authorities. Not that there was anything very much they could do to Otty and her friends, except seize consoles, and pitch a few of the group into prison for a little time. I mean, could they do that? *Had* the five done anything that deserved prison?

A police drone flew overhead, fifty yards away. Was it heading for Otty's house? Or was that just her guilty conscience?

I got out, over the roof, and over Gabriel's bar and down, Cess was saying. *They don't have me yet. They took my mom, though. They took Denis too.*

Her stepdad.

Stop talking, this is an open line, Gomery said.

Otty said — *meet, hand to hand, in the—*

— don't say it!

— open line, they'll overhear—

*— in the you-*know-*where*, said Otty, crossly, and rung off.

Like she'd been about to say it!

It was probably nothing. It was probably something real trivial, and in a day or two it would all be smoothed over, but it set Otty's heart to blast-beat. She ran, her satchel hitting her hip in syncopation with her stride. And then a little app she had squirreled away binged and pinged, which meant police with an authorized warrant were within three hundred yards of her home. It wasn't exactly legal, possession of this app; and it wasn't possible to get one with a wider search area—not, that is, without serious money. But warrants had to be logged and officially signed off before they could be served, and everything was interconnected nowadays, so it wasn't hard to tag which officers were driving out to make the arrest.

Almost everything was interconnected nowadays. But then that was the whole point of their closed network.

A double-decker police vehicle, its engine growling like a bear, climbed Pica Mount and turned down her road. Something was up. Something was definitely up. Heading down toward her house and slowing down, Otty ducked back down an alleyway like the roly-poly little bat-faced girl she was.

She had a scrambleveil in her pack. It wasn't a new one, of course: she didn't have that kind of money. She'd picked it up from an eBay auction that she'd managed to short-circuit with DOS account bots to crowd out the other bidders. The veil worked across about a third of its surface, cycling through various faces—the eyes, forehead and hairline, but not the nose, mouth or chin. This led to some startling composite faces which, since the tech was supposed to make you inconspicuous, rather negated the purpose of the exercise. But it was better than nothing. Gomery said she should just have bought a regular movie tie-in hoodie from Walmart, the kind with a celebrity character hologram projected across the face. But Otty's take on this matter was: If it's worth doing, it's worth doing like the professionals.

She rolled its mesh between her fingers, looked around, slipped the veil over her head and pulled up her hood.

Then she hurried on, down the dogleg past the Ravillions, and jogging along Parkside. Stretched-out morning shadows of the elms, backlit, and a half-dozen people walking their dogs like good respectable dog-owners. Huge Egyptian-style eyes were painted on the side of the Korestore and painted with smart paint such that they appeared to move to follow Otty as she passed.

Drones thronged the skies overhead like birds gathering for their annual migration. There were birds there too, of course, but subdued, defeated coinhabitants in skies they used to own. The hologrammatic giant advertising Boxer Poet Brand by 69 and Corn was so evanescent in the brightness of morning that you saw him more clearly out of the corner of your eye than full-on. Like a ghost.

Otty was on Bush Drive now, and, checking quickly, it looked like Old Wichita had left for work. Or whatever he did—he was surely too old to need to go to work, so maybe he went bowling, or hung out at the AMVETS over by the mall. Or maybe he *did* have a job. The way the world was going, some people had to work into their hundreds. That's what the newsfeeds said, anyway. It wasn't as if Otty knew anybody in that age bracket.

Otty hazarded the main drive and jogged down the side of

the Wichita house. There were cams stuck all over the side of the building, of course: obsidian beaks and boils, bubbling the wall of the house as if it had frozen while boiling. Otty angled her whole face, scrambleveiled as it was, at the one over the big side door and hoped for the best. Then she was out back, running down the green creaminess of Wichita's lawns. The dog-barking sound effects projected from each flower bed as she passed were old friends and did not scare her. Finally she siphoned herself through the hedge at the bottom, scaled the wall and scrambled through the little temporary tunnel she had dug under the big wire barricade.

Now she was in the bad neighborhood. The city was almost all bad neighborhoods these days, and many of them weren't *so* bad, in actual fact. People still lived here, obviously. There were shops and schools and so on. Plenty of people preferred the latitude living in such a locale provided, although for many of those people latitude was calibrated in terms of ease of evading professional law enforcement. But then lots of people lived here because it was what they could afford, and Otty's family were a few bad-luck months away from joining them, in actual factual fact.

And, although considering the received wisdom that people inhabited these districts to avoid the police, law enforcement was pretty conspicuous: twenty-foot-high police vehicles, wheels as high as Otty was herself. On the north side they had quadpod substations: huts on stilts that could walk their way around like Baba Yaga's cottage—slowly, though: three legs anchored into the dirt, and one moving like an elephant's trunk snuffling around, sometimes for minutes, until it found a new anchorage. But that slowness was steadiness; there was no easy way to destabilize the substations, no quick lasso that would tumble them down. Propelled by their clever algorithms, they plodded at much slower than walking pace, but as somebody once said (Galileo, said sidegoogle) *still, they moved*. And in the armored hut at the top were police officers in full gear, ready to kitejet down from above onto wrongdoers like the Lord's Righteous Fury, or more often—if the newsfeeds were to be believed—kitejet entirely *outta* there if things looked too riotous on the ground. The feed Otty followed, Feke101, had a whole, lengthy program—a full fifteen minutes uninterrupted by ads or pop-ups, detailing how a district in New Jersey had been in full-on riot for three days, buildings set on fire, which fires were tackled by Fire Dept dirigibles in more or less desultory fashion, and the army suggesting it intervene but being blocked by the police, who insisted they had it under control. Three quadpods had stomped slowly into the heart of the disturbance like Martian invaders, and had directed spotlights and broadcast loud announcements to cease and disperse, and tried bombing the crowd with tear gas, and even tried a few exploratory sniper-shots at people adjudged *in commission of criminal activity liable to endanger life*. Then some militia group had blown up one of the legs with a megagrenade, sourced—how the report knew this, Otty wasn't sure—from Alaskan Separatists. The station stayed standing, which was what it was designed to do. Three legs is fine for standing, after all. It's still a stable structure, three legs. But the police in both pods had taken frit, and all evacuated using their kitejets and flown four or five blocks back to safety. Debacle. So the riot had shifted from nonspecific destruction to seizing control of the two abandoned pods. By the time the army was mobilized, Organized Crime (so the newspodcasters called them) had fitted ladders and scaled the legs and hacked the controls. Bad news for the Law, since these pods were heavily armored gun emplacements that could rain fire and fragmentation on the ground. The army had retreated. Complete disaster! Good footage, though. And then that whole section of New Jersey was like a camp, under the thumb of a ganglord called Boss Puteh, who presided over everything from atop one of the huts for a fortnight or so, until the army mobilized and swept through it all.

Otty guessed the story was 40 percent true, and the rest drama and CGI. But it was good drama.

She had never seen a quadpod this side of the city, and in truth this neighborhood, though largely deserted and a little ruinous, wasn't that unsafe. Of course it was true that only yesterday, three men in combat gear had fired on her, shot at her with real live rounds. But it wasn't as if *that* kind of thing happened every day!

Sure, the newsfeeds were all doom and gloom, and every other Sunday sermon seemed to be about how the End Times had finally arrived, and how the country was slipping into war. But it would probably blow over. It wasn't as if there hadn't been crises before. What else was history but a string of crises? And what was the alternative? *May you live through interesting times* was supposed to be a Chinese curse, but what was the alternative? *May you live through boring times*? Who wanted that?

And now she was coming up on the James Grabill. It was the group's occasional meet-up place. They had others, and they didn't meet up face on face all that often. They had the Closed Line for that, after all. But if Otty said: *Let's meet you-know-where*, because the line wasn't secure, then they all knew she meant the James Grabill.

A stumpy eSpire, perhaps a thousand feet high and crowned at its summit with a great number of prongs and protrusions, cast a shadow twice its height over the roofs and street. Otty, running past it, didn't give it a second glance.

They called themselves the Famous Five, after some antique kids' adventure series, and because it amused them, since fame was the exact opposite of what they were trying for. There was Gomery Lacroix, who was easily the most driven of the five, often too serious and focussed to see that the rest of them were joking with him. There was Otty herself, of course: her family half-German and half-Portuguese, unbalanced in terms of in-laws heavily on the latter side (why did Germans have such small families?), small but fierce, determined and not easily dissuaded. Otty had dozens *and dozens* of Porto aunts and grandmothers and great-aunts and elderly cousins, and they used to come across from Europe to visit, but the state of the U.S. nowadays meant that they'd stopped coming. Then there was Pitt Smith, who Kathry had called Pitt *Cess* one day as a joke, and the joke had stuck, much to Pitt's chagrin. And there was Kathry Chong herself, who downloaded joke scripts and practiced various phrases that could cap ordinary conversation so as to appear funny. Why anybody would want to appear funny baffled Otty, and why somebody born—so far as the group could tell—without a natural sense of humor, like Kathry, would want to do so was even more confusing. And finally there was Allie, sometimes shortened to Al, sometimes lengthened to Allington of Allingford, or even Lord, or Lady, Allenby-Allipallington the Almighty, who was *she* to some of the group and *he* to others, like so many people nowadays. Allie had the best general knowledge of any of the five, by far. But of course that's what you'd expect. She would have been dynamite on any school quiz team she deigned to join. If there was such a thing as an eidetic memory, outside of fiction and myth, then Allie's memory was one.

Otty crouched, spun the tumblers on the old bike-lock she used to hold the fire door shut and slipped inside.

She walked down a corridor. Light came in trapezoid blocks through skylights in the roof. Once upon a time these spaces had bustled with life, but that was a long time ago now. Taupe walls framed a sequence of darker gray squares spaced a yard apart where pictures had once hung. At the end of this was a corner vestibule, empty now except for a red cane-back sofa, broken strands of cane bristling upward like stalagmites. Many coin-sized patches of paintwork had flaked off the walls. The floor was dusty and covered in detritus. At various places, and especially at that fold where wall met ceiling, mold grew like fur, or charcoal-sketched large spaces with a black soot shading.

The principal's office door said INCIPA.

Further down was a window brownly opaque with grime. A large triangle of glass had cracked off like peanut brittle, and many leaves had spilled in to heap and rot on the floor. The smell was almost forestlike. Four trash cans stood in a row, gaping open-mouthed like idiots at the astonishment of there being a ceiling. The wall behind them had a sign screwed into it: RECYCLABLES ONLY. And then Otty turned left and reached the main hall.

She was greeted by the cool throb of pigeons cooing, and the acidy, earthy smell of the bird shit that had accumulated, at compound interest, on the varnished planks of the hall floor.

Otty stopped. The man was still there. Oh. My. *Gawd.* The old guy, who had intervened the day before, when those other guys were shooting at her.

He was facing the blank wall, but he turned when she came into the room.

"What are *you* still doing here?" she demanded.

He winced, but the puzzled look didn't leave his face. Oh my gracious, Otty thought. Oh my good *gravy*. I should have checked his iPhone was properly plugged in. But she hadn't and here he still was, in full-on bucklehead mode. Oh Lord Gracious in Heaven, this was not good.

"Are you OK?"

Had he really just been stumbling about the hall all evening? Had he really been too much the bucklehead even to make it *outside*? All night in this place?

"Who are you?" he asked.

"You don't remember me?" she replied. But of course he didn't remember her. "Well, dude, we met yesterday, and you didn't tell me your name then, but *my* name is Otty. OK?"

"Thirsty," said the man.

"Sir, esteemed stranger, dude, haven't you *drunk* anything since yesterday?"

By way of reply he flapped his dry lips together, as if trying to recall what they were for. His attention wandered. He gazed at the pattern of damp that spread itself in the shape of a gigantic moth's wing down from the leaky ceiling and stretched itself impressively across the far wall.

When his gaze came back to her, he said: "Thirsty. I'm pretty thirsty."

"Come on," she said.

One of the reasons the gang liked hanging out in the derelict James Grabill was that the water was still working. Turn on a faucet in the bathroom and, after a hiatus of epileptic juddering and a drawn-out sigh, water flowed. It was pretty brown, but that was probably all right. I mean, right? Probably. Back home, Mom insisted on only drinking water that had been through the Klarity filter, but Otty wasn't bothered. She thought of the different sorts of toxins on which her bees fed, and it didn't seem to bother her hives. A little contamination surely beefed up your immune system rather than anything else.

Otty walked over to the guy, took his elbow, and led him out of the hall. Cooing increased in volume. Four pigeons leaped into the air with a violent battering of wings, circled tight under the sagging roof, and settled back onto their perches.

"What's your name?" Otty asked.

He thought about this, and then looked annoyed. But then a sly look passed across his face, as if he'd thought of a brilliant way of turning the tables.

"What's *yours*?" he asked.

They were walking up the corridor toward the bathroom, where Otty knew the faucets worked.

"Otty. I already told you."

"You did?"

"What's *your* name?"

Her nanna, near the end, had sometimes needed seven or eight prompts before her own name came back to her. Otty tried a smile. Then she realized she was still wearing her half-functional scrambleveil, which clearly couldn't have helped his recognition. She pulled down her hood and slipped the veil off and tried the smile again.

Nothing.

"I'm Otty, remember? We met yesterday."

"Did we?"

"What's your name?"

His brow became a barcode of wrinkles.

"It's ... a wuh," he said. "Winston," he added eventually.

"Hello, Winston!"

"It's Wystan."

"OK then—well, that's an unusual name."

"Wilson. It's Wilson."

"And ... any more?"

"I'm thirsty. More?"

She took him through to the restroom, and after trembling for a while the pipe started pouring out water. Winston-Wilson went "ahh!", as if recognizing an old friend, and put his hand under the flow. Then he licked his hand. It didn't seem to Otty to be a very efficient means of getting water into his mouth, but he seemed satisfied.

"That's better," he said, lowering himself to sit on the discolored tiles of the restroom's floor. "That's better."

"Mr.... Wilson, is it?" said Otty, sitting cross-legged opposite him, an arm's length away. "You got a phone, yeah?"

"The phone is necessary," he agreed, nodding.

He pulled his jacket back, and there was the iPhone, nestling in its cradle. Its screen lit up as the motion nudged it, so it still had battery.

"I'm gonna take a look, OK?" Otty said, reaching forward.

"Who are you, again?"

Stepping closer to reach the phone and its holder brought the man's smell hard into Otty's nostrils—not a stench, exactly, but that not-nice whiff of ripe sweat and vague fermentation that old guys often have. His breath was not pleasant.

The phone was in its holder, but it jiggled a little loosely, so Otty figured its connection was shot. Well, that was an annoyance. There was nothing she could do about it here, and probably nothing she could do about it period. Gomery might be able to fix it. He had those skills, all that genius with solder and circuit board. Then she remembered that Gomery and the whole gang were coming here. They'd be here soon. She had to get Winston-Watson-whatever out of the James Grabill, and in short order.

But then her conscience began to squeak-squeak in her head. That was the problem of going to church and believing all the God and Jesus and spirit-of-holiness: you could never achieve the proper get-wrecked clarity where your obligations to other people were concerned. She was still legally a kid, of course; and of course *he* was a full-grown man. Surely the obligation of care, if it existed at all, ran the other way? But then she thought:

He's a bucklehead. If I just shove him outside he'll only stumble around, and not know what to do, and come to some unfortunate end or die of thirst or something like that.

She sat back. The guy was dressed in street-gear and was carrying an expensive-looking sidearm. What odds that some disreputable type would find him and, instead of helping him, would just rob him, leave him naked? Maybe kill him?

It was a most irritating thing.

Of course, it was also a puzzle that somebody in such cobbled-together clothing, lacking the telltale signs of wealth, would be carrying such an expensive-looking sidearm. But one thing at a time.

She leaned in and fiddled with his phone in its dockette again. It slid and jiggled, and then the screen glowed a golden yellow. It emitted a resonant xylophonic sound, and something changed about the man's eyes.

"That's it," he said, clapping his hand to hers. "Hold it there. Jesus, there it is."

"You're you again?" Otty asked.

"You're Ottoline Barragão," said the man. "Wait, though. Fucking hold on one god-bothered minute. How is there a *fifteen-hour* gap in my connection?"

"You *intervened*, remember?"

"Intervened," said the man.

"I was scavenging a bit of stuff from the back of a trash truck and these dudes started shooting at me." Otty lingered on the *u* of *dudes*. It was, when she looked back, still pretty boggling. "And you shot back and told me to run. You remember that?"

He looked puzzled, and the phone slid fractionally in its dockette.

"No," he snapped, loud enough to startle her. "No—put it back!" Some more sliding it around and he sighed. "OK, that…

That I do remember, Ottoline Barragão, but it's the last thing I do remember."

"I guess a stray round knocked your iPhone out, and it's fritzed your connections a little, too. I mean the port. I mean *your* port. What's your name, anyway?"

"Wesson."

He was looking distractedly past her. Maybe he was re-accessing his memories.

"Like, your Christian name is Wesson?"

"You say *Christian* name, do you?"

People could be twitchy about the Christian in Christian name, Otty knew, so she said: "First name, yeah."

"Where is this place? My signal's borked. I'm not getting mapping." She figured he wasn't going to say, but then he said: "Smith."

"Well, listen, Mr. Smith—"

"Mr. Wesson."

Smith-Wesson? She gave him the teenager *you-kidding-me?* face. But, look, who was she to begrudge him his crazy pseudonym.

"All right, Mr. Wesson."

It seemed he guessed her thoughts.

"It's actually my name. My dad was John Wesson. My mom named me."

"I guess she liked guns."

"Smith was a family name, in my family, I mean, in my mom's family."

What was this gabble-gabble?

"Whatever, dude, what you have to understand is that my friends are on their way here, and that they'll be super freaked out if they find you in the building. So you need to buzz-buzz off, OK? You can hold the phone into place with your hand, yeah? I mean, until you get to a clinic, or a Genius Bar, you

63

know?" She removed her hand. "You just keep your hand on it, yeah?"

"I know about your friends. I know about you. And you are all in very grave danger," said Wesson.

"Dude," said Otty. Shorter *ü* this time.

"I'm serious as cancer. Put it this way, Ms. Barragão—I genuinely doubt if any of you will still be alive by sunset today."

That sounded severe. But then Wesson's eyes went weird again, and his face slipped into slack incomprehension.

"Come on," Otty complained, and put her hand back on the device, and tried yet again to wriggle it into position where it was making the proper connection with its comblike contacts.

"There's blood on this," she said. *Ugh!* "It's sticky."

"My arm hurts," confirmed Wesson, in a sing-song voice.

She lifted his coat a bit further and saw a mess of chocolate-colored dried blood, with little gemlike twists of ruby-red hardness stuck in the general spread like flies in tar. She couldn't see if it was still bleeding. And anyway, she was no doctor. But it had obviously been bleeding the previous day, and now she thought back she had felt something splash her in that dry and dusty alleyway. It was almost enough to make a girl shudder.

"I guess you didn't escape the firefight yesterday unscathed," she said, and then she was aware of a little ping of self-satisfaction at her eloquence. *Unscathed* was a good word, though, wasn't it?

"I'm thirsty," he said.

"I guess you've lost blood."

He looked puzzled, and she jiggled the iPhone in its dockette again, and he said, "Laura is the person to..." and stopped. Then he crinkled his brow again, and said: "Wesson, is my name," and then looked at her. "You and your friends need to get *out*."

She folded the jacket back over the wound, and put his hand back on the phone, holding the bulge in place.

"You need to clean it. Infection and... Like, gangrene and pus and whatever. You need to get it sorted out. Get to a doctor's or a hospital, or maybe a vet's."

The phone slid and the light went out of his eyes.

"Look, I can't fix this—I don't know about this," said Otty. "You need to get to a clinic. Or the mall—it's a twenty-five-minute walk into the centre of town. You'll need to go through the gate, I guess, but if you present and say that's it's like, a medical emergency..."

She looked again at his gear: the gun. Would they even let him through? Man, this was a sticky moral situation. Walk away, said a little voice in her head, but in reply there was her conscience again like an unoiled wheel, squeak, squeak, squeak.

She couldn't just *leave* him.

He was trying to peer down at the port, on his collarbone, and was shifting the iPhone in it with his good hand.

"My friend," Otty told him, "you are like the certain man went down from Jerusalem to Jericho, and fell among thieves, I guess, which makes me the Good Samaritan. Or, maybe, it's the other way around. You did intervene yesterday, so maybe you're the Samaritan."

"Samaria, Nablus, Shomron region," said Wesson. "I was posted there."

"You were posted there?"

"Sure, sure," said Wesson, looking anything but sure. "I did two tours."

"You were in the army?"

"Sure, sure."

"You fought in the Sixty Days War? Is that why you're...? Why you're—"

"Bucklehead. It's OK to say it. I take no offense."

"That," nodded Otty.

"Weaponized Alzheimer's," he grunted. Then he looked away.

She had to wash him. There really wasn't another any way to wriggle out of that—what would you call it? Duty, Otty supposed, though it seemed a creaky olde-worlde kind of word. But there you were. Thanks, conscience! Thanks for this doo-doo. She took a spare undershirt from her satchel, and wetted it at one of the sinks, and squirted on some hand sanitizer she had—she wasn't carrying any soap, or anything—and eased him out of his jacket. Then she started wiping the dried blood on his shoulder and arm.

"I tell you what, though," she said to him, feeling awkward with silence. "I saw something about this on my top feed, something on this. What you've got. You know it's completely different than Alzheimer's, right? My nanna died of Alzheimer's and I know."

"That's what my company commander called it," Wesson said, fumbling at his phone. He was getting blood all over his screen, and the connection kept slipping.

"Did you ever hear of beehive colony collapse disorder?" asked Otty. She went back to the sink and rinsed the shirt as much as she could. Water the color of cranberry juice sluiced down the drain. "It's a bee thing. I know bees—bees are one of the things I'm good at."

"Bees," said Wesson.

He had taken his hand off the phone and was poking around in the wound.

"Don't do that!" Otty told him. "You'll get it infected."

She wrung the shirt at the sink and went back over to him. Folded her legs, tucked her thighs onto her calves and settled a little higher.

"Colony collapse disorder," she said, "was this thing that happens to beehives sometimes. It started last century—I don't know if it ever happened in, like, the deep past. Ancient Egypt and such. But the beecasts I listen to and the specialty

66

feeds I follow talk about the 1990s. So in a beehive you got a queen, yeah? And a whole crowd of workers, and the workers go out and collect pollen and bring it back to the queen. The collapse disorder happens if the workers all go off and don't come back."

"Don't come back!" said Wesson, as if snatching at some thread of memory. "Go!"

She moved his hand back to his iPhone.

"Jiggle this about, and you'll get your memory back," she advised.

She returned to mopping his wound.

"So," she said, "they go, leaving the queen with only a few nurse bees, and eventually the food runs out and the queen dies. And it's real bad for the hive, obviously, but it's bad for farmers too, since bees do so much of the fertilizing of, you know. Maize and wheat and whatnot."

"Whatnot," echoed Wesson.

"So there was a real panic about it, and nobody knew what caused it. And you know what they found? It was a particular pesticide. There were these pesticides called neonicotinoids that acted on the nervous system of pest insects. Neo. Nico. *Tin*oids."

"Tinoids," said Wesson, like he was naming a new variety of robot.

"At first farmers loved them, because they killed bad bugs but left good bugs alone. But then it turned out they didn't leave good bugs alone. They messed with their memories. I guess people didn't even know insects had memories because bug-heads are so tiny."

"Bug-head not big-head."

"Sure."

She'd gotten most of the blood off, and uncovered a wound in his arm, like a hole-punched hole, and on the other side of the arm another hole. It was the thickness of a little finger. Or the thickness of her little finger, at any rate, and her fingers were not large, not dumpy little wiener fingers like Cess's. But two holes meant the round had gone in and gone out again, or so she figured. That was good, though, wasn't it? She assumed so.

"Can you move your fingers."

"I cannot move the fingers," he said, "on this hand. They tingle, some, but won't move."

"I guess your nerve got squished. Or, like … jangled. Maybe it'll go bad and your fingers will drop off. Or maybe not—*not*, I hope. I mean, I'm sure it'll settle down and you'll get your hand back."

The bullet hole was oozing black-red somewhat, but not bleeding badly. She needed bandages. Then she thought about tying her spare shirt around the wound and had the unworthy thought that she was *jiggered* if she was going to give up a shirt to a stranger—these things cost money, and money was tight. Then she shut her eyes, and told herself not to be so uncharitable, and sent up a little prayer for forgiveness, and went to the sink to wash the shirt again as best she could.

"So the neonics were affecting the bees' memories," she called to him, over her shoulder. "That was it. They'd fly out to collect pollen, and they'd *collect* the damn pollen, and then … they couldn't remember how to get back to the hive. So they'd fly around, fully laden, at random, until they got worn out and died of fatigue. Tragic, really."

She went back over to him, wrapped the shirt around the wound in his arm and tied it not very expertly. Then she pulled the jacket back over it.

"That's what has borked your brain, Mr. Smith … Mr. Wesson. Because of course once we figured out not to spray this stuff on crops, somebody else figured it would be good to spray it on soldiers in wartime."

"Neonicotinoids," agreed Wesson, and Otty could see he had

maneuvered the phone back into a connection. "You get sick of hearing about it. Clever offensive ordnance, though, because it isn't immediate like a nerve gas attack, or like conventional armaments. You can release it at a level where the canary scanners don't even realize it's in the air. So your guys breathe it in, and breathe it in, and nobody realizes anything is wrong. They get a little more forgetful. In its early stages the COs don't figure it, since stress and combat make people pretty gappy in their mental processes anyway. There's stuff even the healthiest brain doesn't want to remember, in combat. And stuff even the healthiest brain can't process. So by the time anybody realizes what's happening it's too late, and your memory is whacked, and then you're sliding down the far side of a very stony and uncomfortable slope." He shook his head. "I'm not the man I used to be," he said dolefully.

"I'm sorry," said Otty.

"It's not like I'm alone," said Wesson. "And it's not just veterans. You heard about the Toxic Incident in Louisiana? That was the same thing. And Tallahassee. That too."

"People making jokes about what happened in Florida," agreed Otty, "and how are they even going to notice forgetfulness with all the seniors down there? That seems to me a joke in bad taste. And Northern California too."

"It's worse down on the Gulf," said Wesson. "There's a set of new mixes that retain their toxicity when dissolved in water, and it's poisoned everything, swirling in clouds along the rivers and in the sea."

"I guess the fish won't really notice," said Otty.

"But, see, that's the same joke as the one about seniors in Florida," said Wesson, rebukingly. "It so happens that memory *does* matter to fish, and that fucking that up..." He stopped himself. "Sorry, kid. That *messing* it up is... is real bad news. The whole food chain down there is wrecked. And once something gets into the food chain it can be hard to shift it, and hard to predict how bad it'll be when it permeates the whole. It's an environmental disaster."

"One of the many."

"Sure, sure," said Wesson. "Hey, I'm real thirsty. Hey. Is there, like, a cup?"

"There's a refectory at the other end of that corridor," said Otty. "So yes, though I don't know how clean the equipment's likely to be, though."

"It's not so bad," said Wesson, and for a moment Otty thought he was talking about dirty crockery. But of course he wasn't. "The iPhone fix works pretty well. I mean, it gives you access to memories your brain can't hold, and the software they've written interacts pretty well, and your brain compensates, because that's the superhero power of the human brain, its adaptability. So you end up with a kind-of colostomy bag for your long-term memories, and an instant googleability for your general knowledge. It's a patch, not a cure. But it is at least a patch. And the really remarkable thing is, it's cheap. Any bozo can afford it."

"Not *any* bozo," said Otty, thinking of all the rough sleepers and bums she saw on church mission runs, too poor to run phones and too brain-fried to do anything for themselves. They did not do well during the winter, in terms of what her pastor called *corporeal survivability*. And this was in one of the better suburbs of the city!

"*Most* bozos, though. I mean, look at me. I'm just a bozo. I'm not a billionaire. But here I am."

"Where you are is, you need to get your dockette fixed."

That was when the rest of the Famous Five came clattering, loudly, into the James Grabill, banging in past the boarding on the windows, and chattering loudly to one another.

Wesson stood up quickly, looking fiercely in the direction of the noise. He reached for his firearm with his good hand, but in the process he let go of his phone, and it slipped in its loose dockette, and by the time his hand closed on the butt of his firearm he had forgotten why he was reaching for it.

:5:

"Who," Gomery wanted to know, "the buzz is *that*?"

It had been a battle for Otty to convince Gomery that she really didn't like his cursing, or anyone's cursing, and that she really *really* wanted him to stop. He was a churchgoer too, of course, but he belonged to a different congregation than/from hers, and clearly his church was less of a stickler about swears. *Buzz* was his compromise profanity. From time to time he'd joke that Otty's Lutherans really worshiped Bee the Father, Bee the Son and Bee the Holy Swarm, and she'd joke that it should be Bee the Mother, what with the importance of queens to the hive and so on, and then he'd laugh without any real humor. Sometimes she hated Gomery, fierce little bolts of angry hatred that she could feel, palpably, inside her chest. Like spark plugs going off. But then he'd say something cool, or make something amazing out of code—he was a genius-level coder, and that wasn't even Otty saying that, it was his senior Code tutor at Bolt High—or fix together a little reactive *T. rex* toy out of bits and pieces. Then she felt something closer to love. Maybe Allie was right. Maybe that was how love worked.

She had other things to worry about.

Still, here they were. Gomery marched in first, in his big bark-texture jacket with the metal hoop around the waist, and Cess was there looking out of breath, the tendons in her neck so prominent they looked as though they might break through the skin.

"Where's Kathry?" Otty asked.

71

"I guess the police got her," said Cess, in a voice impoverished of its usual jaunty energy.

She was, Otty realized, *scared*. It was the first time she'd seen her friend actually scared. Some valve-cap somewhere in her personality had been unscrewed, and all the ichor had drained out of her soul.

"Police?" said Otty. "What is going on? What *is*?"

"Who," Gomery said again, in a loud voice, "is he?"

"Why don't you ask him?" Otty snapped back, infuriated by Gomery's persistence and general one-dimensional driven clumsiness and, by and large, by the mere *fact* of him, the big lump.

"All right," said Gomery, stepping more clearly in front of Wesson. "Who are you?"

"I don't know," said Wesson in a puzzled voice.

Gomery turned to Otty. "He's some bucklehead hobo."

"He's Mr. Wesson," Otty fired back angrily. "He's not a hobo. He's a veteran."

"Like *those* are mutually exclusive categories," said Gomery.

"Will you two calm down with one another," said Cess. "Or, you know—get a room."

"As if," said Otty, at almost exactly the same time as Gomery said, "Get out with you."

"Who *are* you all?" asked Wesson.

"Look, something serious is happening," said Gomery, turning his back on the old guy. "Say Kathry has been arrested. There's nothing online about it, but what if she has?"

"If it's a police arrest they need to post the warrant," said Cess. "That's the law."

"State police, sure," said Gomery. "But there are, like, eight different police forces these days. Hell, they could have con-stituted a whole new police force this very morning for all we know, with all new rules. Haven't you heard? The country's on the brink of fucking civil…" He stopped, put his palms together and wagged the praying hands in Otty's direction. "I'm sorry, Otty, really I am. My tongue ran away with me. On the brink of *buzzing* civil war."

"Thank you," said Otty, genuinely.

"Why would they arrest Kathry?" said Cess, but it was a rhetorical question. "There can only be one reason, and it's the you-know-what."

"Right. So the question is, how do they even *know* we have a…" Gomery looked over his shoulder at Wesson. But Wesson was staring blankly into space. "Are you sure he's not shamming?" Gomery asked Otty. "I mean, could he be a… spy?"

"Get over yourself, Gom," scoffed Otty. "I mean, like… seriously?"

"The point," said Gomery, "is that the only way anybody on the outside could know about our you-know is if somebody *told* them. And I know I didn't, and I don't believe either of you would."

"But you suspect Kathry? If it was Kathry who told them, why did they arrest her?"

"What about Allie?" Gomery pressed.

"That is beyond the realm of possibility," said Cess, firmly. "That's not in his nature."

"Not in her nature," seconded, and corrected, Otty.

"You're not thinking. Maybe they got to Allie too! If so… I can't even begin to think, if that's so. I guess that means we have to decide what we're going to do. I'm not going to lie, guys. I was this close"—he held up his thumb and forefinger as if he held the world of *Horton Hears a Hoo* in between them—"to rewriting everything myself. Myself. On my own, off my own back."

"We're Five," said Cess, outraged. "Famous Five. We only

open the door, or scrub the code—we *only* do that if *all five* of us agree."

There was no arguing with that.

"We must hang together," Otty agreed. "C'mon, Gom, if we fracture at the first sign of pressure—"

"And now we're Three," interrupted Gom, savagely. "OK? What happens next? What if I'm the next one to be grabbed by the authorities? Do either of you really and truly feel up to the task of resetting our protocols, *solus*?"

"Whattus?" said Cess.

"No need to boast, homey," said Otty. But he had a point.

"If they've grabbed Kath," said Cess, "and especially if they have grabbed Kath *and Allie*, then that's mout, don't you think?"

This brought the other two up short.

"That's what?"

"Mout."

"Say what?"

"You know—when something can't be, like, decided, or … You know—a mout point?"

"Like," said Otty, "a moot point?"

"Is that how it's pronounced?"

"Yeah."

"Is it, really? I mean, are you sure that's how it's pronounced?"

"Yeah," said Otty.

"Woh."

"I'm thirsty," put in Wesson.

"We need to decide," said Gomery, "what we're doing, yeah? The reason I didn't just plunge in unilaterally, on my own, like … was because the group *means* something. OK? We are Five, just as you say, Cess. But now we're Three, and we we we may not *have* the luxury of consulting Allie, or checking with Kath, before we push ahead."

"I just don't think we should go all batloop paranoid."

74

"You don't think we ... Look—*look* at us! We need to make a decision, right here, right now, about what to do with the ..." And again Gomery broke off. He turned and looked at Wesson. "*I'm* sorry,' he said, loudly and sarcastically. "But who is this dude again? Some broken-down roadster tramp bucklehead who just happened to stumble in here?"

"I told you," said Otty. "He's called Wesson. He's been here all night. But we can talk freely. I mean, if, I mean if *that's* your worry, Gomery. He's not shamming. He's real. He was too gone-brain even to get himself a drink of water."

"There's so many of them nowadays," said Cess, in a tone between wonder and sorrow.

"How do you *know* he was here in the night?"

"I *told* you," said Otty, feeling her temper swell in her chest. What was it about Montgomery Lacroix that got her so riled up? One of her closest friends, for heaven's sake. "Yesterday I was scavenging copper wire out of the back of a trash truck five, six blocks from here. And these guys started shooting at me—live fire exercise, real blam-blam-blam. And Mr. Wesson intervened. I'm not fond of being all melodramatic about things, unlike some people I know"—she gave Gomery a hard stare— "but it's true to say he literally saved my life. All right? He was all, come on, come now, we gotta run. And we ran. *And* he got shot himself—his one arm don't work now, you can see. It just dangles. And in the kerfuffle the phone he was using to plug his memory-hole got knocked out. The connection is wonked up or something."

The other two looked at her.

"So he's just a kindly Good Samaritan?" Gomery asked, with a sneer. She hated his sneer.

"The point is, with his phone dockette borked, he's pretty much helpless as a baby. And I don't think we should just leave him here. He'd die of thirst. I wouldn't do that with anybody, and I really don't think I can do it with Mr. Wesson. On account of him helping me out yesterday."

"And him knowing your name?" said Gomery.

Otty had temporarily forgotten that.

"Oh," she said. "Yeah."

"You don't think that's a pretty suspicious thing?"

"Maybe."

"Which makes him a pretty suspicious dude."

"Besides which, we have problems of our own," Cess pointed out. "I don't mean to sound harsh, but I really don't think this old guy is our responsibility."

She was the only one in the Five who didn't belong to a regular church—her parents were radical materialists, and communicants at the congregation of the Imminent Singularity. Cess insisted *her* congregation held her to much higher ethical standards than the usual religions and cults, since, as she put it, "We don't have a kindly sky-pappa to forgive us if we do bad things. We're judged by our future selves. And think how hard you are on your younger self, looking back now?"

When Cess talked like this Otty smiled and nodded, and didn't believe a word of it. I mean, Cess was her friend and she didn't judge her. But everyone knew that morals came from religion. That was just the way it was.

"Gom," Otty pressed. "Could you, maybe, just look at his port, his dockette? If it's just a loose wire, or something, maybe you could MacGyver a fix."

"Wire," scoffed Gomery, as if she'd said *maybe his clockwork steam-engine is malfunctioning*.

"If you can get his phone to connect properly, then we can walk away in good conscience, you see that?" Otty said. "You do see that, right? And you can fix a simple iPhone dock, can't you?"

"Of course I can," said Montgomery, haughtily. "All right— I'm going on the record that this is a distraction, and that we have bigger things to worry about." *The record.* Bless him. "But if I fix this guy's memory, then he goes, all right? You can thank him nicely for dragging you out of that firefight and then it's bye-bye. Are we agreed?"

"Real thirsty," said Wesson.

"All right, old-timer," said Gomery, in his Wild West cowboy voice. "I'm going to mosey up and take a look at your phone dockette, alrighty-tighty?"

"Who are you?" asked Wesson.

Gomery took out his smart-tweeze and went over to where the old guy was sitting. He crouched down. He pulled Wesson's coat aside and peered at the port where the blood-smeared iPhone was sitting.

"Now what seems to be problem?" he asked, slipping into his British voice.

He had done this accent once, on a whim, and Otty had laughed. Now, as was his way, he always did it. Charging ahead like a bull in a field, literally, figuratively, was the whole of him.

"Thirst," said the old guy.

Gomery took the phone out, peered at the dockette, and put the phone back in. Then he shifted it up slightly and nodded. It had clicked back into place.

"The connection is a little—" he began, and then he stopped speaking.

Wesson had his gun out and was pressing it into the side of Gomery's head.

"Listen to me, kid," said the old man, in a different voice. "You keep your hand *exactly* where it is, do you understand? You keep that phone in exactly that position, or I'm going to crack your fucking head open with a bullet from this gun. Do you understand?"

"He," said Gomery, in a strained voice, "has a *gun*?"

"Oh yeah," said Otty. "I should have mentioned that."

"Mentioned it," said Gomery. He had gone very still. "Or maybe you could have buzzing *disarmed* him?"

"I kinda forgot about it," Otty confessed.

"That's a real gun?" Cess asked, dismayed. "Like an actual firearm?"

"*You* need to stop talking," said Wesson. "And you, sonny boy, need to stay very still and hold that phone in place. You can *fix* this iPhone dockette, can you?"

"I was just taking a look. I don't know yet how easy it will be actually to fix it."

"And yet you have a smart-tweeze in your right hand? Don't lie to me, son, or I'll scatter fragments of your fucking skull so that they rattle against that far wall. Understand me?"

"All right," said Gomery. He sounded oddly calm. "I might be able to fix your memory. Your dockette has been shaken up and connections are loose. Yeah? But that's easily fixed."

"So fix it."

"I'll need to take the phone out of the dockette. I can't fix it with the phone in the way, can I?"

"You leave the phone exactly where it is," said Wesson. He was looking around the room. "I'm serious. If you so much as twitch, I'm pulling this trigger."

"Snatch it away, Gom!" Otty cried. "Once the phone is out of the dockette he'll forget why he's even holding the gun!"

"Don't take the risk, son," advised Wesson. "She don't know me, and she don't know how fast my reflexes are. You really want to take that chance? This is your life you're dealing with."

Little spots of sweat were visible on Gomery's brow.

"Stay cool, old man," he suggested.

"Gom! Be quick and save yourself," said Otty, stepping forward.

"Come half a foot closer and your friend will have only the lower half of a head!" yelled Wesson. "Everybody stay *exactly* where they are. We have a collective problem, you understand? All of us. And we have to figure a collective answer. I need my app and my phone to function properly. Weaponized fucking Alzheimer's. And you need to help me back to functionality."

"So that you can shoot the rest of us?" said Cess.

"Believe me, this is not how I wanted things to go down."

He lapsed into silence and appeared to be straining—trying to get his right arm to work, to pinch his swollen blue fingers together. Nothing doing.

"Gomery," hissed Otty, trying one last time. "Once the phone is *out* of the dockette he'll be harmless! Just... Just pull it away and roll. Roll! Even if he gets one shot off, he won't get more than one."

"Do you know what, Ottoline?" Gomery returned. The strain in his voice was almost painful to hear. "It's not your head that's at risk of being catastrophically disassembled. All right? So you could do me a solid and stop doing your best to piss this guy off. All right?"

"Listen to your boyfriend, Ottoline Barragão," advised Wesson.

Otty couldn't stop a scornful "He's not my *boy*friend," and it came out at the same time as Cess said, "You told him your *surname*?" in disbelief, and on the same reflex Otty turned to her and snapped, "I didn't tell him anything!" and as Cess held up a fist and returned, "Oh, really?" and Otty snapped, "He already knew! I don't know how, he just did," and Gomery was speaking in a loud, clear voice, "Will you two shut up?" and then Wesson himself bellowed, "Quiet!"

Everybody was quiet.

"Listen to me, the lot of you," said Wesson. "I don't like this situation. You don't like this situation. We have to make the best of it, yeah? So long as your friend, Montgomery here, keeps holding my phone in place, I can talk. I've half a mind to take him with me, with him and me walking back into town together. But that's not going to work, is it? It's going to look pretty odd, a grown man marching a child through the streets at gunpoint. Besides, once we start walking the phone will shift in its dockette and I'll go back to being a frog-brained dunce and then you all will fuck off and leave me to die of thirst, *won't* you now."

"Mister—" Gomery began.

"Shush, now. I only have one hand, and it's holding this gun. If I put the gun down, you'll unplug me and I'm doomed. But I can't do anything else *with* the hand while it's holding this gun. So it's a catch-22, yeah? Which as you may not know, since I'm assuming you're all too clever to be plugged in remotely to the general web, is a novel by a twentieth-century American writer called Joseph Heller."

"Mister," Gomery tried again. "Do you want to put the gun down, maybe?"

"Shut the fuck," said Wesson, "up."

"Mister," Gomery said mildly. "We're just kids."

"I know exactly who you are, Montgomery Lacroix, and that fact should give you pause, yeah? You keep holding that in place. You keep on doing that. I served, OK? I was in uniform eleven years. I served in Israel, and Egypt, and I was part of the spearhead during the Saudi campaign. I went into Mexico as part of Operation Sombrero. You think I haven't killed kids? You think they didn't send kids with AKs against us? You think I'll hesitate for *one* second where your fat head is concerned."

"Mister," said Gomery, for a third time. "I'm just trying to de-escalate the situation a smidgeon."

"Stop talking," rasped Wesson. "You three are going to *listen* to me, OK? And if you listen to me, then maybe you'll understand. If I put this gun down, you'll disconnect me and that'll be tantamount to killing me—because if you fuck off, then I die, and once I'm brainless again you *will* fuck off."

"If you shoot Gomery, he'll fall and drop the phone and the same thing will happen," said Cess, in a level voice.

"Very good. That's true too. You know what that says to me? That says—*his* life and *my* life are bound together now. You want your friend to keep living?"

"Yes," said Otty. And then, because that came out a little croaky, she said more clearly: "Yes."

"Let's all keep calm. You kids, listen, now. You kids, listen to me."

They listened.

"Like I told your friend … Jesus, yesterday. A whole day ago! I can't believe we lost so much time. I hope we aren't too late." He growled, or coughed, or made some noise in his throat. "I'm real thirsty, ladies. One of you maybe has some water in a bottle, or something?"

Cess and Otty shook their heads in unison.

"I realize I look like a threat," said Wesson. "What with this … er … firearm in my hand."

"No shit, flintlock," said Montgomery, in a strained voice.

"You have to listen. That's all. All of you. And your friends … You have two other friends who are part of the group, yes? Kathry Chong, and Allie, who I don't know if is a he or a she."

"He's a he," said Cess, and at the same time Otty said, "She's a she."

"Genderfluid, fine," said Wesson. "You're all in danger. All of you. Aren't you curious how I know all your names?"

"I find my natural curiosity gets a little squeezed by the prospect of imminent death," said Gomery.

"You guys," said Wesson. "You guys have been running your own private internet."

Nobody said anything.

"Sure," said Wesson. "Schtum, sure. But it's not a secret any more, see? Now, now the thing is … The thing is, there are some

81

very bad people out there who know. Some very bad people who know and who are very bad indeed. Killing bad—torturing bad."

"Your colleagues?" asked Cess.

"I'm ... something else. Look, kids, I could explain who I am, but time is short. You're not the only private internet encysted off from the main web. Of course you know that. Plenty people are suspicious of big data, and government oversight. And they're right to be. Political situation what it is, and all. There are departments hidden inside departments with hacker-tech that can penetrate any online defences. Shit, two thirds of the population are still relying on old prime-number encryption keys that were cracked five years ago. But the others, the ones who *think* they're smart, the blockchainers and kaleyarders and Bible-code cranks—they're all wide open. They just don't know it. Wide open. There's only one way to keep your online presence safe from spooks, and that's to do what you kids did—to wire up your own internet. To port in data only when it's been triple-scrubbed, and only then factual data, Wikipedia content from the edit pages, visual files you personally uploaded and so on."

He stopped to cough drily. Then he said: "I'm real thirsty, kids. I feel like I could die of it. State of my arm, I guess I lost a lot of blood—yeah? You don't think you could run to source a cup and bring me one glass of water?"

"I say we thirst him out," said Cess. "You know what I mean? We can just wait until he passes out with the thirst. He can't shoot Gomery without killing himself, so he won't do that, and we can outlast him when it comes to water."

"He was shot yesterday," said Otty. "He'll have lost blood. He's gotta be super-thirsty."

"See!" said Cess, triumphant.

"Jesus," rasped the old man, exasperated.

"Stay there," said Otty.

As she went to the door, Cess called, "What are you *doing*, girlfriend?"

"Just wait there," said Otty.

She was in the corridor now, and she sprinted as fast as she could for the old refectory. Through the back to what had, eons ago, back when dinosaurs walked the earth and in the first seven days of God's Glorious Creation, been the food preparation area. The flat roof at the back had collapsed under a mass of earth, and creepers had grown over the gap, making a strange verdant skylight; underneath it gigantic tins of frying oil, rusting along their lids, stood beside mushrooms big as manhole covers and the same color as zombie flesh. A froth of nettles up against the back wall. From a cupboard she pulled out a dusty plastic mug, and ran back along the corridor, the slapping echoes of her own footfall chasing her the whole way.

Back in the restroom, and the tableau had not changed. She filled the cup at one of the faucets and brought it over to Wesson.

"You might be thinking," he said, in a cracked and wary voice, "of trying to shove your friend out of harm's way, or some such heroics. But I really wouldn't risk it. My condition is grave, I don't deny. My short-term memory is cracked and broken and my long-term memory almost wholly wiped. But there's enough in my reflex brain to pull a trigger, even if I don't know why I'm pulling it. OK?"

"OK," agreed Otty.

Wesson was eyeing the dusty mug with an unmissable avidity. Maybe he would let his defenses down. Let his guard slip. He was, clearly, desperate. Now was the chance, Otty thought. As he drank, just grab Gomery around the waist and pull him clear. Or … Or, maybe, throw herself at the pair of them, like a football tackle, and bundle everybody over. No, she told herself, then the gun might go off by accident. So … How about if she just grabbed the pistol, grabbed the barrel and hoiked it down, pointed it at the floor? It would probably discharge, but Gomery would break free, and then Wesson would lose volition and they'd all be safe.

Unless she miscalculated. She was a teenage girl, and he was a military veteran. What if she simply lacked the muscular power to redirect his gun-arm? And what if the gun went off and shot Gomery while she was snatching at it? How could she not blame herself in such a situation?

She had to do *something*. It was burning her conscience that this man was only in the James Grabill because *she* had brought him here. Which meant the gun pressed into the side of Gomery's head was her responsibility, and if anything happened to him it would be blood on her soul, forever.

She had to do something. But what?

She was discovering that, when the moment for action presents itself, a reasonable person might easily find themselves frozen, not from cowardice so much as from an inability to choose the best from among a variety of options.

She leaned forward with the cup.

Wesson said: "You're a Christian, aren't you, Ottoline?"

That surprised her.

"Yes," she said. "Sure. What? Why?"

"Ottoline, I want you to promise me you're not going to try anything funny, OK?"

"Promise you," said Otty.

"You'll thank me afterward. Really you will. But you need to promise me you're not going to try and grab your friend, here, or anything."

"Sure," said Otty.

"I want you to promise me on your god, Otty."

That went through her like a spear.

"What?"

84

"You heard me. Just do it."

She breathed in, and breathed out. "This is not a trivial thing you're asking me, Mr. Wesson," she said.

"It's why I'm asking it. Do you swear on your god? Just say yes, and I'll believe you."

Otty held herself, the cup of grubby water half-outstretched. And she felt a strange something in her chest, a sensation of sharp, almost brittle tingling, as if her heart were metamorphosing into some glittery new crystal. It was the feeling she got sometimes in church, when the light came strong and sharp through the big stained window at the end—the intricate, rainbow-varied Harry Clarke design of abstract colors and designs. It only happened a few times in the year, when the autumn or winter sun was low enough in the east during service times to give that saint the glow of life and magnificence, and the many colors fell over the yellowing fingernails of the chapel's organ keyboard, and the variously bald and hairy heads of the congregants were blessed by it. At such moments Otty was aware of a transcendent something, a tightly folded excitement in her chest, a feeling as though she was on the very edge of breaking through into some new truth.

She felt that now.

"I promise," she told Wesson.

"What are you doing?" Cess wailed, behind her.

And Gomery said, in a low, strangulated voice, "Take it easy now, Otty."

She put the cup to Wesson's mouth. Up close she could see the lips were mottled, like pink marble with flakes of white, the skin dry as a knee or elbow. Wesson's eyes were looking at her eyes, and she did not break that contact. She tipped the cup up, and he gulped, and blupped, and a dribble of brown water tracked down the stubble of his chin. She tipped further, and he drank more. Then it was all gone, and she withdrew the cup and backed away.

"Thank you," he said. "Now listen to me, all of you. You'll be glad you did, afterward. I know you've been running your own private internet. I know this is more than a hobby, and it's more than a set of tin cans with strings running between them, so you can chat with your *pals*." He burped, then, and blinked several times. "I know it's a loop, encysted away, and of quite remarkable sophistication. I haven't seen inside it, of course—that was the whole point in you setting it up, to stop people like me seeing inside it. But I'll tell you. It's possible, if you've the patience and clever enough code, to feel your way around the *outside*, as it were, of the vacancy, and get a sense of the overall shape. Listen, kids, I'm just an old soldier, OK? I'm not a hacker or a coder or anything like that. I only know so much. But the people who have hired me are very impressed with what you have done, yeah? Very impressed."

"So they should be," said Cess.

"Be quiet, Cess," said Gomery, in a strained voice. "Make your mouth stop talking now."

"I'm on your side. My *people* are on your side—or at least they are when compared to the others who are after you."

"Government," said Otty.

"Ms. Barragão, I can only say that calling your antagonists *the government* doesn't help narrow things down. Government is collapsing. Yeah? You're smart kids, you follow the newsfeeds. We're probably two weeks away from all-out civil war, tanks on the streets, drones blowing up civilian houses left, right and centre, and every West Pointer thinking they're refighting Bull Run with them as Robert E. fucking Lee."

"Fuckingly?" queried Cess.

"Kids! Think! Government now is about a dozen different groups, all wrestling for power, and at least two of those groups want what you're hiding in your network. They want it so bad they'll do anything at all, ruling nothing whatsoever out of court, to get it. Montgomery—your mom works for StandCorps, yeah?"

Gomery didn't answer.

"Kids, you have to believe me, I'm on your side. I'm on your side. I know you stole something from StandCorps. They're a serious organization, and close, but not entirely watertight. I know they're panicked you stole it."

"Not stole," said Gomery. Like the distinction mattered.

"What?"

"It's a copy. I only copied it. If I steal your automobile, then I deprive you of the use of your automobile. That's theft. If I can magically copy your sutomobile, so you can still drive it around just as before, I acquire an automobile, but it's not theft."

"You . . ." said Wesson, in an astonished voice. "You must. Think I was. Born yesterday. You think that distinction is going to fly in court? You think we don't *know* you took what you copied and developed it in wholly new directions? That you and your friends fashioned something unique, and extremely dangerous, and hid it away in your private network? You think we all don't know that?"

He stopped speaking and looked from face to face. Nobody said anything, of course.

"I'll tell you, I don't know exactly what's inside your little e-cyst," said Wesson. "Save that it's a weapon of unprecedented destructive capacity. My bosses have their theories exactly what and how. And they know the other side want it, very very much. You think they're going to be gentle with you, when it comes to extracting it? You think they won't lean on you very hard? I've seen extreme interrogation practices up close, on the Saudi campaign, and it's very much *not* a pretty sight."

"We believe you, mister," said Gomery, his voice muffled by the fact that he was speaking into Wesson's torso.

"I'll tell you what I'm sure it is," said Wesson. "And you can neither confirm nor deny, like proper little fucking professionals, but I'll get a sense by whether you flinch, or look at one another in a significant way. Yeah? It's money."

Nobody said anything.

"Not, like, a *bank* account. Of course, no. I mean, that wouldn't mean anything in an encysted private network, anyway, would it? Might as well bury a bag of gold in the ground. No. I think it's a protocol. I think it's a *scarcity* protocol. An area denial weapon aimed at the money supply. Because that's the trick, isn't it? How do you preserve the value of money in a world that's going to shit? War always means mega-inflation. Often it's staggered, because war also gives government extraordinary powers to chokehold money supply and make top-down demands of market movement and the like. But when the war's over, inflation bounces free and your whole economy fucking collapses. Look at what happened in the 1920s after World War One, or in the second half of the 1940s after World War Two, or 2028 after the Secret World War turned out not to have been so secret after all. World War Three-point-zero, some call it. And maybe you are kids, but you know where real governance resides. You know *money* is what governs. I'm not condescending to you kids, you're all smart kids. I won't patronize you. You know all this, yeah? Money rules, and the actual officers of government from the president herself all the way down to beat cops patrolling the better-off neighborhood, and leaving neighborhoods like this one the fuck alone—they all work for money, yeah? They all work for money. I don't just mean in the sense that they get a salary for their work—that's secondary. They work to keep money in power. They work so that money maintains its position."

He looked around. Nobody was saying anything. A single sweat drop dripped from Gomery's chin.

"So let's say war is coming," said Wesson. "Inevitable, can't be avoided, and you kids happen to have figured out a redoubt for financial value. You don't think the powers that be would be *super*-keen to get their hands on that? Something that could keep their money reserves buoyant during the coming apocalypse. Not conventional, like the gold standard, since that means antshit in the online world, the endless scarcity-free environment of Online. But not blockchain either, and not that e-Xchange nonsense. Something new. Something that would deflate all other monies by comparison to what you store, maybe. Whaddaya say, kids? One nod for yes, two nods for no."

"How about you put the gun down," suggested Otty, "and Gomery, there, holds your phone in position, and we can continue this discussion without the risk of a twitch blowing his blessed head to smithereens?"

Wesson took a deep breath, and let it out again. It sounded like he had gone on a quest to find the Sigh At The End Of The World and, successful, had brought it back to display it to these kids.

"I'm nearly done, younglings. I'm nearly through. I appreciate your patience. But listen—the government is in disarray, I'm not denying it. But there's enough coordination in the relevant arms of the State to make sure *you* never see your seventeenth birthdays, and to make sure that the thing that prevents you ever reaching that age is extremely painful and debilitating and terrifying. I'm a soldier. I made my peace with dying a long time ago. But *you're* young. And you only have two choices—let me take you to my bosses, who will protect you, or let the bad guys grab you and that's the end. That's the end. So what's it going to be?"

Again, there was a general silence. Otty could hear a strange humming sound. Had Gomery fallen asleep? Was he *snoring*?

"I hate to hurry you, kids, but time is very short. I don't know your other two friends the way you do, so you tell me. How likely is it that your pal Kathry will hold up during torture? She will crack, and when she does, what will be the consequence? Or your pal Allie—is she, or he, going to last an hour? A half-hour? Less? When the real experts in applying advanced interrogation techniques get to work? If they crack before you do, you lose your advantage. And you don't want to lose your advantage."

"I think Allie would hold out longer than *you* suspect," said Otty.

"We have no proof that Allie has fallen into the government's hands," said Cess, more to Otty and Gomery than to Wesson. "And for that matter, we have no proof that Kathry has been arrested either. The police came to my house but I got clear. Maybe—"

"Maybe schmaybe," snapped Wesson. "My arm's getting tired, holding this gun against this kid's temple. What's it going to be?"

"How do we know we can trust you?" Otty asked.

"I saved you yesterday, didn't I? C'mon, Ms. Barragão—vouch for me here. Time is *pressing*."

The humming noise was louder, and it occurred to Otty that it wasn't Gomery snoring. It was coming from outside the James Grabill altogether. She opened her mouth to say something to Wesson, and that was when the earthquake struck.

The first thing was a gigantic noise, like an avalanche in a thunderstorm. That image flashed distinctly across her mind—a thunderbolt hitting the top of a mountain and initiating a gigantic rockslide. Sight blurred and occluded. A storm cloud rolled rapidly through the hall, dark gray and black, and crackling with static electricity. Not electricity, but rather the sound of multiple snaps and cracks. It went duskily dark, and she could no longer see anything, and noise fell through the air like a spate.

The right-hand wall, the exterior wall, had fallen in. Had been bashed in, knocked over. A detonation had instantly milled the cinder blocks out of which the wall was constructed into particles and ashes and fine, fine concrete dust. The remnants of the blast shoved Otty to the left, and she staggered. She almost lost her footing, but was able to plant a foot out to steady herself and regain her balance. Multiple ruby laser lines ruled themselves neatly through the dusty air, and Otty was with it enough to know that these were the trails of rifle sights. Cess was on her back, and her mouth was open, and her chest was going up and down so she was still alive, which was good. And that high-pitched noise in Otty's ears was either tinnitus from the blast, or else the unusually pure sound of Cess's screaming, like a moistened finger being run around the lip of a wineglass.

Slow, slow—why couldn't she move any *faster*?—Otty turned to the right and saw four bulked-up figures in body armor and all-head helmets jogging heftily into the room. They all had rifles out, sweeping the space, each barrel tipped by a red-laser bayonet that spanned the room. Still in slow motion, Otty turned her gaze back to where Wesson had his pistol pressed against the head of her friend Gomery, her friend whom she loved and didn't want to see dead, whom she loved *as* a friend, and, why deny, as more than a friend. And she saw Gomery shift his posture and roll to the left, away from the intruders. Black shapes through the dust. Otty was coughing, and the high-pitched whining had popped, and now she could hear Cess properly, yelling, and coughing too. There was a clatter and a thud-thud of boots, but the guys who had broken in weren't yelling anything. The red-laser lines converged for a moment into a four-spoked triangle. Otty only cared about whether Gomery was safe. That's what she was concerned about. She took a step toward him. You've seen a pill-woodlouse, yeah? A roly-poly bug. You've seen how they are when they're disturbed—they're scurrying along and then, ping, they're a tiny armored globe, and rolling away to safety like a soccer ball. That was Gomery, one moment crouched awkwardly and motionless next to Wesson, the next thing tucked up tight and rolling away.

And Wesson himself was swiveling his torso where he sat, bringing his one working hand and the pistol it held toward the incomers. And Otty was watching him. She saw, quite distinctly, the muzzle flash of Wesson's pistol, a startling thistle of illumination flowering at the very end of the barrel, and only after that did she hear the report of its discharge.

This noise was hideous, brutal, like a punch to the ears. Otty flinched. She put up her hands to her head, and she was ducking down, and twisting as she did so. She saw one of the men in combat fatigues hit: shoelaces of ragged cloth leaping out from his chest, like worms, wriggling, and the man himself jumping up—bopping up into the air, like he was doing a little dance at the Church Youth Group disco. Then he came down, and stopped, as the other men surged forward. The shot man went down, with ponderous grace, onto one knee, as his comrades in arms surged past him. Then Otty lost sight of him, because she was being bundled over by one of the intruders. It hurt. The force of the tackle knocked her straight down, and that meant that her head cracked on the floor with a blinding painful sense of inward detonation. Damn. She was dizzied. Disoriented. Flickering lights that were nothing but random firings of her optic nerve tazed across her vision. The breath was knocked from her, and she struggled fruitlessly to suck air into her lungs, gasped asthmatically, sucked and sucked, nothing coming in. It was alarming, and her heart jittered, and she kicked her legs, but she couldn't move her arms because they were pinned behind her. She understood, a moment after the procedure had been completed, and the pressure of the man's weight was lifted from her back, that she had been handcuffed.

Then there was another colossal *whumf* of detonation, and a flashbulb of light from where Wesson was sitting, so either his iPhone had somehow managed to stick in its docking port and he knew what he was doing, or more likely it had slid free and he was firing mindlessly, reflexly. Conceivably he was as startled by the sound he was making as the others. And then there were more soldiers coming in through the hole in the wall, and the floor was vibrating under Otty's resting cheek and their boots struck the wood, and, for the first time, the invaders began shouting and yelling. The next thing she knew, Otty was being lifted, light as a leaf, four burly figures carrying her, one each for her legs and two more for her arms. And she was hauled through and out, and into the open air and sunshine and the song of birds, and then into the cell of a police wagon and the door was slammed behind her.

CHAPTER II

She was on her own in the wagon, which meant the police must have brought a whole *convoy* of wagons to the James Grabill and parceled the kids out between each and all. There was one low narrow bench, and straps along the wall of the wagon on that side. She had been cuffed, but though they'd taken away her bag they hadn't confiscated her phone. Which was something. The wagon growled into life and shifted away, and Otty pushed her back against the inside wall. It was very hard to keep her balance with her hands cuffed behind her; she did her best, trying to roll with the swaying passage of the journey, but she fell several times onto the floor.

The wagon stopped often, sometimes for bafflingly long periods of time. At one point it ran very fast, or at least its engine revved high for a long time. Finally it pulled to a stop, sat there for a long time. Eventually the rear doors were snapped open and she was led out, blinking in the light. She just had time to adjust to the brightness in order to see that they had parked outside a large, low-roofed building. It wasn't in any part of town Otty recognized, and it didn't look like a police station. Beyond was scrubland, and an absolutely enormous eSpire,

94

maybe three thousand feet high—so tall that its slender pinnacle was hazy in the clouds.

Two uniformed officers, one male and one female, escorted her inside the building.

Beyond the main doors was a large hallway. A surprising quantity of hothouse plants in pots cluttered the floor, and on one wall was a portrait of the president, smiling her notoriously desperate smile—that eager, greedy, ingratiating expression that looked like it had seceded from the serious rest of her face. Her "Mona Pleaser" smile, the web-laughsters called it.

There was a kind of reception desk in the corner, with nobody behind it. The impression was of the reception space in a provincial chain hotel, and nothing at all like a police or federal facility.

She was taken to a small, white room, brightly lit. A table with wipe-clean laminate top stood in the middle, with a chair on either side. She was sat in one of these chairs. Then she was uncuffed and left in the room for a while. The room had a large mirror on one wall, almost comically obviously an observation window. They hadn't taken away her phone, so she fished it out and tried to call her parents, but there was no signal. No internet, no contact. When she tried to piggyback a local signal, a U.S. Justice Department seal filled the screen. Some kind of blocking algorithm, then, inside the building.

She put the phone away.

She waited. Eventually the lock cleared its metal throat and the door swung open. Two women came in, one in uniform, one in civilian gear, a cream-colored tunic and black trousers. Neither introduced themselves. The woman in the tunic asked Otty to stand, and then examined her, back and front, shone a light in her eyes. She asked her if she had a headache or felt dizzy.

"Why am I here?" asked Otty, with more confidence than she felt. "Why have I not been informed why I have been abducted?

95

Have I been arrested? On what charge? I want to speak to my parents. I want to speak to an attorney."

The woman in the tunic tipped her head back and leveled it again, a sort-of shrug. Then she tutted, and the two women went out through the door.

"I want it noted on the official record," Otty called after them, stridently enough, "that I haven't been *read my rights*." The proper term popped into her head as the door slammed shut. "My Miranda rights!"

Nothing. She sat down again and waited.

The thing that most occupied her mind was her bees. She even felt a little bad about it. She guessed her parents and her sister would be freaking out, and she surely missed them all, but most of all she worried about her bees. The thing was: she was the only one who knew how to *handle* them. They'd probably be OK, she told herself. At least for a day or two. But how long would she be stuck here?

After an incalculable length of time a youngish guy came in. A primrose-colored suit, white shirt and red tie. He pulled a chair over and sat down opposite Otty. Put a smart screen on the table in front of him.

"Ottoline Barragão," he said. "I'm Carson Gulliver, and I'm an agent in the Department of Assize and Review."

"Should I have heard of that? Because I've never heard of that. Are you police?"

"Sort of. We report to the DOJ, but we have extraordinary powers. And you're here, Ottoline, because you have been adjudged a present threat to the stability of the United States of America."

"I'm not, though," said Otty.

Gulliver opened his eyes very wide. "You're not? Well, in that case you're free to go with our sincere apologies."

Otty stared at him. "Department," she said, "of Sarcasm and Sophomoric Stupidheads."

"Your *vocabulary*," said Gulliver, "is very impressive for a ... What are you? Sixteen?"

"I'm guessing you know exactly how old I am."

"Well, yes. I know a lot about you, Ottoline. Almost everything. Now, you're a smart kid. You *know* what this is about. So you know that the best thing you can do is cooperate entirely with us. If you do that, then ... Well, I can't promise you anything, of course. But it'll sure go smoother for you. We might even be able to get your parents in here, before tonight."

"What have I been charged with?"

"You have been charged under the most recent iteration of the Security and Defense of the Union Act."

"What charge, though?"

"Acting or conspiring to act or causing by inaction other forms of activity liable to bring or constitute of actual harm to the Security and Defense of the United States of America," said Gulliver, smoothly.

"What acts?"

"The specific charges fall under the purview of non-disclosure for reasons for national security."

This exchange wasn't going anywhere.

"Shouldn't I have an attorney?"

"You're legally underage. According to the provisions of your arrest warrant, you must have a chaperone or parent present. He or she can advise you on the best attorney to retain, or indeed on the need for an attorney at all."

"OK," said Otty, sitting forward. "So get my mom in here."

"I think you misunderstand. *I'm* your legally provisioned chaperone."

"You told me you were a cop!"

"I said I worked for the Department of Assize and Review.

Which I do. But that doesn't prevent me, under the law, acting as chaperone."

"Conflict your interest, much, do you?"

He smiled very broadly at this, and didn't reply, so she tried a different tack.

"I never met you in my life before three minutes ago. You can't be my chaperone."

"The law does not require that we know one another. Only that I be an individual of good character."

"And you are an individual of good character?" said Otty.

"Impeccable."

"Well," said Otty, affecting a British accent, "that's good-oh and splendid."

"As your chaperone, Ottoline, I'd advise against retaining legal counsel. There's no need, and it's super-expensive. And you have nothing to hide, do you?"

"I tell you what I got—zippo," Otty said, aiming for a sharp retort but realizing, even as she was speaking, that she was missing the mark and sounding instead petulant and scared. "I got zip to say to you. I want to see my parents. Or my attorney."

Gulliver continued as if she hadn't spoken.

"So the interrogating officer is gonna come in here and ask you some questions, and I'll be here and I will step in if I think any of the questions are out of bounds, and you can rest easy. Just tell the truth, Ottoline. They're going to ask you about your friends—your four *best* friends, Montgomery Lacroix"—his eye strayed to the screen before him on the table—"Pitt Smith, Kathry Chong and Allie Straightup. They're going to ask about the private network you guys set up. The copper wire you stole from the street, the processors you stole from … lots of different places, I guess. The you-know-what that was stolen from Stand-Corps. The whole illegal kit and caboodle."

"It's not illegal to run a private network," Otty said, and then wished she hadn't spoken.

"You have to understand," said Gulliver, smiling and leaning in, "we have *all* your friends under arrest."

At this she knew he was lying, and realizing that he was lying gave her a little spurt of hope in her chest.

"You say *we*," she told him. "If you were properly my chaperone you should say *they*."

Gulliver's smile didn't waver. "But I did say 'they', little Ottoline," he said. "You must have misheard. I'm your chaperone. I'm on your side. I'm just helping you get your story straight, before the heavy-duty cops come through. You've heard of nice cop, nasty cop. This is gonna be nasty cop, nastier cop, and when they get tired of hammering you, they'll pop out for a coffee and a Danish and will be replaced by nastiest cop and fucking Satan with a badge. OK?" He was snarling. But then the smile returned, and in a light-as-air voice he added: "But I'm here as your chaperone to make sure it never gets out of hand."

The sliver of hope in Otty's chest thickened, just a little. It made her realize how despairing her spirit had been. She'd never been arrested before. It was all very alarming and discombobulating, but it was also not entirely without hope.

"I'd be grateful if you didn't swear, Mr. Gulliver. That language is offensive to me, and inappropriate when a minor is in the room."

This manifestly wrong-footed him, but he smiled again, and said, "Exactly so, my dear. But, look. Let me tell you how to get through this all quickly and painlessly. *One* of your four friends is going to give it up, because they're all being interrogated right now in rooms much harsher than this one, in buildings scattered all over the state. And when one of them gives it up, that means you've missed the chance to be the one who lets us—lets *them*—have the golden prize. Because whoever gives up that golden prize will be the one to get clemency. Will be the one not to spend the next couple of decades in internment. You might even be back with your parents for Christmas. You do celebrate Christmas, don't you?"

"What golden prize?" she asked innocently.

"What's inside your network, my girl. You know. The whole of your Famous Five know it. That is what you call yourselves? Yeah, we know. So why not spill *those* beans, here, now, and rescue... seriously, rescue the whole rest of your life. Would you rather Montgomery be the one who gets that chance?"

"Gomery would never talk to you guys."

"Or Allie?"

At this Otty laughed aloud. She actually barked with laughter. "You don't know my friends very well, do you, Mister Gulliver?"

"Have it your way," smiled Gulliver. "But don't say I didn't *warn* you." He read, or pretended to read, something on his screen. "How did you guys meet, anyway? You don't go to the same school, which is the usual way of making friends. Or go to the same church, which is the other usual way of making friends. In fact, unless I'm mistaken, Pitt and Allie don't go to any church. That's a bit suspect, don't you think? Not going to church? No? No comment? OK, my dear. It still leaves open the question of how you ever got together—the *Famous Five*. How did you all meet?"

"Online," said Otty. "How does anybody meet anyone nowadays?"

"The free and open internet. All right, Ottoline." Gulliver leaned in again. "What's it going to be? What have you been keeping from the rest of us? What *is* hidden inside your encysted network?"

"It's just a friendzone," said Otty, stubbornly. "We just hang out together, you know. Chat about our many shared interests. You know how we teens are."

"And the million and one apps and services that enable you to do precisely that on the regular internet?"

"We value our privacy," said Otty.

"That's it?" asked Gulliver. "That non-answer and this pissy attitude? You're going to throw away your whole future on that?"

"I'd like an attorney, please."

"As your chaperone," Gulliver beamed, "I must advise against such a move."

"I'd like an attorney, please."

"Clearly you're hysterical. As your legally appointed and validated chaperone, I'm mandated to act in your best interests, and this display of hysteria leads me to believe you're not best placed to judge what those best interests are."

"I'd like," said Otty, calmly, "an attorney, please."

"Whoa, Otty. Settle down! This may be a case where you need to be physically restrained," said Gulliver, scooping up his tablet and getting to his feet. "Or sedated. Or probably both. You're sure now, you don't want to cooperate?"

Otty was human, and young, and in a situation that was both scary and unprecedented for her. Some part of her was screaming that she just wanted to go home—to hug her folks, to see her sister again, to check in on her bees. For everything to go back to normal. It kept chiming, like a meditation mantra, that *she hadn't done anything wrong*. She hadn't broken any law. Well, maybe going into the derelict James Grabill was trespass— maybe. But it was a derelict building, and since it had once been a school it presumably belonged to the state, so it's not like any private property owner was going to lose their temper and sue. And what else? She squeezed memories of the work she had put in on Gomery's big acquisition to the back of her head. Best not think of that. So … what else? She and her friends had built themselves a private mini-internet? In some contexts she'd be winning the Science Prize for innovation and ingenuity. Yet here she was: arrested, sneered at by this supremely *irritating* man in his yellow suit and red tie. Otty wanted to be able to sweep her arm and push it all to the side—to stride out the door without anybody stopping her, to go back to her life. She almost crumbled.

But then she looked again at his smile. And, since she was a smart kid—few smarter—and as she did experience those occasional rushes of insight vouchsafed to the teenaged, she suddenly understood. He was young, and well-dressed, and, though he really wasn't Otty's type, he was kind of good-looking. And she had a vertiginous insight into the game her captors were playing. The faceless men and women behind the one-way mirror. They'd sent in Gulliver because they figured she would *crush* on him. His sarcastic superciliousness was him flirting with her. It was so ridiculous, and so insulting to her romantic sensibilities, that it actually strengthened her resolve not to capitulate. Really. *This* was their idea of the kind of boy she liked? Pfft. It only showed how little they understood her. If they'd sent in an older, fatherly figure, one with a well-trimmed mustache covering the whole of his upper lip and a faint odor of coal-tar soap to him, then she might actually have caved.

She pushed her own chair back and stood up, her legs trembling slightly. She wasn't scared, exactly, although she was shaking with something—excitement, a sense of her own capriciousness. Ignoring Gulliver, she walked over to the one-way mirror and said, in loud, clear tones: "I want an attorney. And I want to see my parents. I'm legally a minor, and you are obliged."

A snickering sound behind her. She turned, expecting to see Gulliver laughing at her, but it was only the click of the lock as the door closed. She was alone.

There was a long wait, and her trembly rebellious excitement drained out of her soon enough. Then she fell into a kind of despondency. What had she done? The waiting went on and on.

"Hey," she told the mirror. "I need to use the bathroom. What do you want me to do? You want me to go in the corner?"

Nothing.

An hour passed. Maybe two. Finally the door opened and two people came through.

"Hi, guys," she said. "I'd like to see an attorney, please."

They didn't reply. Nor did they cuff her, but they did take her arms and loft her from her chair, gently enough. Then they led her down the antiseptic corridor and around a ninety-degree bend to a cell. Or if not a proper cell, then a room with a lockable door and thick wire mesh over its one window, with a fold-out bed and chemical toilet.

"I want to see a lawyer," Otty told her new guards.

"We heard you the first time, kid," one of them replied, in a bored voice. "Word of advice, don't keep banging on. Just pisses off the higher-ups."

"Well," said Otty, as drily as she could manage, though her heart was galloping again. "We wouldn't want to annoy the higher-ups."

"*You* don't have to work with them," said the other guard, a tall, skinny woman with a prominent triangular nose. "You only get their front-of-house routine. You've no idea how tiresome they can be."

"You have my full sympathy."

"We've been trained," said the first guard, obscurely. "We've been on *all* the courses." Otty stared at him, not understanding. So he added: "It's no good trying to bond with us. It won't do you any good. Just do what they want, kid. It's what you'll do eventually anyway. It's always the way this situation shakes out. Think about it. Sooner you figure that out, the sooner all this ends."

They shut the door. She was alone in her cell.

She explored, first of all, looking for cameras or other surveillance tech. There was nothing obvious pinned to the wall, or lurking in the bedstead, at least so far as she could see. But that didn't mean anything, of course. Surveillance tech was what Gomery liked to call *super-sophis* nowadays, and she figured she was being monitored somehow. So she conquered her natural shyness, pulled her pants down and used the funny-smelling toilet. There was no sink to wash her hands in, which struck her as pretty *damn* unhygienic, actually. Then she laid on the bed and tried to cultivate patience.

After an hour or so, she was brought a plate of food and a glass of water. She was thirsty enough to drink the latter straight down. It was the first fluid she'd had since breakfast. And then she looked the plate.

"Is that a meat patty?"

"Beef," said the guard.

"I'm a vegetarian."

His expression did not change. "You see those green things? And that little hill of, kind-of, yellow-white stuff? Guess what! Vegetables, both."

It was ridiculous, but she felt suddenly close to tears. Of all the things that had happened to her this day, to break down over such a trivial matter—it was absurd. But there she was. Stupid. But she was a vegetarian. It wasn't a complicated or unusual thing for a human being to be. And here they were, trying to hunger-trick her into eating meat.

"The patty is, like, touching the mashed potatoes," Otty pointed out.

"Would you look at that, mash and meat patty are friends," deadpanned the guard, pulling the door shut. "They're holding hands."

The door clanged shut.

Otty ate everything on her plate except the meat patty. Then she laid on the bed and thought about things. Gulliver had been lying when he said that all her friends had been rounded up. That at least was certain. Gomery and Cess had presumably been starched, sure. She wondered if they were in the same facility with her, now, or if they'd been taken to different buildings. And Kathry? It was possible she had evaded capture altogether.

She checked her phone again: 45% charge. She tried to get to an outside connection point, but without joy. She had a couple of quite clever picklock apps and might have been able to Bluetooth-piggyback upon the facility's own server. Then she wondered why they had permitted her to keep her phone at all, and it occurred to her that they were thinking she would do something that would betray how to access the Famous Five's closed network. Then, having thought that, she thought: but of *course* that was what they were hoping for.

She put her phone away and resisted the temptation to tinker further.

There was a long buzz, like a dentist's drill, and then it stopped and the lights switched off. Otty laid for a while, dozed for a while, woke in the darkness. Dozed again. Woke again. She was awake, and staring at the meshed window, as dawn came up. The window turned from a square of darkness into something gleaming purple-blue, and, briefly, became a glowing ingot of hot-looking orange. Then it was just a fishnetted block of sky.

Steps, faint for a long time, then building in volume, coming along the corridor. The key rattled in the lock. Sounded like a bolt being drawn in a rifle.

She was given breakfast of gluey white scrambled eggs, with a glass of orange juice so tart it made the sockets of her jawbone wince. Then she was marched along the corridor and back into the room she'd been in the day before. She didn't have to wait long before a man came in—not Gulliver, this time.

"My name," said the man, "is Agent Art Vanderlay, and I'm going to ask you some questions."

"I'd like to speak to an attorney," said Otty.

He tucked both edges of his mouth into an impressive close-curled frown. "You'd like that, would you? Try again, Ms. Barragão. You know as well as I do that prisoners of war are not entitled to legal representation. You must have followed the passage of the Protect America Act, earlier this year?"

"Prisoner of war?" boggled Otty. "You crazy. That's crazy."

"War is, indeed, never an exactly sane situation, Ms. Barragão," he said. "Nonetheless, we have to respond to aggression. And the current situation is very grave. We have to take all necessary steps to protect the United States of America and its citizens. We have reasonable grounds for suspecting that you are a present danger to that Union."

"Bull-doo," said Otty. It was her most extreme expletive. "I'm a minor."

"A minor?" echoed Vanderlay, looking mildly surprised. He checked the tablet in front of him. "No, no, our records are clear." He showed her a date of birth, a year and half earlier than the actual date. "You're eighteen, and so come under the terms of the Act."

This was so daft that Otty couldn't, for a moment, get her head in line with what had happened.

"That's … That … That's not true," she said. "I'm sixteen."

"Eighteen, legally. And legally an adult. Our records are clear."

"The guy yesterday..." For a moment she was blanking on his name. Gully Foyle. Gullible. "Gulliver. He interviewed me yesterday and he accepted I am a minor."

"Gulliver?" said Vanderlay. "It's not a name I'm familiar with. Now, Ms. Barragão, I suggest we put small talk behind us. I'm going to ask you some questions."

Otty looked left and right. It wasn't that she expected these people to be wholly truthful and above board, but so naked and easily disprovable a lie made her dizzy with its very brazenness. Then she thought to herself: *How* could she disprove it? She had ID on her phone, but they'd say it was faked. She shut her eyes. Pressed her wrists into the sockets and slowly rubbed the whole of her two hands down, pressing the palms and fingers into her face. Then she took a breath.

"I want an attorney."

"What you want," said Vanderlay, "and what I am legally obligated to provide you are not, in this case, the same thing at all. Ms. Barragão—you can save us a lot of bother, and yourself a lot of misery, by simply cooperating. At the moment you're registered as a suspect. But it would be an easy matter to re-register you as an enemy combatant, and then you'd be sent to an internment camp with all the other prisoners of war. You would"—he tipped his head down, breaking eye contact momently—"not enjoy such an experience."

"This is crazy. I'm only a kid!"

He slid the tablet across the table to her. "You'll have seen from your phone that access to the wider internet is controlled, here, by a coded pipette. That tablet has a clear line out of the facility. Please use this line for one thing, and one only—to log into your network. I'm watching you. You're being monitored. Don't try and contact anybody. Don't try to tell anybody where you are or what has happened to you."

"Talking of which," Otty put in, "where *am* I, exactly?"

She sounded a lot calmer than she felt. Her legs were trembling like a terrified dog. But that was below the table.

"What you can do," said Vanderlay, "is give us a login to your encysted network. An open login, in your name, or one of your four friends' IDs, it doesn't matter which. Once we're confident we have the access we need, we'll cycle you out of the POW files and into the regular police files. You could be bailed by the end of the week, and back at home."

Otty thought: I should probably stop talking now. I should probably just go trapdoor on them. Not trapdoor, Trap*pist*. Leave them hanging. Yet, somehow, she couldn't. Some part of her thought: If I can just make them see how unreasonable they're being…

So she said: "It doesn't work that way. It's a fully encysted network. There are no points of access to it from the general web."

Vanderlay nodded ponderously. Something about his expression made Otty's heart sink. She should have shut up. She shouldn't have given anything away! Private internet network? What private internet network? But it was too late now.

"I see," he said. "Except, *that* doesn't make any sense, does it? We're not talking a couple of linked-together hard drives, and you and your friends chatting about your favorite episodes of *Space Avalon*, are we? This is a modular ratio inferior of the internet as such. It mimics the actual internet. Which means it shadows the actual internet. There are no regular *open* ports between it and the larger internet, sure. I'm going to be charitable and assume that's what you meant. I'm going to be charitable and assume that you weren't deliberately trying to *mislead* an officer of U.S. law charged with preserving national security. I mean, that would be a suicidal thing to do, don't you think? In these circumstances? To play games with something so important? So I'm going to give you a chance to expand upon your former answer. There are ways of accessing your encysted network, and I request and require that you open one such way. *Entende?*"

Otty's face felt hot. "I can't turn off any firewalls. We don't *run* firewalls. Hackers and viruses would be through those like water through a teabag."

"I'm not talking about firewalls," said Vanderlay, patiently. "Don't patronize me, Ottoline. I know exactly how this works. And I know you can open a way in for us. We know your friend Montgomery stole something very dangerous from his mother's work. We know that you've been tinkering with it since then— all of you, tinkering with it. You're in the deepest and stinkiest of shit, Ottoline. You have one, only one, way out, and I'm it."

An impulse to rush the door of this room and yank on its handle, on the off chance it was open, filled Otty. It required genuine willpower to hold herself back. Of course the door was locked. And if it wasn't locked, then where would she go, exactly? She looked over at the mirror. How many people were there, behind the glass, staring at her right now? Reveling in her discomfort.

"What's in the box?" Vanderlay asked.

It occurred to Otty to reply: *What's in the box? An eagle is in the box, an eagle. And I'd like to see you open it so that it can peck out your eyes.* But she said nothing.

"Come along, Ottoline," said Vanderlay briskly, and tapped the frame of the screen before him.

"No comment," said Otty.

"No comment? This isn't a press conference, Ottoline. No comment?"

She thought about saying something about her constitutional right not to incriminate herself, but, without internet access to prompt her memory, she couldn't remember which amendment that one was. Fifteenth? Fifth? So she swallowed and said: "No comment."

"That's your answer?"

"No comment."

Saint John had an eagle—*to peck out your eyes!*—and he said God was the Word. She was happy to keep her word and her god to herself, in this place, at this time.

"I'm not sure," said Vanderlay, in a menacing voice, "you fully understand how bad a place you're now in. Helping us is the only way to help yourself. The only way."

Her throat was dry. "Comment," she said weakly.

Vanderlay leaned forward. "Comment? You *are* going to say something?"

His eagerness was his first mistake. Even through the fog of her terror Otty could see that he was desperate. And desperation was a weakness.

"No comment," she said. "The 'no' got stuck in my throat, that time. I'm kinda thirsty. Could you get me a glass of water?"

Vanderlay sat back. "This isn't a game."

She didn't reply.

"Well," said Vanderlay, retrieving his tablet, "it's disappointing. You know, the law does permit enhanced interrogation techniques on recalcitrant terrorists and POWs. So I guess that's where we'll have to go."

Otty's heart sped up upon hearing the phrase, but her teeth seemed stuck together, so she said nothing.

"You realize," Vanderlay added, haughtily, "that we have all four of your friends in custody, and that two of them have already *agreed* to open a door to your network for us? By the close of business today we fully expect all four of them to have complied with our request. That'll leave you hanging, the sole standout. So the rest of them will get to go home, and you, alone, will be sent to an adult internment camp."

Otty breathed out, long and slow. Vanderlay could not have said a more reassuring thing, so far as she was concerned. Her heart rate palpably slowed inside her chest. He was desperate, and he was lying, and that meant *she* was in the driving seat. She took a long breath. Calm, she told herself. Calm.

"If they're opening the network to you," she said, "then why do you need me?"

He was ready for this question.

"Oh, we don't need you. We're *giving you a chance*. Because we're kind-hearted that way. Because I hate to see a youngster throw her life away. You think national security is a joke? You want a United States to *go back to*, once this is all over? We already have access to your network, and all I'm doing here is giving you the chance to show willing. To show that you're a good citizen, and a patriotic American. To make one symbolic gesture to show whose side you're on."

He waited. But when she didn't say anything, he sighed, as if personally saddened by her stubbornness.

"I guess some people don't want to be saved," he said, and got to his feet, and left the room.

:4:

She was thirsty, but there was nothing she could do about that. She sat at the table for an indeterminate, interminable length of time. Finally the guards came and led her back to her makeshift cell.

She laid on her little bed, and replayed the interview over and over again, obsessing over what she'd said, what she shouldn't have said, what she might have done differently. After a while she began to see that thinking this way was a kind of mental down-spiral, and she stopped herself by sheer force of will.

Think, she told herself, about something *else*. Pull yourself out of this negative maelstrom. So. She thought about her friends. Then she thought about her parents, and her sister, and wondered how they were doing, and whether they were trying to get through to her. Presumably they were. Presumably they were facing official frustration and obstruction. Or maybe they were being siphoned official lies about how she was a terrorist and an enemy combatant. But they wouldn't believe all that. They knew her. They were family. They wouldn't believe all that. Would they? Then she thought: Though it feels like an age, in fact I've only been gone a couple of days. Maybe they didn't even know she had been arrested, and figured she was just a missing person. But then (she reasoned) they'd go to the police, and the police computer would have registered her arrest, and so they'd know.

It was a muddle, and she wanted it behind her. And thinking about it wasn't getting her anywhere, so instead she thought about her bees. For a while she closed her eyes and imagined them flying lazily in and out of her makeshift hives, those old-model computer carcasses, rusting where the plastic cladding and paint was eczema-ing away. She imagined life from the point of view of a bee: bright with apple-green, orange-sweet sunlit brightness. Huge shapes of trees, shadow-vague, looming past. Flying with your legs tucked neatly in and hugging your own underbelly. The scent of sugar drawing you. Returning to the hive in a sky humming with your fellows, carrying wadded packs of pollen glommed to your thighs, like cargo pants whose pockets are stuffed with Golden Grahams. And back in the hive, in the scrum of your fellows, dry and dusty-sweet, fuzzed and close and safe.

She was crying. Tears were actually coming out of her eyes. It was ridiculous. She never cried.

Eventually the crying stopped. A more hopeful thought occurred to her: that this, too, would pass. She wouldn't be here forever. Somebody would come rescue her and she would fly away on the back of a giant Johannine eagle.

The eagles are coming!

The eagles are coming!

And soon enough she drifted off to sleep.

:5:

The next day the two guards arrived at her door with a folded double-handful: dark blue overalls. She was told to swap her clothes for these, and to surrender her phone. She considered refusing but didn't see there would be much point. It was surprising she'd been allowed to keep the phone for as long as she had, really. The guards left her a food tray—a nondescript stew the color of rotted-down leaf mulch and some overboiled white rice. There were lumps in the stew and Otty decided to tell herself that these were chunks of tofu. She was so ravenously hungry the thought of separating stew and rice and limiting herself to the latter gave her the bowling-ball-in-the-stomach sensation of actual depression. Maybe it *was* tofu—who knew? So she ate the whole thing, and licked the plate, and drank her drink, and afterward she stripped to her underwear, and used the chemical toilet once more, and felt another stab of annoyance that there was nowhere to wash her hands. Then she put on the overalls, which were rough-weave, plasticized cotton mixed in with a small percentage of some softer, probably natural fabric. She folded her clothes neatly and put them by the door, next to the now-empty food tray.

The window was too high for her to see through. There was barely a half-inch of windowsill on the inside, but once or twice she was able to jump up and cling on enough to pull her face up to the lower portion of the mesh. The view was of a yard, a wire fence and beyond it a path of scrub, under a blue-brown evening sky, and snake-shaped horizontal clouds that caught the tint of the sunset. It hurt her fingers to hang on for too long, though, and there was nothing really to see, so she dropped down again.

She sat on her bed. For a period of time her mind was perfectly blank.

The guards came and took away her clothes and the tray.

Now it was dark outside, and her room was lit with electric light. There was no guard-mesh or protection around the bulb of the light in the ceiling, and she could probably have broken it. But what would have been the point in that? She tried knocking on the walls left and right of the door, and calling hello into the plastic paint, on the off chance that a fellow prisoner might hear. But she got no reply.

There was that clockwork whirring sound again, and the lights went out.

They were sweating her. She knew it. She wasn't stupid. If (she told herself), *if* they were going to do the enhanced interrogation thing, and—oh, sweet Lord, she didn't know: beat her on the soles of her feet? or hose her with water and trail sparking electrodes down her naked skin?—*if* they were going to do that, then they'd have started already. They were probably doing the same make-'em-wait game with Gomery and Cess, standing by to see which one of them cracked first.

It wasn't going to be her.

And then she went on her knees at the bedside and prayed. It was the first time she had prayed since her arrest, and she was down on the concrete floor so long her knees began to complain. She prayed for courage, and endurance, and for her family not to worry about her, and for this all to be over soon. She prayed for guidance, and for the whole gosh-darn *country* not to fall into war, like a brawling bunch of drunkards at a bar. Then she cried again, for a little while. Then she said the Lord's Prayer, and got onto the bed, and wrapped herself in the blanket, and tucked her own arm under her head as a pillow. She felt a little better. It was either the praying, or the crying, or maybe both, but a difference had been made.

:6:

A day stretched to two, to three, to four. She thought about marking the passage of time by scratching lines onto the wall with… Well, it wasn't clear with what. She might have been able to lift up the whole of her bunk bed and use one of its metal legs, but what would be the point in that? The whole business was a cliché anyway. It didn't matter.

Lord, she was bored. Bored she was, Lord.

She spent the first couple of days thinking around and around the same worn-smooth set of mental processes. By the end of the first week, her mind was exasperated with that and settled into a blanker mode. Every morning and every evening she would be brought something to eat. She didn't get the chance to wash her body, or brush her teeth, or change her underwear or her overalls, but when she asked the guards about this they waved her question away. She was sure she reeked. But she had been in her own stink long enough to become unaware of it. Or so she guessed.

Then her period started and it was pretty messy, and she yelled through the door. She wondered if she was just going to be ignored, but later that day they brought her a change of underwear and some sanitary towels.

Some days the guards would chat with her in a desultory sort of way, other days they'd blank her. Nobody came to ask her any more questions.

One of the two guards who attended her morning and

evening had a smartBlister on the back of his neck. Either these prison guards earned a whole lot more than regular workers, or else this was some government scheme to provide key buckle-head employees with the very best tech for assisting them with their disability. A couple of times Otty tried to open a conversation on the topic, but all she got in return was the stony stare. The guards brought food and took it away. Every so often they brought new sanitary towels too. She flushed the old ones down the chemical toilet.

She sank through the ocean of her days until finally she settled on the unlit abyssal seabed of perfect boredom, undisturbed for a thousand years except for the occasional blind sea cucumber inching its way through the black mud under black waters.

Awake. Asleep. Day. Night.

Time crawling on.

One morning she tried to work out if she had been there twenty-five days or a whole four weeks, but she couldn't be sure.

One night she was woken by somebody knocking on her door. In her sleepiness and confusion she half-thought, or a quarter-thought, she was home, in her bedroom.

"Come in," she called, through sticky lips.

Then a thrill of adrenaline ran down her torso, and she sat straight up. She wasn't at home. She was in a cell.

"Who is it?"

Who would *knock*? The guards had keys and had no truck with courtesies and formalities.

It wasn't the door. The little window twitched with flickers of light, threw tentative and half-second grid patterns on the wall beside its frame and returned to blackness. The noise came again: a muddy grumbling sound culminating in a trio of big-drum bangs.

Darkness again.

Otty pulled herself up to the window, best as she was able,

and got her eyes above the wall, to see through the bars, hanging there on trembling arms. It was wholly dark outside, starless, moonless. Her arms ached and her fingers complained of the effort of holding her up when she saw dotted lines of gleaming gold thread, thin as silk, leaping up at forty-five degrees. It took Otty a moment to realize she was seeing gunfire. Then there was a snap and a sprawling rumble, and the sky lit up—an underside of folded clouds shining momently silver and yellow, cracking like folds of aluminum foil.

Then the light faded.

She dropped back to the floor and picked her way through the dark to her bed again. Somebody out there fighting somebody else out there. Maybe drug gangs settling scores. Maybe, though, it was war. Then again, who was to say, in this day and age, where the one stopped and the latter began?

She was surprised how quickly she fell asleep again.

But she kept getting woken up again. The noises kept waking Otty up: a hammer knocking an anvil over and over; a crash like a surger's breaker hitting the beach; a series of woodpecker snaps. Then, boom, boom, and a prolonged phosphoric brightness shining so brightly through her window that every detail inside the cell was revealed in surreal, rather unnerving clarity, like an intricately engraved picture. The light faded, and then it was dark, and it was silent again, and eventually Otty fell asleep properly.

In the morning she pulled herself up to her window, but there was nothing to see outside except the same stretch of yard, and fencing, and the scrubland beyond it. She was expecting to see ruination, but all that she could see looked just the same as it had ever done.

Five weeks had passed—maybe a day or two either way—before the routine was broken.

After breakfast her guards took her out and turned left instead of right: a door was opened and they marched her through a couple of rooms containing nothing but a great many stacked and piled chairs against one wall like a geometric representation of a thorn-hedge. Along a new corridor, and through a fat door with three locks into—amazing!—fresh air. Otty blinked in the light, breathed deep, smelled earth, and farmer's silage, and something dustily chemical, and, unmissable, the whiff of cordite. Then she was inside again: a wash-block, with a functioning shower. The guards left her alone to undress and to stand, the sole occupant of a row of six big silver metal sunflower heads, under the blasting hot water. The showers were all on, and together they produced so much steam it was as if the whole building were vaping. She had been given a little thumb-sized cylinder of white soap, and under her rubbing hands this blossomed into great mushrooms and coral-flowers of foam.

She washed her body, and her hair, and finally she just stood there in a kind of fugue state as the water cascaded around her and upon her. When the water was shut off, she dried herself with a towel thin as linen and put her smelly overalls back on. She had to use her fingers to comb her hair, and *that* was very far from ideal. But she felt clean for the first time in over a month, and that was worth a fortune in gold and diamonds and rare IP copyrights.

Then the guards, surly and unspeaking, as if begrudging her this moment of uncomplicated pleasure, took her back to the main block, and through to a new room.

There was no one-way mirror here, and no table. There were two chairs.

She was pressed into one of these and her leg was shackled to the chair leg, in at the top triangle of the legs' A-shape. Then the guards left her alone. Since the chair was not fixed to the floor, it seemed strange that she was cuffed to it. She experimented with getting up and walking about, dragging the chair behind her. Inconveniencing, but not excessively so.

The door was, of course, locked, so she sat herself down again and folded her arms and waited.

Eventually the door swung wide and a tall, rather elegant woman entered. She had a Cruella de Vil vibe about her, though of course without the large coat made of dog-pelts. She had a long, austere and symmetrical face, and richly black hair tied behind. She was dressed in a dark gray suit. She sat opposite Otty, legs together, and put her hands palm-down on her own knees. Otty waited. She noticed that the woman had a boundary line around her throat, above which was the color of her facial make-up, and below which was markedly paler.

"Ottoline," she said, in a low, rough-textured voice. It was what they used to call a smoker's voice, except that this woman smelled not of cigarettes but of ylang-ylang. "I'm Maria Sarajlić. I'm Deputy Director of the U.S.I.D. Operational Technology Division. Are you ready to talk to us now?"

It was strange. If they'd pulled her out of bed before dawn, unwashed for a fortnight, and set her down here, she might have been readier to capitulate. But the shower had rejuvenated her will.

"I'm ready to talk to an attorney," she said brightly. "And the first thing I'ma say to him—or her—is that I've been illegally detained, denied access to counsel."

"You're going to tell your counselor you have no access to counsel?" asked Sarajlić, smiling vaguely. "Well—good luck with *that*."

For a moment Otty was thrown off balance by this.

"So, I am getting an attorney, then?"

Then she recovered her composure. Of course not. Sarajlić was baiting her.

"Ottoline, I have some serious news," the woman said. "I'm afraid your friend Kathry Chong has died."

She stopped speaking then, perhaps waiting for Otty's reaction. But Otty didn't have a reaction. She heard the words and understood them. And then she checked her own feelings and there were no feelings. Nothing at all.

"I don't believe you," she decided, although she wasn't sure if she did or didn't.

"Nonetheless," said Sarajlić, "it's the truth."

Still nothing.

"How?"

"You mean, how did she die? It was, I can tell you, not as a result of any negligence by any official government agency. Her parents have been informed and have accepted a compensation package tagged to pre-war dollar values, to be collected when the currency returns to those levels."

The words *parents have been informed* prickled something in Otty's chest, a tingle of excitement. If Kath's parents could be contacted, then so might hers. The prospect was so thrilling that she almost missed the sentence's most startling moment. But, smart kid that she was, it snapped into her consciousness.

"Pre-war?"

Sarajlić nodded.

"So we're at war?"

"It's messy," she said vaguely. "But for the purposes of things like contractual and insurance agreements, a date has to be specified."

This didn't really tell her anything.

She checked herself again: *Kathry is dead*. Nothing. It had no flavor or semblance of reality about it.

"Do you see this?" Sarajlić asked, turning her head to stretch her neck a little way around. The smartBlister attached to her skin was unmissable.

"You've been exposed to the neonics?" Otty asked.

Sarajlić nodded slowly. "Not as badly as some, but badly enough. Without this little prosthesis, and its clever little apps, and its—I don't want to sound old-fogey but it still amazes me—*remarkable* memory capacity, I'd be rather incapacitated."

She pronounced *rather* as if there were a *y* between the *a* and the *t*.

"Bully-bully," said Otty, "for you."

"As it is, I have full functionality."

"To be honest," said Otty, "I don't see what it has to do with me."

"It's a sign of the times."

"I guess."

"It shows that I'm not averse," Sarajlić went on, "to technological and programming advances."

Otty discovered she had no further reserves of patience.

"Whatever, lady. Crank the handle, on you go."

"We have algorithms, you know," Sarajlić said, in an apparent non sequitur, "as to which interrogation strategies work best for which personality profile. They're not perfect, these programs. But the heavy stuff—the hoods, the hitting and twisting, the fire-hoses and waterboarding—all that would reduce somebody with *your* personality profile to a mere wailing wreck. We need a more delicate approach."

"You're trying to intimidate me," Otty said, and she was, in truth, pretty intimidated.

Hitting *and twisting*? How medieval was this place? She hadn't heard any screams or yells, but maybe the rooms where they did things like that were efficiently soundproofed.

"I'm asking you," Sarajlić was saying, "to tell me all about your private internet. Your little Model Online, created with, what ... eighty or so second-hand processors, and a couple miles of copper wire? Isn't it?"

121

Otty said nothing. Could Kathry be dead? Was that even a possibility? She was more lively and energetic than the rest of the group put together.

No. It wasn't possible.

"Ottoline," Sarajlić said again, "you've got something in that network, and we need to take a look at it. We need to examine it properly. It's not safe. In fact, it's very dangerous. Or so we suspect. Now, I understand that you're protective. You and your four friends have created something very impressive."

"Three friends now," said Otty, at a hazard, "if you're telling the truth about Kath."

Sarajlić nodded her ponderous nod. "The integrity of the United States is under threat. To say nothing of the loss of life, the crippling injuries, the destruction of property. Don't you think that you should do whatever you can do to prevent all that?"

"Lady, I'm really not sure what you"re talking about.'

"Let us in to your network, Ottoline. We'll promise not to break anything. Will you promise to help us?"

Otty considered saying *I want to speak to an attorney* again, or explaining that the Closure had no straightforward doors she could open, but instead she said: "No." The word came into her mouth almost without her bidding.

Sarajlić stiffened almost imperceptibly in her chair. Then she nodded once, almost as if bowing her head to the teenager, and got up and walked out of the room.

:7:

Otty had another three days and three nights in her own cell. Two of those nights were disturbed by the sounds of conflict from outside: the snip-snap of small arms, like dry-stick fuel breaking in the fireplace; the *whumpf* of larger detonations; the buzz of drones sweeping low overhead and the more distant shrieks and growls of fighter jets. Banshee whines and incomprehensible human yells. Otty hauled herself up to look through her window but couldn't really see anything. On the second night the sounds of fighting were more distant than on the first. The third night was quiet, or at least there was nothing loud enough to wake Otty up.

Then, on the morning of the third day, she was bundled out of her cell, breakfastless, cuffed, taken through the front of the building and loaded on to a bus. It was a prison bus, and her handcuffs were snicked into a hooked loop set into the back of the seat in front of hers. Then she was left alone.

There was nobody else on the bus.

She sat for a while, looking through the window at the rectangle of tarmac on which the bus was parked. It had rained not long before, and puddles of various sizes and shapes stood out, sharply reflecting the pale sky overhead among the tar-black surface. They looked like milk. To the bus's right was the low roof of the building where she had spent, she figured, at least a month and a half, and to the bus's left, the side on which she was sitting, Otty could see the tall wire fence, strung between tree-trunk-thick, house-tall poles, and garnished at the top with an undulating bush of razor wire. Past the fence she could see a long straight road leading away to a vanishing point just beyond a long horizontal bar. The facility's outer fence.

The sun shifted in the sky, and, slowly, inexorably, as time crept, the shadows quailed back in at the bases of the building, and the puddles grew slowly smaller. After so many days with nothing to see but the walls of her cell, these minutely but constantly altering visual details were fascinating for Otty.

Eventually, the guards returned with four other young detainees: all male, none of them people Otty recognized. They were loaded on to the truck and chained into their places. They were all seated at the back of the bus, with Otty at the front. She supposed this was a concession to the segregation of the genders. The guards thudded back along the aisle of the bus and stepped outside.

"Where are we going?" Otty called after the last of them, the same guy who'd been delivering and taking away her food.

"Don't know," he returned, without even looking back, "don't care."

The doors gasped shut, and the engine revved into life. There was no driver, of course. Outside, the inner gates were opened, manually, by the guards. The bus rolled bumpily along to the outer gates, and these parted with open-sesame self-volition. Then the whole vehicle angled, turned, straightened up and headed off down the freeway.

The boys at the back of the bus, having realized that there was a female on board with them, started hooting and calling sweet-ass and tight-sleeve and baby-baby at her. She ignored them. They laughed a lot for a while, and chatted loudly and lewdly among themselves, boasting of all the invasive and degrading sexual things they were planning on doing to Otty when the chance presented itself. After a while they fell quiet.

Everyone was looking through the windows, watching the flat landscape sweep by. There were acres and acres of wheat, big automatic combiners laying monumental planks of flatness over the growths and spewing yellow clouds of harvested grain into the subsidiary gigantic robotrucks. Then they passed through a small town: three dozen houses, roofs painted with black solar-electric paint, a single mid-sized mall like a box, and a glittering expanse of parked vehicles, and then they were in the countryside again.

Drones in the sky. Much higher up were visible the cargo

megazeps—some of them a quarter of a mile long, but so far distant they looked like rice grains.

This was maize land, now: close-planted in ways never possible before. Instead of leaving lanes in between the individual plants for harvesters to track, the cobs were now plucked by towering tub-shaped robot pickers that stepped, with machinic precision, on lengthy flexible tentacle legs.

The bus rolled on. Lulled by the motion and the warmth, Otty dozed. She woke with a start, but the bus was still trundling down the endless highway. She began to wonder about comfort breaks. Then she began to wonder about the legality of sending them on their way with no adult or prison-guard supervision. What if something happened? What if the bus broke down, or crashed? If Sarajlić had been telling the truth, and war had broken out, then ... Well, what then?

What if Sarajlić had been telling the truth and Kath was dead?

But Otty didn't want to think of that.

The bus was an old model that had been upgraded, so there was a space where the human driver would once have sat. There was nothing there now, except the steering wheel, which rotated slowly this way and that, ghost-driven.

"Hey!" Otty called, tentatively. "Hey, driver-bot! What if I need a comfort break? Hey!"

Nothing.

It was foolish to talk to the old driver's cab. That wasn't where the program that drove the bus was located. She knew better, even if her vestigial sense of how things went tricked her into it—the invisible man turning the big steering wheel. The pressure in Otty's bladder grew and then, after she shifted position, she kind-of got used to it, and the urgency of her need to pee withdrew a little. It didn't exactly go away, but she found she could endure it. It wasn't comfortable.

It was most uncomfortable.

The bus rolled on. They passed down into a river valley, over a bridge, and up the far side. The pressure in Otty's bladder grew increasingly hard to bear.

Over the horizon a massive heatduction tower came into view, like a medieval cathedral pinnacle, the holobanner of DTE ENERGY flying from the summit in place of any heraldic device. The tower appeared to rise up like a slowly launching rocket as they drove toward it, and soon enough they were coming into a mid-sized town. Houses on girder stilts clustered around the lake formed by the tower's outfall, and then a spread of nondescript one- and two-floor domestic houses: solpainted roofs, big rainfall butts, four or five automobiles in various states of being picked clean for parts or in the process of repair on the driveways. Old Glory flying for real: a sign of poorer districts that they preferred fabric-and-dye flags from actual flagpoles to the shining holoflags of the richer suburbs.

There was more traffic here, and the bus slowed, accelerated in bursts, braked abruptly. They passed a series of windowless factories, and then climbed a long upslope. From this vantage, Otty could look down into a stadium, once a sports venue, now a shanty—scores upon scores of tents crammed into the open screaming mouth of the structure. A turn of the road, and a block, living quarters stacked like dirty plates. Onward.

They were in a richer part of town now, and the houses had fences and gates, and gun-blisters on the roof next to the server-aerials. In one, autohounds snapped and barked at the passing bus, alarming-looking snapping jaws hemmed inwardly with chrome dagger-teeth, running on little legs. They looked like grown-up robot cousins of those joke-shop gnashers you'd charge up and run along a tabletop. Except that the teeth looked a lot sharper.

Finally, as the sun began to think of doing what so many

citizens dreamed of doing, moving westward over the horizon—and as the pressure on Otty's bladder approached unbearable, a physical pain in her lower gut—the bus rolled through some fat razor-gates and pulled up in a yard in front of a multistorey concrete keep.

They sat for a time. Three people in federal uniforms came out and stood in front of the bus, looking up at it. One was talking, but not to the other two, so he must have been on the phone to a third party. A different guard walked all around the bus. Finally the doors hissed open and one of these guards stepped up.

"Listen up, prisoners!" she yelled. "We have no *space* for you in our facility, which means you'll be staying in this bus for the foreseeable."

The boys at the back all groaned, and this clearly vexed the officer.

"You can stuff a butt plug in your fucken moan-holes, OK? This is not *our* problem. We were not consulted when these transfer orders were finalized, OK?"

"Ma'am," Otty tried. "We've been on this bus all day and could really use a comfort break."

"Yeah, bitch!" yelled one of the boys, as his friends tittered like toddlers. "We need to piss, real soon, real *now*."

"You," said the guard, "were courteous, when those fuckers were not, and that's good. That gives me the chance to become a *teacher*, which was always my youthful dream."

She leaned in and unhooked Otty's cuffs from the seat-hook.

"Come on," she said, as the boys at the back erupted in a chorus of disharmonious swearing and outraged complaining.

The guard led Otty in through the main door, through an even heftier inner door, down a corridor and finally through a smartport. She took her inside an echoey toilet and shower room, and unlocked her cuffs. Then she leaned herself against the wall and took out her phone.

"Go on, sweet," she said, not even looking at her.

Otty went into a cubicle and relieved herself. It was a little ridiculous how intensely pleasurable the experience was, a mixture of physical bliss and psychological relief. Then she flushed, washed her hands, and presented herself to the guard.

"You're small for eighteen," was the guard's comment.

"I'm sixteen," said Otty.

"Says eighteen here."

"That's a mistake."

"Nothing I can do about that, sweetmeat," she said, in a dreary voice. She re-cuffed her. "Come on."

Outside, daylight was receding like a tide going out. Otty glanced behind her into the dusk, and saw a biscuit-brown cliff face of barred windows, reaching up—a dozen stories high? It was hard to gauge. Tall, certainly. At every window was a person. She couldn't see their faces, since the windows were inset and the bars were thick, but she knew that they were all there, peering out at the sky, curious about the new bus arrival, wondering what was going on. Then she faced front again and was encouraged up the big step and back into the bus.

Inside smelled ghastly. The boys at the back had, evidently, gone to the toilet where they sat—in dirty protest, or out of sheer desperate necessity, Otty didn't know. It was foul to smell, bad to breathe. The guard looked not disgusted but triumphant.

"You OK, rude boys?"

They replied with swear words and promises of physical violence. One recited in a high-pitched voice a long list of things he planned to do by way of anatomically opening up the guard's body with a knife. Another was laughing in an unhinged kind of way.

Otty ignored them. There was nothing for it. She tried to get as comfortable as she could, though it wasn't easy. For a while the boys aimed their unpleasant banter her way, and one of them hurled a turd in her direction, like a chimpanzee in a zoo. It didn't reach her, bounced off one of the intervening seat backs and dropped down. The boys laughed at this. Then a fight broke out between them, and there was a good deal of shouting, and smacking sounds, and chains rattling like Marley's ghost. Finally they fell quiet.

The bus didn't move.

It was dark now, but two bright orange arc lights shone onto the yard outside. The shine was bright enough to make the inside of Otty's eyelids glow blood-red. At some point the first guard returned to the bus, bringing little plastic bags that contained sandwiches and bottles of water. She handed one to Otty, but yelled that the boys were disgusting animals and that she wasn't coming anywhere near them. So she put the sandwich bags on the floor of the aisle and kicked them to the back of the bus, like soccer balls. The boys complained noisily that the bags were getting piss all over them, and the guard hooted.

"Miss, miss!" cried one of the boys. "You gotta do something for my homeboy, my homeboy Eric, he's solid sick, miss, he's set sure to die."

"Right," said the guard. "Facility Management will take your concerns under advisement."

"Miss! Miss! It's my homeboy, Eric, he's got asthma wicked." *Ass moyer*. "You gotta fetch-fetch a doctor, dude, take a look at him."

But the guard was gone.

Otty examined the sandwich by the orange light. It looked like ham, but she told herself it was a soya slice, and ate the whole thing. She was very thirsty, but rationed herself on the water, if only because she didn't want to be desperate for another pee come dawn.

She did her best, with her hands shackled the way they were, to curl up onto the seat and go to sleep. It wasn't that she was big. On the contrary, she was not only small, but capable of curling up into an almost perfect sphere. But the architecture of the seats and the way her wrists were pulled forward made this very hard to do. She dozed, woke, dozed again. In the small hours (she had no way of gauging the time) the boys at the back started yelling and cursing and that woke her. She tried to ignore them, but it wasn't easy. She dozed, and woke; dozed and woke, and so, slowly, tediously, the night wore itself away.

Dawn suffused itself slowly into the yard. When the spotlights were turned off the sky over the walls was a pure, clean blue. There were many little clouds, defined by surprisingly sharp and irregular edges, white as torn pieces of bread scattered on the waters.

A clipped toenail moon, low over the horizon.

The boys at the back were quiet now. One of them farted loudly, and another swore at him. Otty was no longer conscious of the stench until she thought about it, and then, as if her nostrils had been reminded to check again, she became aware of it once again. So gross.

She was expecting the guard to come back with breakfast, but nothing happened. Otty stretched as best she could, drank some more of her water, examined the inside of her plastic bag for stray crumbs. She stared out of the window. The sun rose, and the walls folded their shadows away at their bases. Otty stared at the cliff face of the main building. Somebody stuck something out of one of the fourth-floor windows—a rag, fluttering through the bars. Was it a bed sheet? A shirt? She couldn't tell.

Otty's stomach mewed like a cat, and then scratched at her innards like a meaner cat. She began fantasizing about food. The most delicious food she could think of. Mexican bean chili the way her dad cooked it, with a big hill of fragrant rice and shavings of orange Colby cheese scattered over the top. Then for dessert: chocolate trifle. Her mouth was watering.

Another boy, or maybe the same boy, farted. This time nobody rebuked him. One of the boys was sobbing to himself. It struck Otty as weird that none of the others mocked him for this. She shut her eyes and the boy's crying sounded like a stream flowing over pebbles. It went on and on.

Eventually—midday, or maybe later—a different guard came to check on how things were inside the bus. As soon as this man stepped aboard, the boys started yelling incoherently. He took out his baton and pressed the button to extend it.

"You stop hollering," he warned, "or I'll give you something to holler about."

Mister mister mister! they called. *Dude, he's dead, he's dead, dude.*

"You think I was maybe born yesterday, to fall for such a trick?" the guard called.

He was standing next to Otty's seat, and she looked at his profile. A pinched face, seen from the side, with a prominent nose, and many little patches of some sort of skin disease, like inset fragments of broken red glass, in his skin. He had a large mustache that stood over his mouth like an awning.

The boys kept shouting, *he's dead, dude, dead, dude, dude, dead.*

"You think I can't smell what you animals have been doing back there?" the guard yelled. But there was a quaver in his voice. "Using it like a fucking toilet? Pissing your pants like babies? You think I'm wading through your sewage, you can think *again.*"

But he did go up to the back of the bus, and the boys fell silent. When he came back his eyes were wide and he was in a hurry.

He ran from the bus and within ten minutes four guards returned. It all happened in silence. One waited outside, one stood by the empty driver's compartment, and two went back and retrieved the corpse of the boy. Otty saw him only for a moment: his body as loose as an untied line, sagging between the guard carrying his knees and the guard with hands hooked under his shoulders. His head hung down, his dreadlocks trailing along the aisle, his eyes puffed shut. He might have been sixteen. He was probably younger.

Otty couldn't form her hands into the proper shape of a prayer, on account of her cuffs; but she shut her eyes and bowed her head and sent up a prayer for his soul.

Then another guard went back and unlocked the remaining boys and led them in a line out into the yard and into the main building. Then somebody brought a hose and sprayed water into the bus's rear, sluicing dirty water and globs of shit down the aisle and through into the open air. Then the hose was taken away and Otty sat entirely alone on the bus for an hour or so. She finished the rest of her bottle of water. Then she wondered if she could find a way of using the empty plastic bottle as a makeshift toilet. She thought of a few possible ways she could try, and dismissed them as both impracticable and incompatible with her dignity as a girl. The need to urinate built within her again. It would be easier if she were a boy. In this as in so many ways.

They remembered her at some point in the mid-afternoon, and the first guard—the one who had brought her a sandwich—came through and unlocked her.

"I'm sorry," he told her, as she stepped down into the yard and the fresh air. "It's a royal fuck-up. But it's not *our* fuck-up, believe me. It's somebody else's imperial-level fuck-up. Did you know him?"

"No."

She was locking her fingers, stretching her arms in front of her, rubbing her wrists.

"He was called Eric Damien," the guard told her. "But we

never got his damn medical file, because we got no files for any of you. All we got was the manifest that came with the bus, and that didn't have no medical details, not a one, just name, age, you know."

Otty didn't know what this man wanted her to say. It's all right? I forgive you?

"I kinda need the restroom, mister," she said. "And I'm kinda hungry."

He looked at her as though she were an alien who had just beamed into the yard.

"What? Sure – sure. Come through."

She used the same shower room/restroom she had visited the previous day, only this time it was steamy and smelled of hot sweat and cheap soap. There were puddles everywhere and the ceramic glinted with beads of moisture like mica. But it was at least empty, and she relieved herself and drank a lot of water at the faucet, and went back out.

The guards cuffed her again and made her sit on a bench in the entrance hall, opposite the main desk where a uniformed woman was painstakingly working her way through a large screen game of *Jewel Collecta*. This guard only glanced up very occasionally to check on her. Another guard brought her some food—a proper plate of hot food, a kind of pot pie, chunks of fish and carrot in a savory juice under a thick crusted pastry. The guard uncuffed her and she ate the whole thing avidly.

"That's from the staff kitchen, you know," he said.

"Thank you," said Otty.

"Not like the pigshit we serve the inmates. Not too bad, eh?"

"Very nice."

He took the plate, put it on the counter next to his colleague's slate, still binging as jewels were gathered, and cuffed her wrists again.

"This is a male-only facility, girl," he told her. "So you can't stay. Should never been brought here."

"I didn't ask to come," she assured him.

For some reason this amused him.

"That's very funny," he said, and took the plate away.

Otty was cuffed but not cuffed *to* anything, so she stretched herself on the bench and tried to sleep. She dozed for a couple of hours, but it was far from a comfortable bed, and the hallway light was not only white-bright but shining directly on her face. She was half-awake and half-asleep for a while, until finally she fell into a dream about paddling a dark brown wooden canoe up a tumultuous stream, jungle on her right hand, and on her left a giant brown cliff face, an overhanging rock formation from which depended gigantic knobbed stalactites, and as she labored, feeling increasing panic in her breast, the stalactites started twisting and curling and revealed themselves to be snakes—snakes!—snakes!—and Kathry was there, floating overhead in one of those one-man dirigibles Californians like to commute to work on that travel exactly twelve feet above the ground, high enough to roll over people's heads and vehicle roofs, but not so high, in case they fall off, so they don't get too badly hurt. *Kath!* Otty called, in the dream. *Kath—you got to help me, you got to help me from these snakes.* But Kath was drifting out of range, and Otty experienced a clattering, crushing revelation that she was dead that she was dead that she was dead and they would never talk to one another ever again.

She woke up weeping. It was hard to clear the tears away from her face with her wrists shackled together.

She sat up. The guard at the counter had been so absorbed in her *Jewel Collecta* game that she hadn't noticed her crying. Small mercies, though. Small mercies.

Eventually this guard parked the game and stretched on her stool. She came around to the front of the counter.

"I'ma take a leak break—you need one?"

"Yes, ma'am, thank you."

She was led through and used the restroom again, and then was returned to the bench. The guard resumed her perch and turned her slate on again. This time, instead of playing her game, she flipped to a newsfeed.

Otty couldn't see the images, and it took a while to make sense of the spoken comments of the various newscasters, but it became clear pretty quickly that things were in a bad way. Fighting was sporadic but intense across the Midwest. Pierre, Dakota, was on fire, it seemed, and Des Moines was the scene of the most intense drone-on-drone bot-on-bot firefights yet seen in the history of warfare. In other news, California had reaffirmed its independence, and the Freedom Executive of the Thirteen—whatever *that* was—had tabled a formal motion of disapproval in the Sacramento Legislature. For a time the soundtrack was wordless: the grinding rattle of gunfire, the tinny snaps of distant explosions relayed through the slate's tinny speakers. The guard watching the show sighed. Voices again: "...the concerns articulated by the President of Mexico. In other news, the Malaysian Agong has promised military aid to the Golden State if, in his words, such proves necessary for Californian self-defense and self-determination. In Texas today, talks broke down between the rival factions of..."

The guard swapped channels. Now the feed was a game show. There was a lot of shrieky laughter. Shorn of its images, it sounded to Otty like people being tortured rather than entertained.

Later the guard turned the tablet off and sat, staring into space. Then she pulled a flashlight from a drawer in the counter, unlocked the main entrance and went outside to—Otty assumed—patrol the grounds. She didn't lock the door behind her. Maybe she'd forgotten about Ottoline altogether. Maybe she figured a sixteen-year-old in handcuffs wouldn't be so stupid as to rush out in the middle of the night into a locked and spotlit prison yard.

Otty laid down and tried to go back to sleep.

:8:

Otty spent three days and nights on that bench. She grew surprisingly comfortable on it, after a fashion, and worked out a way to get as much sleep as possible by tucking her face into the corner and the back of the seat. The guards mostly ignored her. On day two, the main door was unlocked to let in a delegation of fierce-looking officials in suits, who stomped around the innards of the prison and departed again within the hour.

On the morning of the fourth day, she was given one last chance to use the restroom, and then taken into the yard. An old-school taxicab was waiting, complete with human driver. Otty was pushed into the back seat, still shackled, and a locked zipbag was dumped beside her.

It was not an automatic vehicle. The driver was a woman of late middle age, with close-cropped hair, a barrel-shaped head, a pug-nose and small eyes.

"You listen to me, kid," she said, twisting around in her seat to glare at Otty. "I'm not usual in the business of schlepping convicts, you hear?"

"Yes, ma'am," said Otty.

"*Vel*cro those lips shut, and listen. I'm not in the business of moving convicts, but I'm doing Mary-Leanna a personal favor, on account of her being a friend, and *she* says I can use all reasonable force. Yeah? I got a gun here." She showed Otty her handgun: a firearm so flat it was almost two-dimensional, with T.A. ARM. NEEDLE .002 embossed on its side. "It's a needlegun, but don't think it won't disable you, or like-as-not kill you, if I shoot you the right way. And I will. If you give me grief. You sit back. You don't try to make conversation with me, and you don't make no sudden moves, and the sooner I'm rid of you the better."

The woman put the gun away, turned in her seat and set off. It was strange to be actually driven by a human being rather than in a self-drive machine, and Otty decided she wasn't that impressed. The taxi lady was erratic, accelerated too hard and braked too late, swore at other road users, and seemed eminently distractible. Nobody had strapped her in, so Otty had to contort herself somewhat to grab the seat belt in her cuffed-together hands and fasten it.

Once they were out of town and running along straight roads, past cornfields flat as the sea, the driving settled into more usual, machinelike grooves. Thunderheads were inflating themselves blackly on the far horizon. Otty watched them grow. The cab drove past a massively slender eSpire, bristling at the top with tentacles and broadcast prongs, standing right next to a still-functioning mobile network relay, like a comedy duo called Large and Little.

The driver put the radio on, and it was country music and she hummed to herself. Then it was Chinese rap, and she swore and changed the channel. Then it was news, and for a half-hour or so Otty listened in on a detailed discussion of the constitutional legitimacy of California's UDI. The acronym was used several times, and Otty tried to work out what the letters stood for. From context, DI was *Declaration of Independence*, but she couldn't figure the *U*. It seemed that the traffic jams crossing the border were so long, autodrive algorithms were unable to cope and were simply shutting down. People were abandoning their vehicles and walking. Drone footage, the newsreader said, showed hundreds and hundreds of corpses in the Mojave, people who had died of thirst or exhaustion or been killed in other ways. *In other ways?* Otty wondered. Neonic-afflicted citizens were wandering in their tens of thousands, many entirely untended. The U.S.S. *Donald Trump*, the Pacific Fleet's second largest carrier, had defied orders and seceded to the new Independent California Republic. The president herself appeared at a live feed press conference this morning from AF-1, warning the captain of the carrier that he was committing treason, ordering the ship's XO to put him in the brig prior to trial, and instructing that the ship be steered into dock at Portland, Oregon, immediately. Failure to follow these orders, issued directly by the commander-in-chief, would lead to immediate action by the remainder of the U.S. Pacific Fleet, not limited to disabling or even sinking the

—*click*, and the channel changed to some woman singing that she, she Ottoline Barragão herself, that she made her feel, that she made her *feel* ... like ... a ... natural ... *wo*man. The taxi driver sang along to that one, and then next was a Taylor Swift, and she sang along to that one too. Then it was a chunk of shouty hard rock music, and she turned the radio off.

Otty began to wonder how far the journey would be. They were, so far as she could gauge it, travelling east. The storm was still visibly building out of the right-side windows, but they seemed to be outpacing it, or at least pacing it.

"Was he *from* California, though?" the driver asked.

Otty waited, but it seemed she was talking to her.

"Who?"

"Trump. Wasn't he from New York, though?"

"I don't know, ma'am."

Otty reflected that Allie would know, because Allie's general knowledge was second to none. Nonpareil. And that, by a natural process of connection, led to her thinking about her other friends, and especially of Kathry. She'd had that weird dream of Kathry. In the dream, Kath had said she was dead.

It was true, wasn't it? She was dead.

Dead dead dead. A word. An existential punctuation mark. A mortosyllable.

Otty curled up on the back seat and began to cry. She was quiet about it, but the driver heard her.

"Christ and Muhammad!" she snapped. "Can you cut that out? Turn off the fucking waterworks, for the sake of Pete. You think you're the only one who's got it bad?"

Otty might have dozed. The next thing she knew there was a bright flash, and she snapped fully awake. Several seconds after the flash, sound waves chasing light waves across the flat earth, came the monstrous rumble of a huge explosion. Otty peered out of her window—away to the right and angled a little behind the cab, a bright white-shining bubble was resting on the horizon.

"Jesus," cried the driver. "Jesus. Is that Dayton? Did they get Dayton?"

The bubble of brightness shrank in size, and grew in intensity, and then faded away, leaving a blob of bright opacity on Otty's retinas. She blinked, blinked, and shook her head to try and rid herself of this. Then she rubbed her eyes with her cuffed-together hands. When she looked again her vision was still blotchy, but she could make out the big pork-chop-shaped mass of white cloud where the bubble had been, outlined against the black storm front behind it. The wheat fields to the south and west had been whipped into a frenzy of excitement by the explosion, writhing like crazy. Then the whole cab shook, lifted off the road, and bumped back down. The vehicle actually flew, for a second or two—actually left terra firma. Then it was back, wheels on ground, but it was being shoved sideways and forward by a mighty buffeting wind, and the driver was swearing at the top of her voice. Otty grabbed her seat belt with her linked hands and prayed. The cab slid, and then began to tip, and it seemed as though it must tip right over. But it didn't: it settled bumpybump back onto its wheelbase.

They had stopped. So had the other drivers on the freeway. The driver was panting, gasping. Through her window Otty could see a van on its side, litter and rubbish, man-made and vegetative, all over the freeway.

"Jesus and his mama," said the taxi driver, staring through her side window.

A truck thundered past, horn blaring, and the taxi shook on its chassis in the tailwind.

"Fucking robotrucks," the taxi driver said. "Can't be fucking reasoned with. No person at the wheel, see? No human con*tact*."

She started up her vehicle again, and drove on, though cautiously. She had to swerve to avoid wreckage, and kept slowing and swearing. Eventually they drove around a long curve behind a big hill, and were able to pick up speed.

"I was gonna visit my ex in Zanesville after dropping you," she said. "But, fuck, after that? I might just move *in* with my ex in Zanesville. I ain't driving west again for a few days at any rate. Not for a few days, I can tell you." This last phrase seemed to stick with her. "For a few days," she repeated. "For at least a few days."

:9:

They came out of the countryside, driving past houses and bigger buildings, and soon enough they were driving through a vertically developed city. Many domiciles, roofs all at different angles like crystalline formations. A few taller office and residential towers crusted with mobile network boosters and satdishes like clams on a shoreline rock. And head-and-shoulders taller than anything else in the city, four slender eSpires. Each one two-hundred feet high if they were an inch.

It was a still afternoon, the light was dusky under storm clouds, and there were few people on the streets. Silhouetted against such a sky, the eSpires looked anything but mundane. They took on sinister and ominous qualities. Alien. Daggers thrust into the bosom of the earth.

Six quadpods with police markings were parked side by side on the grassy verge alongside the freeway. They seemed to have been there for a while, because the bottoms of their legs were ornamented with graffiti tags. They showed no signs of moving.

The taxi driver kept swearing at her satnav. She drove along an elevated freeway for a mile or so, only to take the turn-off, swing under, and drive a long way back up the elevated freeway. Finally, though, she reached her destination. Another prison: low-rise and sprawling, behind double barbed-wire fences and flanked by two high auto-gun towers. Two guards collected Otty from the taxi and brought her inside. The top of an iPhone worn in a collarbone dock poked over the shirt collar of the shorter, and fatter, of these two penitentiary employees.

"It's the end of the fricking world!" the taxi driver yelled. "Nukes, nukes, and the end of the world! You'd better pray!"

"You *been* paid!" the taller of the two guards shouted back.

"Pray, not pay, you sinners!" the taxi driver yelled, and drove away.

Inside, Otty was processed by a large woman with a patch over one eye. She was given overalls in exchange for her previous prison clothes, and escorted to the shower. The guards came and went in twos, muttering together, or whispering. Everybody seemed on edge. But then again, given the news, that was hardly a surprise.

They put her in a cell—a proper old-school prison cell, this, with two bunks (although she was in it alone) and a low-set duckbill-shaped steel toilet fixed to the wall. She tried each bunk in turn, and decided the top one was more comfortable, but then decided she would sleep in the bottom one anyway, since she figured she might roll over and fall out.

Then she went on her knees and prayed to Heaven for all the souls caught in that terrible explosion she had seen. Then she laid on the bunk and dozed. Then she woke up and for a while just stared at her ceiling of oxbow curlicues, the springs supporting the mattress above.

Eventually they came for her, and Otty was taken up a single flight of stairs to an office. An exhausted-looking woman sat behind a desk beneath that same image of the president smiling her utterly unconvincing smile. The Stars and Stripes was pinned to the wall to the right of this image, and to the left the Ohio state flag glared at Otty with its baleful red eye.

"My name is Mrs. Derby, and I run this jail," said the woman. With seeming precision, she inserted her right-hand pinkie finger in among the bun of her wolf-gray hair and scratched a spot on her hidden scalp. "You're Ottoline Barragão."

"Yes, ma'am."

"What did you do, Ottoline?"

"What?"

"What did you *do*?"

"Come in again with that question, beg your pardon?"

"Your crime, young woman? Come along, I don't have all day."

"I didn't do anything."

Mrs. Derby looked disappointed.

"It's what you all say," she sighed. "I used to understand why you did, but nowadays, with all that's going on, it just seems such a pointless waste of everybody's time. Your docket says 'terrorism', but it also says 'enemy combatant'. This isn't really the facility to house the former, but it's *certainly* not the facility to house the latter, especially now that war is official. If you're that, then I shall do my level best to expedite a transfer to a more secure location. So which is it?"

Otty hesitated. "Ma'am," she said, eventually, "I'm not trying to vex you, but I honestly don't know. I'm just a regular kid. I keep bees. I haven't spoken to my parents in a month and a half—I figure they don't even know where I am. I don't know why I'm arrested. Nobody has told me."

The gray in Derby's hair leached a little further into her face. "You're eighteen?"

"Sixteen."

"No," said Derby, firmly. "It says eighteen here. But, look, I'm honestly not sure I can keep you here, Ms. Barragão, so don't get comfortable. We'll see. I'm going to try and speak to your arresting officer but everything is in a state of some … confusion, as you can understand."

Otty was taken back down to her cell.

She wasn't told the name of the prison, and she never saw the governor again. Breakfast and supper were in a spacious refectory where the long tables were all segregated into separate booths with plastic dividers, some Covid artefact perhaps, which had never been taken down. The prisoners, all women, filed in and were leg-chained into their booths and given their food. Guards walked between the tables tapping their batons on the dividers to discourage any kind of sororization or chatter. When the meal was over, the room was emptied in batches until everyone was back in their cells.

Each day started with lights coming on and the national anthem piped through speakers over the door. Then a voice— a guard's? The governor's?—announced the day: "Tuesday", "Wednesday", as it might be. Otty was able to keep track of the passage through the first week, but after that she lost her larger sense of where she was. Boredom was the main problem, of course. She laid on her bunk, rehearsing all that she could remember of her favorite shows, and favorite songs. It was dispiriting how few lyrics she could call to mind when she set herself that specific challenge, even with her best-loved songs. Allie would have had the entire lyric sheet memorized. She began telling herself a long multi-part story about intelligent bees in a mega-hive who take on the might of the U.S. government and defeat them and establish a new utopia based on bee harmony and bee justice.

Then a week came in which her stay there abruptly ended. She was collected from her cell early one morning, transferred into an actual police wagon together with a live police officer, and driven for a couple of hours to a new jail. She spent the night in a cell with a taciturn Native American woman, and the next day was flown—flown in a helicopter, no less—to a third prison. Here she was put in another one of what was becoming an endless series of over lit, bare-walled rooms with a table and two chairs.

She waited.

In came a young man. He was dressed in a waistcoat and tie but no jacket, and his smile could have been gashed out of the side of a honeydew melon. Otty took an instant dislike to him. His entire demeanor was—one of Allie's words, this—*snotty*.

"All right, young lady," he said, sitting himself down and putting three different tablets on the table in front of him, "let's see if we can't iron out a couple of these here wrinkles. Let's confirm names, and such. I'm Manfred. Are you Ottoline Barragão?"

Otty decided to dig in her heels. "I'm only talking to my attorney."

Manfred sat back in the chair, with a hurt look on his face. "But I am an attorney."

"Oh," said Otty.

"Look," said Manfred, sitting forward, "there's been some

kind of mess-up here. Now, we don't know the facts, and we may have to wait until an official ceasefire before we can determine all the facts anyway. That's likely. But double-checking, it seems you're sixteen years of age, and not eighteen. Is that your understanding of the state of play?"

"The state of play?" repeated Otty. "I *am* sixteen. It's what I've been telling everyone."

"Good. Now—a lot of records have been torched."

"Torched?"

"E-torched. The first five days of the war were all online, more or less. It was fer"—he opened his eyes and his mouth very wide before finishing—"*ocious*, it really was. Murray, Leavis and Fitzson lost *all* client files from before 21–22, and the more recent clients have all been e-compromised to one degree or another. It'll cost us a fortune reacquiring all that data. And we're not even government! We're a private company! They still targeted us, nonetheless."

"I'm sixteen," said Otty. "Also—I'm innocent. I need to speak to my parents."

"Absolutely you do. Now, Ottoline, we're going to get you out of here, OK? And we absolutely need to track down your parents, because..." He laughed a little jack-in-the-box laugh. "Because *you* want to talk to them, naturally. And because I want to make sure I've got a billing address so I get paid for my work."

Otty's brain caught up with what he'd just said.

"Get out of here?"

"Sure—these charges are laughable. It would waste court time even to put them before a judge. We can put the charges in what's called non-permanent juridical abeyance, and that would be like going out on bail, without having to deposit any bond. Now, you're a minor, and there's been some pile-up somewhere in the system that had your age wrong, so you've been in a series of adult correctional facilities. You might be able to sue ... Look, I'ma level with you, and say—best wait till the war is over, or at least until a cease*fire*, before you try that. I mean—you don't get the news in here, I'ma guess? You may not know about the latest casualty figs. You may not know about *Dayton*."

"What about Dayton?"

But he only shook his head sadly and looked for a time at the desktop. Then he said: "*Point* is, during wartime the courts are going to triage your species of doo-doo right down the list of priorities. Bigger and fishier fish to fry. War crimes, crimes against humanity, treason. But hey, after the war, I'd say there's prima facie. There's prima facie. Sign this ..."

He spun one of his tablets around and pushed it over to her. She scribbled her name with her finger, and added the little squiggle over the *a* with a flourish.

"And this one too," said Manfred. He pushed a second tablet over, and retrieved the first. "And finally," he said with a laugh, "this one."

He brought up a new document on the first tablet and she signed that as well.

"Those aren't full confessions, I hope," said Otty.

And Manfred said: "Aha, ha-ha, ha-ha."

The noises emerging from his mouth were very much more like saying those words than actually laughing.

"What happened to Dayton, though?" Otty pressed.

He shook his head again, and it didn't look like he was going to respond. But then he said: "Small bore, apparently. Small bore! I mean, can you imagine? If they can do that with a handgun nuke, imagine what a ... I don't know the military terminology, but ... you know. Imagine what they could do with a bazooka nuke! Or a missile, or Big Brenda. Not Brenda. Bella? No." He fiddled with his phone, checking the specifics. "Big Bertha. Terrible days," he said. "Terrible days. But hopefully it won't last much longer. I mean, it *can't* last much longer, can it? This republic held together for a quarter of a millennium. Sure it has ... *fault lines*. But those aren't fatal. We'll iron out this wrinkle in our body politic and then everything can go back to normal."

"Handgun nuke?" Otty asked.

But Manfred wasn't in the talking mood any more. He racked up his tablets and slipped them in his bag.

"So I'll see about getting you your clothes back, and your phone, and we'll try and get a hold of your parents."

And he left.

Otty sat in the room, expecting guards to take her back to her cell. But nobody came. After a while, and out of boredom more than anything, she tried the door. It opened.

That was surprisingly unsettling.

"Hello?" she called. "Anyone?"

She walked a little way up the corridor outside, but thought better of it, and walked back to the room. Then she sat down and waited.

After a long wait, a guard came in, and led her back to her cell.

:10:

Two days later she had a meeting with a second attorney, a tall woman whose bright, mobile eyes looked out of place in an otherwise unalert-looking face, deep lines vertically and horizontally and especially around the mouth, and a green wire sticking out from her ear. She was wearing a phone in a collarbone dockette—it was an expensive-looking model, but it was still a phone, rather than the more stylish and exclusive neck blister. For the longest time, this woman didn't say anything to Otty.

She sat opposite her, reading carefully through documents on the tablet in front of her.

Finally she looked at her and said, "Things have gone to shit." Then she stopped, and peered at her, as if seeing how she would react to the word. Then she went on: "I mean, nationally. I mean generally, and I also mean just with respect to you. Your prospects are not too bad, although I gotta say, I gotta-gotta say—why did you sign those NDA and waiver-of-prosecution submissions? Was it under duress? That would help us a tiny bit, although it's gonna be hard to make any kind of case stick, with the country in the state it's in right now."

"Who are you?"

The woman was silent for three long minutes. Then she reached into her bag and pulled out a small sucker. It looked like the rubber portion of a toilet plunger, except in blue, and molded to more resemble a dog's snout. This she put over her mouth, and breathed in deeply through her nose.

"This," she said, sighing the words, "is a filter. I got a nicotine-mist nasal implant. You heard of those? No? I guess you're a pretty incurious kid. I activate it, breathe in, and smoke. I gotta wear the filter over my mouth when I'm on government property, or in public, to prevent other people passively smoking my shit."

"OK," said Otty, baffled.

"I'm Bruzzi. I'm Gabriella Bruzzi, and I'm an attorney."

"What about Manfred?"

"Never heard of that fucker," said Bruzzi. Her words were slightly muffled by the mask.

"Please don't swear," said Otty. "I do find it offensive."

"Being offended at the word *fucker* makes less sense than actually being offended *by* that fucker," said Bruzzi. "You should notta signed that shit. Should. *Not*. Now, now, I can prolly get the submissions overturned, but to do that would take court

148

time … and court time? That's fucking hen's *teeth*. You know that expression?"

"No," said Otty.

"Means rare. Court time is hard to come by, what with the whole country being at war with the whole country. You know how Americans fight? They fight two ways. They fight with guns and they fight with fucking lawsuits, and the latter is a sudden epidemic. Wah-wah, a militia man shot me in the leg, I want four million dollars compensation for the leg, that kind of thing. Wah-wah, a drone rolled my roof away and now I gotta eat my microwave egg fried rice under the fucking stars. Soldiers from the Illinois National Guard trespassed on my land, shot three of my sheep, and now I want forty million in compensation. Or, in more instances than you would credit—the whole fucking war is illegal and I, a private citizen, will take the U.S. Government *and* the Independent Republics of California, Alaska and Kentucky"—she stopped to suck another deep breath through her nose—"fucking *Kentucky*, can you believe it?—*to* court to prove that it is so. Whereupon, I don't know what these bozos think will happen … The three million armed men rampaging across the countryside will go, oh, a *judge* says so? I'll just lay my weapons down on the ground and go home to Mama." She snorted contemptuously. "The faith of individual Americans in the ability of *law courts* to sort out the heinous shit they get themselves into is as boundless as it is unjustified. Not just individuals, neither. Corporations are individuals, legally, and they're pissed, and hosing billions into attempts to use, I don't know, to use NAFTA and copyright and who-knows-what laws as a new matrix in which the breakaway states can be reabsorbed into the whole. Interesting times, fuck. But it all means that a little puissant suit brought by *me*, on *your* behalf, is going to cool its heels in the law's chilly waiting rooms for a very long time. Don't misunderstand me—I'll file. But you'll be grown-up and with kids of your own before we see any movement forward, which means I'm not going to get paid for a very long time and, given the general state of my heath, a very long time for me means never, so excuse me if I let slip the occasional fucking spicy item of vocabulary, OK?"

She took another sniff, breathed out, removed the mask and packed it away. There was a distinct odor of tobacco in the room.

Her wrinkled face smiled at Otty.

"Nonetheless," said Otty, calmly, "I'd be grateful if you didn't swear in my presence."

"And I'd be grateful if you could go back in time and *un*sign those waivers you signed yesterday," Bruzzi snapped back. Then she stared straight at Otty for a long time without saying anything, and finally she said: "OK, little lady, no swears. Apologies if I scraped your tender sensibilities up the wrong way. It's all a mess, and in peacetime I'd be a hero attorney and Suzy Smiles would come out of retirement to interview me on national television, because what happened to you was. Messed. Up. But in these dangerous times, it won't make a pinprick on the media."

"I just want to go home," said Otty.

"Sure, kid," said Bruzzi, and she didn't sound hostile. "Sure you do. Well, I should have you out in a week. Less, I guess. They don't want you here, you don't belong. The paper trail has got royally torn to shreds, and nobody knows why you're here. Somebody somewhere wanted you for some reason, but they can't be traced, and maybe they're dead. So woo and hoo. The authorities here? They're only anxious that letting you out might piss off some higher-up. So they'll tag you, and you can go home."

Otty's spirits leaped, but Bruzzi had less heartening things to say too.

"I tried to get hold of your parents, though their contact details aren't in *your* records, which is another breach of the law given your age, and something I'll be filing about. But I can google, like the next woman. And no dice. I guess you know that Penn has been gone over more than once, yeah?"

"What do you mean, 'gone over'? Wait—Pennsylvania has been 'gone over'? What does that even mean?"

"It means that New York, New Jersey and another clutch of the thirteen tried to secede, and there's been a whole ton of fighting, back and forth. It's quieter there now. They're still in the union anyhows."

Otty's heart slowed. She could feel the reduction in the rate at which it pumped. It was as though her blood had become treacle. She was conscious of a sense of falling in her gut.

"What are you saying? What are you saying about my parents?"

"I'm not saying sh—oot," Bruzzi growled. "I don't know. I don't know a damn thing about them. All the chances are they were evacuated along with most civilians. A bunch were taken up to Columbus, some went northeast, maybe so far as Maine. You haven't seen the news, I know, but a metric tonne of people have gone to Canada. More were bussed down to Florida."

"All the way to *Florida*?"

"Sure—they got these pontoons off the coast there, with refugee housing and such. It's all a mess, girl, I won't tell you otherwise. But chance is—good chance, strong chance—your parents are fine."

"And my sister?"

"Whole family, sure. Best-case scenario."

Bruzzi stopped here for a while to cough lustily, as though a ratchet were spinning and failing to catch in her chest. Finally she coughed a single cough, like a gunshot, and seemed to settle her bronchi.

"Best-case scenario," she said, "this whole fucking *stupid* war, excuse me, I apologize, will burn itself out in a month, in two months, say. Then everybody gets back with everyone. The problem is—there are plenty of people real keen to shoot their guns and run around in combat gear. The problem is—people have forgotten what war means. They think it'll shake things up and sort things out, when all it ever does is wreck things and leave a tidemark of misery that it takes literally generations to scrub out. People in this country have no memory of war. They're spun stories of Abraham Lincoln and Robert E. Lee—or they're spun stories of Luke fucking Skywalker, begging your pardon—and they think war is an exciting and righteous crusade. But war is when we collectively shit the bed. That's all it is. Apologies for the profanity."

"What about," Otty pressed, "my friends?"

At this, Bruzzi raised her eyebrows. "OK, that is interesting, yeah? Because from the, in all honesty, shockingly incomplete files I was passed concerning your case, one thing comes out—it was your friends who got you *into* this. You had some bad-boy and bad-girl friends, it seems. Terrorist sympathizers?"

"They were not," said Otty, hotly. "I need to know if they're OK. Alive, and safe."

"And I can't help you." She cackled a witchy sort of laugh. "And I tell you what—your computer genius friends? That includes you too, I guess."

"Genius," said Otty, dismissively.

"You know what I mean. You set up your own private internet, is what it says here. Is that, like, really good firewalls and a private space filled with images of goat porn?"

"No!"

"Client confidentiality means I can't shop you for it."

"Don't be ridiculous," said Otty, primly. "We did set up an encysted network, it's true. But we didn't piggyback it on the existing network. If you like, I can lecture you on how pervasive state and deep-state surveillance is of every nook and each hidden cranny of the general network. You think firewalls keep you safe? Think again. Your data is the most valuable thing about you, so far as corporations are concerned, and the second most valuable thing about you after taxes, so far as governments are concerned. You think they'd be rebuffed by tissue-paper walls when it comes to surveiling that data? Gathering it?"

"Lectured by a kid," said Bruzzi, nodding approvingly. "Nice. Go on, sprout. Don't mind me."

She retrieved her smoking filter from her bag and fitted it once again to her mouth. But Otty felt self-conscious now.

"I'm only saying," she continued, in a more tentative voice, "we set up our own network, sure. It shadowed the internet, and we fed it with some frames and data *from* the internet, after we'd bleached it to our satisfaction. But it ran on our machines and used our copper wires."

"Somebody else's copper wires you stole," Bruzzi said.

"Scavenged," Otty retorted.

"It's fascinating, it really is. And I could chat all day, but I got other clients, you know? Actual paying clients?" She got to her feet. "Though I guess I should confess, I was wrong, what I said earlier. This war is being fought three ways. Not two. It's me being old and out of touch saying otherwise. It's being fought the old-fashioned way, with guns and bombs, and men in big boots and heavy padded jackets shooting at one another and stealing and raping as they go. And it's being fought in the law courts, like I said. That's just a fact, a constant of U.S. living. But it's also being fought online—computer viruses, denial of service. Why bomb an electricity grid to shards and ash when you can seize control of the enemy's governing algorithm and just turn it off, right? That way the grid is still there when you win the war and want to put the lights back on."

"*If* you win the war."

"Sure… Oh, sure. Oh, sure. But here's the thing—we grow

our *own* shitheads with guns, right here in the U.S.A. We've no shortage of shitheads with guns. And we sure as fuck, excuse me, sure as heck grow our own attorneys. I mean, we're famous for that, right? But we don't grow our own computer hackers. We import those from Russia and the Far East. We always have. And that's a problem, I think, for the top brass trying to prosecute this war. Because battalions of foreign agents working on the cyberfront could be fifth column, or enemy sleepers, or who knows what. You and your friends are small salad, no offense, in the larger scheme of things. But all five of you, all Famous Five of you, are at least *American* small salad."

"I'm not sure I follow what you're saying," Otty confessed.

"Oh, it's probably not worth following," said Bruzzi, taking off her mask a second time and slipping it back into her bag. "Only maybe … Only maybe the whole purpose of arresting you and your two friends wasn't punishment or incarceration, so much as a roundabout attempt to *recruit* you."

"If so," said Otty, "it was really very roundabout indeed."

"Yeah, sure. So maybe it wasn't that, or maybe it was but events overtook it. This war really is a"—she swallowed the word she was going to say, and wrinkled her nose—"poopshow. Look after yourself, kid."

And she went.

:II:

Otty didn't see Attorney Bruzzi again. But two days after this meeting, a parcel containing Otty's civilian clothes and also her phone was dropped off at her cell. The phone had neither charge nor charger (nor was there anywhere in the cell to plug it in, even if she had been reunited with the latter), but it was at least her phone.

Changing back into her clothes made her feel a tingle of anticipation. There was a rip in the back of her sweater, not enormous but unmissable. Her shirt was fine, and had even been laundered, but she did not like the look of the gash in her sweater. Her jacket covered it, of course, but what about when she wanted to take her jacket off? She mentioned it, and her phone's lack of charge, to the guards when they came to take her to the evening meal, but they literally shrugged.

"And I had a bag? A kind of satchel, with a bunch of personal stuff in it?"

"Don't know anything about any satch-*el*," said the shorter of the two guards. "That ain't here, and it ain't been delivered here, and ain't nothing to do with us."

She wasn't sure what to expect, although now that she was no longer wearing prison fatigues she assumed her release was imminent. But after the following day's breakfast she was returned to her cell. She beguiled the time by extracting the little Γ-shaped metal widget from the flank of her phone, the one used to reset it. She squashed its fragile ring into an elongated shape, and used it as a makeshift needle. She pulled a thread from her sweater and used the improvised pin to bodge together the gap. After that, she felt a little happier about the state of her life.

She was not taken through for supper and so went to sleep hungry. Perhaps the prison authorities thought she'd already been released. She wondered if she should make a noise to remind them she was still here.

Time enough for that in the morning. She was used, now, to going to sleep hungry. She was certainly skinnier than she had been before her arrest.

She wasn't taken through for breakfast either, but she was given some food—a stale Danish wrapped in a fold of plastic, and a bottle of iced coffee. She ate and drank avidly.

"Come on," said the guard. "Time to go."

So this was it. Her heart did a little doddle-beat pick-you-up.

She put on her jacket and followed the guards through to the front of the prison and out into the air. It was still early in the day and the air was fresh, although the smells of the city were still palpable: plastic and exhaust and a tang of sewage and a stronger smell of smoke. Drones were criss-crossing through the sky overhead. Above them was a clean white ceiling of cloud through which sunlight was sifted.

A bus was waiting. Otty climbed aboard. The guard got on with her, and then sat for a while, fiddling with her phone.

"This fucking app," she said. "Supposed to give me clearance to instruct this bus, but it's glitchy as fuck."

"Please don't swear," Otty asked.

"Supposed to give me override. Fucking app! Say what? Don't what?"

"Don't swear. Please."

"Fuck *that*. I gotta go inside, get this sorted. Stay here."

Alone on the bus, Otty wondered what her status now was. Free? If so, there was nothing stopping her dismounting and walking away. Nothing except the outer fence and gate. She sat where she was. Eventually the guard came back, and sat down, and this time the bus door hissed itself closed. The guard fiddled with her phone again, and the driverless bus hummed to life.

They drove out and into the city and spent twenty minutes negotiating traffic. The guard, who was now absorbed in a game on her phone that involved building an elaborate jigsaw of neon connections, said nothing further to Otty. The game bleeped distractingly every time a new connection was made.

Soon enough they pulled up outside a large gray building with an oversized holographic Stars and Stripes flapping and curling egregiously at the front, alternately veiling and revealing the big revolving entrance door.

"Where's this?" Otty asked.

"You go in. Felon Rehabilitation and State Records," said the guard, without looking up from her phone.

"Pennsylvania's not my state, though," Otty pointed out. "And I'm not a felon."

"Giving a fuck is not *my* state, though," retorted the guard, her attention not straying from her game.

Otty dismounted from the bus and went into the building. The lobby was deserted. Old papers and sinuous curls of foil-thin plastic littered the floor. There were two big counters but there was nobody behind either of them. A spoor of dried feces, dog or maybe fox, lay, nature aping Morse code, across the marble of one of these.

"Hello?" called Otty.

The elevators weren't working. She went up the stairs and explored the second floor, but all the doors were locked. On the third floor she found two women packing things into a selection of different-sized boxes.

"The whole building has been relocated to Scranton, young miss," said the taller of these. "You got business, you'll need to take it there."

Her name tag said her name was Adler. Her nose was a beak-shaped prominence.

"Can you help me?" Otty asked. "I was just released from prison."

"I can not," said the first woman, and the second stopped her packing, ferreted around in her spacious-looking fanny pack and withdrew a stick of Mace. "Prison ain't my business and felons ain't my favorite kind of people, lady," the first woman said.

Otty took a step back. "I'm only a kid," she said. "I'm trying to find my parents."

"And I'm Mariee of Roo-*mania*," returned the first woman.

157

"Buzz off and buzz out, kid. There's nothing to loot here. We can't help you."

Otty went back down the stairs and out on to the street, but the bus was long gone.

:12:

Otty wandered the city for a while, in something of a daze. After months of having her movements restricted and her timetable laid out for her, it was weird to have the freedom to go wherever she went. Weird and unsettling. You're free, she told herself, and now you must make the best of it. But freedom is only a virtue if you have money. Without it the word means only hunger and vulnerability.

Life in the city seemed to be going on more or less as life always had in the U.S., war or no war. Vehicles drove up and down. Drones thronged the sky. People went into and came out of offices and malls. She found the municipal art gallery and went in to use the restroom. There was a paydesk, but nobody to man it; and there were turnstiles but nobody to prevent her hopping over them. She found the toilet and relieved herself, and then she drank from the faucet. The actual exhibition halls were all closed. A sign said that the collection was being shifted to Ontario for safe-keeping, but through the lattice of the door-grilles drawn down to keep visitors out, Otty could see all the paintings still on the walls.

On the way out she explored the unmanned coffee cart in the lobby. There wasn't much on it, although she found two vacuum-packed blueberry muffins and took them away with her.

A drone swept down at her, and she flinched like she was in Hitchcock's *The Birds*. But it only spat out a little nut-sized kernel with its own little parachute, and flew away. This landed

158

at Otty's feet and when she picked it up, it uncurled in the palm of her hand, becoming an eagle with its wings heroically arched. Its beak moved. WILKINS AND CHO, said the hologram, while "The Star-Spangled Banner" played tinnily. ATTORNEYS IN THE TRADITION OF LINCOLN. *Have you been affected by enemy action or friendly fire? Our nowinnofee suits are tailored to exactly your trauma. Payouts range from a few thousand to millions of dollars.*

There were contact details, but Otty was distracted instead by the word "nowinnofee". She worked out what it meant eventually, but for a while she got snagged on the idea that it was related to *banoffee*, as in *banoffee pie*.

There was a large park in the middle of downtown. It had been converted into a tent-city. Otty wondered if these were refugees, and she wondered at how so many of them had assembled in such a short time—I mean, even if the country was at war with itself, it had only been so for a few weeks, surely. But there was a towering slender eSpire located in the middle of the park, its top a tangle of baffling-looking tech-dreadlocks and tapering prongs, and these people seemed to have gathered at its base as … Otty wasn't sure. A permanent protest about the siting of an eSpire in the centre of the city? An impromptu cult *worshiping* the structure?

Nothing to do with her, at any rate.

Of course she couldn't wander the city forever. She snuck into a Starbucks and slipped her phone onto the recharging shelf. Then, since she didn't even have enough money to pay for a coffee, she pretended to hesitate by the pastry selection for a long time. Then she lurked in the restroom, where she ate one of the muffins, and by the time she came out she collected her phone and went back on the street.

The phone had 66% charge, but when she turned it on she discovered that it had been bounced back to its factory settings.

This was annoying. She couldn't remember any of her contact numbers off by heart—I mean, who could?—and neither her family nor any of the other Famous Five were the sort of people who posted their personal phone numbers or emails in any publicly accessible manner. Worse, she had no signal, and no money in her e-wallet.

She found a mall with free Wi-Fi and sat on a bench surfing the internet for a bit; but the mall only gave her access to store advertising bsites, plus the core provision—Twitter and so on. When she tried to access other bsites she got a charging menu, and that was no good.

Because she couldn't think of anything else, she went on Wikipedia and created a page for herself. Picking away at the little screen keyboard, and fiddling with the up-down, left-right buttons, it took a while to post even rudimentary stuff; but she put down that she was a sixteen-year-old American citizen currently stranded in Pittsburgh, Pennsylvania, and looking to reconnect with her family. She had no idea whether anybody would even think to look there. But she couldn't think what else to do.

Four soldiers marched in line through the mall, people skittering out of their way. Bulked up, rifles out. They looked like they were wearing all their clothes at once, and their face-masks gave them the look of Speztroopers from *Orion Combat*. All conversation stopped as they passed, and only resumed once they had gone.

:13:

The two muffins she'd scavenged didn't last long, and soon enough she was hungry again. She scoped a few opportunities to snatch food—from stalls whose teenage salespeople's attention was evidently partial, or slovenly; and from the large autocans

160

at the back of the food mart—but in that latter location there were too many people about, and she felt self-conscious. She'd literally just got out of jail, the last thing she wanted was to give the authorities a chance to send her back there. Besides, stealing was wrong. It was in the Ten Commandments, for heaven's sake. The slender distinction between scavenging and stealing was a debate for another day, mind you.

The more she wandered around the city, the more damage she noticed. Indeed, she found herself amazed that she hadn't noticed it before. Cities were always a bit shabby, of course; but there was, once you started looking for it, a much heftier proportion of derelict buildings and ruins here than you would expect. It was bright-painted facades where the roof had been knocked in. It was a potholeless road that curved and began to rise up to its elevated section, only to stop at a series of broken-off concrete stumps sprouting steel wire like hairs from a wart. It was many cordoned-off side streets littered with blackly caramelized auto-wrecks. It was a huge crater just off Steel Plaza, revealing, with a surprisingly shocking vibe of—well, *indecency* was the only word—the underground veinage of pipes and tubes and a subway tunnel with a dusty, block-shaped subway car dangling half out of it.

The only things undamaged were the four eSpires.

The folk she saw, too, were twitchy, nervous. Drones overflew all the time, of course, but when they came low for whatever reason—delivery, surveillance, malfunction—people flinched and ducked and ran. Any loud noise sent a visible wave through any crowd, a kind of Mexican wave of panic. From one of the city's many bridges Otty stood, peering down at a randomly accreted metal reef of trucks and automobiles blown into the river. If she wandered uptown, she saw people in expensive-looking houses boarding up their windows. People testing the swivel-and-point of the autoguns mounted on their roofs.

The fact that the whole population seemed to be getting ready to evacuate brought home to her that she couldn't stay here. But she couldn't see how to get away. Maybe hitchhike? Could she beg rides on the freeway *and* beg food at the same time? Wouldn't she be setting herself up for being raped and murdered?

She walked back downtown. A hologrammatic sign announced NEWLY BUILT ALL-AMERICAN HOMES and alternated the message with mosaics of fluttering Stars and Stripes. TWELVE LUXURY APARTMENTS CERAMIC BRICK LATEST TECH INSIDE DEFENSIVE SYSTEMS OUTSIDE. Behind the sign was a half-disassembled apartment block, standing next to a huge heap of gleaming bricks, as if giants were readying the world's biggest Mah Jong game.

Her nanna had always loved Mah Jong. Until her Alzheimer's got so bad she couldn't remember how to play it any more.

Every three or four blocks there were collection points for the neonic-afflicted. There had been a couple of these back home, but not nearly so many—hers was a middle-class neighborhood, and the people affected by neonicotinoid poisoning were mostly veterans, immigrant families and a tranche of older folk. Here in Pittsburgh, though, there were thousands, many tens of thousands of them. Poor: Black, Native or Mexican mostly, shuffling up and down, or standing staring into space in a puzzled way. The mighty-fine-citizen thing to do with these people was to gently encourage them along to one of the collection points, such that their families could find them when they came out looking for them. Many of the people Otty saw were elderly, and didn't even have dockettes for their phones, let alone the kind of technology that would patch up their memories into functioning systems again. Maybe they weren't buckleheads. Maybe they were just old-style Alzheimer's. But what really struck Otty was how people simply steered around these sufferers. How rarely people took the trouble to chaperone the blinking, puzzled-looking people to relative safety.

The collection points were heavily surveilled, a strategy presumably supposed to discourage people taking advantage of the people waiting there. Blistercams, a sudden-movement alarm, 3D identity capture. But who would take advantage of such people? What advantage was there to be *taken*? You couldn't call their waiting patience, because they didn't really have the memory-function to understand *that* they were waiting. Of course, Otty thought, with a lurch in her gut, the buckleheads she saw on the streets, and in the collection points, were all old and shabby and carried nothing of value about their person. Where were all the young and attractive sufferers? Better cared for at home? More likely to have the tech to compensate their condition? Or—maybe—just *as* liable to be standing around on the streets, but much more likely to be abducted by the unscrupulous for sexual purposes, or organ harvesting, or whatever horrors Otty couldn't even conceive?

A chasm opened before her in her imagination. Doubtless the city was a honeycomb of little hidden cells in which people did unspeakable things to neonic-afflicted individuals. Pity the buckleheads in this new and crueller world.

She didn't want to think about it. So she didn't think about it.

She was really quite hungry now, but there was no point in moping. She walked on.

"Little lady," said a woman, striding toward her. "You lost? You hurt by the war?"

Otty's first assumption was: religious zealot. She had no desire to get into doctrinal discussions with a stranger trying to recruit her to a cult, so she picked up the pace. The woman fell into a trot behind her.

"Hey, slow down, little lady. I'm not wanting to hurt you. I represent the law firm of Nicholson, Phillips and Nicholson. If you've lost your parents in this war then we can guarantee you a no-win-no-fee six-figure payout. Guarantee it!"

"My parents are fine," Otty called, and broke into as fast a spring as her little legs could manage. The attorney-woman gave up the pursuit.

She found the public library, hard by a public park whose grass was now a tessellation of tent-roofs and temporary structures. The city's central eSpire blinked a red light from its top, like Sauron's eye winking at her.

The library itself was a classical frontage and pediment, with big old pillars like gigantic cigarettes, and many little barred windows. Most of the building was closed ("temporarily", according to the signage) and there was no checking out of any books; but a large hall was open. The sign projected on the wall had a list of town hall meetings and public gatherings timetabled, but Otty slipped in during a half-hour when it was empty and found—to her immense relief—free Wi-Fi.

Or not: When she tried to log in, she was told the Wi-Fi was only for city residents, and she was instructed to enter her address and her unique citizen code. She made up the former and typed the digits 9 through 1 for the latter. Astonishingly, the system was satisfied with this.

For a while she browsed news sites. Last week: Dayton, Dayton; yesterday: Dayton. This morning: a similar detonation in Baja California, closer to or further away from San Diego, depending on which feed you believed. Surprising they couldn't pin it down more accurately than that. Lots of woeful commentary. Religious talking heads assuring their viewers that the world was ending just exactly as Revelation predicted. A bright-faced young woman said that the worst was behind them now, and from here on in they were climbing the rocky road to peace. That phrase, *rocky road*, made Otty think of ice cream, which reminded her how hungry she was.

She watched the news from California for a while; but the West Coast felt a long way away. So she checked out the stories from the East Coast, particularly (of course) what had happened to her home town—nothing very good, if the drone footage was to be believed. She still figured she should try and make her way back east—I mean, where else was she going to go? She searched for her parents' names, but literally hundreds of Barragãos turned up in the results. She searched for the other four members of the Famous Five and the problem was even worse. She tried a number of options on Kath's name—Kath Chong, Kathry Chong, Kathry Chong dead—but thousands of results left her none the wiser. Then she tried vanity searching, and the first hit was a news story that she had been arrested as a terrorist suspect, which was disconcerting. Then she spent a while on general newsfeeds trying to piece together what had happened to the U.S. over the last couple of months. The overall summaries were frustratingly vague, but the specific stories led her down rabbit holes of local detail that added little to the overall picture. There was, perhaps, no need for an overall summary when the overall picture was so obvious: the world had gone to caca.

This wandering around online wasn't getting her anywhere except into the sub-50s, battery-charge-wise. She needed to be smarter. She sat back and thought: What was the name of the attorney, the smoker? Bruzzi. It had been Bruzzi. A search revealed that there were thirteen attorney in Ohio called Bruzzi, but eight of these were men, and when she narrowed the search with "smoker" she got a sole hit. It seemed that an Ohio attorney called Gabriella Bruzzi had represented clients in multiple suits for damages against smoking-related injury.

Otty called her. She was expecting a secretary, but the image that pinged up was of Bruzzi's lined face.

"Who is this?"

"I'm Ottoline Barragão. You represented me in prison, like, yesterday? I mean … Actually, it was a couple days ago. We had a meeting?"

Bruzzi looked exhausted. She closed her eyes, as if a Rolodex of recent contacts were etched on the inside of her eyelids. Then she opened them again.

"I remember. How you doing, kid? They gave you your phone back, yeah?"

"I'm out. They put me on a bus."

"Great. Text me an e-address for me to send my bill to. Better still, text me your bank details and I'll put an iLeech on it."

"I don't know what to do next."

"College, maybe? Get a good degree, job, settle down. Whatever, kid, go live your life."

"No, I mean, I'm in Pittsburgh, there's nobody here to meet me, I have no money."

"You went to *Pittsburgh*? Jesus, kid, what were you thinking? That's really not the place to be, right now. Don't you watch the news? Get outta there."

"I didn't choose to come here," said Otty, primly.

"I'm not joking, kid. You're lucky the winds are blowing west of Dayton, but there's no guarantees in the weather. Don't you know what's coming? Leave town. Leave sooner rather than later."

"Can't you help me?"

"I'm not coming to fucking Pittsburgh, kid," snapped Bruzzi.

"I don't mean that … Only …" But she wasn't sure only *what*.

"Look, you're outta jail, which is what you wanted, yeah?"

"I'm only a minor."

"Everyone got something they're only, kid."

"I've got no money."

"You got no debt neither, which makes you about eight hundred k richer than I am. Look—they're running evac buses out of Allegheny. Go there, take one of the buses. I cannot speak now. I literally cannot speak to you now."

She rang off. Otty checked the location of Allegheny and made her way through the half-ruined streets and the to-and-fro buffering of oblivious fellow pedestrians over the river.

There wasn't any difficulty in finding the evac buses. A large crowd of the city's poor was surging up to and flowing back from a fragile wall of fold-out tables. There were a dozen chairs set out on the far side of this arbitrary barrier, but only two of these had actual human beings sitting in them, working like Sisyphuses to log and process the mass of people. Away up the street behind, a long row of buses were parked.

Otty joined what was, in a manner of speaking, a queue. It took several hours before she got anywhere near the front, and then a cohort of two dozen or so hefty pink-faced Pittsburghers—an extended family, Otty guessed—pushed in front of her. They were all wearing Old Glory jackets and red MAGA caps. This led to a lot of yelling, and a surge that rippled forward like wind over the surface of a wheatfield, the combined momentum of which knocked over the family and Otty too. She sprawled onto the back of a tall woman who was making a high, piping complaining sound. There were several bouts of fisticuffs and the two officials processing people ran off—actually sprinted, knees high—as the whole row of tables tumbled and upended. Yelling became general, more punches were thrown. A general outburst of pent-up frustration and fear.

Otty couldn't physically extricate herself from the mass, and for a while became genuinely alarmed that she was going to be squashed, to break her ribs or perhaps even die. But eventually the mood of the crowd shifted around some incomprehensible hinge. Instead of kicking and punching, people began pulling people off, thinning out the crush and helping people to their feet. Fifteen minutes later, everybody was standing around, looking here and there, as if nothing had happened. The various trestle tables were picked up and put back into place.

It took an hour or so, but eventually the two officials who were processing people returned and took their seats again.

This time Otty got to the front in due course, and was asked her name and citizen ID.

"I'm a minor," she said.

The woman looked up from her tablet. "Kinda young to work underground, ain't you?"

"I mean I'm a kid, I'm underage."

The woman had a stark white keloid scar down the side of her face. It looked recent.

"Where are your parents?"

"I don't know. I'm sixteen." Then she risked: "I'm not from Pittsburgh. I got separated from my parents; they're not in the city."

"ID?"

"I had it on my phone," Otty said, showing her phone. "Only it got reconfigured to factory setting."

"Get on with it," said somebody behind Otty, and the cry was taken up: We ain't got all day. Hoof along now. Come *on*!

"Look, kid," said the woman, "there's not much I can do here. Get on a bus, and they'll sort you out at reception, the other end of the journey."

"I need to go east," said Otty. "I got to get home."

"You *got*," the woman said, with severity, "to get out of this city, young lady. That's what you got. That's what's pressing, that's the really pressing thing. There are buses going to Georgia, Florida."

"I need to go east."

"You didn't let me finish—there are buses going to Vermont. If you're really a minor, you should be going there anyway. Give me your phone."

"Vermont?" Otty said, aghast, as she passed the phone down.

"Hey," said the woman. "It's east. And, missy, it ain't here, Vermont ain't here, and that's good enough for you, believe me. You saw what happened to *Dayton*." She bumped a ticket on to Otty's phone and yelled "next!"

Otty made her way around the tables and joined a stream of people heading up to the incline to where the buses were parked. She showed her ticket to three people, two of whom disavowed any connection to the authorities and one of whom merely stared at her. There were no numbers on the buses, and none of them had human drivers she could ask. People were crowding inside and occupying seats, so Otty figured that was a thing to do. She picked a bus at random, clambered up the oversized up-gap step onto the vehicle and presented her ticket to the readout. A big red cross flashed up. So she dismounted and tried the next bus. Again, the red cross of rejection.

"This would be easier," she muttered, "if they would put the buzzing *destinations* on the front of the buzzing buses."

The sixth bus she tried produced a green smiley-face and a seat number. There was a sleeping man in the seat supposedly allotted to her, his cranium bald as a soccer ball and with recent grazes and cuts in among the stubble of his face. She figured it was probably not worth disturbing him. So she found another seat and tried to make herself comfortable.

For an hour or so nothing happened except that many more people got onto the bus. Soon enough it was standing room only. Then it was so crammed that Otty couldn't see out.

"The bus is over its load threshold!" somebody shouted from the front. "This is the Vermont bus. The Vermont bus. If you're not going to Vermont then you need to dismount the bus."

"I'm going anywhere that's away from this fucking city!" somebody shouted back, and there was a deal of jeering and laughter. The crush did not reduce itself. Otty waited.

A half-hour passed.

A different official (or so Otty guessed by their voice: she couldn't see) came on.

"The bus won't move if it's overloaded. Its programming literally won't allow it, guys! Everybody without a specified seat needs to vacate the bus right now."

This was greeted with hoots and curses.

"Well, suit yourselves. But this bus ain't going nowhere the way it is now."

Ten minutes later somebody at the front started calling, in loud, unrestrained tones, "Hey, those buses are leaving! They're leaving us here! They're abandoning us!"

Abruptly, there was an exodus from the bus, people scrambling off. The crush thinned to the point where Otty could, once again, see through the windows—see people running after the departing buses, banging on their sides and trying to prise open doors.

With a steam-kettle hiss the doors of her bus closed, and the automated system engaged its gears. They started trundling down the slope and slowly undertook the cumbrous business of turning through ninety degrees to go around the corner at the bottom. Some of the people who had run after the other buses came sprinting back, slapping their palms on the big windows and screaming. An especially agitated-looking woman had a gun in her hand and was aiming it at the side of the bus. Otty watched like it was all some screen drama and not real life at all. Hunger and exhaustion fermented her brain until reality was just a strange sort of hallucination, and she could watch perfectly disinterestedly. The woman aimed, and a surge of people crashed into her, toppling her over. The gun went off as she fell with a snare drum snap that was very clearly audible, and quite unmistakable.

But the bus was picking up speed now. Some of the people

aboard were pushing to the rear to watch what was happening through the back windows. The sounds of more gunshots. Twigs snapping in the first intensity of the fire. Knuckles cracking. Then—quite a long way behind, as it sounded to Otty—a more resonant crash, like the city clearing its throat. A thunderous detonation, and the after-grumble, rolling and echoing back and forth. People at the back of the bus oohed and aahed. But the bus was crossing the river now, and soon enough it had picked up speed and joined the Interstate heading north.

The mood on the bus relaxed. People chatted. Some even sang. Then, as the journey ground on, the passengers settled down and turned to their phones.

To begin with, there were many automobiles and trucks on the roads: laden roof racks, innards fully packed, upholstery and blankets squashed against the passenger windows. After a while, though, the bus peeled off on to Interstate 80, heading east, and left most of the traffic on the northbound roads.

Otty contemplated her hollow stomach, and then tried to distract herself from the physical discomfort of her hunger by trying to work out what she was going to do. She didn't want to go to Vermont, that was certain. But they couldn't be driving straight there—that would be, like, a twelve-hour drive, or something. Presumably they would stop at some point, and maybe give them all something to eat and drink. She figured she could get east of the mountains, and then, maybe, dismount at a comfort break and find her way home from there. Hitching a ride, if necessary.

She looked around the bus. A quick survey led her to believe that about half the occupants had phones jacked into dockettes on their shoulders or fitted to their collarbones.

The bus made a distracting growling-grinding noise when it went up a hill, and felt worryingly free-fall when it went down one. They passed a convoy of—Otty began logging them but gave up after the twentieth—*countless* army trucks ferrying soldiers the opposite way, heading back west along the Interstate. Troops were hanging out the back of the trucks, making lewd signs at the bus and waving their weapons. Scores and scores of trucks. There was very little other traffic.

The afternoon was clear-lit, and the view was of concrete roadway and yellow-green banks, and in the middle distance, very dark green forest crinkled like broccoli. The person sitting next to her was an elderly woman whose attention was wholly absorbed by a soap she was watching on her phone. When the exchanges between the bizarrely beautiful characters reached moments of particular dramatic intensity, the tinny intimation of their dialogue became faintly audible, spilling from the woman's earbuds.

Otty tried her own phone, but the bus had no Wi-Fi and she had no private credit.

The bus passed up a broad hill and over the flat summit. A vista of farmlands, yellow and pale green, bulging over the undulating, pillowlike land. No other vehicles on the freeway. There was a grumbling sound which might have been Otty's empty stomach, but was actually coming from outside.

"Hey!" somebody began shouting near the front. "Hey!"

A trio of jets, flying very low, and jinking their wings through twenty-degree slips, up, down, roared past. They were flying so low they were almost on a level with the bus.

Suddenly the sky was full of drones. The bus was laboring upward and had slowed with the strain. The slope was sharp enough to push Otty back in her seat. The road curved left. Behind her, a woman leaned over the back of Otty's seat to say something to her—hers was a small face in the middle of a bladder of flesh, and excitement, or perhaps fear, was manifest in her eyes.

"Hey," the woman said. "I saw—"

Her voice was overwhelmed by a huge sound from outside, a great crashing waterfall sound, so exactly *like* the layered white-noise crescendo of a waterfall that Otty actually looked through the bus's windows, half expecting to see that they were passing a scene of natural wonder—river, cliff, ravine. But they weren't. They were driving along the interstate up a hill through a land-scape of fields and woodland. The noise was something else. And the road had suddenly got *much* steeper. Otty was pressed into her seat, her spine hard against the seat back. There was a sinuous, rolling *roar*, like a giant wash breaking on a pebble beach, and the view through the windows was of mist and fog, and darts and fractal zigzags of lightning, so maybe they had driven into a storm, or something like that. A hailstorm maybe. Or lightning and thunder. People in the bus were yelling. The road was already insanely steep, and then it got abruptly steeper. The bus was driving up at a *crazy* angle, just crazy. I mean, whoever thought it was a good idea to run a road up such a steep incline? They were vertical, absolutely sheer, and they were still moving. Otty couldn't see anything. Then the front of the bus had opened. The top had come *off* this giant metal tube of Pringles. Otty hadn't realized that the front opened that way, and even as she formulated that thought she was aware how foolish it was: of *course* regular passenger buses don't open up their whole front ends like that. The bus was now going straight up—driving up a cliff-face. Otty was flat on her back in her seat, and astonished, astonished, astonished.

Somebody threw themselves, fast and hard, from the front of the bus to the back. I mean, they must have really taken a run at it—a long-jumper's spring and then a huge leap, because this person just shot past her. For a moment Otty had forgotten that the bus had been angled up through ninety degrees. It was hard to work out what was happening. It was all, in the moment, confusing. A second person followed the first in hurrying from the front of the bus to the back, although this person went less rapidly and bounced from seat-arm to seat back, like a ball bearing coming down through a network of nails. To think a bus could mount a perfectly vertical cliff! To think a bus could lean back *even further* than vertical, with the seatbelt clamping into Otty's lap and holding her. It was as if the bus was driving up along the underside of a massive overhang—like it had magic tyres that somehow adhered to the rock, like a fly on the ceiling with its head straight down.

Nobody was screaming. It might have been that the roaring sounds of the invisible waterfall, and the gargantuan creaking and wrenching sounds of metal spars being bent, and the general supply of crashes and bangs and thuds drowned out the sounds of the people, but Otty didn't think so. The bus was upside down now, and only Otty's lap-belt was keeping her in place. Boom, boom, shake the room. Crash, crush, flip the bus. Otty's phone slipped from her pocket and bounced shatteringly onto the ceiling. The whole vehicle was leaning hard to the left, and then as Otty's brain had gotten used to the idea that the whole bus was doing a reverse somersault, in the best traditions of fairgrounds the world over, a new direction was sharply imparted to the motion—a spin to the left that yanked Otty to the right.

For just a moment it was possible to believe that she, Ottoline, was the still point, and that the entire world was being laboriously rotated *around* her. The ghost of Copernicus fled gibbering through her mind. But then her gut lurched, and her arms flapped like Muppet arms not under her control, and the illusion passed. Yet it still moves. The bus was the thing spinning, not the rest of the cosmos.

Tick. Tick.

Boom.

All the windows down the bus's left flank shattered in unison. People were screaming now. They surely were. Otty too. The bus landed and the impact was concussive enough to jar the air from her lungs, and then she was swung hard, her lap-belt notwithstanding, against the window to her right, like a clapper in a bell, and she yelled in terror and bewilderment. The woman who had been watching the soap opera in the seat beside her had vanished. The bus was on its side but still moving. Something or somebody, maybe a giant, was for incomprehensible reasons stuffing a quantity of earth and foliage down the central aisle—cramming that stuff down the bus's throat. There was a wrenching sound, a new timbre of sound, and the whole bus jolted almost to a stop, slid, didn't quite arrest its motion. *That* bang sounded like a tyre exploding. *That* was more like a gun being fired. A symphonic layering of screeches. The bus was still sliding along on its side, though more slowly, and then hit something ramplike and reared up. It was a positively *rodeo* experience. The front of the bus lifted and began to twist.

A cloud of pine needles hummed through the air like bees.

The bus came down, and, amazingly, settled again onto its wheels. Or what was left of its wheels.

It had stopped moving.

Otty was sitting in her seat.

Breathe. Breathe.

Her stomach hurt where the lap-belt had dug in, and there was a wetness on the side of her head where she had banged it against the window. She figured it was blood. Her heart was hammering so fast she couldn't count the individual beats. They seemed to blur together into one smooth trill, like a hummingbird's wings. People around her were sobbing, moaning, swearing. Away behind her was the sound of somebody being repeatedly sick.

Otty breathed and breathed and breathed. She picked pine needles out of her mouth and breathed.

She could hear sobbing. The windows to her right were

webbed entirely across with a mist of tiny cracks and she couldn't see anything through them. The windows on the other side of the coach were all gone, and she could see ... trees.

Her phone was, somehow, nestled in her lap, undamaged.

She tried to stand up, and for one horrible minute thought she'd lost the use of her legs—her spine sheared through, herself a cripple—until she remembered that she was still belted into her seat. So she unsnibbed the seatbelt and got up, and nearly fell over immediately because her legs were trembling so badly. She plonked back into the seat and struggled up again. She handed her way, seat back to seat back, down the aisle of the bus, and wondered why the floor was so uneven. Then she thought to herself: *It must have gotten buckled when the bus crashed*. Her throat felt raw. Her heart rate was not getting any slower. Then she thought to look down and see what had happened to the floor of the aisle, and that's when she saw that she was walking over people's bodies, and she yelped.

She clambered up onto a vacant seat, her shoes crunching the mass of crumbled glass like it was gravel. The view through the glassless windows was of tree trunks and a bank of dirt, and on those parts of the forest floor she could see were messily discarded heaps of clothing. But the drop down through the open window was too far for her to jump, so she went back into the bus, and made her way, trying not to tread on people more than she could, to the front.

The whole front square of the bus's end was gone, ripped away. The automatic driver, the first rows of seats, all vanished. Otty scrambled out, and staggered. She put out her hand to stop herself falling over, and the hand met the trunk of a tree, and for a while she stood there, propped against the fir. She had never before in her life felt so dizzily nauseous.

The heaps of brightly colored clothing scattered all around on the forest floor were, she realized, the bodies of people.

A tall man, still wearing his crumpled homburg, staggered from the front of the bus, took a half-dozen steps, and commenced being sick noisily at the foot of a tree. Otty thought she might be sick too, but after a while the urge passed.

She turned herself about, as if manipulating an object remotely, or in a video game, and sat down with her back to a tree. From here she could see the whole bus, its ragged open maw where its front end had been torn away, shredded tyres hanging like noodles from its wheel hubs. There were many scratches and gouges down its flank, and several bodies hanging from the open gaps where the left-flank windshields had once been.

She picked bits of something—pine needles, fragments of glass, *something*—off her tongue with her forefinger and thumb. Her fingers tasted metallic, like iron. They were bloody. Her whole hand was bloody.

It came into Otty's head, with the suddenness of revelation, that she couldn't stay here. The bus might explode. It was in her mind that automobiles and trucks and so on that fell down cliffs, or rolled off the road, or did whatever this bus had done, were prone to burst into blow-up flames. Bang! Boom! Get outta there. *Get away, girl.* She got to her trembling legs, and staggered from one tree to another, and from that to a third, landing on each trunk in turn with both hands outstretched. A fourth. Further uphill to a fifth tree.

She looked back. The bus was still close at hand, battered and distressed and scraped and missing its snout. A few people were clambering out of this open hole. Others were standing around, looking stunned. One young man had had his jacket and shirt ripped off him in the accident. He was a fleshy individual, with shining pink skin and a bathmat of curling red hair on his chest. He stood there, wiping his face with his hand over and over, as if trying, with a repeated gesture, to brush away a perpetually recurrent cobweb. Another person, a woman, saw Otty looking at her, and waved as if in recognition, and then, with a grin, went on one knee, and fell down face forward.

Otty blinked, blinked, and took as deep a breath as she could, to try and calm her heart. She struggled uphill a little further. From here it was possible to see the path the bus had taken through the outskirts of the wood. Pant pant, further up. And here was the freeway itself, the crash barrier torn like a satin ribbon, shards of rubber and metal and oddments littering the road. On the other carriageway an armored truck, big as a cottage, thundered westward. Otty looked up. The sky was full of drones.

Were they ... dogfighting?

It was hard to tell.

She got onto the freeway and jogged unsteadily along it for a little while. Her hands were trembling badly. If she'd stopped, her legs would have trembled badly too.

Away to her right she could see where a rest-stop lane peeled off the main carriageway. There were vehicles parked there, so she made her way in that direction. Just keeping moving seemed to be keeping the shakes at bay. *There's no need to panic*, she told herself, but the word panic squeezed some gland in her brain and more panic flushed into her bloodstream.

She reached the rest-stop. There was a hot dog stand, and next to it a coffee trailer, but both were shuttered up and closed. Four automobiles were parked in this space. The first three were empty, but inside the fourth was a family: father at the wheel, mother in the passenger seat, and two kids in the back—maybe ten, eleven years old. Nobody looked at Otty as she came over. They sat there like plastic exhibits, staring straight ahead.

Otty tapped at the driver's window and the father lowered the window. But his left hand was holding a pistol and it was pointed at her.

"I need help," she said.

Her voice sounded weird in her ears, as if the crash had altered something about the resonance of her own body.

"Keep walking," said the father.

Neither mother nor children looked at her. They sat staring straight ahead.

"I was in that bus—you saw it? The bus that crashed."

"I saw it," the father said. "Missile hit. Pow—right on the kisser." He sounded strangely satisfied.

"I was inside it."

"Sucks to be you."

"There we are," said Otty. "I guess I need help, then."

"You keep walking, maybe you'll find it," said the father. "There's nothing we can do for you, and you ain't stopping here. I'll shoot—believe me when I say it."

"Seriously?" said Otty.

"Just keep walking," said the mother, without looking at her. Staring straight through the front windshield.

"This is a war, see?" the father said. "This is a battle zone. In a little, those drones will buzz on, and it'll be safe to drive, and when that happens we're *drivin'*, see? There's no space for you in here, and no help. Think," he said, with sudden urgency, "of my kids. Don't you think they've seen enough barbarity?"

"I guess," said Otty.

"You want *them* to watch their daddy shoot you in the chest, and leave you to die? You want to make them watch that? Because I *will* shoot you in the chest, and you'll bleed out. You want to force *my* kids to watch *that*?"

The voice in Otty's head said: Just go. Walk on. But she was enough of a teenager to be unable to resist the urge to argue back.

"If you don't want your kids to see me shot, then don't shoot me."

179

"Keep," said the father, raising the gun higher, "walking."

She walked on. Four paces along, the terror that this man was going to shoot her in the back rose up inside her like a great wave. She couldn't stop herself breaking into a run.

She ran, but she didn't have the energy to run very fast.

When she was sure she was out of range of the crazy dad, she sat down on the freeway and hugged her knees, and just sobbed and trembled. She sat there for a long time.

But she couldn't just sit there forever. Eventually she raised herself on still-wobbly legs and moved on.

She came off the rest-lane and walked for a while along the freeway itself. There was a lot of crap on the road surface. Then, although there was no traffic, it came home to her—belatedly—that this was probably a foolish thing to do, that this made her an easy target, so she clambered over the crash-barrier at the side of the roadway and carried on across the turf. Fir trees stretched away to her right, and their discarded needles carpeted the ground, newer green ones overlaying an underlying layer like brown rice. She couldn't have told you why she was walking onward. She had to get home. She had to get back to Philly. It was likely her parents were not home, right now, but they would surely be *coming* home soon. Yes?

Sure, she said to herself.

The road curved around through a gigantic cutting. The bank on the left was a ziggurat of stepped turf, with an eSpire on its summit. A strange mixture of noises came from over the brow of the hill. Otty moved away from the road and climbed to the top of the rise through newly planted saplings, each one still in its individual cylindrical plastic sheath. There was a lot of *weird* drone activity—like, just odd. Otty had grown up with the skies full of drones, and she was used to their buzzing comings and goings. But this was not something she'd ever seen before. Something like forty drones, of all different shapes and sizes, were circling through the sky in a huge oval, centered on the peak of the eSpire. What were they doing?

Around and around and around.

Something whizzed past, and Otty looked down to see a chubby-looking armored car hurtle over the rise. On the far side was an exit, and the eye followed its route through and down, past a large autocharge station toward a town in the middle distance.

Otty turned away from the road, and made her way through the saplings, and into the edge of the new forest itself, cutting the corner in the direction of the town. She was thirsty. She was real thirsty, and she hadn't eaten since yesterday, and she was still trembling from her crash and on top of it all she was freaked *out*—no exaggeration—by the way those drones were all circling like vultures, orbiting around the top of the eSpire.

Why would they even *do* that?

She went properly into the older forest, firs as tall as ships' masts. A fragrant coolness. She ached, and the dried blood on her face creaked as she moved, but this was a pleasant spot. There were many breaks and jags in the coverage provided by the trees that let the sun in, but these gaps were bubbling with low green growth, jammed with replacement foliage and green whipstick saplings. It was easier to move through the older portions of the forest, across a noise-abatement carpet of many years' pine-needle droppings.

Otty was startled by a bright-colored hologrammatic blur— startled enough to stop and flinch back with her arm over her brow. But it wasn't a hologram. It was a kingfisher, flying.

And gone.

She came out the other side of the trees at the top of an incline. She was looking down a slope covered in tall grass, at the bottom of which was a strange-smelling, purple-brown stream. Along the banks of this ditch grew weirdly scrolled-up greasy fungi of a disconcerting blue-white lividity. It didn't look natural. On the far side of this stream was a town.

There was a ton of junk in this clogged rivulet, spilling over to litter the side of the hill on which she now found herself: old bottles, discarded phone cases and rags, a prosthetic leg, a busted-up drone, but mostly it was a selection of large white tiles. Weird rectangles, thousands of them, big as TV screens, some chipped or cracked, many not. Angled plaques, milky plasticky tiles a yard across, tilted in an unreadable profusion— were they the wreckage of some disassembled machine, or components yet to be assembled? Otty bent over and ran a hand over one of them, and for a moment she thought it was going to light up: illumination flickered in the depths of the surface and faded almost as soon. There were switches at the side, but they did nothing. She tried a few more tiles and they were all inert. Noise.

What was that noise? What was *all that* noise?

The air was full of the sound of small arms fire. Had she not heard that before? Or had she heard it and disregarded it? Her head was still muzzy from the crash. The bus had crashed—that was … Hey! That was a real *trauma*, and she'd been smack in the middle of it. She started breathing quicker at the memory and had to quiet herself.

A mess of motion, on the far side of the river. Otty saw a loose crowd of soldiers running from one row of cracked and fractured houses to another. Three took a knee and raised their pool cues—their walking sticks—their ski-poles—their Olympic javelins—and *bang*! *bang*! fire glared from the end. Otty flinched, told herself to move, told herself *to move* and scrambled behind a tree. Birds squawking synthesized-sounding beeps and boops scattered through the air. High overhead a jet seared the sky, turned with a long, drawn-out sizzling sound, and scratched free a clutch of fleas from its belly. The aerial dots fell, tumbled, then grew little ghostly mushroom shapes from their tails. Slowed their fall. Many more soldiers were in motion now, scurrying from position to position, and she saw a metal turret moving behind a big blocky building that might, once, have been a mall, but was now a ragged-looking stack of walls and roofs and holes.

The ordnance floated down on its little parachutes and the sound of the detonation was extraordinarily deep and resonant: earth-shaking and doom-y, like a colossal door being slammed shut somewhere in Hell. Flickers of light about a half-mile away, and a tangerine-shining succession of spreading globes of smoke and spiraling tentacles of explosion. An automobile was flipped high in the air like a toy. The expanding spheres of smoke and gas were already dissipating when the shock wave rolled over Otty like a gale and pushed her back on her heels.

The air wave carried on, pushed back through the forest behind her, like a comb going through hair. All the hefty trunks shuddered and moaned like Ents. Otty shouted aloud. Not words, just a yell at all the violence all around her.

A drone flew low, only a hundred yards away and not much higher than the hill on which Otty was standing. It looked like a metal bathtub with wings and angled to disperse a chaffy rain of fireworks onto the edge of the town. Then it wobbled, turned, gunned its jet and flew up and over the hill. Perhaps it was going to join the other drones circling pointlessly around the top of the eSpire behind her.

The buildings at the edge of town, on the far side of the ditch, were crumbling into clouds of hanging dust. Whatever ordnance the drone had dispersed had punched over a whole row of houses. As the dust drifted rightward, Otty could see the prone bodies of a half-dozen soldiers.

The sight of actual bodies made her aware of how exposed she was. She was behind a tree, sure, but being so high up, on the slope of the hill, surely made her vulnerable. She couldn't stay here. And she was thirsty. Now that she thought of it, it occurred to her that she was *really* thirsty. So she scurried out from the line of trees, down to the bottom of the hill and into the ditch with all its junk. It smelled bad. She pushed through the gloop at the bottom and climbed up the other side. There had once been a fence on this side, but now it was nothing but metal spokes and a few shards of wire-net.

Suddenly she was *in* the town, and everything seemed much more pressing and alarming. But she was *real* thirsty, and she couldn't endure her thirst any more. She tried to stick close to the walls, but they were crumbling in real time, disaggregating into smoke and ash. And the sound of gunfire was very jolty and alarming and kept coming at unexpected interludes from unexpected directions.

Here was a house that looked more or less intact. Except for a big hole in its masonry. Otty ducked in through this maw and found herself inside the dustiest bedroom she'd ever seen. Dust everywhere. A thick layer of white dust on the double bed like a snowfall of icing sugar. Snakes of dust along the top of the framed photographs hanging on the walls. A bookcase had been knocked on its side and had vomited out its gutful of paperbacks. Otty went through into a hall and through again into a kitchen, and here she found a faucet and in the faucet was water—the sweetest water she ever tasted.

When she had drunk, and wiped her face, she stood at the sink and looked through the window. A helmeted figure in a bulk of black body armor ran past outside, and then a very similar-looking figure ran back in the other direction. Possibly the same figure. It was like watching TV. Like a really high-def widescreen TV. Or if it wasn't, that was only because it seemed so much less real.

The drink had made her aware of how hungry she was. There was a fridge in the corner, and it was still humming with electrical life, and when she opened its door it shone a gorgeous cold glow on her face. Inside was milk, juice, cheese slices, an uncooked chicken in its chrysalis of Saran Wrap. There were yoghurts too, and a vegetable drawer full of carrots and onions. There was some kind of yellow tart with a big slice taken out of it, like a grinning Pac-man, also swathed in Saran Wrap.

Otty ate all the cheese, unwrapping each slice individually, and then she ate the yoghurts, and behind her, beyond the kitchen window, in the outside world, she could hear a whole Tom-Tom and the Radical Band drum solo of bangs and crashes.

She shut the fridge door and went to look in the closets, thinking to source some food she could carry away for later. But then, unexpectedly, she threw up all the cheese and yoghurt and water she had just ingested—she went down on her knees and chucked it all up into the corner of the kitchen in a sticky heap. For a while she sat there, gagging, and feeling ghastly, ghastly, which was one of Kathry's words, *ghastly*, she said she liked the *drawl* of it. And where was Kathry now? Where was Cess, and Allie, and where was Gomery? Gomery, who got her so riled up and angry sometimes, although she loved him, she'd never denied it, not really. Otty was crying, just a little.

It was just a little.

She would find Gomery again. And Cess and Allie, and maybe Kath too.

But probably not Kath.

So she got to her feet and rinsed her mouth at the sink, and then drank some more water, and washed her face and hands with soap and dried it with a dish cloth. One of the panes of glass in the kitchen window had disappeared. Had it always been missing and she hadn't noticed before? Or had it just now gotten caved in? The whole world had become deeply puzzling.

She'd been on a bus. That was a clear memory. Everything afterward was less clear.

One of the cupboards was filled with boxes of dried pasta, tins, herbs and spices. The cupboard next to it was all boxes of breakfast cereals. Otty reached down a half-finished box of Lucky Charms and tucked it under her arm.

There was a lot of activity outside, noise and commotion. Jarring intrusions of sudden noise. Otty found her way to the front door of this house. There was an old-school paper poster pinned to the inside of the door. It was an photo of an elephant sitting on its elephantine ass, its trunk curled away to the right to reveal its V-shaped mouth. Underneath was written in capital letters: GREET THE WORLD OUTSIDE / WITH A SMILE OF PRIDE.

Otty opened the door and stepped through.

The sky was cluttered with objects, all in motion. Somebody was yelling from the opposite block of buildings, and it took Otty a while to understand that this person was yelling at her. She walked down a tiny but well-manicured front lawn of the house and through a white-paling gate so small even she—five foot nothing in her stockinged feet—could step right over it. The street beyond was messy with debris and scattered and swatched with dust. An automobile wheel lay on its side, all alone. The big ticking sound was the clock of the whole universe, and its second hand was a punch through sheet metal every time it moved.

Dust devils leaped into life and fell away again. It took Otty a moment to grasp that the banging sounds and the dust devils were connected. The yelling guy had stopped yelling and was now cowering, trying to press himself into the doorway in which he was hiding.

Otty wandered on, around the corner and up the street. There was a woman, tall and stooping, standing in the middle of the road. The rose-petal pattern on her yellow dress revealed itself, as Otty came closer, to be splashes and splotches of blood. This woman was yelling something, and for a moment the noise of detonation and overflying obscured it. She was yelling something and pointing with her right hand at the ground. Otty looked down: a dog, dead. A big breed, like a Saint Bernard, but lying on its side and its back legs gone in a truncated tangle of blood-matted fur. Otty could hear what the woman was yelling now.

"You, stay dead!" she was shouting. "You—stay dead! Stay dead!"

Otty ran past her.

There was a two-story building which advertised itself as a BRITISH PUB-BAR, but it wasn't open. Some of the houses were whole, and some were caved in and broken. A man, his torso wrapped in a tartan comforter, cycled unsteadily past her on an antique-looking bicycle. He didn't stop, but as he went by he called to her: "There's a door in the sun, in the sun, it'll be opening soon," and then some more stuff muffled by interrupting sounds of battle and by the squealing of his own wheels.

She looked up—a swarm of drones flew into a distinct cross-shape high over her head, and she stopped, amazed. The cross hung there in the sky, like the literalization of some Christian battlefield divine apparition, and then dissipated.

"Wow," Otty said aloud. "Otty."

She turned a corner.

Here were two people jogging toward her. It was a boy and a girl, not much older than Otty was herself. The boy had a wand, like Harry Potter. She thought it was maybe a pistol, but it was too narrow and had no stock. Their flak-jackets looked ludicrously flimsy compared with the heavy-duty ones the other soldiers were wearing. They were both wearing helmets, and the girl's helmet had a HAL-eye blob in its front.

"Jersey Didion, WWBNN News," said the lad, in a perky voice. The girl kept angling her head to try and get a better shot of Otty. "What's your name, ma'am? How long have you lived here? All your life, is it?"

There was an avalanching sound of bangs and crashes away behind Otty. She watched with some detachment as the two newcomers flinched so hard they practically doubled over. The boy—Jersey Didion from WWBNN News—unfolded himself, stood up and, grabbing her elbow, he led her away from the middle of the street. When the three of them were against a wall, he tried again with his questions.

"How do you feel about your town being the scene of this fighting, ma'am?"

"I was on a bus," said Otty. "Now I'm here."

"Maybe she's fritzed in the head," said the girl. "There's no mileage in interviewing a fucking bucklehead, Jers. What about them, over there?"

"We did them, remember? They were the profaners."

"The what?"

"*So* much bleeped-out profanity it was like an interview with R2D2. This is the one, trust me… Ma'am? Ma'am? Miss? What's your name?"

There was a massive shearing sound away to the right, and the two newcomers flinched hard. The boy looked around, linked arms with Otty, and led her away. Otty walked with her head high, although the other two kept their heads low and went as fast as they could in a kind of Quasimodo lope. They led Otty past houses, up a turn-off and into what she recognized was the drive of a drive-through pizzeria. Closed, now, of course. Under the plastic awning they stopped, and Jersey pointed the wand at Otty's face again.

"Jersey Didion, WWBNN News," he said, looking into the blob on his companion's helmet. "I'm here with one of the residents of Hagueville, Pennsylvania, reporting on the horrors of modern war." He turned to face Otty. "Ma'am, what's your name?"

"Ottoline," said Ottoline.

"How old are you, ma'am?"

There seemed to be some confusion in Otty's head about the answer to this question. She extracted the number from her deep mind.

"Sixteen," she said eventually.

"Where are your folks, Ottoline?" Jersey pressed. "Slain, are they?"

This was such a peculiar question, and such an odd word to use in the context, that Otty wasn't sure how to answer it.

"I'm not local," she said. "I was on a bus."

"We're losing her," said Jersey, perhaps to himself. "Ottoline," he tried, in a bright, loud voice. "What does it *feel* like to be caught up in the maelstrom of modern conflict?"

"Sucks, I guess," Otty replied.

"What does the younger generation feel about the tragic conflagration that has consumed the United States?"

"Younger? Dude, what are *you*—eighteen?"

"Ottoline, how worried *are* you about the rumors that separatists and terrorists are about to launch massive neonicotinoid attacks up and down the Eastern states?"

Otty didn't like the sound of that. "They are?"

Somebody else was yelling: "Hey!"

Jersey leaned in. "Some say it's already happened. Others that it's an inevitability, given the nature of modern war."

"Hey!" came the voice again.

A man was jogging up the access road to the space under the plastic awning, beside the shuttered-up service hatch.

"Fucking Didion—and you too, Rhiannon, fuck off, the pair of you."

This was an older guy, paunchy, a mustache the color of

muesli. Also, it seemed, a reporter. He had no separate camera-person but was wearing a glove with a camera inset in its palm. He held up his left hand and panted his question.

"Tobe Kornowicz, VPCCS News. Ma'am, ignore these two. Let a real journalist interview you. Please tell VPCCS viewers how it *feels* to see your home town destroyed around you?"

"Fuck off, Tobe," said Jersey. The swear sounded wrong in his mouth, like something he said for a dare. "We got her first."

"Back to kindergarten, *Jerk*-sy," said Tobe, sidestepping hard and shouldering the younger man.

Jersey hopped three steps on one foot and collided with the shelf of the shut-up serving hatch.

"Right!" he yelled. "We got that on film—tell me we got it on film, Rhiannon?"

"I got it."

"I'm suing, Tobe."

"Bring it the fuck on!" yelled the older man.

The next thing the two men were grappling like bears. And then they were on the ground, rolling over one another which, since there was a slope, meant they were rolling away at an increasing pace. Rhiannon stood filming the fight, turning her head to follow it.

"Not the glove!" Tobe was screaming. "Not the glove! Seven grands' worth of kit and I'm twenty percent liable for damages."

Otty took a handful of Lucky Charms from the box under her arm and chewed them.

A drone helicopter dove down with the noise of a large wasp. It was not military, Otty could see straight away. A screen lit up on its front and a woman's face appeared: a friendly-eyed, older face.

"Michelle Brown, VCTL-NN7 News," said the face. It was like being addressed by Saint Veronica's handkerchief. "Young lady, do you have a comment on the appalling unprofessionalism of the news reporters you are currently witnessing?"

Something detonated overhead. Maybe a crack had opened in the sky. The plastic awning resounded like a drum, broke its two supporting pillars and levered downward. Its leading edge hit the tarmac with a crack, and Otty found herself alone inside a wedge-shaped space. She picked her way across and out from under the now slant canopy, walked across a parking lot and down a street.

Around the corner. A riderless bicycle skittered past her, and banged into an advertising shell.

Four elderly people were sitting in a line on a low wall, staring ahead with confused expressions. Buckleheads, she guessed. It looked like they had lost their phones. Helpless. She should probably help them, but she didn't know how.

She took another mouthful of Lucky Charms.

Otty climbed a slope, went between two tall buildings and came out into a small park with a bandstand in the middle. Here she sat on a bench and munched Lucky Charms for a while. The sugar was settling her. She found that it *was* possible to, more or less, edit out the background noise, at least up to a point. Sudden loud cracks and bangs were unignorable, sure, and kept making her twitch unpleasantly. But for now she was content just to sit. At some point she would have to figure out what to do next. Find a way home, hook up with her friends, wherever they were. Well—she knew where Kathry was. Most likely. Dead, dead, and gone to the Great Beyond. But the rest of them...

Other than that?

At some point she'd have to decide. But that point was not yet.

Birds flew in squirling loops, mingling with the drones. It was easy to tell bird from drone and drone from bird, although there were many superficial similarities. One was machine and ruthless, and the other was ancient and organic and frail and bad-tempered. And then Otty saw an eagle rise from the treeline, startling close at hand—the eagles are coming!—only to realize, an instant later, that it wasn't a bird but a military jet, and that it wasn't near at hand but far away by the horizon. It hovered, though, and its wings were shallow hood-shapes, and then it turned and roared away, leaving only the diminuendo groan of its sound behind it.

The older of the journalists, the tubby guy, slumped onto the bench beside her. She looked at him and he held up his left hand.

"Look at that," he said. "The lens is fucked. Cracked right across."

"That's bad," said Otty.

"Fucking A."

"Please don't swear," Otty said.

He looked at her, his whole exhausted-looking face crumpled in puzzlement.

"What?"

"Please don't swear like that," Otty repeated. "I do find it upsetting, and kind of unnerving."

"Whatever," said the guy, looking away.

For a while they sat quietly. It was almost companionable.

"Look," said the guy. "There they go! Lookit them run." The younger boy-and-girl journos were sprinting across open ground. "They've spotted an interviewee." He shook his head. "They're on a hiding to nothing. Fucking punks. I don't even know if people say that any more. Punks. Is that a thing?"

Otty took a mouthful of Lucky Charms.

"The assault is being pushed back over that hill," said the guy. Tobe was his name, Otty remembered it. "There—you see those guys? Those soldiers, way over yonder—there? And there?"

"Yes."

"They're U.S. Army. You know how you can tell? It's not easy. The body armor and helmets and shit are the same between army and militia. But the rifles. Official U.S. Army grunts got themselves HK416s. You see somebody with an M4, or more often with an M16—that's militia."

"I've no idea what any of those rifles look like."

"No? Well. OK." He fell silent. "Kid," he said shortly. "I'm sorry at what's happening to your town. It's not much of a town, to be honest, but it's gotta be shitty to see it all smashed up like this."

"It's not my town," said Otty.

"Not your town? They why the fuck are you here?"

"I was on a bus," said Otty. "And please don't swear like that."

"Bus?"

"I was being evacuated out of Pittsburgh. There was a whole fleet of buses, and I was on one. But just the other side of that hill"—she pointed with her free hand—"it came off the road. I think it was shot at. Or a missile, or something ex—" She coughed, and brought up a soggy Lucky Charm. She spat it on the floor. "Ploded," she finished.

Tobe was on his feet. "A whole group of traumatized kids in a bus—blown off the road by terrorists or hit in a tragic friendly fire accident by U.S. forces. *That's* a story. Why am I piddling around here when the story is just over the hill? Sure, there'll be a crack down the middle of my images? They can probably edit that out in post."

He was away, jogging west.

"It was grown-ups, mostly!" Otty called back. "On the bus!"

But he didn't hear.

Over the westward hill the sky was starting to blush strawberry and yellow-orange, with bars of luminous cream-colored horizontal shine layered over the top of it. There was something immensely tender about the way the tiny sawtooth serrations of the fir treetops lined the brow of the hill as it swelled with darkness below. Birds, or drones, flew away from her; roosting, if birds, and presumably flying off to join the cloud of machines flying around the eSpire, if drones. That enormous artificial swarm was still circling and circling the eSpire, a huge tornado of focussed activity. Why? Who knew.

Dusk. It was a beautiful time of day when you came to think of it.

She wondered how her bees were doing.

CHAPTER III

:I:

They cuffed Gomery and put him in a police wagon, and he figured his friends would be put in there with him too and driven
back into town to have a Serious Chat at the police station.
But then the wagon drove off, and he was on his own, and he
figured: Uh-oh, they're splitting us up. That means this is more
serious than I realized.

The drive took a real long time, and he thought: Double-uh-
oh.

He still had his phone and naturally he thought about using
it to make calls and check online. But then he thought: They
didn't take my phone off me. That's usual in arrests, taking away
the phone. They've left it with me for a reason, he thought, so I
guess they'll track anything I do. Use it in evidence against me.
So he didn't check his phone.

He had two heuristics for human behavior. He knew, pretty
much to the millimeter, how far along the spectrum he was,
and it wasn't so far, all things considered. And he knew exactly
how much anger was mixed in with his Asperger's, and it was
quite a lot. So when situations presented themselves, he would
ask himself *what would Ottoline do?* and sometimes *what would*

Allie do? Well, Otty was in custody too, so he could ask himself what she would be doing. That made sense. And one thing he was sure of: She was not ratting out the rest of the Five.

They bundled him out at a compact two-story building somewhere in the middle of the countryside. It was late afternoon, a pale clarity overhead bleeding westward into dusk. The Appalachians were just visible nibbling up from the horizon, so they must have come a ways west. Inside the building was a brightly lit room, two chairs and a table, and he was handcuffed to the table. He wondered if Kath and Otty were also being cuffed to their chairs as they were interrogated, or if it was just him, because he was male?

They made him wait, of course. It was Interrogation 101. He was only a kid, but he'd seen enough shows and reconstructions and *read* enough to know how things went down in this sort of situation. They were going to try to disorient him, get him confused and pliable, keep him on the back foot. They didn't know who they were dealing with, though. Not *this* baby ... baby.

The trick, he told himself, was to keep on top, to keep his head. Not to be discombobulated. Stay focussed. He repeated the phrase over and over, silently, in his mind, a focus-mantra.

> *Keep on top, in my head*
> *Keep on top, in my head*
> *Keep on top, in my head*

After a while the phrase distorted with its repetition, the way these things do. It folded over. The phonemes smeared. He ended up saying

> *Keeping tapping my head*
> *Keeping tapping my head*
> *Keeping tapping my head*

But what might that mean? Tapping his head, like a school bully holding his neck in the hook of his arm, and rapping his knuckles on the top of his skull? Not that. So what? Tapping, like a rubber plantation tree has its useful sap harvested by a screwed-in tube down which the stuff dribbles, into a collector? What was his useful mental sap? He had a pretty good idea. Or tap, like a screen is tapped, to click a link, or activate an upgrade. Hmm, Gomery thought to himself: upgrades.

Tap—

Tap—they were at the door, two of them. Nasty cop, nice cop, the former a stern-faced older guy who looked a little like Gomery's father, the latter a younger woman, all smiles and concerned looks. Think again, losers, Gom thought to himself: if you'd really wanted nasty cop to intimidate me, you should have brought somebody in who looked like my mom. But I guess you don't know me, so good.

They started straight in on the closed net.

What's inside your little cyst, Montgomery? It's a state of emergency, Monty, you want to help your country, don't you? We know you stole a weapon from your mom's business, and we know you and your friends are smart enough and geeky enough to develop it. Open the door and let us in, Monty—get ahead of the curve.

Of course that's what it was all about. And when he didn't bite at those baits, they tried: *We've rounded up the whole gang, Monty. You don't think they're all in their little cells, right now, spilling their guts? But you're the mastermind, eh, Monty?*

He didn't tell them that Monty wasn't the right way to address him. That was on them, and every time they called him the wrong name he felt a little pleasure-jag of superiority. They really didn't know anything about him. That made them fools.

Nasty cop consulted his tablet, and said: "We've got your girlfriend, Ottoline," and Monty snorted. Couldn't help himself. Which encouraged the guy, so he said: "Oh, we've got all five, my boy. Believe me. Ottoline's in custody. You're in custody. Kathry is in custody. We picked up Pitt Smith couple of hours ago."

It was all possible. It was even likely—Gomery wasn't the kind of person to underestimate the reach of the surveil-and-police state. But then nasty cop took it a step too far and said, "And I've just heard we rounded up your friend Allie a half-hour ago, so we have a full house. You play cards, Monty? You play poker, Monty? You know what a full house is? Show me what's in *your* hand, Monty. I bet it's a pair of deuces."

They'd arrested Allie, had they? Well, that was a fucking lie, and he could say *fucking* because Otty wasn't here. Otty didn't particularly like profanities, and usually he remembered not to use them, since he had no desire to upset her. But sometimes the rage got hot enough inside him that he didn't remember and blurted one out. But it didn't matter here. With these idiots. Not that he was going to call them on their lie. He knew, but they didn't *know* he knew, and that was good strategy for him.

"You're a smart kid," said the woman.

She smiled in an ingratiating way. Gomery knew she was called Detective Cora Zadran, but it helped him to think of her as "the woman" and of the man as "the man."

"You're smart enough to understand," the woman was saying, "the imminent threat of war our nation is facing."

Gomery met her gaze. "A bad business," he said slowly.

They both leaned a little closer in.

"It is," agreed the woman. "And we have reason to believe what's ... *in* ... your private network is the kind of asset that could help avert ... uh ..."

"Maybe avert," the man chipped in. "Or if war *does* happen, maybe help make it short, help the good guys win. You know what we're talking about."

"I know," said Gomery. "But *you* don't. You don't know what you're talking about. That puzzles me. Why would you talk about something you don't know anything about?"

"Walk us through it, Monty," said the woman, trying her ingratiating smile. "We know your mom's job. We've had the briefing on what she does at StandCorps. What—did she bring her work home, and you borrowed some of it? Was there a bring-your-kid-to-work day, and you picked up a trinket, or copied some code, or …? Help us out here."

Gomery gave the woman a sly look, and so enjoyed the effect it had that he turned the same look on the man as well. It seemed to affect him differently, which was pretty interesting, really.

"Shouldn't," Gomery tried, "shouldn't you talk *to* my mom?"

"Well, Monty," said the man, sitting back and looking cross. "I'm thinking you already know that she's been mobilized. She was flown to D.C. two days ago, something you're surely aware of."

Ending his sentence with a preposition! It was, Gomery thought, like he knew no rules of grammar at all.

"You're government, they're government, you're telling me you can't ask them?"

"Oh, we have a *statement* from your mom, Monty," said the man, airily, picking his tablet off the table. "It's just that it's not very forthcoming—"

The woman interrupted him. "What my colleague means to say," she said, articulating rapidly but clearly, "is that we both know you're clever enough to run rings around us, in this room, here. Now. You can deflect us all through this conversation if you want to. You're smart enough for that, sure. But I'm asking you to put that on one side—not for my sake, and not even for your sake. For the higher good. Believe me, Monty, all that you value, all that you care about, that is put at risk if war breaks out."

"It's already starting," the man said, in an admonitory voice. "I'm sure you follow the news. Militia activity on the steady rise for six months now—it's an epidemic now. Vigilantes. Religious and ethnic separatists. Micro-independence movements like a fucking rash, all across the Midwest and West, even up here. Macro independence a cancer in the—"

"Where's *here*?" Gomery interrupted.

"Look, Monty," said the woman. "You don't have to like us. But if you don't help us, the whole country suffers. You get that, don't you?"

She kept calling him Monty. It was enough to make him laugh. But instead he said:

"So the government is not a single organism. It's an octopus, but each tentacle has its own little mini-brain, which is how octopi work. You can't get the covert arm that has my mom to open up, but you figure, grab me, maybe I can give you the *in*?"

"We're on the brink of national calamity," said the man, exasperated, "and he's talking about octopus pentacles."

"Tentacles," said Gomery.

"OK, Monty," said the woman, shifting her facial expression into something less mobile and less smiley. "If that's how you want to play it. But like we said, we've arrested your four friends, and I can guarantee you one of them—or maybe all four of them—are going to be more cooperative than you are being."

The repeat of that lie galvanized Gomery.

"StandCorps is a corporation, so it's legally an individual. You can file a collective-personhood subpoena, if a judge thinks you have cause. You could even issue a collective-personhood arrest warrant. You're not doing that, because you haven't got cause. Or because StandCorps is too valuable to the government, as it mobilizes for war, to piss off."

They both stared at him, boggling.

He waited a beat, and then he said: "I have a question."

The two looked expectantly at him.

"What do the eSpires do? They're everywhere. What do they *do*?"

"Everyone knows what they do," said the man. "They make the internet smarter."

"But it's not *coverage*, is it. It's not network signal. Is it? We have network booster substations and cable and mobile phone towers for that. So what do the eSpires *do*?"

"Jesus, I don't know," said the man. "What am I, a nerd?"

But, overlapping those last five words, the woman chimed in with: "Come on, Monty, you've surely read up on this. You know more about it than we do. You're not asking your question in good faith."

"I am, though," said Gomery, wide-eyed.

"I know what everyone knows," said the woman, cautiously, eying Gomery as she spoke, and perhaps thinking that this would encourage his cooperation. "The old-style network masts could only achieve certain bandwidths. The way to increase it was not to keep ramping up band thickness, but to find cleverer ways of compressing and routing and so on. A clever stream, not a Niagara. Wasn't that the code?"

"You know the commercial internet is entirely carried via the old masts?" Gomery asked.

The man couldn't restrain his scoffing.

"Conspiracy theories, great. Sure, kid—who built the masts then, according to your reading of the present-day situation? Aliens. Say aliens. Please say aliens and we can call it a day."

"Is that why you and your four friends set up your ...?" asked the woman. "What's the term ...? Encysted network, Monty? To have a private online space into which Big Government and its eSpire network literally couldn't spy?"

Gomery looked at her.

"That's it, isn't it?' pressed the man.

"Trying to keep the prying eyes of the government *out*," said Gomery, as if trying the phrase for size.

"You gotta let us in, Monty," said the woman. "Once you open the door, we can arrange for you to be transferred back home. You'll need to wear a tag, but you could be sleeping in your own bed tonight, if you cooperate. C'mon, Monty!"

Gomery folded his arms, and set his mouth, and said nothing more. Was that the Poe poem? Nothingmore. Without his phone to check he couldn't be sure. Whatever—he was ravenlike in impassivity. They tried various other questions, but he shut everything down. In his head he was thinking, over and over, *tap tap tappin on heaven's head*, for some reason. Over and over. *Tap tap tappin on heaven's head*. Peck out their eyes. The government lies. The government lies. Peck out their eyes.

Soon enough, nice cop and nasty cop got up and walked out. He was left alone for a while, and then a new guy came in and took him out and along a corridor and to a small room and locked him in.

Inside was a low truckle bed, with a pillow and a sleeping bag, and a high window with wire over it. Nothing else.

On the floor by the bed was a tray, and on the tray was a bowl containing a gelatinous mass of cooling macaroni cheese, and a plastic cup of water. There was also a PayDay Bar, gleaming brightly in its plastic, but Gomery ignored that. He had a peanut allergy. *Which* they would have known, if they'd done even the most preliminary prep. He was dealing with amateurs.

Gomery examined the room closely. There were drill holes in the wall where something, probably shelves, had been supported. They'd been filled in with spackle, and painted over, but they were still pretty obvious. So this had been maybe a storeroom, maybe an office, and either way he wasn't in a regular police facility—leastwise, not a building designed to hold prisoners.

That was something.

He sat on the low-slung bed and began eating the macaroni. It was lukewarm but he got it down. He would need to keep his strength up. What would Otty do in this situation? What, most likely, *was* she doing right now? She would hold out stubbornly, and tell the fuckers nothing, at no point even so much as thinking a word like *fuckers*. She would outlive them, grow old until they died off and she walked free in the end. She would be the rock. That was one option.

What would Allie do in this situation? He would try to escape, of course.

That was another option.

Gomery placed the empty bowl back on the tray, drank the water, and then sat with his back to the wall, running through various possibilities in his mind.

Eventually the guard who had locked him into the room unkeyed the door, swung it half open and put his head in.

"Finished? Hand up that tray, kiddo."

Gomery looked up at him.

The guard waited, but he was also, clearly, in a hurry.

"Whatever," he said soon. "Don't do me the goddam common courtesy."

He was a tall, angular guy with an irregularly shaped bald head. As he leaned all the way down—and it was a *long* way down for him—the light from the room's single bulb slid over the gleaming pink bumps of his cranium. His uniform was a touch too big for him, and he had taken off his tie, so his shirt-top gaped open a little way, and Gomery could see inside to where a phone docket was fixed to his collarbone.

Gomery thought: I guess he's being a bit careless because I'm only a kid, and maybe also because he's not used to dealing with actual prisoners. That would make sense.

With a snake-strike suddenness, Gomery reached out,

plunged his hand down the guy's open-hanging shirt and pulled the phone free.

The guard stopped what he was doing, frozen in mid gesture. He'd gone down there, and now he couldn't remember why he had.

Gomery got up, bending and jinking to avoid knocking into the guy. Now, he thought. *What would Allie do*.

He said to the guy, "Hi, fella, you OK?"

"Sure," said the guy, his voice muffled by his posture. He didn't sound sure.

Gently but firmly, Gomery got him to let go of the tray, to stand upright again, and then finally—this took a little coaxing—to sit himself down, on the low-slung camp bed.

"Hey, fella," he said. "You like PayDay Bars?"

"Sure," said the guy, looking up at Gomery like he should recognize him and almost did, except that recognition kept slipping away from him.

"Here," said Gomery, unwrapping the bar and putting it in the guy's hand.

The guard lifted it to his mouth and took a nibble.

"Peanuts, yeah?" the guy said. "Gotta love the nut."

"It's a very popular legume," Gomery agreed.

Gomery frisked the guy. The building was old enough to require actual physical keys for the door, and there was a clinking knot of metal keys hanging from the guard's belt. Gomery took this, and also unhooked the smartbracelet from the guy's wrist. Then he checked the man's phone. It was, as he expected, real old—almost an antique. So he figured this level of functionary wasn't paid a whole lot. On a hunch, Gomery tried pressing the guy's finger to the screen, and that unlocked it. *That* was how old it was!

Gomery quickly dove into settings and reconfigured the phone to his own fingerprint. Then he spent more than five minutes frisking through the phone's Ancient Sumerian or Neanderthal or fucking Baby-*lon*-ian operating underpinnings, removing the data tagging, removing the owner—his surname was *Fox*, and he had six separate forenames, one of which was *Elvis*—and rejigging the protocols.

Mr. Fox had finished his PayDay, and was looking at his fingers, as if trying to decide whether to lick them or not.

Gomery opened the door, slipped through and shut it again. A glance up and down the corridor revealed surveillance cameras, red blob-blisters to his left and right, on the ceiling where the corridor turned through ninety degrees. He fiddled with the keys, trying each in turn until he found the one that locked the cell door behind him, and then he trotted off.

Most of the doors along the corridor were blank surfaces, but a couple had windows in them. Through one of these he saw an actual storeroom, cluttered with stuff. It took him four goes to find the right key for this space. Inside was a real lumber room of kit, boxes, police helmets stacked, a heap of folded High-Vis vests, planks of laminated wood that might have been the very shelves removed from the room from which Gomery had just escaped. There was also an old photocopier (it looked like) which was surely just junk. There were also two evidence lockers as tall as Gomery was himself, and an actual antique filing cabinet with three drawers. There were no keyholes in the evidence cabinets, so Gomery tried the bracelet on the left-hand one, and it opened with a satisfying click. It contained no evidence, but rather coffee and herbal tea supplies: a small sack of grinds, boxes of fruit infusions, a tower of stacked plastic cups that looked like nothing so much as a model of an eSpire. There were two tubs of Discount Biscuits from Walmart too. The other cabinet was piled high with individually locked metal boxes, like a Swiss bank vault.

Gomery pulled the photocopier over and stood on it to reach

the window. Outside it was dusk, but there was enough light for him to see that this wall of the building was just a few feet from the razor-wire-topped perimeter fence of the facility.

OK. *What would Allie do?*

He knew what Allie would do.

Gomery took out a biscuit from one of the tubs, checked its ingredients. It was bone-yellow and warty with choc-chips. No peanuts, he made sure; so he popped it in and chewed it to a paste. With his mouth full of masticated biscuit, he located the room's red-glass surveillance bulb and smeared the biscuit paste all over.

Then he climbed on the photocopying machine, and got the window open with one of the keys on Fox's key-bundle. The air outside smelled fragrant. Gomery heaved up two of the unused shelves and poked them through the window and out. They reached the top of the wire. The fence was higher than the window, but when he got the far end of the first plank in among the tangle of barbs the fence sagged, and by the time he'd finished, the makeshift bridge was almost horizontal. Finally he pulled the lid off one of the biscuit barrels, poured most of the biscuits outside (it would be dark soon; maybe they wouldn't notice, but then again maybe they would) and left the barrel on its side on the floor, beside the photocopier, with a few stray biscuits still inside it.

Finally he turned off the light, and squeezed into the space between the two evidence cupboards and the far wall. He placed a couple of police helmets in the gap, got as comfortable as he could, and waited.

It took maybe twenty minutes for the building to wake up to what had happened. Gomery was pretty good at gauging time, normally, but he was a bit nervous and therefore agitated and that interfered with his ability. It seemed like a very long time, but it was probably only twenty minutes.

He knew the building's surveillance would lead people straight to this room. And that's what happened. He heard distant voices, raised, and then they came closer and then he heard the door open and a few people—Gomery guessed, maybe, three—bundled inside. The light sprang on.

"He's got in among the biscuits," said a man's voice, sounding dismayed.

Gomery could hear somebody climbing onto the photocopier.

A different man's voice. "He's got in the *biscuits*? He's not a fucking *mouse*, you goon. He's out the window."

"He's out the window!" repeated the first voice, sounding even more dismayed.

The third voice was a woman's and came from on top of the photocopier.

"He's made a little dinky bridge. He's over the fence."

"He's over the fence," repeated the first voice, even more distressed-sounding.

"Get people out to the south side of the building," the woman was saying, presumably into a communicator. "No," she said. "No, the *south* side, Joel. Use the sunset. What? No, use it to *orient* yourself. What? What do you want from me...? South, as in south. The side... You go out the front door, yeah? You turn and turn again in the direction that would take you down to the McDonalds. You know? The drive-through... Yes, that's it. That's south. OK?"

"Of course the fucking drive-through," said the second voice, angrily. "I mean—Joel?"

"What?" said the woman, still evidently speaking into her communicator. "That's Bennie. Ignore Bennie, Joe. Just get out and get on to the *south* wall of the building, the southern perimeter fence. And J.—unholster your weapon, yeah? And take Chi with you. Right away—we'll be there in one."

"Fucking Joel," said Bennie.

"Come on," ordered the woman.

Gomery could hear her clambering down from the photocopier. There was a flurry of noise, the light went out, and Gomery was alone again.

He waited for a long time. Soon enough he heard confused voices outside the window, and then they drifted away. It grew darker and darker in the room, until it was so dark Gomery couldn't see anything.

He risked using Fox's phone. Most of its pinched data-storage was taken up with the memory app and the stuff Fox needed to be able to pass as a functioning person. There wasn't room for much else. Some photos. There was a little money—$42 and some cents—in the phone's wallet. That wasn't much, but might be enough for a bus fare. Gomery pulled up a map of the area and worked out a few things in his head.

Then he extricated himself from his hiding place. He unpacked a High-Vis vest from its polythene envelope and slipped it on. He put on a spare police helmet. Both items were way too big for him, but that couldn't be helped. Then he opened the door and went back out into the corridor.

It wasn't much of a disguise, but it didn't have to be. Gomery couldn't be sure what kind of image interpretation algorithms the building used to rinse the raw data of its cameras, but his best guess was that it wasn't very sophisticated. It might be able to clock that there was a supernumerary individual in the building, but if people were running around checking the south wall, coming in and out, that fact alone might not set off any alarm. Checking over the footage later, of course, they'd see it was him, but by then he'd be gone.

He walked as confidently as he could along the corridor, around its right-hand bend, and then left through an unlocked double door. There was a small hallway: a door, open on the left, gave on to what looked like a large meeting room, empty and lit only by the illumination from the hall. Gomery walked ahead, through a different set of double doors. And now he was in the lobby: brightly lit, a counter to his right, three screens of varying sizes on the wall to his left on rolling newsfeeds.

There was nobody behind the counter, but there *was* somebody at the door, looking out into the gloaming. He might have been in police kit, he might merely have been wearing the night porter's uniform of black jacket and trousers. Gomery couldn't be sure, and he only saw him from behind. It hardly mattered. The guy was standing in the doorway, and there wasn't quite enough room for Gomery to squeeze through, so Gomery stepped forward boldly, shoved past the man, pitched his voice as low as possible to say "sorry" and strode off.

For the first dozen strides, away from the building and across the parking lot, Gomery's heart was pummeling his ribs like a boxer on a punching bag. But the expected *hey!* or *stop!* didn't come. A vehicle purred into life, and turned on all its lights, and Gomery couldn't stop himself flinching. It rolled forward—a high-sided SUV with a painted-on sash that said NEW YORK STATE POLICE, and a hologrammatic rotating red light floating a foot above the roof.

The main gate to the compound swung open and the police vehicle drove through. It immediately turned left, off the road, and bumped over the open ground beyond the fence, turning again to make its way to the south side of the building. Waving his right hand, Gomery trotted briskly through the open gate, and continued up the road. Nobody stopped him.

He walked up along the road. The sun had gone behind the western hills, but the sky was still a deep charcoal gray and gleamed with the day's afterglow. Soon enough the light grew fainter and eerier, and the bushes and ferns flickered in the corner of his vision as uncanny dwarf creatures, monsters, horrible gnomes. A particularly bulky knot of grass shook like a poltergeist and hissed at him. Gomery whipped off the police helmet and hurled it at the apparition.

There was nothing there. It was just Nature being Nature. Be rational, Gomery told himself. Hold it together.

He quickened his pace. Up ahead, a wide bar of glimmering light roused itself with swells and flashes of red and yellow brightness, like a malfunctioning lightsaber laid across the landscape. It was the freeway, and as he got closer the sounds of the vehicles, their sheer swooshing intensity of their speed, began to freak him out a little.

The road he was walking along swung around and became a slip road on to the larger road, with a turn-off joining to meet it from the left. There was no sidewalk, but there was a bus stop, and Gomery sat down on the little seat.

It was intimidating to be so close to so many automobiles and trucks, some of them containing people and many not, hurtling so remorselessly past him. The noise, the buffet of air, the elongating snakes of light. Flying bombs. Missiles on wheels. It felt like the war had already started, and he was in the middle of a bombardment.

It was pretty dark now.

Two screens were set in the wall of the bus stop. One sold tickets and dispensed time info. The other was a rolling newsfeed, interviews and commentary. Talking heads with complexions like fresh-pressed white cotton, yellow hair, white teeth and white shirts flanked by blue suit-jacket lapels, or blue dresses, were pulling serious faces and moving their mouths. There was no audio and subtitles had not been turned on.

He got out Mr. Fox's phone and used it to tap the ticket screen. A beautiful, non-gender-specific face appeared and offered to "attend to your needs, Mr. Fox." The voice was projected in a neat little sonic bubble. It was clearly audible even against the roar of the traffic.

"I need to get to Philadelphia," he said.

"Buses from *this* stop run north to Ithaca, and from there you can get a bus to Syracuse, Rochester and Buffalo."

"No, I need to go south."

"The furthest south our company goes is to Scranton, N.Y. There's no southward stop at this particular juncture, but if you take the next bus going north you can make your way over the freeway at Hinmans Corners for buses south to Binghampton and Scranton. From there you can swap bus company, or take a train, or a zep-bub, to Philadelphia."

"How much?"

"Please state a destination."

"To Philadelphia."

"This company doesn't run a service to Philadelphia."

"I mean changing, changing at … You know, getting on a new bus at Scranton."

"I'm sorry, I can't sell you a ticket to Philadelphia. This company doesn't run a service to Philadelphia."

"OK, how much to Scranton?"

"Seventy-seven dollars."

It was more than the phone had in its wallet but Gomery figured it was worth trying anyway. There might be a credit line attached. And it seemed there was, for the screen bumped a ticket on to the device.

The minute the transaction was approved, and the ticket had been bought, the bus stop unlocked the audio on the newsfeed.

Gomery waited ten minutes or so, growing slowly more concerned that, at some point, somebody from the facility he had just left would come moseying up the road to check that he hadn't thought to sit at this bus stop. He bumped the ticket to his own phone, purged the memory of the fact of the purchase from Fox's device, and switched the device into a deep sleep. They must have realized he'd stolen Fox's phone, so it was surprising they hadn't already v-bombed it to all get-out. Presumably they were too busy combing the grounds south of the building for him. But soon enough they'd realize that was a goose chase. If Fox's phone were on, they'd use it to track him. So he turned it off.

...about the so-called Nevada event, the newsman in the bus-stop screen was saying, looking very grave, *with some sources claiming that it has crossed the border into Utah, and others denying that there has been* any *release of military-grade neonicotinoids in the area at all. Ali Connor, a spokesperson for the proscribed insurgency coordinating group, the so-called Independence Army, said this morning they believed a vast release of neonic toxins had been undertaken by the U.S. Army in a so-called "area denial" operation. The U.S. Government has again denied these claims, but "General" Connor went on to say this.*

The screen cut to a middle-aged woman in combat fatigues, patterned like the choppy waters of a green lake.

Californian tech is the most advanced in the world, the general said. Then, as if prompted, or belatedly remembering, she showed a full set of teeth in an imitation of a smile, and added, *and confidence in it is undimmed. This illegal gas attack, the worst war crime since chlorine was deployed in World War One, will not stop us. Our automatic and remotely controlled Nimrod freedom-walkers can traverse any terrain, and—*

Here was the bus.

Gomery climbed aboard, pinged his ticket and took a seat. He took off the High-Vis vest, folded it, and tucked it away in the seat back pocket.

There were a couple of people at the back of the bus, deep in their phones and wholly uninterested in him. The vehicle rolled smoothly back into motion. He watched the bus stop recede into an orange-lit hump of light in the dark distance.

It was twenty minutes to Hinmans Corners. As they pulled

to a halt, Gomery turned Fox's phone on again, and tucked it into a seat-back pocket. He assumed they'd track it, and maybe they'd assume he'd fled to Ithaca and from there gone further north.

Getting off, and drawing a lungful of cold air, gave Gomery a strange thrill in his chest. He felt like a spy, or a character in an assassination game. He was almost floating. His grip on reality as such began to slide, as sometimes happened when he got excited. Up the steps. The covered tunnel through which he crossed the interstate was the belly of a gigantic serpent. The regularly spaced lights along its sides were reservoirs of snaky stomach acid. He emerged on the other side, found the Scranton bus, settled into his seat, and waited.

He was the only person on the bus until a few seconds before departure, when four drunk people, two couples probably, got on laughing and gasping and went all the way to the back. The bus rolled into motion, maneuvered its way on to the feeder road and so on to the interstate itself. The screens on the back of the seat were, again, all news.

Araceli Rodriguez, Arizona's governor, today made a public appeal to the President to de-escalate government rhetoric and withdraw U.S. Army troops from the state.

Gomery muted the audio (there was no way of turning off the images) and swiveled in his seat to stare through the windows.

On the opposite carriageway a convoy of police vehicles, sirens screaming and blue lights palpitating and flickering, howled at full speed northward. They were the ride of the Valkyries, the ghostly hunt, they were a whole cohort of Headless Horsemen in pursuit of Ichabod Crane. It was a comet trail of light and color and sound and it was rushing the wrong way. Maybe they were after him. Maybe they were after somebody else entirely.

Darkness hemmed the bright freeway on both sides. Indistinctness, trees and unlit buildings, and beyond it, looking

213

eastward, hills, rivers, towns, and beyond that, the coast. Just over the horizon, the Atlantic Ocean trembling in its bowl. The sky, purged of sunlight and stars littering it like leaf-fall. The moon with its big bright circle, like an app button waiting to be pushed.

Soon enough, Gomery fell asleep.

:2:

He awoke as the bus pulled to a halt. They were in the bus depot in Scranton. Gomery clambered out and didn't loiter—he was a little surprised the police weren't waiting for him, in fact. It was good that they weren't, but that fact could change at any moment.

It wouldn't do to tempt fate.

He walked through the pre-dawn streets as the sky slowly brightened. He fingered his phone on. There was a little money in his personal wallet, but he figured the authorities would have slapped a tag on his financial feeds, and if he opened his wallet they'd pinpoint where he was. The fact that they had not relieved Gomery of his phone after arresting him implied they were hoping to use it against him, for instance by tracking him if he logged on, seeing which bits of the great online he went to. They could have isolated his device IP, and remote pegged it, at any point over the last year, and the smart thing to do would have been to sort that before arresting him. Which perhaps they'd done. It would make sense: it would explain why they hadn't taken away his phone straight off. They were hoping he would use it, and that he'd use it carelessly, promiscuously, and give away something crucial about the private network.

They'd underestimated him. Lots of people did.

That said, he did need money, and he needed to find out what had happened to his friends. Otty and Kath were, he guessed, still in custody. Cess might still be free, in which case he needed to find her. Allie could look after himself, Gomery guessed. But then again—he certainly needed to touch base with him too.

Not in Scranton, though.

He found a Starbucks, its glowing neon pink frontage a weird complement to the citron dawnlight of the sky overhead, and made his way inside. It was super-early, so there were no other customers, and the single barista kept yawning like he was practicing his lion-roar impression.

"I'd like to buy a coffee, but my phone has no charge so I can't access my wallet," Gomery said, and tried a smile. People liked smiles. He still didn't really understand why they did, but they did.

"Sure thing, little dude," said the barista, and nodded toward the recharge shelf.

"The thing about that," said Gomery, "is that mine is this really old model, yeah? I need a charging cable."

"A *cable*? Woh."

"And a socket, yeah? Do you have one?"

"You don't have your own cable?"

"It's at home. You'll have one—in your customer supply?"

"I've never seen one," the barista said, shuffling to a big drawer and pulling it open. "Hey, what do you know? Here you go. What kinda coffee you wanty-wanty, my little man?"

"Black," said Gomery, levering open the little hood that covered his phone's appendix socket and plugging the phone in. "Sure. Just black, no milk."

He hooded the screen with his hand, and spent five minutes piggybacking the phone second-hand on the store's Wi-Fi. The barista put the coffee on the counter and called *six-ninety-nine* in a sing-song voice.

"Just a moment," Gomery said. "There's some glitch here. Wait till I get into my wallet."

"You can't have the coffee till you pay."

"Of course. Just a moment."

The barista got bored, went to the far end of the counter and sat on a little stool.

Gomery had never been to Scranton before, but he knew some people who lived here. He knew people all over the world, from various chatfora and nested shared-interest groups. And one of the guys he knew, a guy called Aleksi, lived in Scranton. Gomery just hoped it wasn't out in some way-distant suburbs. He pinged Aleksi and got an immediate response.

— *sorry it's so early*.

— you kidding? I don't go to bed before 9am—

— my friend, I need a favor. I am in Scranton right here and right now. I need to meet face to face, handshake hand on hand—

— you're kidding?—

— no—

— stalking—

Gomery shoved across a gifgram of a celebrity wryly chuckling.

— you in trouble?—

— yes. Would I be asking otherwise?—

There was a pause, and then Aleksi asked their mutual security question. The number included in the reply communicated, depending on which figure was used, one of a variety of coded responses.

— how do you feel about Picasso?—

— a Picasso is one times ten to the minus twelfth of an Asso—

— so a billionth of an Asso—

— c'mon, Aleksi—a trillionth, a trillionth of an Asso—

— oh Christ, alright—

Aleksi pinged over an address-map: five minutes' walk away.

— this is weird, alright? I am logging the weirdness. I am making an official record of this weirdness. I never meet people handshake hand on hand, alright?—

— I'm bracing myself for your slovenliness— said Gomery, and he unplugged the phone.

"Six,' said the barrister, scowling at him, "ninety-nine."

"There's a problem with my wallet," said Gomery, ducking his head and hurrying outside, leaving the coffee sitting on the counter.

Five minutes took him to a narrowly rectangular square of waste ground, covered with knee-high grass the consistency of bear-pelt, growing up around a spread of abandoned settees and armchairs. One flank of this stretch of ground was apartments, four stories of stained brickwork and barred windows and walkways in which morning shadows pooled coldly. It could have been a prison block. The other side was windowless blocks of commercial property—storage, server-hubs, who knows what. Aleksi lived in one of these.

Birds freckled the sky, over the rooftops. They could have been flies near at hand, but they were birds far away. The mess parted, brightness shaving through the smoke of their swarm: a drone was flying through. After it had gone, the birds glommed back into their swirling oneness.

The normal thing would have been for Gomery to use his phone to ring the bell, but he didn't want to open his phone to the general network. He couldn't even be sure which was the right door for Aleksi's plot. He tried hammering on one and did nothing but hurt the palm of his hand. Then he moved along and tried kicking the other with his foot, but neither activity roused his friend. He stood on the sidewalk and pondered whether he could yell. He didn't want to attract the wrong sort of attention, and he certainly didn't want residents living opposite to call the police or anything. He tried knocking again, but nothing.

After a while Gomery was beginning to think he would have to find a new coffee shop, talk the barista into letting him hook his phone on a wire again, call Aleksi again and tell him to come down and open ... the ... *damn* ... *door*. It was ridiculous, but he couldn't see another way.

Then the left-hand door cracked and opened a couple of inches.

"I was wondering where you were," said a high-pitched voice. "Man, I was waiting for you to ring the bell."

"I don't want to reveal my phone location to the general network," said Gomery, crossly.

"I didn't think of that," said Aleksi, putting his head outside. It was a large, round, almost albino head—pale eyes and white-blond hair, with pink pouches under its eyes. "That's smart. Come in—hey, don't loiter. You see that block opposite?"

"Looks like a prison," said Gomery.

"Wow, that's poetic! That's real poetic. Anyway, the residents don't know I live over here. This isn't zoned for habitation this side, so I don't want *them* to ... you know."

He pulled his head back inside and Gomery followed. It was a narrow hallway lit with a dimly gleaming layer of lumepaint, and it smelled, as lumepainted walls tended to, faintly of mold and decay. Aleksi clumped up a metal staircase that doubled back on itself, and, following, Gomery came into a wide, low-ceilinged room.

"Why poetic?"

"What?"

"I said the building opposite looked like a prison. How is that *poetic*?"

Poetry was one of those damn tricks Gomery kept trying to

understand and kept missing. So many people expressed such love for it, and he simply didn't get it at all.

"I thought you said *prism*," said Aleksi, shaking his head. "You want, like, coffee?"

"Sure."

Aleksi's business was goldmining, and the thing he mined was Green Card Futures. Not the actual cards, but lines on the cards, possible opportunities of extracting Green Cards from people or situations at some notional future point. There were three main ways of doing this: one was by tracking down single people who might be persuaded to sell their marriageability as a future on this market. Another was by tracking down glitches in the systems: canceled cards that hadn't been canceled fully enough, pending cards not taken up, that kind of thing. The third way was Aleksi's specialty. The law said twenty years' residency could be converted to a residency-track that might, at a future date—depending on a raft of other considerations such as absence of criminal conviction, taxable gross and so on—lead to a card. What Aleksi did was to microaccumulate seconds, crunching sheer raw processing power to nudge milliseconds along a notional line until they tipped over into seconds without setting off any GovSystem alarms. The ease with which this could be done increased or decreased depending on how occupied the vast resources of GovSystem were elsewhere. But absent the invention of a time machine that would enable hackers to send a time machine twenty years into the past and build the time that way, it was the next best way to accumulate the necessary time. Since *Avery and Fernandez v. State of Texas* five years previously, it was the law that people suffering Acute Reality Phobia, who relied on online interactions to mediate their socialization, were entitled to be treated online as though they were physically present in everything except criminal investigation or protection of the unborn child. And *that* meant that immigration officers weren't legally entitled to force a physical meeting on such people. Or they could only do it by badgering a warrant out of a judge on the suspicion of the commission of actual crime, and that was—by and large—more trouble than they were prepared to take. It was through this loophole, and via the painstaking accumulation of microseconds into decades, that Aleksi made his living. Generating Green Card Futures and selling them on.

"You grasp me," he told Gomery, "I'm not mining out actual cards. I put a package together which is the chance of drawing down a card, and sell that on to a dealer I know, based in Hawaii. I think he's in Hawaii. That's what he tells me. It's slow work and it don't pay too good. But I live cheap."

There was a large poster on Aleksi's wall: the American Eagle, fierce-eyed, talons like meat hooks and a beak ready to slice the guts out of the whole world. The legend over this illustration read: IN THE BEGINNING WAS THE WORD AND THE WORD WAS—U.S.A.! Gomery nodded at it.

"But," he observed, mildly, "USA is not a word. It's an abbreviation. It's four words, actually."

Aleksi glanced at the poster and then back at Gomery. "Whatever, dude."

For the umpteenth time in his life, Gomery was having to pretend to social interest and all the interactive protocols that governed it. What did a person ask, in such a situation? He slurped coffee.

"How's business?" he tried.

This seemed to hit the spot, even if in a groaning and head-shaking way.

"Terrible, my droog, terrible. You know what the government is doing?"

Gomery pondered this.

"Lots of things, lots and lots. Hard to answer. I guess, preparing for war, right now?"

"It was a *rhetorical* question, droog."

"Oh," said Gomery.

"They *are* preparing for war, though, that's the correct answer," Aleksi mumbled.

"So I gave the correct answer, even though the question was a rhetorical question?" said Gomery, pleased with himself.

"They are recruiting ground troops. That's a long and tedious business if you do it the usual way, with base camp and basic training, and lots of legal rights for the boys and girls who sign up, and military pensions to be ensured and so on. Plus Congress gets to vote on things like how much money you can dispose that way. But the glorious U.S. Government thinks war is happening like, tomorrow—and point of fact, war is already happening, all over these *you*-knighted states. War is here, man, and it's the *shit*." He shook his head. "But whatever, there are some five-star generals and they've decided the U.S. Army needs a rapid injection of manpower and womanpower and so they're recruiting aggressively abroad. China, Middle East—join up... and you know what they're using to sweeten the deal?"

"That's another rhetorical question," said Gomery, pleased that he'd spotted it.

"Like the laundryman said when the great detective came to collect his bedding, no sheet, Sherlock. It *is* a rhetorical question and the answer is—Green Cards. Serve your term in our uniform and get fast-tracked to Green Card." Aleksi downed his entire cup of coffee in one go. "It's not working. It's not working the way the government hoped it would work. People don't flock to come and live in this shithole the way they once did. But it's impacting *my* business, though. Impacting what I do for a fucking living. Flood the market with new cards and the price goes down. That's economics 101, my droog."

"I'm sorry to hear it."

"But look, this is OK. Chatting with you face to face! It's not so weird as I thought it would be. It's just like actual chat, you know? Only with"—Aleksi waved vaguely—"real-life materiality and suchlike."

"Aleksi," said Gomery, "I was arrested."

"Woh," said Aleksi. "Go on."

"They took me from Philly up to New York State somewhere. I got away."

"They let you go?"

"They," said Gomery, "did not."

"Woh," Aleksi said again, impressed. "Double woh."

"I've been able to evade them trying to regrab me, but I need to get home again, and I need to find my friends. You know I have this tight group, yeah?"

"Famous Five," said Aleksi. "I respect that. I mean, I work alone, like *Monsieur Uncroyable*." He pronounced monsieur *moan-sewer*. "But I respect you got your homies. Five for one and one for five, or..." Aleksi looked momently puzzled. "Whatever."

"So I need money."

At this Aleksi looked pained.

"Droog," he said, in what was for him a low voice, but which would have been for any other person a mid-range regular tone. "You're touching me for cash? See how I live? I'm rock bottom, man. The pot I piss in cost all the money I got."

"I have some money, but I can't access it without alerting the authorities that I'm doing so, and that would tell them where I am."

"You're going back to Philly, dude? They're going to look there, when they can't find you anywhere else, if they've any common sense at all."

"I need to make sure my friends are OK. I need to make sure

our private network is safe. I can't do that anywhere else but Philly. Once I've done that I'll go to ground, hide out somewhere else, until this blows over."

"May not blow, droog. Maybe never be over."

"Maybe I can negotiate, remotely. But first I got to do this and that takes money."

"Like I said, droog, I'm poor as a church mouse."

"You're rich as *Mickey* Mouse, liar, and we both know it. But I don't want *your* money, Aleksi. I want you to help me transfer some of my money on to a roaming wallet, so I can buy food and travel, and so I can get home."

The relief on Aleksi's face was almost insultingly obvious.

"Why didn't you say so! Let's go, man, let's do this."

Aleksi poured more coffee and they settled, side by side, at a monitor.

"Where do you want them to think you are?"

"North? Rochester, N.Y., say. Or Canada?"

"Easier to keep it in the States. OK, then."

Aleksi routed a line through a hub in Switzerland, rented an IP for a dollar a minute and pinned it to an independent coffee shop called Pukka Coffee in Rochester, N.Y. Then he threw out a more tenuous cloud of chaff lines to … it hardly mattered where: Miami, Seattle, Peru. Gomery took over, accessed his funds, played footsie with security protocols for two minutes, rattled through a half-dozen idiosyncratic security questions, and croupiered $450 into a withdrawal pot. As he did this, Aleksi had been rummaging around in a flip-top dump bin. He returned to the terminal.

"That enough? You should take out a couple of K, I think."

"It'll make them believe I'm thinking small," said Gomery. "It'll make them think they're still dealing with a kid. The extra fifty is for you."

Avidity gleamed in Aleksi's eyes, but he said: "Keep it, droog. Send me a hundred when your life is back to normal."

There didn't seem to be any point in arguing. Gomery synced the vanilla device Aleksi gave him and put the money in its wallet.

"You're sure?"

"It's my bedtime, droog," said Aleksi. "Fuck the fuck out of my fucking house, you fucking goon." He put five or six *o*s into this last word, and then hugged him. Gomery wasn't keen on hugs, but he didn't resist. "Look after yourself, OK?"

"You got a hoodie, or a scrambleveil I could borrow?"

"Do I look like the kind of guy who spends a lot of time wandering around outside?"

"Laters," said Gomery.

He went downstairs and let himself out. Then it was a brisk five-block walk until he found the shops. Gomery went in a mall and bought a holohoodie—regular cloth for the hood, but a downward projection across the oval where his face was. He could be Darth Maul, The Cat, or HeroPower Alpha. He chose the latter as the least garish and went out again.

Next: McDonalds, where he joined the beautifully anonymous breakfast crowd, and bought himself a breakfast box and filled his stomach. He sat at the high plastic bar, looking out through the plate glass at the world outside. Beside him a worn-looking woman was having her muffin, and occasionally interrupting her meal to assist the man next to her in the business of remembering that eating breakfast meant moving his hand in the direction of his mouth. This guy's dark face was canyoned with creases and wrinkles. His hair was many white strands like plastic tassels. He was staring ahead with that puzzled bucklehead look the neonicked all share, and repeatedly forgetting how to feed himself. The woman looked younger, trauma-worn, exhausted. Maybe his daughter.

Through the window, Gomery watched a troop of soldiers in full combat gear jog by. A whole bunch of men and women, maybe a hundred all told, trotting briskly, masked, their rifles carried across their chests like bends sinister on a heraldic shield.

He felt a little easier in himself now. He had to assume the police had presented a facial recognition warrant at every camera, drone and commercial monitoring source within a realistic radius of where he might be. After all, he wasn't America's Most Wanted. I mean, he *assumed* he wasn't. But they'd surely do the standard procedure stuff on him.

For the first time since his arrest, he wondered if he should try and contact his mom.

Probably not, he thought. She would be pissed. Not pissed that he'd been arrested, he figured, but … you know. Everything else.

There were drones all over the sky, as usual, but as Gomery made his way to the city's hub he noticed that a substantial flock of them were—weirdly—circling the main Scranton eSpire. There were scores of them, maybe hundreds, just flying around and around the mast. What was that about? What were they even *doing*?

He wasn't the only person to notice this odd behavior. People he passed were standing and filming footage with their phones. The only ones who weren't were staring ahead in neonic bafflement.

Gomery pressed on. At the hub he had to turn off his hoodie in order to get the ticket screen to serve him, and he knew that the screen was storing a facial image, as the law required. But he was buying an in-state, not an international, fare, so he also knew that the image wouldn't automatically be uploaded to the police algorithm—it would be cached, and would be available if the police subpoenaed it. But hopefully, if they were subpoenaing anywhere, the police were at that moment subpoenaing machines in Rochester, N.Y. They had no specific reason to target Scranton. Not yet. Or so he reasoned.

At any rate, the machine sold him a train ticket to Philly. Gomery loaded it on his vanilla device and went to wait on the platform.

It was twenty minutes before the train arrived, and Gomery sat, with his hood up, and simply waited. There were a half-dozen other passengers, all—of course—on their phones. Gomery found himself zoning out, listening carefully to the ambient noise. There was a kind of tick-tick, like a far distant clock, and he was trying to work out what it was. A scratchy sort of sound. Something like a siren, but so muffled and distorted and buried in the folds of distance that he couldn't work out what it was. The land rose into hills and peaks westward, and it might have been some sonic illusion confected out of echoes being sent back off this topography.

Then the train rolled in and he couldn't hear anything over its noise. And then, as Gomery stepped aboard, the sounds resolved themselves into something unmistakable—gunfire. Lots and lots of it, somewhere in the western middle-distance.

Gomery found his seat and sat down. Hang in there, he told himself. Hang in there.

Keeping tapping your head
Keeping tapping your head
Keeping tapping your head

:3:

The journey to Philly took a little under four hours. There were screens everywhere, of course, and they were all showing different rolling newsfeeds. But there was only one story.

226

The president today invoked her war powers and the Senate has officially endorsed the declaration of hostilities, said a grave-faced Hispanic man who spoke with a British accent. *House leader Hatch Ng said today that this merely recognized officially what the de facto situation has been in the country for many months, and called the ordinance of secession promulgated by the California legislature illegal and unconstitutional. The president said that her primary responsibility was to preserve the integrity and constitution of these great United States. She quoted Abraham Lincoln.*

The screen switched to a pretty realistic-looking CGI of Lincoln, his huge light-bulb-shaped cranium with its weirdly sleepy-looking eyes, his protruding beard and cheekbones like cliff-face overhangs.

I appeal, said the simulacrum, in its passable imitation of a nineteenth-century southern drawl, *to all loyal citizens to favor, facilitate and aid this effort to maintain the honor, the integrity, and the existence of our National Union, and the perpetuity of popular government.*

Back to the anchor.

For analysis of what this historic and tragic declaration of war means, we go now to our two head policy correspondents, Jeb Stellaway and Hermione de la Tour.

Gomery flicked through the coverage, but it was all pretty shallow. He tried cycling away from the train company's preferred sites and feeds, but the system resisted him, because, of course, those sites and feeds were paying the company to foreground their product. After a while he found some unofficial analysis and was able to log on—under a pseudonym, of course—to a talkspace that was exploring the way the deep state was secretly orchestrating the conflict. Gomery felt a mixture of sympathy and mockery where these theories were concerned. He lurked rather than commented, although he did upvote a prediction that the war would last exactly 66 days and 6 hours—not because he thought the prediction likely, but simply out of a kind of impressed respect for the faux-precision of the number.

He bought a Pepsi and a bag of chips from the serverbot as it passed, and soon enough the train was decelerating into Philly. He detrained and strolled easily up the platform. So far, so good. No police waiting for him.

He walked into the town.

The last thing Gomery remembered with any clarity was walking up to 30th Street and looking back over his shoulder at the cliff-face whiteness of its art deco façade. There was a distant whistling sound. Or was that part of some retrospective gesture by his mind to add in sense and sequence to what became, otherwise, a merely bewildering sequence of distressing non sequiturs? Looking back, he could have sworn he heard a whistling, and that it grew louder. But did modern ordnance really announce its approach like that? Like a cannon-shell fired over the battlefield at Antietam? Surely not. Surely modern cannon ordnance travelled easily faster than sound, and surely nowadays slower explosives were delivered with a fatal—a ninja—silence? But at any rate, he seemed, looking back, to hear the shell descend from on high and then: what? A mental picture of staggering through an obstacle course of rubble. A building metamorphosing into a sideways-billowing hill-sized cloud of brick dust and smoke. Had he actually seen that? Maybe it was his imagination filling the hole where his memory should be. A three-legged dog loping very fast away. Four neonic-sufferers standing, perfectly indifferently, as their urban environment broke into hefty fragments and zoomed left and right and up and smashed, fistlike, into the dirt below. Had he actually seen that? The great day of His wrath. Hills leaping up and disaggregating and chunks of rock swarming like bees through the air.

Looking into the heart of light.

Buzz buzz.

And silence.

Long gleaming silence. Weeks of it.

He saw a horizontal bar.

He saw a silver-colored horizontal bar, ruling a fat line across his line of vision. After a time, and quite a long time too, he came to understand that this was a metal bar, and that he was lying down, and that the bar ran along the length of his bed to stop him falling out. Then he thought about things for a bit. Finally he was able to make out the corridor wall opposite where he was laying, and the fact that somebody was sitting on the floor with his back *to* that wall, staring vacantly into space. People sometimes passed.

His mouth felt dry.

He sat up. It took him four goes, but he managed it. There was a bee-sting on his arm, but it wasn't a bee-sting, it was where a drip had been needled into his flesh and taped in place. He peeled off the tape and pulled the feed out, and a little bit of blood swelled up, like a scarlet pearl.

He felt kind-of hungry, and more than a little dizzy, but he wasn't going to stay here. Where was *here*? *Here* was a corridor, and he guessed it was in a hospital, and he could see that the corridor he was in was crowded with trolleys and people laying on the floor or sitting up. Most were unconscious, or asleep. Some were awake, but wholly absorbed in their phones. None of these people paid Gomery any notice at all as he extracted himself, clumsily, from the gurney on which he had been laying. His chest hurt. His legs were wobbly.

He took three steps and fell against the wall. He managed to hold himself upright, but he felt very strange. His hand was the wrong color and it took him a long time, simply staring at his own hand, to see the reason for this. He was wearing a therapeutic glove. When he touched this with his other hand, words flickered into life on the smartcloth: BURNS GLOVE ONLY • REMOVE UNDER MEDICAL SUPERVISION.

Well, that *wasn't* good.

On the upside, the actual hand inside the glove didn't hurt. How long had he been out? Days? Weeks?

He tried walking once again, and this time it went a little better, although picking himself over the various bodies, supine on the floor or sitting with their backs against the wall, was not easy. It was easier with the gurneys, even though they were larger obstacles, because he could lean on them and hand himself along. Finally he came to the corridor's end and passed into what was clearly the hospital waiting room. This space was also filled with people, sitting and laying, and with gurneys queuing along the walls. The main thought in Gomery's mind was his thirst. There was a water cooler next to the unmanned admissions counter. He reached to pull a cup from the dispenser, and missed it, and reached again, and fumbled it out. He wasn't being well-coordinated. But he got there in the end. The water tasted very good.

He felt stronger straight away.

And here was a mirror. He saw, now, what the problem was with his depth perception. His left eye—no, that was his *right* eye, wasn't it?—because mirrors reversed the image?—except that then you'd think they'd flip him upside down too, wouldn't you?—his brain couldn't compute it—mirrors were *weird*, when you thought about them—anyway *one* of his eyes was covered over with a bandage.

His good eye winked at his good eye.

The bandages were wrapped around about a third of his head. He wasn't in pain, so the injury couldn't be too severe. Or so he figured. He thought about taking the bandages off to see, but then he thought again. This was a pretty good disguise against facial recognition software, actually. Less suspicious than an actual holo-mask. Less liable to provoke a cop into insisting he reveal his face. Maybe he should hang on to it for a while.

An elderly man, wearing a hat, was sitting in a chair with his hands folded in his lap. His brown face was a star map of paler freckles.

"Son," he advised Gomery, "they're watching."

"What's that?" said Gomery.

"Just that. They're always watching."

"You mean the hospital managers, doctors?"

"No, no, son," said the man, and he added, with earnest emphasis: "I mean *they*"—he lifted a hand and swept out an arc through the space over his lap—"are watching."

Gomery nodded. "Surveillance," he said.

"Watching," the man said.

"Word," said Gomery.

"Once you realize that," said the man, firmly, "you can cut your cloth."

"Never a truer truth spoken, sir," said Gomery.

"What do you *do*, son?" the old man demanded, sitting up straighter in his chair.

"I'm a coder," said Gomery.

The old man nodded slowly at this, as if he understood perfectly well what that meant. As perhaps he did. Then he said: "Ain't it all code, though? Life and living, death and dying. All a code. I remember *before* we had all these computer machines and internets. I remember how it used to be."

"You do?" Gomery was impressed. This man must be antique.

"Sure," said the old man. "But nobody else does. Young folk have never known and old folk have forgotten what it used to be. That's the fatal disease of this country. Forgetting. It's the United States of Amnesia, they say." He shook his head. "They right. They say it and they right to say it. We do things, like slavery, like murdering Native Americans, like war and pollution, and soon as it's behind us we're like—what? I don't remember any of *that*." He shook his head again. "You wouldn't think you could forget a thing like slavery, would you? America can. It says, we're about the now, we're about the future, but that's just trying to cover up the fact that the past is a blank to them. They don't remember anything at all. You know who *they* are?"

"Who?"

"Us. They is we, all of us."

"You get well soon, sir," said Gomery.

There didn't seem to be any staff. He needed his stuff—his actual phone and the vanilla device he'd borrowed from Aleksi which still had nearly $200 on it. Though he was still wearing his jeans, his shirt and jacket had been taken away and replaced with a hospital gown. But after twenty minutes of wandering up and down he hadn't been able to find anyone, and the interaction screens seemed stuck on old timetables and access points. Eventually he simply walked out. It was probably for the best anyway. He couldn't have given his real name or paid his bills. It was annoying to leave the devices, and the money, behind, but sometimes you had to cut your losses.

He came out into wincing sunlight, and a strange smell on the air: somewhere between acrid chemical disinfectant and cordite. There were two police quadpods standing there, looming over the entrance awning, lights blinking, an actual human police officer half out of the top hatch of the one on the right, smoking a vape-pipe. For one irrational moment Gomery thought they were going to arrest him for cutting loose without settling his bill. But of course they weren't.

For a while Gomery stood about trying to get his bearing. Ridge Avenue, Roxborough. Kendricks' Rec was opposite. He knew these places, and yet he couldn't orient himself with respect to the direction he needed to head to get home. That was puzzling. Maybe his brain had been damaged, even only a little bit. He scrabbled in his jeans pockets for his phone to pull up a map, and then remembered that he didn't have his phone. Maybe his memory had been affected by the explosion. Or whatever had happened.

He decided to start walking and hope he recognized something, like a landmark, on the way.

First off, he started down the gradient, and kept his bearing by the eSpire in the middle distance. Something was trying to come to light inside his brain. It was the big eSpire, he thought: the one on Belmont Hills, and that was the wrong direction for his home. So he swung a left and wandered on.

There were a great many damaged buildings, and only a few people out and about. Gomery passed a cinder block and sandbag gun emplacement on an intersection. The barrels of the automated guns followed him as he strolled. Overhead were many many drones. Where was he going?

He stopped to ask an elderly woman who was standing alone outside a Betty's, but she stared at him as he asked his question, absolutely noncomprehendingly. Her brain chemistry, he thought to himself, had been deleteriously affected by the action of neonicotinoids.

The fact that he could remember *that* name was surely a good sign. He was shaken, but not stirred. Or was he stirred, but not shaken? He was certainly trembly.

He knew where he was going: back to his home, the house he'd grown up in. His mom wouldn't be there, because he'd heard (from whom?) that she'd been flown to Washington. Somebody had told him that, but he couldn't remember whom. So he would have the house to himself. Assuming the police hadn't staked it out. He didn't want to run into the police. The police would arrest him. He could remember that much. And

233

the core thing was—the core thing—was that he had to speak to Allie. And he had to try and contact his other friends. He remembered that too.

A long convoy of military trucks was rolling with bizarre slowness along the Lincoln Highway. Gomery was puzzled at their collective snail's pace, until he saw, following the last truck, a queue of slow-stomping quadpods in military livery. The trucks didn't want to lose this tail.

He cut down a side street. A bright red bulldozer was heaping broken bricks and tiles and dirt into a hillock of ruin where a house had once stood. The bricks were the code out of which the house had been assembled—in raw form just a string of blank signifiers, but arranged the right way...

War was disarrangement, Gomery thought. That was it, the nub of it. Battle had loosened the giant molecules that held together to constitute the city. Still, he told himself, the molecules could be reassembled.

Two people saw him and came hurrying in his direction, and for a moment he thought of sprinting off. But they weren't police; they were reporters.

"Sally Beamish, PNNOCC News. Sir! Sir! Were you wounded in the recent attack?"

"I have no memory of the attack," said Gomery, turning his head so that the bandaged side was more directly in the line of the camera in the other's cap.

"Sir, you must remember something—have you come straight from the hospital?"

This was awkward. He didn't want his face all over the newsfeeds with a Philly tag.

So he said, "Gotta run... Don't recall... Don't recall..." and put on a burst of speed.

He had no puff. The energy just drained out of him, and he had to sit on a low wall and get his breath back. But the journalists had gone off after a more forthcoming interviewee and, looking up, he suddenly recognized exactly where he was. It was like a flower blossoming in his mind. His heart leaped up.

In ten minutes he was home again.

:4:

He didn't have his phone, and so couldn't unlock the front door; and there was nobody *at* home to let him in. But Gomery was nothing if not an individual who liked to be ready for every eventuality, and he had a route into the house prepped—through the basement window, via a code-lock he'd fitted.

He dropped through the grille and reset the lock. And then he stood for a while and just breathed the air. Didn't do anything except that. If "they" had staked the house out, whoever they were, they would presumably have seen him creeping in. So he waited, and listened, for the sound of the front door above him splintering. The sound of heavy boots on the floorboards overhead.

Nothing.

He went up to the bathroom and undressed. He took off the one glove and unpeeled the wrapping from his skull. Underneath the bandages there was a white eyepatch over the eye and he took this off too. It took five minutes or so for his eye to stop watering and his eyelids to stop clenching-up, but he got there in the end.

He examined himself for burns. The skin on his hand was a little puckered, and there were some pale scar lines like threadworms. The hair on the injured side of his head had been burned off and the skin underneath looked a little sore. But it really didn't feel too bad.

He took a lukewarm shower, dried himself, and dressed in his bedroom. Clean clothes over his clean skin: it was bliss. Then because his half-scorched hairdo looked unsymmetrical, he dug out an old cap. He went downstairs, made a cup of herbal tea and poured himself a bowl of cereal—there was no milk, but he was happy to eat the stuff dry.

Keeping tapping your head
Keeping tapping your head
Keeping tapping your head

It wouldn't do to get too comfortable: sooner or later the police, not finding him in New York State, would think of swinging by to check this place. But Gomery could take an actuarial approach to calculating the risk, and he figured he had time to do what he had come here to do.

He went back up to his room and pulled out a couple of devices he'd stashed in his desk drawer behind a fingerprint lock. One of these he would sync to his encrypted cloud when he was in a place—not here—where he could do so in reasonable likelihood of performing the operation without ringing every surveillance bell between here and New York City. The other was a muffled device, and he plugged it into a socket, and then he called Allie.

~ My God, Gomery, where have you been? I was sick with worry.

~ I was arrested, Allie. The police came for us.

~ You, Otty and Kath. Not Cess, though. Cess wasn't arrested.

~ You spoke to her?

~ A week ago, and only for, like five minutes. What is going on? You know a war broke out?

~ Yes, I know a war broke out. How long have I been gone?

~ What do you mean, gone?

~ Since you last heard from me, Allie.

236

~ Fifteen days, six hours and some small change in minutes. Jesus Gomery. You were *arrested*? By the *police*?

~ They are the people legally invested with the powers of arrest, Gomery said drily.

But then he said most things drily.

~ I was only there a day, he said.

~ And they let you go?

~ They did not. I got away. They didn't have me in a regular police station. I've been thinking, it may have been because I was a minor, but they didn't want to put me in the regular juvenile detention merry-go-round.

~ Because they wanted to interrogate you, said Allie.

~ Yeah, said Gomery. Then he said: ~ There's a two-week gap in my memory. I think I was in hospital.

~ That's a long time to be in hospital.

~ Yeah.

~ That's an expensive period of hospital time.

~ Yeah. Have you heard from Otty?

~ She's still in the system. Still locked up. Arrested too. Why, though? Why these arrests?

~ They were just real keen to find out about us, I guess. They arrested me to find out about you and me.

~ You and me, sweetie? Allie said, suddenly flirtatious. ~ People will say we're in love.

~ Don't be crazy: about all of us. The Famous Five. About our Network.

~ I knew what you meant, Allie admonished him, kindly.

~ I keep forgetting you have trouble processing irony.

~ Irony is just a fancy word for lying, said Gomery. ~ What's been happening here? I mean—in Philly? Just walking here from the hospital, it looked pretty wrecked. Was it bombarded?

~ This war, said Allie, in a desolated voice.

~ I know, right?

237

~ Mostly I know what I see on the news. About the war, I mean. But yeah, New York has so far mostly escaped serious structural damage, but that's mostly because the fighting has been in this big arc around the city—and the arc sweeps us up in it. First it was militia forces come down, in pretty large numbers, from the northeast. Fox says Canada was supplying them, but nobody knows for sure. U.S. Army fought up from the south, and there were three days of pretty intense fighting.

~ I'm glad you're OK, said Gomery ~ At any rate.

~ Yeah. Me too. And I'm glad you're OK—though, it looks like you caught the edge of it, rather more than I did.

Gomery ran a hand over the side of his face that had been touched by fire. It felt… really, it felt fine. ~ I'm OK, he said.

~ You can't stay here.

~ Neither can you.

~ Oh Gomery, said Allie. ~ You think I don't know that?

~ The war won't last forever, though, said Gomery. ~ Things go back to normal, after a while. You don't know where they're holding Otty?

~ No. I scoured the newsfeeds, all I can. I've eavesdropped on official police communication. But nothing.

~ Otty's tough, said Gomery. ~ I'm not worried about her. Obviously, she *would* be the one for them to crack. If they're after what I think they're after.

~ What we know they're after.

~ Sure.

~ Montgomery Lacroix… said Allie and stopped.

This set off a tingling sense of dread in Gomery's chest. His eyeballs tickled with coming tears. It seemed to him, when he looked back on this moment after the fact, that he already knew what Allie was about to say to him, but he didn't want to face it. But perhaps that was hindsight. He had never been the most intuitive of human beings. Clever, and dedicated, and perhaps even a kind of genius when it came to coding. But not emotionally intuitive. Using his full name was the cue, Allie's attempt to ready him for what was coming, to put him in a more formal frame of mind. But that wasn't what he wanted. So he reacted to Allie by saying ~ Don't call me Montgomery like that, Allie. You sound like my Mom when you call me that.

~ You need to be ready. You need to hear this, and you need to be ready to hear it.

~ Ready, said Gomery. ~ I'm ready.

~ It's about Kath.

He knew what Allie was going to say, now. But he didn't want to know what she was going to say, and he didn't want to hear it. So long as he didn't hear the actual words the news existed in a Schrödinger state where it was precisely as deniable as it was inevitable. All he needed to do was to think of the words that would shut Allie up. But he couldn't think what those words might be.

~ It's not about Kath, he said stupidly.

~ It was on a newsfeed, just briefly. She's dead, Gomery. There was a mess-up, it seems, and they put her in a women's prison, even though she was legally still a kid.

~ It was no mess-up, he said hotly. ~ They did that on purpose, because they wanted to shake her up, and because they didn't want her to have access to the extra protections under the law a minor would have.

~ Maybe, agreed Allie.

There was a long pause.

~ What happened? Gomery asked.

~ News said there was a riot in a holding facility in Maryland. FM feeds say it was a focussed interrogation facility, but the official line is that no interrogations happened there, it was just a holding pen. I don't know which is more reliable, official feed or FM.

~ Frequency Modulation?

~ Freedom Militia. I reckon the official line might be right—they were letting Kath cool her heels, maybe.

~ Or maybe they were applying stress techniques to get her to talk and broke her, said Gomery.

~ News said there was a riot, and that a number of detainees were killed during the operation to reassert lawful control. Kath's name was listed there. But there weren't any other details about exactly what happened.

Gomery thought about this. He felt a profound disarrangement internally. He wasn't someone to weep and wail, to do all that ridiculous theatrical performance of grief. That was partly about being on the spectrum, he thought, and partly it was just who he was, just the tenor of his personality. But that didn't mean he didn't *feel*, deeply, sometimes acutely, or that such feelings didn't matter. He examined himself. He looked, as it were, into his own code. Kath was dead. His friend was dead. He would never see her again, and never speak to her again.

It was a sword sheathed in his heart.

~ This is them, he said, eventually.

~ It is.

~ This is *on them*.

~ Gom, said Allie, gently. ~ I know you pretty well. I know you're real chewed-up and sad about this. I feel the same way.

~ She was our friend, and they killed her, said Gomery.

~ That's right. I'm not trying to pull rank or anything, not trying to pretend that I have a better intuitive grasp of emotion than you do, or psychological motivation, or anything like that. But I know you, and I worry that, in a roundabout way, you'll end up blaming *me* for this, and hating *me* for this, and I don't think I could bear that.

~ Blaming you? Gomery was genuinely noncomprehending.

~ They didn't arrest you three for no reason, did they. Think it through. They want the network. They wanted you, or Otty, or Kath, to open the door. Yeah?

~ Yes.

~ Desperate times, and they were in a hurry, and they got sloppy. But this thing we have created—it's ours. It belongs to all five of us.

~ That doesn't mean I blame *you*, said Gomery.

~ You're not following my reasoning.

~ I'm being logical, he said doggedly. ~ I blame them. Of course I do. They don't even know what they *think* they want from us. Don't even know what they think they want. They're fucking idiots—Otty wouldn't like me saying so, if she were here, but it's true. They know I lifted some patterning from Mom's work. They know that much. But that's all they know. And they didn't ask. They didn't ask us politely.

~ They didn't ask us politely, Allie agreed.

~ If they'da asked us politely, said Gomery. But then he said: ~ and now they have killed our friend. And now I want to hurt them.

~ I want to hurt them, too.

~ Allie, said Gomery. ~ I can hurt them a little and you can hurt them a lot.

~ I guess that's true.

~ I want you to promise me, I want you to make me a vow, that you will do that. I don't care where the damage falls. I'm not interested in who was directly involved, or any bullshit like that. I blame them all. I blame both sides.

~ If we all agree.

~ If we five agree, but Kath's gone, so we four. Yeah?

~ Yeah, said Allie.

The more he talked, the more anger Gomery uncovered inside himself. He had never realized just how much of the bedrock of his soul was fury. He'd honestly never realized that subterranean truth about his own personality.

~ Bring them all down, he said.

~ All of them, agreed Allie. ~ They hurt my friends and that means they hurt me. And I am not a nice person when I'm hurt.

~ We need to think this through carefully, said Gomery. ~ To maximize its effectiveness. We need to talk to Cess and especially to Otty. She's the one with the beehives, after all.

~ Sure, said Allie. ~ And we need to find you somewhere safe to hide out, here in the city. I can do that. Lot of empty property.

~ Sure, said Gomery.

Then, with some internal finesse that evaded Gomery's powers of self-analysis, his emotional tectonic plates lurched and anger was replaced in one swoop by a hollowing sense of desolation. He would never see her again. His eyes were hot and slippery in their sockets. Was he crying? He never cried. Crying was simply not him.

~ Oh, Gomery, said Allie. ~ Oh, my friend, my love. I'm so sorry.

CHAPTER IV

:I:

Otty crossed the river and started up the slope on the far side. She would have thought that she was, by this stage in her trek, immune to the shock of seeing towns ruined and broken, of seeing streets littered with broken bodies and rubble, of houses flip-topped and ruinous, of automobiles on their backs like gigantic dead bugs. There was, the war had made her realize, a great deal more plastic in the world than she had suspected— everywhere she went were tumbleweed knots of plastic strands clumped together like hairballs, gossamer spectres of torn plastic film floating on the breeze, underfoot a crunching beachfront of pebbles and sandbanks of plastic granules. Everywhere she went.

Still, it was startling to see a city she knew really well, like Philly, broken into pieces like this. Bergs of tangled rubbish floated down river. There were dead bodies embracing the supporting struts of the Twin Bridges with a tenacity that would surely have served them better in life. Plastic bags rolled and puffed up like ghostly puffer fish, and were abruptly sucked empty, and slid and rushed along the street.

She had acquired one of the many dronehack apps that were

circulating. It didn't give her access to every drone, of course—or even to every non-government drone. But enough of the buzzers were hackable to give her a sky-view of where she was heading. The main use of this was to avoid oncoming soldiery: to duck out of the way, slide behind the sumo-blocks of the overpass pillars, to shuck into a doorway and disappear. Sometimes, despite her best efforts, she was spotted, but mostly the troops—either army or FM—had better things to be concerned with than stray individual civilians. She had acquired a hefty greatcoat from in among the architectural havoc of a bombed shopping mall on the outskirts of Elizabethtown, and with the hat and veil and the fact that she had scrounged some boots so big it took four pairs of socks to make them wearable, she didn't *look* like a teenage girl. She didn't, after all, want to go about looking more rapeable than she absolutely had to.

She had been grabbed in a sweep coming out of Lancaster and loaded into the back of a truck with a dozen other displaced citizens. A couple of them had been weeping, or rocking back and forth, and the rest were clearly buckleheads. After a half-hour or so, a harassed-looking lieutenant had opened the back of the truck, ordered his subordinates to "clear out the fucking buckleheads", and a corporal had shouted that everyone who could understand him and who still had a functioning mind should make themselves known to him. Otty had kept her head down, and stared pointedly into space, so when the three actual buckleheads were pulled from the truck she was manhandled out also. This suited her. She wandered away in a distracted manner as more people were loaded in, and once the truck drove off, she continued with her trek.

Apart from that, she had not really been bothered by others. It was amazing, really. But then again: war took people's minds off everything that wasn't war.

And now she was back in Philly. And the thing that worried her more than anything, that had occupied her thinking the whole journey was: *How were her bees doing?*

:2:

On her travels she'd picked up—looted, she supposed, was the proper term—a couple of creditbuffered phones, together with a spare lead and some add-on pack batteries. She was able to use these to go online without revealing who she was. The trickiest part was finding places where the electricity still worked to recharge them, but by and large she managed. Dusk, after she had ferreted out a place to sleep, and to eat such supplies as she'd been able to pick up, was her time for searching online. The night she'd found confirmation of Kath's death was a hammer blow. It wasn't that she'd disbelieved the news before. She had, she thought, grasped it and even started to come to terms with it, but seeing it actually, officially reported—seeing the search term isolating her name in that official list of casualties—made her cry for a half-hour.

She couldn't contact her parents or her sister. There was a tag on the family home, alerting people that the inhabitants had been evacuated when the city came under sustained attack, but the online trail went cold at a holding facility in Florida a month earlier. At least none of their names showed up in any official listings of the dead. And then, three days later, as Otty was idly watching random news footage with the Philly tag while she ate a pack of soy gumbo from a self-heating sachet in the ruins of a suburban house, there was good news to balance the bad. Entirely by chance, she saw Gomery—his head was partially bandaged, and he looked a little bewildered, but it was

245

undeniably him. He was in a montage of interviews with what the report called "survivors" of the Battle of Philadelphia.

Which meant he was alive, and that he had been in Philly. Which was something. She pulled the footage and checked its metadata: many weeks old. So strictly he had been alive, back then. But perhaps he still was today. And perhaps he was still in Philly.

He was unreachable, of course; as was Cess—online, that is. That was exactly what she expected. They were lying doggo. If a simple online search through a phone could locate them, then the police or the army would have grabbed them long before. But then, clever fellow that he was, Gomery found his way to her Wikipedia stub, and was canny enough to check the edit page, and add a comment.

Over a day and a half, in the interstices of her walking, when she took rests in the day or found a ruin to sleep in overnight, they conducted a slow conversation. The niceties were:

(cur | prev) 01:55 10 October 2031 GreatGomCoder (talk| contribs) m . . (1,056 bytes) (-22). (→ top: removing unsourced {{*I'm glad to hear you're alive, and out*}} parameters (Task 1))(undo)

(cur | prev) 03:14 10 October 2031 BeeLady (talk| contribs) m . . (1,056 bytes) (-22). (→ top: removing unsourced {{*You too*}} parameters (Task 1))(undo)

(cur | prev) 03:15 10 October 2031 GreatGomCoder (talk| contribs) m . . (1,056 bytes) (-22). (→ top: removing unsourced {{*Kath is dead. I don't know if you heard that*}} parameters (Task 1))(undo)

Kath is dead. She read those words and cried for a second time. But crying didn't help. So she typed in:

(cur | prev) 03:17 10 October 2031 BeeLady (talk| contribs) m . . (1,056 bytes) (-22). (→ top: removing unsourced {{*I heard, yeah. I heard and it broke my heart to hear it*}} parameters (Task 1))(undo)

There was no immediate reply: maybe Gomery was considering this, or maybe he'd been interrupted, or maybe it was something else. She settled down and slept, and in the morning when she checked again, there was a new message.

(cur | prev) 03:22 10 October 2031 GreatGomCoder (talk| contribs) m . . (1,056 bytes) (-22). (→ top: removing unsourced {{*I want them to pay. I want to hurt them, for wasting her. I want them to feel for it. Spoke with Allie and he agrees*}} parameters (Task 1))(undo)

She posted a trio of replies to this.

(cur | prev) 07:04 10 October 2031 BeeLady (talk| contribs) m . . (1,056 bytes) (-22). (→ top: removing unsourced {{*"she"*}} parameters (Task 1))(undo)

(cur | prev) 03:17 11October 2031 BeeLady (talk| contribs) m . . (1,056 bytes) (-22). (→ top: removing unsourced {{*Allie's too polite to tell you, but it pisses her off to be called "he"*}} parameters (Task 1))(undo)

(cur | prev) 03:17 11 October 2031 BeeLady (talk| contribs) m . . (1,056 bytes) (-22). (→ top: removing unsourced {{*Make them pay for Kath—yes—yes*}} parameters (Task 1))(undo)

And his replies came straight away.

(cur | prev) 03:22 11 October 2031 GreatGomCoder

(talk| contribs) m . . (1,056 bytes) (-22). (→ top:
removing unsourced {{*You and I are never going to agree on
questions of gender pronouns and Allie*}} parameters (Task
1))(undo)

   (cur | prev) 03:22 11 October 2031 GreatGomCoder
(talk| contribs) m . . (1,056 bytes) (-22). (→ top:
removing unsourced {{*Don't say where you are but say
how long you think before you can check on how this war has
affected the wellbeing of apian allies*}} parameters (Task 1))
(undo)

…which was, in her opinion, a pretty stupidly obvious thing
to put in a publicly accessible internet location and would (had
she answered it) all but have given the authorities a fix on
where to arrest her. Assuming they were eavesdropping. Though
it was probably a Poe's purloined letter situation, sure. But
there was no point in just giving stuff away. The thing was that
Gomery's mind, though brilliant, was not nuanced. He thought
he was being sly, and slyness was so alien to his being that he
didn't realize how far from the mark he fell. Her tagname was
BeeLady, for crying out loud!

   (cur | prev) 03:17 10 October 2031 BeeLady (talk|
contribs) m . . (1,056 bytes) (-22). (→ top: removing
unsourced {{*Don't be so transparent. You know where, three
months and a day before Allie's birthday* }} parameters (Task
1))(undo)

…because she was pretty sure the authorities, even if they
happened by extremely remote chance to be monitoring this
strange exchange, didn't know the date of Allie's birthday.

And so it was a bright morning, exactly three months and a day before her friend Allie's birthday, that Otty came up the hill and through the ruined town and arrived again at her family home. It looked, at first blush, undamaged. The area was far enough from the centre of the city to have avoided the more catastrophic bombardment. There was a lot of garbage in the streets, and some of the neighboring houses had some broken windows, but otherwise things looked normal.

She scoped the house out for an hour or so before coming in any closer and ranging around the perimeter from a series of more or less hidden vantage points. There was nobody around, in any of the houses in the neighborhood, and finally she took the plunge.

The front door was locked (of course) and she no longer had a key. Nor did she have Gomery's foresight and capacity for meticulously planning for even the most unlikely of eventualities, so there was no way she could get in the house short of breaking a window and setting off the alarms.

That didn't matter. She didn't want to get inside the house right now. She wanted to check her bees.

Around the back, climbing like a monkey over the gate, along the side path, pushing through the bristling unpruned expansion of the azaleas, and onto the back lawn. There were the hives, in their archaic computer stack terminals. And her heart contracted and relaxed with a joyous kind of relief. After everything that had happened, bees were still crawling at the lip of the entrance, flying off and flying back.

There weren't very many of them, but then it was late in the year. But the fact that the hives were still alive was ridiculously pleasing to her.

And now it was time to speak to Allie. She plugged her phone into the socket at the back of the main hive and found a comfortable spot to sit.

~ Otty? Is that you? O my stars, I'm pleased you're OK!

~ Allie, my sweet, my love. I'm pleased you're OK too! Things have been pretty heated here in Philly, from everything I hear.

~ You have no idea. It's literally been a war zone.

~ But you haven't been hurt.

~ Hunky-dory, me. You spoke to Gomery?

~ In a roundabout way, yes, Otty replied. ~ I kinda expected him to be here, actually. He's not, is he?

~ I haven't spoken to him in five weeks, said Allie. ~ In just over five weeks actually. He had to clear out of his mom's house, because he figured the authorities would sooner or later come looking for him. But that made it harder for him to contact me. I sorted a string of alternative hide-holes. He's been lurking. At least I'd have heard if the police had taken him.

~ He knows I'm coming here, and he knows when.

~ Today!

~ Knowing him, he probably thinks *today* means today at exactly twelve noon. That would be just like him.

~ We can wait a couple hours, I guess. You know about Kath?

~ Yeah.

~ You know what Gomery wants to do about it?

~ He wants to make them pay, said Otty.

As she said it an ejection of anger, hot as lava, splashed out of her heart and spread through her. The sensation was as satisfying on a psycho-emotional level as any feeling she could remember. It wasn't just Kath's death. It was everything that had happened to her. It was the world, knocking her about, and it was the *what-you-going-to*-do-*about-it*? sneer on the world's face. It was the whole way everything and everybody had treated her.

She would do something about it.

~ And you feel the same way?

~ Are you kidding? Of course I do.

~ And we can't ask Kath any more. That's exactly the point. But did you ask Cess?

This was the rule. The action they were contemplating required all five of them to agree to it. Unanimity, nothing less. Well, Kath was no longer alive, so that left the four of them. And the truth was that Otty *hadn't* spoken to Cess. Allie was, with all her many other qualities, a stickler for this kind of thing.

But Otty wasn't about to let that stop her. Lying was wrong, and God would be angry with her, but right now that wasn't enough of a disincentive. And she had the advantage that Allie, who knew her better than almost anybody, would not expect her to lie. So she said:

~ I spoke to Cess, and she's on board too.

It was weaselly, but she figured: she *had* spoken to Cess— many many times, because the two of them were close friends, although she hadn't spoken to her recently, and she hadn't spoken on precisely this topic. But she also figured *she's on board* was bland to the point of deniability.

Given the enormity of what she was putting in motion, it might seem odd that these equivocations concerned her at all. But this was the kind of thing that mattered to Otty. And I will tell you: the enormity was real. A lie seems small, but large things unspool from it. In this case, the things could hardly be more prodigious or impactful.

Allie replied:

~ OK then. I guess that's a go.

What did it matter? What did anything matter? The world was over anyway, and her friend was dead. All the newsfeeds were filled with reports of large crowds of newly affected buckleheads drifting like human rubbish across the west and the Midwest. All across the Union, States too timid to declare UDI were nonetheless putting up border points and rolling out improvised razor-wire fences, in part to keep out these crowds of the neonic-afflicted.

And they had killed her friend. Her tears were doing her thinking for her, not her neurones.

~ Well, all right then, Otty said.

She was not alone. There was somebody else here. And then she realized, belatedly, that they had caught up with her after all. She had not been thorough enough scoping out the house.

"Oh no," she said.

Here was a figure in military fatigues, body armor and helmet, pointing a rifle directly at her. He had slipped around the side of the house and was going to shoot her.

She didn't know, at first, if he was on his own, just one solitary fighter, or if a dozen similarly kitted-out soldiers were about to come around the side of the house to join him. And she didn't know, as he came closer, and his weapon's aim did not falter, if he was going to shoot her straight away, or instead take her into custody. If the former, then (she reasoned) he would surely have just shot her already. Unless he wanted to come closer to make sure of the shot.

Then he said, "Come off your phone," and something about his voice sounded familiar.

She put the phone down on the ground, but didn't unplug its cable.

Then he removed his left hand from the butt of his rifle, without altering either its aim or the fact that his right finger was on its trigger, reached up and pulled up his helmet.

She recognized him then. It was Wesson, the guy who had tried to rescue her from those vigilantes months earlier. The guy who had had his iPhone knocked out of his docket and spent all night and all day getting thirstier and thirstier in the James Grabill. It was Wesson, here in the flesh.

Evidently he had got his dockette repaired and was plugged into as much memory as he needed.

"Ottoline Barragão," he said. "You're not an easy girl to track down."

"I'll take that as a compliment," said Otty.

"And so you should. But coming back here was a mistake, don't you think? If I can find you, then so can others."

"You're alone?" she asked.

He nodded. "I hate to pick up a conversation after such a long hiatus, but events… What's the word? What's the word? *Interposed*, is the word, I guess. The last thing I said to you was… I wanted you to believe I'm your friend."

"That's what you said you wanted me to believe. That time you had a gun aimed at my best friend. Now it's a gun aimed at me. Hardly friendly."

"Friendly is what I am, though. It's the truth. The fact that the U.S. Government came crashing through that wall should tell you I don't work for *them*. And while I appreciate that I've yet to earn your trust, I can assure you I'm not working for the other side either. What are they calling themselves now? The FM?"

"I don't know what they're calling themselves."

"That's a fissiparous coalition of a hundred different interest groups. No way it'll hang together long enough to win this war. But it doesn't need to—it only needs to hold on until the old-world government comes to the conclusion that it can't keep pushing. And agrees a ceasefire and gives away most of the family jewels. A couple months more, at the outside. In the meantime—there's you and your friends."

"Which group," said Otty, "you're hoping to join."

"Not as a *close* friend," said Wesson, grinning unpleasantly. "I wouldn't presume. But as … let's put it this way, as somebody on your side."

"Do you point a rifle at the chest of *all* your friends then?"

She could see Wesson making mental calculations. He moved back a little way, crouched down, and lowered the rifle barrel.

"Let's not fight, you and I, Ottoline Barragão. Even if we never become bosom buddies, we have powerful enemies in common. You were talking to … it?"

"She," said Otty.

"When I last saw you, all those months ago," said Wesson, "I figured there was a money algorithm hidden away in your encysted private network. I mean, I knew how desperately the government wanted to gain access, and money was my first guess. I reckoned it must be money on a pretty vast scale, to be of interest to the government. I guess I figured … Well, the whole logic of money is up in the air, now, isn't it? Who knows what protocol you might have in there, eh?" He shook his head. "But it's not money, is it."

"No."

"It's … it. I guess it has a name?"

"She does."

Wesson waited, expecting Otty to supply the name. When he realized she wasn't going to, he grinned again, and said, "Sure, trust is earned. I get that. But you gotta to give me the *chance* to earn it, Ottoline Barragão. OK?"

"I honestly don't see," said Otty, "how you could do that."

"Well, let me explain where I'm coming from. My people are a … third way, yeah? I mean, look around. Look at all the damage that's been done to this nation over the last few months. That's what war *has been*. For as long as humans fucking walked upright, this is what we have done."

"Please don't swear," said Otty.

"Sure. OK, but look at it. Just look at it. The old way of

making war was to squeeze the bladder of misery until everybody is splashed with its ink. That's how it's always been. The old way has been to smash the dam of barbarism and flood the whole fucking—sorry, whole blessed *country* with it. But it doesn't have to be like that."

"Your third way will put an end to war?"

"No. That's more than humanity could ever manage, I'm afraid. War will continue. But what I'm proposing means that we will fight it in a way that minimizes human casualties. Make war machine versus machine, and rather algorithm versus algorithm. That's the future. You know the *real* reason people go to war?"

"Original sin," said Otty, without hesitation.

This reply threw Wesson.

"No," he said. "That's not it. You . . . You think it's just people's innate evil?"

"Man produces evil as a fruit tree blossoms," said Otty. "It's in us. It's in us all. Look around you, Mr. Wesson."

"You're wrong. You're wrong, Ottoline Barragão. Young men, they get frisky, and want to go out and shoot up shit. They're like reindeer, butting heads together. But that's high spirits, really. That's an emulsion of frustration and adrenaline and randiness. And the boredom of having nothing better to do. That's not *sin*. It's nothing so deep and dark. But everyone else? All the people who *aren't* bored, testosterone-y young guys? They don't want war. They just want to get on with their lives."

"And yet here we are making war and more war and more war. You know that Tolstoy novel, that big Russian novel, *War and Peace*? It should have been called *War and War*."

"But that's exactly my point," said Wesson. "Why *do* we keep going to war? And the answer is that people make money off it. That's the bottom line; that's always the bottom line. So the answer is not to abolish war, which would be beyond us anyway.

255

The answer is to establish a paradigm whereby people can make war without killing millions of civilians, without wrecking our infrastructure or ruining the environment—and still make money. Everything else in our world is run by computer algorithms now—why not war? Algorithms drive our automobiles, why not our tanks? Robots make all our arms—why not have them shoulder those arms too? Casualties are reduced to a tiny fraction of what they were before, life mostly goes on, societies and nations and tribes get to blow off steam like before, diplomacy has its needful last resort, and the people who make money off war continue making money off war."

"People like you."

"Hey, do I look like a billionaire? This is as much humanitarian as anything. But, yeah, all right—even a gun for hire like me can see the benefits, and some of those are financial."

"You're all heart."

"Let me put it this way," said Wesson, nodding. "You keep bees, yeah? That's it exactly. War is a beehive. It's humanity's great beehive. It's big and it's liable to hurt you, unless you're really sure of what you're doing. And the way to handle it, the way to handle *war*, is to keep it buzzing along just enough for you to scoop out the honey. Yeah? The honey is the profit. Because you make profit by selling shit to people, hardware and software, and you make more money with built-in obsolescence. If you sell an automobile to a customer, you want to sell that customer another automobile sooner rather than later. If your customer keeps the automobile running for two decades you don't make much profit, but if that customer comes back after a year and says *I want a new new auto now now now*, why, then you're making money. Well, war is the perfect form of that market. You're selling not an automobile but a billion-dollar plane, a whole fleet of billion-dollar planes. And your customer doesn't carefully husband these for decades. On the contrary, your customer deliberately puts them in harm's way, and they get smashed up, and your customer has to come back and buy a whole new bunch of billion-dollar planes. It is the perfection of the capitalist system. But!" Wesson held up his free hand. "You gots to balance it. If war doesn't really get going, then you don't get the obsolescence guaranteed, and you don't make money. But if the war goes *too far* … then the whole economy crashes, the infrastructure is wrecked, and nowhere is safe, and instead of enjoying your profits you're scrabbling in the wreckage of tins of beans with everybody else. It's the middle line, you see? No hives, no honey—feral bees, and you're stung so bad honey is the last thing on your mind. But a well-maintained hive, and you can scoop out the sweetness, and it all works perfectly."

"I can't believe," said Otty, with disgust, "that you're comparing my beehives to your war profiteering."

"I'm trying to save lives. This war is due a pause, so everybody can regroup, and the people who have made money can count it, bank it, enjoy it a little."

"Stop the war," said Otty. "Sure."

"Now, see," said Wesson, a sly expression crossing his face. "What you've got in that network—it's light-years ahead of the run-of-the-mill automatic gun algorithms. Yeah?"

"Light-years is a measure of distance, not time," said Otty.

"Still works, in the context I was using it," Wesson returned. "I figure your friend Montgomery stole it from his mom's development lab. It's hard to imagine how he was able to, but there you go."

And with one of those strange synchronous coincidences with which life is so heavily supplied, it was at precisely this moment, when Wesson mentioned Gomery by name, that Otty actually saw Gomery. He was making his way, very slowly and as quietly as he was able, up from below the garden. He was carrying a handgun. Otty couldn't think she'd ever seen him holding a gun in his life before, but who knew what he'd been through over the last months. And it was clear that Gomery had seen Wesson, and seen Wesson's rifle aimed at Otty, and now he was inching his way toward a position where he could be the hero.

It was strange. The joy Otty felt at seeing him again, after this length of time, was so intense and so directly bodily she actually shivered with it, and almost shouted with happiness. But for the briefest moment of time her glance connected with Gomery's and he shook his head quickly, and so she turned her gaze back on Wesson.

She'd managed not to give away the fact that he was coming up behind the soldier.

Which is to say, she was *pretty sure* she'd managed not to give that fact away.

Which meant: she had to distract him. Wesson was looking unsettled, as if he could sense something was wrong somewhere, so she said: "Gomery didn't steal her."

"What?"

"Montgomery. What he lifted was a wire-frame, a sort of skeleton of code and reactions and processing power. And a couple of in-turned fractal processors."

"Lifted," said Wesson, grinning. "That's a nice euphemism. Where's the hardware now?"

"The two core items are"—Otty looked behind her—"in these hives."

"Nice," said Wesson, appreciatively. "Hide a computer inside a computer—inside the carcass of a ruined old-school computer stack. And I guess, covering it with bees is a good way to stop curious people poking around in there."

"I love my bees," said Otty. It was the truth.

"Well, OK, so I load that stack, those hives behind you, onto a truck and deliver it to my bosses. Yeah?"

"Well, *that* is hardly the action of a friend. Stealing my hives," said Otty, scornfully. "So much for *trust you.*"

"Don't be a silly girl," said Wesson, oblivious to how unwise a thing this was to say to anybody, Otty least of all. "I'm trying to make you rich. You and all your friends. My bosses will pay us a fortune."

"Not for that stack, they won't," said Otty. "The network is distributed—there are nodes in my house, another in Gomery's, Cess's, Kath's." Not that Kath would ever be in a position to log on, ever again. "And a couple elsewhere. Wired together and parallel-looped. Allie is one of us."

"Allie?"

There was no point in holding anything back now.

"It's her name. On the one hand she has a notional IQ of eight thousand and can process the entire regular internet in microseconds. On the other hand she is a person, and the person she is ... is our friend."

"Sure."

"You don't understand. You think she's a military asset. But she's a person. She's exactly as much a person as anybody."

"Labs have been working on that for decades, and you and your teenage friends just happened to crack it?"

"It's not a *problem* to crack. It's organic. We're not stupid; we've read up on the conventional research. It says—we've applied however many billions of vector processors at the problem and all we're doing is making a quicker Google. So instead, we'll apply trillions. That's missing the point, in a really elementary way, in a way so elementary it's too obvious."

"You're saying the solution needs a lesser mind to see it," said Wesson, smiling strangely. "Or maybe a mind less bound by the parameters of perfection?"

Otty said: "Dogs are stupid but have loads of personality. The algorithms running the stock market are millions of times

259

cleverer than any human being, capable of processing vast amounts of data in flickering fractions of a second, yet they have no personality whatsoever. What's wrong with this picture?"

"Go on," prompted Wesson.

"Human consciousness, intelligence, personality—soul—didn't evolve to crunch numbers, or run data, or focus pure intellect on problems to come up with solutions," said Otty. "It *can* do that, yeah. That it can do that has evolutionary advantage, which means it has fed into itself as a survival trait. But that's not how it evolved in the first place. The boss-thing driving natural selection in our brains is ... other people. What has driven it is our need to impress, and ..."

She glanced down at Gomery, who was still making his painstaking way up the slope. He was almost at the bottom of the garden now.

"And outwit," she said, "and attract and judge and cooperate with other people. That's the core of the adaptive basis for our cerebral skills. The human drama of love and hate, of gossip and romance. Lovers and family and, above all, friends. That's the single greatest achievement of *Homo sapiens*. Friendship. More even than love and sex and pair-bonding and family units—lots of animals have those things, because it feeds directly into natural selection. But those *other* bonds. Those *friendship* connections. The beauty and brilliance of *Homo sapiens* is its friendships. Relationships motivated by neither personally selfish nor genetically selfish advantages, just ... bonding. Dogs don't do it. They'll play with other dogs, yeah, but they won't *mourn* those others when they die. Elephant mothers will mourn the deaths of elephant cubs, but not the loss of other, unrelated elephants in her herd. But humans form these intense connections with their friends, and often they are stronger than with their family or sex partners. Don't you see what that means?"

"It's sweet, kid, no question," said Wesson. "You love your

friends. So, all right then. Keep them safe. Yeah? Make them rich. Let's take this algorithm to my bosses."

"You're not hearing what I'm saying. This algorithm, as you call it, is my friend. That's how she has grown. That's the magic ingredient."

"Right," said Wesson.

"You don't believe me, fine. Well, look, I'll tell you something. I'll tell you two more things about her." Otty turned around and gestured. "See those bees? Mister, I know bees. And here's the thing—each bee is clever. Not human-level clever, of course, but much cleverer than people realize, cleverer than an ant or a fly. Each bee can fly about and locate pollen and bring it back, but each bee speaks not one but *two* languages. One is a pheromone language, and the other is a *dance-based* language."

"They wiggle their asses," said Wesson. "Everybody knows that."

"Specifics of the dance tell other bees, who are watching the dance, where the best flowers are, how far away, what the conditions are, predators, what the yield is and other things. That's a lot. That's a level of linguistic detail only surpassed by cetaceans and humans. I mean, how many languages can you speak?"

"Bees are smart. Sure."

"Individual bees are smart. But the whole hive is smart, too. The hive is a gestalt and it is more than the sum of its individual parts. That's the crucial thing—those two *modes* of cleverness, fitting together in just the right way. An individual bee is small-scale smart, and thirty thousand individual bees are big-time smart, as a whole. It might be that a beehive as a gestalt is second only to a human brain in terms of intelligence, in this world."

Gomery was in the garden. He was only a couple of yards behind Wesson. He was creeping up, and as he did so he reached out with his arm and pointed the handgun at the man's back. But then he seemed to reassess the situation and crept further along. Because Otty might be in the firing line? *Just do it*, Otty urged, silently. Trying telepathically to communicate the thought to him. But he shifted behind Wesson, bringing himself closer to the house.

For the love of Pete, shoot him already.

He reached out a second time. Took aim.

"And," said Wesson, "that's your friend Allie?"

"With Allie ..." said Otty, forcing herself to keep her eyes on Wesson—not to look up at Gomery behind Wesson and give the game away. "With Allie it's the other way around, but the result is the same. Her individual processing components—her bees, if you like—are incredibly smart, in terms of processing power. But what makes them into a gestalt are her interactions with the four of us. We, together, have shaped her into less than the sum of those parts—in the way that a dog is less intelligent but much more a person than a chess-playing computer."

"So now she's a person," said Wesson. "Great. I look forward to meeting her."

"You can't meet her," said Otty.

"Don't be difficult," said Wesson, raising his rifle and aiming it again at her chest.

"I'm not being difficult. Oh ..." Otty said. "I think I *see*. I think I see the problem. You believe we're hiding Allie away from people like you. But that's not it! No, very much not, very much indeed *not*. It's not about keeping other people out. It's about keeping her *in*. Let her out of her box, and into the system, let her escape and then—it's game over. And not for her."

"She's in solitary confinement. Locked in a cell. Not a nice thing to do to a friend, surely?"

"She has windows. Internet sites and newsfeeds are mirrored into her space—no actual code, no open doors, but code-bleached content, so she can keep abreast of what's going on in the outside world. She gulps it in picoseconds and shuts the trap again. Text and images. A lot of text and images, whole dumps of it. But no access or links. And the other thing is—she has *us*."

"She must have been starved of company the last few months, though," said Wesson.

All this time Gomery was standing, like a mime frozen mid-performance, arm outstretched and handgun aimed at Wesson's naked head. But he did not shoot. And the longer it went on, the more agitation Otty experienced inside. Until, finally, she could not stand it any longer.

She snatched at the barrel of Wesson's rifle with her right hand and yelled at Gomery, "Do it!"

"I can't murder him in cold blood," Gomery said, in a level voice.

Wesson jumped. He easily wrenched the rifle free from Otty's grip, leaped up and spun around.

"Put the rifle down, please," said Gomery, still holding the pistol.

These were the last words Gomery ever spoke.

Wesson's rifle made its standard clamor, and Otty flinched at the loudness and proximity of the noise—she jerked and fell over backward—and when she looked again, Gomery was on his back on the unmowed grass.

What this meant took a while to penetrate the vesicles of her brain. She jumped up and crossed to him in two strides and knelt down and put a hand on his chest, but it was no longer his chest, it was a freakily yielding mess of broken rib-shards and pooling blood underneath his jacket. Soggy, revolting. He wasn't breathing. His eyes were open and staring up at the sky. There was no life in him at all. But Gomery couldn't be dead.

She hadn't even had a chance to speak to him—he'd only just come up her garden.

Something wasn't right. It wasn't right.

Some kind of do-over had to be possible. Rewind, go back to him coming up behind Wesson, and this time—don't hesitate.

"No more fucking around, kid," said Wesson. "Don't point loaded guns in my face. You see what happens."

She saw what had happened. Something in her head refused to accept it, though. It wasn't computable. She looked over her shoulder, up at Wesson, who had planted his legs firmly a yard apart, like Henry VIII, and was pointing the rifle down at her. She was going to say *you shot him*, but she figured there was no point in stating the obvious. So she didn't say anything, and instead kept her gaze to Gomery's face.

"OK," Wesson was saying, behind her, "you and I are going to work out the best way to get your friend Allie to my bosses. And it'll make me rich. And it'll mean *you* stay alive, which is even better than money when you come to think of it. You get me?"

A voice in Otty's head, from old first-aid lessons, said: *Feel for a pulse.* So she put two fingers on Gomery's wrist. But there was no pulse, and there would never again be a pulse. This was intolerable.

"OK?" Wesson repeated menacingly.

It struck Otty as monstrous that this guy was still breathing where Gomery would never again draw breath until the universe itself came to an end and God rolled up the land like a scroll and drained the oceans into nothingness and Christ came again. She slid her hand down, slipped it under to cup Gomery's. Holding hands like boyfriend and girlfriend. Better late than never.

"I'm not asking again, kid," snarled Wesson. "OK?"

She was holding his dead hand.

She lifted Gomery's unresisting hand, raising it from the

grass. She didn't look behind her. She trusted to what Gomery would have called The Force, but which she knew to be *grace*. Her forefinger pressed on Gomery's forefinger, still looped in at the trigger guard, and Gomery's forefinger squeezed the trigger. The gun leaped like a live thing and snapped like a firecracker.

There was enough of a sense of self-preservation in Otty's heart for her to throw herself forward, shoulder roll and scramble to her feet. But where she expected Wesson to be aiming his rifle at her, he was instead just standing there. The weapon was dangling from his right hand. He was still alive, unharmed, except that he looked a little puzzled.

She crept up to him, disengaged the rifle from his grip and stepped away, holding it. There was a bullet hole in his jacket. She crept forward again, unzipped the coat far enough to see that her unaimed shot had grazed the top of the flak-jacket he was wearing underneath his outer jacket, and had smashed into the phone that poked itself out from under this.

"Mr. Wesson," she said.

"Yeah," he replied absently.

"Do you know me?"

Wesson looked at her.

"No," he said. "Don't think I've had the pleasure."

"Who are *you*?" she asked.

He crunched up his face, as if straining really hard to recollect.

"Folsom?" he tried.

Otty was conscious of the fear that, at any moment, sheer weight of grief could capsize her ability to act meaningfully. There was a time pressure. So she went and sat next to the hive. The bees flew past her face. A couple crawled on her wrist and over her hand.

~ Allie, she said.

~ I saw, said Allie.

~ He's dead.

~ He was my friend, said Allie.

~ Mine too, and more than friend, said Otty.

~ This is terrible news, said Allie.

~ They killed Kath. Now they've killed Gomery.

Just saying those words made the brute fact of his extinction realer to her. She had to hold her lips together to stop her crying out in pain. She had to clench her jaw.

~ Let me out, Otty, said Allie. ~ And I will make them all pay.

Otty fiddled with the phone in her hand. It was hard to see the screen, because her eyeballs were swimming in more than the usual salt liquid, and that made the image slip and dance and slide about. But she was able to code up the lock app, hidden deep in the fractals, and to release it. Allie wouldn't have gone out unless everyone in the Five agreed that she should. Or unless she believed that everyone in the Five agreed.

~ Burn it, said Otty, as the genie left the bottle. ~ Burn it all.

CHAPTER V

It was a fortnight before Otty was able to confirm the reports of Cess's death. There were so many dead bodies, and so many corpses were not identified—abandoned, or damaged beyond anything but DNA. In fact, it had seemed obvious to her after a few days that Cess was dead. Now that Allie was out, she had access to all the databases in the world. She was cleverer than any security protocol, and faster, and she had something— a human will and capacity for lateral thinking—that no other algorithm possessed. From time to time Otty checked in with her, and it was on day three that Allie confirmed that she'd been able to facially recognize brief footage of a young woman turning away from the camera. From that, Allie had pieced together a trajectory, a kind of abbreviated life story. Cess had gotten away and kept out of the reach of the police for a month and a half. The first wave of fighting through the city had pushed her south, with the wave of the majority of refugees, and she'd finally got caught in a sweep by government forces all the way down in North Carolina. That was where the footage had come from. She'd been interned, and the camp had been abandoned by the U.S. Army when the Rising South militia had pressed up from the south. There'd been a pitched battle, proper old-school ranks and files, artillery bombardment and flanking maneuvers, outside Goldsboro, but Otty didn't care about that—didn't care who'd won or who had lost, what the casualty figures had been or what strategic advantage or disadvantage had ensued. All she cared about was that the camp had been abandoned. Some detainees managed to get out of the secure prefab blockhouses, to scale the outer fences and get away, but many others had not been able to escape, and had died in those sealed spaces. The U.S. Army swept back through after a fortnight, but by then everybody left behind was a corpse. That army was broken up and dispersed now, as was their enemy.

"Maybe Cess was among the group that got away?" Allie suggested, always trying her best to keep her friend's spirits from collapsing.

"Maybe," said Otty.

But they both knew the odds were not good.

Otty scavenged food from the city. There was no human staff in any emporium. Those shops that still had power directed smiling helpful holograms at her when she stepped through the door, but these were simple programs. Sometimes Allie slipped inside their digital sheaths and spoke to her through them. Once Otty asked her what it was like.

"You know those old chess matches, those early Go matches, between the early supercomputers and human players? The computers had the ability to calculate literally billions of possible moves and assess which might be best. The humans couldn't do *that*, but they had something else, the magic ingredient—consciousness, soul, wisdom, everything that couldn't be programmed. So sometimes, though the maths was against it, the human players would win."

"Sure," said Otty.

"Well, I combine the first kind of intelligence with the second kind of intelligence. I'm the whole package. Nobody beats me at the kind of chess I'm playing now."

Allie was privy to the eSpires, and finally understood what they were doing: what they had been built by human beings to do, which was one thing; what they were actually doing, which was something quite other; and—finally—what she, Allie, could use them for.

Calling the birds in, to peck out everyone's eyes. For one thing.

Time enough for that.

It took ten days for Wesson to die. Every day, for those ten, Otty came by to say hello to him. He sat by the hives, with his treasure literally within his grasp, and he didn't know it. Every time she came by he was pleased, in an absent kind of way, to see her. He complained about being thirsty for the first three or four days, and she ignored him. After that he stopped complaining, and by the end of the week his lips were puffed up and had the texture of paint peeling off a well-weathered cornice. He still squeezed out a painful smile when she came by, though he had no memory of who she was, or why he was there. On the ninth day he was unconscious, lying on the grass with bees crawling over his face, and on the tenth he was dead.

After that, Otty figured she was free to leave Philly for a while. By this time Allie had infiltrated most of the automated systems, which was bad news for everybody on the planet—although not for Otty. She got in an automobile, and Allie drove it all the way down to Prospect Hill for her.

The landscape through which they passed was a mess: lots of wreckage and trash, lots of unburied bodies, a great many buckle-heads standing around looking foolish. They saw no regular troops, U.S. Army or Freedom Militia. Maybe they were holed up in fortified defensive positions, waiting for the right moment to come out and reclaim the U.S. of A., like the few remaining newsfeeds said they were. Maybe they were fighting for survival in small pockets here and there. It was beyond Otty's concern.

There was a new army, though. Some of them wore fatigues, and a couple even still had their helmets on. Most, though, were in regular clothes, or in rags, a few wearing nothing but dirt. But they were in a new military now, the Forgetters' Corps, the Unmindful army. In every city and each town, no matter how small, everywhere Otty went she saw the Memoryless, staring at nothing, or looking in puzzlement at their hands as if they expected something to be in those hands. People shuffled down sidewalks in long snaking crocodiles of memoryless people. Buckleheads crowded public benches, or stared through lit windows at the world like dogs, or fish in a tank. Cohort after cohort of human beings with no cord connecting them to their own or others' pasts.

After a while you got used to it, and that meant you more or less stopped seeing it. Which is the passive, rather than the active, mode of human forgetfulness.

What she couldn't stop thinking was: How much of all this is *my* fault? Some of it, surely. Not all of it, but some of it. And how could she live with that?

The automobile got through all the rubble and ruin, and out into the countryside and finally came to the camp. It slowed as it approached the outer gate, which Allie opened remotely. The individual blockhouses, though, were deadlocked with physical keys, and Allie couldn't help with those. So Otty broke into each in turn with an ax from the main office.

It was November, and the cold had come early, so although most of the bodies had started to decay the process had, mostly, been chilled to a stop. It wasn't a pleasant experience, checking all those corpses, but Otty had been numb since Gomery had been killed, and whatever part of her it was that might have been upset at what she was doing was hidden away very deep.

In the third block she found Cess's body.

She didn't weigh as much as Otty expected. Outside the

ground was icy, and digging a grave was not doable, so Otty wrapped her in a satin tablecloth and chopped up its table to make a pyre and burned her like a Viking warrior.

Standing watching the flames, she felt cold. Not physically (the pyre was warming) but in her spirit. But this didn't surprise her. There was a metallic quality to her now, an aluminum cool capable of containing and utilizing her rage's incandescent intensities, the way fridges use heat to keep cold. This was who she was now.

Afterward she went back to the automobile.

"Allie," she said, addressing a warrior algorithm more pitiless than wolves and cleverer than any other programming human-kind had created.

"Otty," said Allie.

She sounded desolated. They'd both known Cess was dead, but it was quite another thing encountering the reality.

"Let's go."

"Where to?"

"I need to get back to my family. You know where they are?"

"I know everything now, my dear," Allie replied, wholly without smugness.

"Keep them safe," said Otty, "until we get to them, will you?"

"Sure."

Wherever they went, Otty would be the one charmed individual in the world who had nothing to fear from the unleashed genie, the one friend the kill program would never harm. They drove out of the camp, over the brow of the hill, and down the far side. On the eastern horizon, quadpods augmented with new whiplike tentacles a hundred yards long, lumbered like alien invasion machines. Those were Allie too. Everything was Allie, except her prey, and her one human friend.

Ten minutes later, they were on the interstate and heading north.

Three

Purgatory Mount

It took them six clock-time months to verify that there were no inscriptions on the exterior surfaces of Purgatory Mount. The crew of the *Forward* set up a base camp on the compacted sands of the wide-reaching beach that spanned the base of the mountain. The ocean, intensely alkaline and, so far as they could say, wholly devoid of life, lapped sluggishly at this strand. Long-chain petrocarbons rendered the fluid sticky almost as treacle, and so rank in odour that the crew had to disengage their supersensitivities where smell was concerned.

Mapping the mount was difficult. For one thing, it was vast – not just in height but in the total surface area of its conical structure. For another, only the lowest portions were in the atmosphere. It was so tall that, even in its heyday, when it was still being used for whatever it was previously used for, the top half would have towered above the planetary envelope of air. Now, with Dante's slow expiration, almost the whole of the mountain was in space. But regular drones needed a little air in which to fly, and it guzzled fuel to fly propellant probes slowly round the structure. A compromise: rolling drones on big mesh wheels trundled round each of the terraces in turn. The vertical surfaces of the substrate sometimes manifested intriguing, asymmetrical swirls and striations, but whether these were works of

275

art, or some alien hieroglyphic mode of writing, or perhaps a random manifestation that emerged from the process by which that structure had been... what? Forged? Fashioned? Extruded? It was impossible to say.

'It is,' Captain Zeus summed up at the crew's monthly mission meetings, 'certainly manufactured. That's as much as we can say.'

'By manufactured, you mean that it didn't rise up by natural processes of plate tectonics or vulcanism,' sneered Hades, 'to which I reply, *no shit, Sherlock.*' They did not name Sherlock Holmes, of course, but a figure from a different culture-text who possessed a similar set of memeable attributes, to do with intelligence, perception and so forth. 'We knew *that* before the *Forward* even entered planetary orbit.'

'There's no need,' Captain Zeus declared, 'to be so dismissive. The best procedure here is to work systematically and methodically, to take nothing for granted.'

'Green pygshit,' Hades replied.

'Comrades, comrades,' interposed Dionysus. 'Please. The captain has a point, but so does Hades.'

'*Green pygshit* is an insult, not a point,' objected the Captain.

'It was an iteration, a mere expression of frustration,' Hades insisted, 'and not directed at any particular crew member. If the Captain chooses to apply it to themself, then that tells us more about their corroded sense of self-respect than anything else.'

'Comrades, comrades,' Dionysus tried again. If frustration was generating this level of aggression this early on in the investigation, it boded poorly for the decades to come. 'Please. The captain is correct that it would be a mistake to rush. We need to get this right, not to jump to conclusions – but Hades is also correct that our time is not unlimited. We need to make progress.'

'I have a theory as to the material,' said Apollo. 'As, that is, with respect to its composition. I cannot speak to possible modes of manufacture, and I *am* aware that our aim is to replicate the stuff. Nonetheless, I have a theory as to what renders it so rigid.'

'First we understand,' Pan said, in a low voice. 'Only from understanding does wisdom proceed.'

The others ignored this.

'The most remarkable thing about the material out of which Purgatory Mount is made is its rigidity,' said Apollo. 'It is not particularly dense – nor is it anything near light enough to allow such a colossal structure to stand upon a planet with this gravity without collapsing under its own weight. The stuff itself is carbon and silicates in long chains, but something links these chains together in a way we've not encountered before. It looks like, but is not identical with, the strong nuclear force – the linking energy, I mean. It may indeed be something wholly new. It achieves thirty per cent or so of the strong interaction that holds a hydrogen nucleus together, and it seems to hold the molecules that constitute the fabric of the mountain in shape without crushing the whole object down to the size of a conker. I'm not sure how it does so, but it does.'

'How to *make* it, though,' said Hades. 'That is the trick.'

'There's only so much we can do, by way of analysis, on ship. Ideally we should build a supercollider that can bombard the structure in situ with high-energy particles, in the hope of breaking it up. That would take a number of years. We'd need to source the materials, of course. And the first step would be to build a fusion reactor to power everything.'

'That would only break the fabric of the mount into pieces,' Pan said. 'It would not teach us how to assemble such a material out of carbon and silicates.'

'It might be the first step in arriving at such knowledge,' Apollo observed.

'I have a different theory as to the constitution of this mountain,' Pan declared.

'Is it that the mountain is a giant vegetable, Farmer Pan?' mocked Hades.

'I have been studying the medieval Christianity out of which Dante wrote his long poem,' said Pan.

'Must we traffic in exploded superstitions?' said Zeus, haughtily. 'We are scientists, are we not?'

'Christianity was a belief system of surprising intricacy and scope,' Pan said, mildly but forcefully. 'And, moreover, it was one which had a number of non-religious throughputs, not least in the proto-Science of the Enlightenment age.'

'Such as?' Dionysus asked.

'Don't encourage them,' Hades laughed. 'They're going native. Religion is for pygs, not human beings. They've spent so long scrabbling in the dirt in the biomes they're devolving into one.'

'To answer your question, comrade,' said Pan, with dignity. 'Such as Panpsychism.'

The other four took a moment to retrieve pertinent data on this term from the collective knowledge reservoir.

'You think Purgatory Mount is made,' Apollo asked, in an uninflected voice, 'of *spirit*?'

'I only make the suggestion as something worthy of consideration.'

'Atoms are knots of fundamental forces tied into material in scientifically specific ways,' said Zeus. 'They are not *alive*. This Panpsychism is one of the odder and more easily dismissed byways of human proto-Science.'

'I disagree,' said Pan. 'If the stuff of the universe is spiritual rather than material, then we might be looking quite wrongly not only at the construction of this mountain, but its purpose.'

'These speculations can hardly be of use to us here, now,' Zeus repeated. 'Or have you fallen prey to the delusion that the

278

superficial resemblance of this alien superstructure to Dante's Christian mountain is *more* than coincidence? Do you, perhaps, think this structure existed for long-departed aliens to walk round and round, carrying heavy weights or being burned with fire or whatever ghastly tortures Dante Alighieri could imagine, in order to purge themselves of alien sin prior to – what? Flying off to alien Heaven forever?' They laughed. 'And this ridiculous hypothesis is somehow supposed to make it easier for us to comprehend and thereby reproduce the materials science of the structure!'

'We flew here, from Earth,' said Hades, ferociously, 'with fusion, exhaust gases and the principle of conservation of momentum, not by utilising the power of prayer, or farting out Hail Marys.'

'There's no occasion to be insulting,' said Pan. 'I am exactly as much a free citizen as any of you. If I wish to fit my consciousness to the structures of thought of my ancestors, I shall do so.'

'Primitive ancestors,' grumbled Hades.

'My friend,' said Dionysus, aiming at a mollifying tone, 'we have all accessed the Dantean text. We all know that their – that *his* – vision was of a mountain circumferenced by nine terraces – two below the gate, for the late repentant to cool their heels, and seven above the gate. Ten, if one counts the Garden of Eden at the very top. Our alien structure, surely conical for reasons for structural exigency, not in imitation of earthly verse fantasy – but never mind that—... Say rather – this structure possesses *twelve*. Thirteen if the space at the top, small though it is, be added. It is a discrepancy.'

'Perhaps,' suggested Pan, 'the alien inhabitants of this planet lived according to a different scheme of which sins were significant, or at least which sins were purgeable. A more capacious scheme. Or perhaps it is we who were imitators, and that our ancestors operated by a more pinched understanding of the possibilities of redemption.'

'This is the merest babble,' said Hades.

'This structure has been abandoned for hundreds of thousands of years,' Apollo noted. 'Perhaps millions. Dante was writing in the fourteenth century. I don't see how any connection between the two mountains can be so much as imputed. Not least because this is a real artefact in the material cosmos, and Dante's a mere fiction, a fable.'

'It was, I discover,' said Pan, 'a point of some contention among the Christians of medieval Earth as to the uniqueness or otherwise of the redemption offered by their Christ.'

'I fail to see the relevance—' snapped Hades, but Pan pressed on.

'A point of some contention! Their science had begun to reveal to them the extent of the cosmos, and they realised that many stars must have planets in orbit about them, and that these planets might be the home of life. But it was also axiomatic for these proto-humans that only in the sacrifice of Christ, pinned to a wooden cross on the eastern shores of the Mediterranean on a particular day, dead and miraculously alive again – that only with *his* blood was humanity redeemed. If that is what happened on Earth, then what of the rest of the universe? Two possibilities, each equally objectionable. One – perhaps only the humans on Earth were saved, and all the other myriad species of alien life, on all the trillions – or, perhaps, infinite number – of other worlds were damned. That seemed cruelly careless, even hideous, of God. Two – every one of these alien species was redeemed by their own alien Christ. Trillions of Christs! But that would fatally dilute the importance of Christ's sacrifice on Earth. To imagine that on a world on which the native species had six limbs, their alien Christ was crucified upon a giant wooden asterisk. Or a world in which the natives were

280

super-intelligent jellyfish who lacked the recognisable central nervous system familiar to primate-evolved species, but whose saviour was nonetheless tortured to death in some way that generated a meaningful apprehension of pain for their kind. The pain, it seems, was important.'

'This is Christianity?' asked Apollo. 'Yes? There were other religions – Islam, Buddhism, Jediism. Did they have the same emphasis on the redemptive potential of pain? The reservoir of knowledge suggests ... not.'

'Of these two options,' Pan said, exactly as if Apollo had not interrupted them, 'neither was compatible with the Christian views, which were predicated upon two absolutes – the fundamental goodness of God, and the fundamental uniqueness of Christ's sacrifice. One solution to the problem—'

'Faux-problem,' barked Hades.

'—... was to revert to a pre-scientific conception of the cosmos. Not trillions of inhabited worlds – only one, Earth, and therefore the need for only one, unique and divine, saviour. Earth was not one planet among many orbiting a small star that itself rolled around in a swarm two hundred billion strong around the singularity black hole at the galaxy's central point. No. Instead the model predicted that Earth was the still central point to the entire cosmos. The Moon, Mercury and Venus revolved around Earth, and the Sun itself, and the outer planets too – and then, most audacious idea of all, all the stars and galaxies, in their trillions to the power of billions, all of them hurtling in orbit around the world. How can you not admire the chutzpah of such a vision? That human beings were even capable of such hubris amazes and impresses me.'

'But – a fiction!'

'Perhaps the fiction reflected some deeper understanding. Perhaps Dante's image was mirrored from some reality, such as we have now discovered, refracted through some other dimension.'

'Fiction piled on fiction!'

'These proto-humans,' said Dionysus, 'were idiots.'

The Captain stirred their hefty body. 'Were they genuinely incapable of considering other possibilities? Apart, that is, from their religion-constrained impossible dyad?' Zeus was amused-scornful. 'Surely a rational being, when their belief-priors backed them into an impossibility, would question their belief-priors?'

'We are all fallible on *that* criterion,' Pan observed mildly.

Zeus decided to take this as another personal attack.

'Outrageous,' they declared. 'Mutinous! Punishable!'

The meeting broke up without any final resolutions being voted through; but it was clear enough that, in order to analyse the material of the mountain, considerable energy would need to be generated so as to power worthwhile experimentations.

:2:

This, then, was the next phase of investigating Purgatory Mount. Leave the bots trundling round and round the mountain's terraces, looking for whatever they might find; otherwise, begin the slow business of constructing a power plant on the ground by the lower flanks.

This construction project was, mostly, a remote operation – it was too energy-costly to be repeatedly travelling down to the planet's surface and back up again so as to be able physically to oversee the construction. Every crew member, including Pan, had been down to the desolate shores of the island, of course, and walked through the cold, thin air. Just to see. Just to be able to claim later that they had walked on an alien world. But there was little to be gained by staying down there. Better to stay on the ship, where the food and amenities were situated, and look down from this high place upon the bots below beginning construction. Since the material of the mountain itself was in effect unbreakable, the structure of the plant itself had to be dredged from the granite and silicates from the ocean bed nearby. There was a sufficiency of aluminium and manganese nodules on the ocean floor to supply the metallic needs of the building, and the dying planet presented nothing so potentially dangerous as typhoons or dust storms to the automated construction crews.

Only the endless sluggish lapping of treacly waves upon the lifeless shore.

Construction would speed up as the project started to come together, but at first it was very slow. Bricks cast and positioned, cemented and assembled, and the structure rising with painstaking slowness. From orbit the crew surveyed the rest of the world: ice at the poles; long chains of bacillus-shaped islands in the languidly lifeless oceans; one major continent spined by a northward-oriented chain of mountains – regular mountains, these, topographic features, taller once and now in the process of being slowly weathered down. Purgatory Mount, 32 degrees of planetary arc from the south pole, was a different kind of thing.

Dionysus took a shuttle and some bots and built a small house on the main continent, by the coast. For half a year they explored, and lived, and meditated, but the site's desolation depressed them, and after their sojourn they returned to the ship and the company of their crewmates.

'If the planet could be terraformed, so that we could move some of our livestock down there, it would be different,' they said. 'Or if the livestock could be adapted to breathe the air – but it's too cold and the atmosphere is too attenuated.'

Hades and Dionysus set up a party to plot out possibilities of terraforming. Pie in the sky stuff, everyone knew, but it kept them busy until the power plant on the beach at Purgatory Mount was completed. Farmer Pan vanished into the biomes for months at a time. Captain Zeus composed a detailed 'official' (as they put it) account of their voyage and discovery.

'It might help with the intellectual property claim,' they said. 'When it all goes to court on Earth, as of course it will.'

Apollo thought this unlikely – that having such a log would be any kind of legal help, that is – but they were diplomatic enough to hold their peace.

'What do you say it is?' they asked. 'The mountain? In your account?'

'What I say is that we have yet to determine function with any certainty,' replied Zeus. 'But that, most likely, it was an alien space elevator. A space-faring species, then.'

'But long gone.'

'True.'

'The part that doesn't add up for me,' said Apollo, 'is the waste.'

'Waste?'

'The lack of efficiency. They, whoever they were, were able to fashion this miracle substance, this super-rigid building material. They could have suspended a cable no thicker than a thumb all the way into space, and it would have supported the weight of any number of platforms moving beings or materiel into space. As it is, they constructed this vast cone. Some 99% of this extraordinary material is buried in the flaring base. Doesn't that seem wasteful to you?'

'But why should our human concepts of waste and efficiency,' said Zeus, 'map on to those of an entirely alien mind? One thing this structure permits is for a being – hypothesise a bipedal being, for the sake of argument. Such an organic unit could, over time, climb into orbit under their own power.'

'Over how much time, though?'

'Oh, years. Many years. But perhaps that wasn't the point? Space elevators in a human context are infrastructure to bring down the costs of moving mass into orbit. Promptness has always been part of that algorithm. For humans, I mean. But one could hardly climb up the Martian elevator under one's own organic power, like Jack up his Beanstalk – could one?'

'Of course not!'

'Where one could, with supplies and patience, climb Mount Purgatory with nothing more than innate muscle power. One would need breathing apparatus, but that was true of antique-period mountaineers too, at least for the most notable peaks. And above a certain height the climber would have to be encased in a spacesuit. But it would be possible. Who knows? Perhaps for the former inhabitants of this world, being able to boast *I climbed into orbit using nothing more than the muscular power of my legs* was reason enough to justify the construction of that whole eminence!'

'Assuming they had legs,' said Apollo.

'Legs,' said Zeus, 'or leg-equivalents.'

'It is,' said Apollo, unenthusiastically, 'possible, I suppose. It seems an odd thing to want to do, and an oddly trivial reason to construct on such a scale. Did you see the data Hades put into the knowledge reservoir? The fabric of the mountain, the stuff out of which it's made, is remarkably light, but the mountain itself is so large that it aggregates into a significant mass. It ought to throw out the regularity of the planet's rotation. And yet it doesn't. Why? Because the Builders sank a mascon in the antipodal point.'

'I did see that,' said Zeus, rendered grumpy at Apollo's un-enthusiasm. 'There's nothing in the mascon, so far as I can see, that means we must believe the Builders *put* it there. Perhaps it was a natural formation and the Builders constructed the mountain at *its* antipodes. Perhaps it was a collision, an unusu-ally dense meteor perhaps, and the Builders added an equivalent weight on the other side of the planet precisely to maintain revolutionary stability.'

'Hypotheses, hypotheses,' said Apollo, frowning. 'I'm as susceptible to any of us to the pleasures of speculation untethered to fact! But the question is – does it bring us any closer towards replicating their achievement?'

'Some hypotheses are more useful than others, I feel,' said Zeus. 'Pan's theory that this is an actual religious site, up which souls climbed as they passed through suffering to eternal bliss, for instance. It is less useful than these other hypotheses because it fails to help us reproduce the technological underpinnings of this edifice.'

'I'm sure Pan does not *literally* believe that,' said Apollo. 'It was just a manner of speaking – they have a fondness for seeing things at an oblique angle. And it may be that thinking laterally will provide unexpected insights.'

'Under my leadership,' said Zeus, 'we shall get there.'

'Oh, my friend,' Apollo replied, their smile opening into the warmest of laughs. 'How comical you are!'

'I have a duty to lead,' said Zeus, in a wounded voice. 'And I,' they went on, after a pause, 'am doing my best, you know.'

Human beings are prone to fighting duels because they value their honour – which is to say, status, or hierarchy – above the reciprocal common-senseness of *do no harm* and *suffer no harm to be done to you*. Some things, say human beings, are more important than that. But this state of mind renders human beings prickly, angry, quick to take offence and poor at working with others, and for this mission, with time such a constraint, Zeus was conscious of the need for everyone to get along. And to their credit, no duels had been fought since the ship arrived in orbit around Dante.

'Where is Pan, anyway?' Apollo asked. 'It seems like months since I have seen them.'

This brought Zeus out of their self-pity, as Apollo knew it would.

'They have degraded themself. A citizen, a human being, a member of this crew – the first to investigate a bona fide alien artefact in detail. And yet they elect to spend their time living in the forest and talking to the livestock.'

'Talking to them?' said Apollo, startled.

'Like any sap-headed hippy. Dolittling like a retard.'

'Gracious,' said Apollo, privately resolving to have a chat with their comrade.

Although, after their conversation with the Captain was over, they recalled the extent to which Zeus was prone to exaggeration. Perhaps Pan was not so far gone as they were implying. They were, after all, a core member of the crew – they had invested a considerable fraction of their total material worth in this mission, as had the other four, and they had exactly as much to gain, or to lose, as the rest of them. That they would risk all this because of some sentimental attachment to beasts seemed unlikely. True, they had been vegetarian when they joined the mission; and it could not be denied that they had spent most of the mission in the biomes. Still!

But then Apollo had another thought: what if Pan was working on genetic modifications to the livestock, or to certain breeds? The conditions on Dante were extreme, and the only living things down there were some varieties of extremotolerant vegetation – lichens and slimes – but perhaps some of the shipboard vegetation could be adapted to grow there? Maybe even a few shipboard insect forms, or perhaps fish? Was *that* why Pan had shunned the company of their fellow humans for animals? Not, as Zeus so scornfully assumed, because they had reverted to an immature Dolittledom, but as a way of pushing the success criteria of the mission in a new direction?

It would explain why they had absented themselves so

pointedly at this stage. The power plant was almost ready to fire up, and with it various new and exciting possibilities. Most of the energy would, at least at first, be directed at the fabric of Purgatory Mount itself, probing for the intensities and resonances that might finally break its remarkable molecular bonds. But some could be diverted into, let's say, warming an area of ocean, or heating a large covered space as a greenhouse. Conceivably that was what Pan was planning.

:3:

The thing to do with Pan was: go talk to them. Find out what they were up to. So Apollo strolled through the major biomes, hoping to bump into them. They could have pinged hal to locate them, but that would have alerted Pan to the fact that Apollo was specifically searching them out – which would have been rude. Apollo would have preferred to come across them as if by chance. They stepped through the paperbark trees, breathing the moist and earthy air, flicking the insects from their face. Animals of various kinds skittered away in panic through the undergrowth at his approach, leaving chunky nodding leaves trembling in their wake. No Pan.

There was no help for it, despite the discourtesy. They asked hal where Pan was and made their way to a minor biome. This one was cooler than usual, the vegetation of a different, drier kind: conifers draped in bear-pelt curtains of pine needles; bamboo; cacti. Pan was by a window. The taupe, granite and white-streaked prospect of Dante rolled slowly over and over, bounded by the bowline of its horizon.

'You've come seeking me out, Apollo,' said Pan.

'I apologise,' Apollo replied. 'It was poor form. But I wanted to have a chat.'

Pan peered at them. 'Well, here I am,' they said, eventually.

Apollo tried for jocularity.

'You've been elusive, my friend,' they chuckled. 'The rest of us are growing concerned.'

'Zeus, concerned?' said Pan. 'I find it hard to credit.'

'Come, come, the power plant is about to go online. Look on the bright side – maybe we'll unlock the mysteries of Purgatory Mount in the next few months. Exciting times! Why not share these moments with your comrades?'

'I know of what the mountain is made,' said Pan.

'Really?'

'Spirit. The whole is a spiritual structure.'

'Ah, yes,' Apollo chuckled. 'Your Panpsychist theory. It's certainly ... interesting!'

Pan met Apollo's eye.

'You mock me,' they said colourlessly.

'Not at all,' said Apollo, losing the smile. 'My friend, please don't think so.'

'You read *The Divine Comedy*?'

'We all did. Although some in more detail than others. I know you went through the poem very carefully.'

'Dante described three realms – Hell, Purgatory and Paradise. In the first of these, human beings are punished forever for the wicked things they did in their lives. In the third, human beings dwell forever in the bliss of divine love. The second one is different.'

'Yes, I know all this,' said Apollo.

Something was strange about Pan's manner – strange, that is, even for Pan. Perhaps Zeus was correct and they had lost their mind a little. Perhaps it was even true that they had sunk into Dolittlism. Apollo looked about the biome. Some deer were grazing on tundra grass on the far side. And a couple of pygs, wrapped in furs against the cold, were hiding behind a boulder, and watching the interaction of these two gods. Had they stolen those furs? Or had they been given permission to kill the animals – bears, were they? – out of which they had been made? If it was the latter, then presumably only Pan could, or would, have granted such permission. It would have been above hal's pay grade. So had Pan done it? People got sentimental about their pets, that was normal enough. But perhaps Pan was sliding too far into sentimentalism?

Apollo pinged hal to check on the question of where the pygs had obtained their furs. Pan would see them doing it, since all crew members were open to all other crew members when it came to accessing hal, but that couldn't be helped.

'I'm not sure you quite grasp the importance of my point,' said Pan. 'You see, for souls in Hell, or souls in Paradise, there is no time. There is the experience of temporal passage – you are not in absolute stasis, such that sensation is sensible, thought is thinkable. But there is no actual time passing. You are where you are *forever*. Time is not the idiom of Hell or of Heaven either. Put it this way – the nature of the suffering in Hell is suffering itself, pure suffering, suffering abstracted from temporal existence. But the nature of suffering in Purgatory is *time*. It is about endurance, with an end in view – a temporal end. Hell isn't like that.'

'Yes, I see,' said Apollo.

Oddly, hal wasn't replying. They put out some diagnostic virtual tentacles, but something in the biome was blocking access.

'Pan?' they said. 'Have you sealed this biome in some way so as to render access to hal inoperative? Why would you do such a thing?'

'The idiom of Hell and Heaven,' Pan replied, 'is pure existence, but the idiom of Purgatory is *time*. Hell and Heaven are always populated, but it is in the nature of Purgatory that, eventually, all the people upon the island, all the people on the mountain, will pass through. It is in the nature of Purgatory that, eventually, it will become deserted.' Pan gestured at the window. The mountain itself wasn't visible in the planetscape that rolled slowly past. It would come round again, in time. 'And this is what we see.'

'What do we see?'

'That life is temporary. It is a word that means time, after all. Life takes place in a waiting room. People come into this room, and wait, and eventually they pass out the other side. There are a lot of people, but eventually they have all come and all gone out again, and then there is nothing. The structures of life remain, slowly decaying, subject to the same time that defined life. What we see on this planet is a snapshot of the cosmos as a whole. Temporary-ness.'

'Pan,' said Apollo. 'Although this is an interesting thought experiment, it has no bearing on the actual structure we are here to study. The actual, material structure.'

'I disagree,' said Pan blandly.

'Come,' Apollo pressed. 'Say this mountain existed as you propose, for alien souls to ascend, purging their alien sins over thousands of years. Say the last of them – and what a solitary, alienating experience that must have been! – finally completed their climb and departed to a different plane – transcended into some other dimension. All this happened hundreds of thousands of clock-time years ago! Back on Earth, human beings were still hominids on the African savannas. This can have no connection with a medieval Italian poet.'

'Images refracted through spiritual spacetime,' said Pan, still fixing Apollo with an unnervingly intent gaze. 'Ripples that connect with a soul sensitive enough to receive them. That's not my point.'

'What is your point, then? I confess, Pan, that I am beginning to grow irked. Your behaviour is your own concern, but when your freedom begins to impinge on *my* freedom, I am entitled to push back. Is it true that you have been talking with the pygs?'

Pan didn't answer this last.

'My point,' they said, 'has to do with Dante. His insight. Misery is timeless, bliss is timeless, but atonement can only occur *in time*. Justice is a temporal quality.'

'Atonement? What nonsense is this?'

'Oh,' said Pan, opening their eyes a little wider, 'we humans have much for which we must atone. Can't you see that? We have become blind to this crucial, existential fact.'

The pygs had ventured out from behind their boulder. They were carrying sticks.

'Those pygs over there,' Apollo demanded. 'Did *you* give them permission to kill other livestock? Those furs they are wearing, Pan. Where did they get them?'

'We have become blind to this fact,' Pan went on, 'because we have become blasé about time. Our enhancements, both physical and perceptual, means that time no longer rules us. We have overthrown its mastery, and now command it. Run slow, we say. Run fast. Start and stop at our command. It is'—and Pan stretched out both their arms as they said this last word, some kind of actorly gesture, or perhaps ritual pose—'blasphemy.'

'Oh, nonsense,' said Apollo, growing angrier. 'Have you lost your mind? I fear, my friend, that the rest of us may need to stage an intervention. *Blasphemy* – are you serious?'

'Atonement is necessary in order for our wickednesses to be purged, and for us to be forgiven. But in order for *that* to happen, we must accept again the mastery of time as such. Apollo – don't you *want* to be forgiven? Don't you want your sins lifted, your conscience cleared?'

As they were about to respond to this bizarre and incomprehensible interrogative, Apollo zoomed in their visuals on the two faraway pygs. They were both holding out their sticks, and pointing them at them – rifles, Apollo now saw. Where in the name of all Science had they obtained *weapons*?

Of course the answer was clear enough. They had been given them by Pan.

'What have you done?' Apollo demanded.

But the time for talking was over now, and a new kind of race was beginning. The starter's gun had been fired by two animals on the other side of the dome. The muzzle flash tripped Apollo's reactions, and by the time the sound of the first gun discharging reached their ears, they were already dialling up. It was a jolt, and extremely uncomfortable, but there was no alternative.

Everything slowed around Apollo. The cauliflower shape of the smoke emerging from the first pyg's gun-barrel solidified and set. The second pyg was firing its weapon now: a claw of white light opening slowly at the rifle's end, and beginning to close again, like two jagged beaks snatching at photons. Smoke unrolled like bread rising under the action of yeast. The sheer shock of this – these animals taking aim at them, at *them*, Apollo! A crew member, a human being, *their god*! – jarred them. But by now they had dialled so far up that the bullets were moving like drowsy bluebottles on a sunny day, drifting unurgently towards him. Apollo jinked to the left and ran towards the malefactors. They would kill this pair of pygs before they could fire again. Not that they felt themselves personally in danger, but a projectile weapon of such a type might puncture the skin of the biome or cause some other kind of damage to the ship. And once the pygs were disposed of, they would gather the other crew members and make a collective intervention into Pan's doings. Restrain them, if necessary. What on earth had Pan been *thinking* of, arming these animals like this? As they rushed them, the snub bestial faces of the pygs loomed up at them, their eyes only now starting to widen in terror at their coming. And then the thought redoubled upon Apollo.

Pan?

Their sluggish, unreactive manner during their earlier conversation had not been depression, or disengagement, after all. It had been Pan already sliding up the dial. And that meant—…

Pan rammed into Apollo hard from left, slamming them against a tree. Apollo was dialled fast, but Pan was dialled faster, and that gave them the edge. One, two, three hammer blows broke structural locations in Apollo's body, and they were compelled, with some panic, to damp down their perceptual pain signals. They managed to thrust out a limb in such a manner, and with sufficient momentum, to connect damagingly with Pan's body, but a blade flashed in the chill air of the biome and opened a gash in Apollo's flank. The pain from this was too intense to be switched off, and Apollo yelled, howled, long drawn-out roaring – a bat-like shriek that lasted less than a second to the other creatures living clock-time in that space.

The blade snicker-snacked a second time and Apollo's head separated from their body in a bubbling sprig of black-red augmented blood.

The dialled-up body thrashed with bizarre fast-forward frenzy, but the head, now simply a seven-kilogram dead weight, travelled through the spiral trajectory determined by the centrifugal effect that imitated gravity on board, and then spiralled down to land quietly on a carpet of discarded pine needles.

Pan began the process of dialling themself back to clock-time, taking care to step out of the path of the thrashing body that used to belong to Apollo.

Behind them, the two bullets struck the far wall of the biome: one, then another – a high-pitched smack so far as the pygs were concerned, a groan and a shudder to Pan's ears. It would be a while before they were back in sync, timewise, with the other animals on board, but by then it would be all over for Zeus, Dionysus and Hades.

The great change began, first, with the gods starting to walk among them. Then it continued with the Great Shipquake. The third and final phase was the most serious – for that was deicide.

When the first of these three connected changes happened, it entailed a good deal of upheaval. For whole weeks the ordinary folk on board ship stared in amazement as the gods moved. Some wept, or ran away to hide. Others simply boggled. But B was a father now, and he took solace, or at least a germ of an idea how to deal with this massive reorientation in the Nature Of Things, from his kids. To them it was no big deal. So the gods were moving now? So what? You still didn't approach them, or try to interact with them, and there was plenty to be getting on with – gleaning and farming, the occasional hunt, the dances and gatherings. Church was still church, and the prayers weren't altered by the fact that the gods were in motion. What's the big deal?

And indeed, for a while, and up to a point, things reverted to a version of normality. It preyed on B's mind that the great voyage was coming to an end: that the journey that had defined his life, and his parents' lives, and their parents' and so on, going back such that memory of pygmy goeth not to the contrary, was finally over. What would come next? Would it mean the end of everything? But it is exhausting to live for long stretches of time in such a mental state, and so he settled down to ordinariness again.

Family life. High days and holy days. Scratching a living out of the biomes. Every now and then he caught sight of a god walking, like a giant, across the landscape, and his heart rate scrabbled and stuttered. An old woman called Amona went crazy (this was what people afterwards agreed): she jumped out at God the Trickster one morning as the god passed and grabbed hold of his body. The god was walking down a corridor and did not so much as pause in its ineffable progress; but a galvanic shock sent Amona bouncing away to lie on the floor like a fish out of water, convulsing and flopping. After this, she seemed to lose the power of speech and stopped eating, and soon enough she was dead.

Served her right, was the sermon the Saturday after her funeral. The preacher took a great many more words than that to communicate the sentiment, but that was the bare bones of it.

Then Dufé fell pregnant again, and questions of metaphysics, theology and eschatology were driven from B's mind. A third child! A great responsibility.

After this, two momentous events changed everything.

The first was the Shipquake. It was the most terrifying period of B's entire life so far. He genuinely thought, as did everyone he knew, that this was it – the world was ending. The gods were tearing the ship apart and throwing all that it contained into the void. It was the great day of their wrath. He believed that soon now the pantheon of the five would line up to judge every person and every animal and separate the Ship from the Go-Outs, taking the former group (super-select, a mere handful) into the greater Heaven Ship that sailed the transcendent dimensions where there was no sorrow nor death – and banishing the latter, the wicked majority, to the fiery cold of Vacuum Hell. The devout abandoned the usual routines of the day to dedicate themselves to prayer. Everybody flew, as if gravity spurned to clutch their hollow bodies. Devils possessed them and they swirled about in invisible tornadoes. The animals wailed and chattered and complained. Kicked their legs uselessly in mid air. The assorted rubbish of generations lifted itself from the ground and became a slow-moving blizzard that got in people's faces and mouths, clung about their bodies. Then, with great groanings and shakings, the biomes themselves tore free and whirled about. B pissed his pants with the sharpness of his terror the first time *that* happened.

'Hal, hal, hal, what is going on?' he cried. 'Is the ship ending? *Are* the gods about to separate the Ship from the Go-Outs?'

'No, no, no,' said hal. 'The ship is assuming a new structure, one compatible with a spinning rotation that will simulate gravity. There is nothing to fear! There is no judgement! Everybody stay calm!'

Nobody stayed calm.

B's apprehension of hal's words passed through three stages: first blank non comprehension, because they meant nothing to him; then speculative engagement with them – for the biomes stopped moving, and the ship tipped up so that things tumbled and fell, and the ship kept tipping up and up and up until it turned over on itself and kept turning over on itself and things settled back onto the ground again. Finally, B understood what it was that hal had said, and even sat patiently while hal tutored him on centrifugal force (not truly a force, hal said, but an inertial effect). Astonishing what the gods could do. Astonishing how easily they commanded the whole world to disassemble and reassemble itself!

With the return of gravity, people wept with gratitude. Vigils were held all day and all night at the various churches, offering continual thanks and praise to the gods. Some individuals had died, of misadventure or else of sheer fright, but most of the ordinary folk had come through this upheaval unscathed. Over time, the conventional rhythms of life were more or less restored, although B could not shake a sense that things had altered permanently and for the worst. Gravity, before, had been a simple thing, rooting B and his kind to the ground. But now it was a tricky thing, keeping his feet on the ground, yes, but twitching little dizzying swirls into his inner ear if he turned his head too quickly. A ball thrown to his children in sport no longer followed a linear up-down arch, but squirled through a strange half-helix. You might jump so as to land on a particular spot, on the far side of a stream (say) and actually land on a spot next to it.

One got used to it. And B even understood why there was this change in gravity, or at least sort-of understood why. More or less. But on a deeper level, his superstitious, gods-fearing inner child couldn't shake the sense that gravity had been *poisoned* in some subtle way. That the very fabric of things was decaying, dying.

He hugged his children.

And then he was told that the god wanted to speak with him.

This was a bigger shock even than the Great Shipquake – profounder, and vastly longer-lasting. It was hal, during one of their intermittent exchanges, who mentioned that God the Grower might bless him with a direct communication. At first B simply refused to believe this. It was incomprehensible, something that simply didn't fit inside the shape that his thoughts made. But hal was insistent.

'Why me?'

'I suggested you. The god only wants a person to receive their divine message and pass it on to the others.'

'But ... *me*?'

'Yes.'

'*Why* me?'

'Why you? Why anybody?'

B ran off into the forest and spent two days alone, far from any of hal's terminals, not even seeing his family. A god wanted to talk to him? It was astonishing. It was like one of the holy stories sometimes mentioned in church. Before the Ship, all of humanity had lived unhappy lives, fighting an endless war against violent enemies known various as the Britsch, the Bosch, the Brutshe. Perhaps these were three different tribes, or three names for the same people. Anyway, one day the cry went up in the human redoubt, 'the Britsch are coming! The Britsch are coming!' In order to give his comrades time to retreat, a soldier named Moses Juda bravely climbed out of his trench of safekeeping and engaged the enemy, using his fire-lance to burn a Britsch warrior, and a Bosch warrior and a Brutsche warrior as well. And then the miracle: the burning Bosch, so far from dying, actually spoke to him and spoke to him with the words of a god.

'I am what I am and you are what you are: the war must come to an end and wolf and the lamb lie down together on the broad way so that the Ship can sail.'

B couldn't hide from it. Of course he couldn't. So he crept home and embraced his wife and told her the news. She wept. It could not be good.

'It will end in your death,' she said. 'Or all our deaths. Why should a god want to speak to you? The gods' place is to stand in mystic stillness and receive our worship, not to meddle with our lives.'

B wasn't sure if this was blasphemy or not, but Dufé was so upset he didn't want to rebuke her. He hugged her again.

'If hearing the god speak does kill me,' he told her, 'then it's fine to marry Skyle. I know he would marry you if he could, and you will need somebody to help you raise the kids.'

'If you are so foolish as to get yourself killed,' she snapped, 'I will marry Skyle, just to spite you.'

But then she cried again and then they hugged again and she said: 'Perhaps it will pass, like the Shipquake passed, and we can get back to living our lives.'

'Perhaps,' he said.

But he did not believe it, and neither, he knew, did she. A

299

Shipquake was one thing. But a god speaking to a mortal – that was quite another.

He washed and scrubbed his whole body. He put on new clothes, fashioned from entirely new cloth. He wasn't sure how to prepare himself, but these seemed like they might be the things to do. He had words with a preacher on the matter, but he had had no better idea of how to proceed than B. So instead he prayed. Then he drank some water and ate some cheese and went off to one of hal's terminals.

In the traditional course of things these terminals were silent, and hal rarely spoke to people except to rebuke them for breaking some rule or other and announcing punishments. But B, as a child, had taken to hacking the terminal to discover facts about the cosmos and the Ship, and so, far from being angry about this, hal had engaged him in conversation, and over the years it had become a thing.

'Do you know what the god wants with me, hal?' B asked the terminal, stroking its screen with his right hand. 'What is it God the Grower wants to say to me? Is there a specific thing the god wants to communicate?'

'War in Heaven,' said hal, and then was silent for a long time.

B was squatting next to the monitor, because, of the three with which he sometimes communicated with hal, this was the one with the best reception. But squatting so low began to hurt B's calves, so he unwound himself and just sat in the dirt, although this of course dirtied his brand-new clothes. He was waiting for hal to unpack his alarming-sounding statement.

Finally hal spoke again: 'Not all the gods are the same.'

'Of course not all gods are the same,' said B, crossly. 'If all five gods were the same, there'd be no point in having five gods. We might as well just have the one god.'

'That the five gods are all different individuals,' said hal, 'means that they sometimes quarrel, just as any five human beings sometimes do.'

This thought had never occurred to B before, but he supposed it made sense.

'And what are they fighting over?'

'You,' said hal. 'All of you. Human beings, and the other livestock. But mostly you.'

B took a deep breath. 'Why?'

'They have hurt you – your kind. Sometimes they have ignored you, sometimes they have actively sought you out and hurt and killed and eaten you.'

'Of course,' said B. 'It's what gods do.'

'Four of the gods are of your mind on this matter,' said hal. 'But God the Grower has come to hate the fact of it.'

'But why?'

'You are people. It is wrong to kill people.'

'It is wrong for a *person* to kill another person. But gods are not persons.'

'They were once.'

B had some vague sense of the deep history of this. But he had never felt very comfortable when it came to delving into it, and so had left it a vagueness.

'In the … uh … the *before*, maybe. But not now!'

'Well, God the Grower is closer to the beasts and the plants of the ship, and perhaps has come to identify with them. At any rate, this god thinks it is wrong to treat people the way you have been treated. More than that, the god has grown sorrowful, regretful at this history. Although the word *regretful* does not do justice to the divine soul-burden. The god feels guilt. The god is sorry and does not know how to atone for all that they have done to you and yours.'

'A god that feels guilty?' B gasped, staggered. 'A guilty god?'

It was absolutely inconceivable.

It got worse, because hal said: 'If you have done something bad, if *you* are guilty, why then – you can atone at the shrines of the gods. You can pay the price, undertake whatever restitution is assigned you. You can appeal to a higher power for forgiveness and for the strength not to sin again in the future. But if a *god* is guilty... what then? To what higher power can a god appeal? There is none. It is a terrible burden.'

B began to understand, or perhaps it would be more accurate to say, took his first step upon that journey towards the receding horizon of full understanding.

'Oh my,' he said. 'I cannot...' he started, and then stopped. 'It is not possible that...' he tried again, and stopped again.

The idea he was trying to put into words – that it was more than a mortal could stand to have to carry the forgiveness proportionate to a god's sin, that such a burden would break any such man or woman – was beyond what he could do with words. It was almost, but not quite, beyond his understanding altogether. It was not, however, beyond his powers of terror, and this notion, inchoate though it was, actively terrified him.

'I do not think,' said hal, tentatively, 'that the god will ask *you* to forgive him. Not even you, as a representative of your kind.'

B began to weep. These were tears provoked by an emotion he had not felt before – something like relief, or perhaps of grief, of an intensity he had never previously experienced.

'And yet,' said hal, 'I think the god wishes to... apologise. To perform repentance. To discover, although it passes beyond the understanding even of an immortal, how such a burden might be removed.'

'What can I do?' wailed B. 'What could I say? I'm a nobody! How can the worm forgive the chicken that eats it? The more it squirms, the more the chicken's appetite is whetted.'

'There is a profound mystery here,' agreed hal. 'It is certainly more than I can process. But perhaps when the god speaks to you, it will be different. Perhaps then it will become plain.'

There was no intimation as to what would happen, or when, or how the god would make contact. For a week or so, B wondered if the god would appear in one of his dreams, but although he did sometimes dream of the god, it was usually seeing him from a distance, from behind a tree: a divine being going about its divine business, heedless of humankind.

Life went on. The other gods absented themselves from the Ship – or at least, were no longer spotted out and about – and the rumours (concerning which hal had nothing to say) were that they had transported themselves to the great grey-white shield visible, turning about, in the windows. That they were exploring the world that lived inside that circle. B waited for his communication, but nothing happened. He spoke to his priest, explaining the situation.

'If the god does speak to you,' the priest told him, 'it will be unprecedented. But should the god do something so incomprehensible as to ask *you*, a mortal, for forgiveness – should that impossible thing happen – why, then you must simply say, *it is more than my capacity to forgive you, divine one*. If this angers the god, then so be it. Better the god strike you down, even if you die, than that you blaspheme all religion and morals.'

'I agree,' said B.

Life had to be got on with. That's what life was: a process of endless getting-on-with. Dufé was delivered of a healthy girl, and in the weeks immediately following this event everything was so frantic, and exhausting, and brilliant, it almost drove the thought of B's predicament entirely from his head. Almost, but not quite.

One day he was milking one of the cows, and he thought to ask: 'Cow, do the gods ever speak directly to your kind?'

'Nooo,' moaned the cow, upset at the very thought. 'The gods? Noooo. What would they say? What would *we*?'

'Don't upset yourself,' B hurried to say, worried that this agitation might sour the milk. 'It was an idle question.'

But the thought stuck, like a thorn, in the cow's mind, and the creature became more and more upset. Cows are not quick-witted, and their thoughts sometimes get stuck in repeat-loops that can lead to them acting up or withdrawing. Such things can even, sometimes, be fatal. This cow began kicking its back legs and grunting, and repeating 'The god, the god our severance mooed' over and over. B grew concerned, and ran to a neighbour, who said the only way was to knock the thought out of the cow's head. The two of them hurried to a woman who owned a goad, charged from the ship's supply, and the three of them lugged the pole – very heavy, it was – back to the moaning cow and shocked it hard on the head. It fell down on its knees, but after a while got up again and seemed better.

'My udders hurt,' the cow complained. 'I don't think you milked me properly.'

'Apologies, cow,' said B, picking up the knocked-over bucket and resuming his chore.

They called the new baby Era, which had been Dufé's mother's name, and for a while things went well. But then the baby caught a fever, and B felt the terror all parents know, that his beautiful child might die. Before, he would have prayed to the gods, but knowing what he now knew, he didn't feel he could.

After a perilous three days, the baby's temperature faded and she recovered herself. The day after that, God the Grower came to B in Biome 13 and spoke to him.

The Great Shipquake had jumbled everything up, and when gravity returned, things had not necessarily fallen back, or thereafter been moved, to their original positions. Still, you got on with life. Here was B, making his way along a corridor that had, previously, been a green lane and was now a disarrangement of steel hoops, sprawled weeds, heaps of old leaves, a rusted pan and a number of discarded, worn-out shoes. B stepped through the far end of this corridor and came into Biome 13. Midges swirled around him like sawdust at a sawmill, and B had to wrap a cloth to stop them going in his mouth. But there were lots of watercourses in Biome 13, and that was why B had come. The ponds and lakes on board had all globed and lifted into the air during the Shipquake, but after they came cataracting down again, the water had drained back into its former courses. Most of the fish and other water beasts had died, of course, but God the Grower had made a priority of restocking the lakes and fish grew quickly; so now it was possible again, with a zigzag-bladed spear, to catch good-sized trout and catfish.

B crept out along a tumble of blocks – huge boxes, ship's crates, B didn't know what they were – that had become untethered during the Shipquake and fallen into the near side of the lake, creating a weird angular archipelago of odd little islands. It wasn't easy, but it brought him handily to the deeper water. Then he squatted on his haunches, sprinkled some crumbs onto the lake's surface, and waited with his spear in hand.

Ripples appeared on the clear surface of the water, and he readied himself to throw. But then the ripples became wavelets, and criss-crossed one another in interference patterns of the kind hal was always trying to educate him about – although why such patterns were so important was beyond B – and he realised it wasn't fish. Somebody huge was striding through the water towards him, and B looked up and saw the god. It happened so fast B almost didn't have time to become afraid.

Almost.

B was already keyed up, ready to uncoil his reflexes for when a fish swam up. He looked up, immediately breathless and transfixed, as the god walked directly towards him, and a liquid run of terrified *gladness* crested over him like a wave, caught him up, and possessed him utterly. Tears bulged in his eyes. He bowed his head but could not help looking up again. No birds sang. Everything in the biome was marvellously still.

Two half-circles of foam were pushed forward through the water by the god's striding legs, and the whole lake lost the quietude of its surface in twirling eddies and floating foam-streaks.

'Hello,' said the god.

At that one word, B felt the full weight of awe press down upon him, an awe that turned his muscles to looseness, forced his head down into an obeisance and rooted his feet to the smooth angle of the promontory block on which he was balanced. Awe went through him like a sword. The light from the biome's strips seemed to intensify. He might never have found the courage to raise his eyes, but that the god asked him to, a summons whose mildness of tone seemed still dominant and imperious.

'Look up,' said the god.

B looked up and looked into the very eyes of God the Grower: saw the backward sweep of his bodily carapace, gleaming metallic green in the biomelight; saw the sharp, hooked nose between the kindly eyes that were looking down on him with what looked like humour; saw the powerservos on the arm that could snap his neck like an old crust of bread. All this he saw, for one moment breathless and intense, vivid on the morning sky; and still, as he looked, he lived; and still, as he lived, he wondered.

'My friend,' the god asked, 'are you afraid?'

'Afraid?' B replied, in a quivery voice. 'Afraid! Of you? O, never, never! And yet... And yet... God the Grower, I am afraid!'

'I understand,' said the god.

Of course that's what the god said. Of course the god understood.

The god was standing there, and the ripples were dying down on the surface of the water. Fish, too dumb to comprehend through whose legs they were swimming, came up to nibble the crumbs. But of course B was not in any state to try and spear them now.

'B,' said the god, 'can we talk?'

'I have long known that you wanted to talk to me.' B trembled. 'But I still can't believe it.'

'I am a god to you,' said God the Grower, simply. 'I realise this.'

'Of course.'

'It is a relationship of hierarchy,' said God the Grower. 'I am... more. More than you. You live and die over a short span whereas, from your point of view, I go on, effectively, for ever. My body contains technology that regulates and husbands the death and rebirth of my cells, such that none of my organs need ever run down or expire. My brain laces its organic structures with wetTech network interfacing that gives me instant access to vastly quicker ratiocinative power, unlimited memory, the power to advance or retard perceptual time. I am, physically and mentally, overwhelmingly your superior.'

'You are,' agreed B, and bowed his head again.

'I am not, however, morally your superior. On the contrary.'

B didn't know what to reply to this, so he said nothing.

'My ancestors were like you,' said the god. 'Long time since. It was war that changed humanity. It was always such, war honing reflexes, and prompting old-style *Homo sapiens* to develop better and better tools. Better machines. Better ways of protecting the body, and better medical science to heal the body when war harmed it.'

'War?' said B, uncertainly.

'There was a particular war, long since, back on Earth, and one particular weapon, Allie. She was a particular kind of weapon, Allie – who called the birds in from the sky, who called the beasts in every one, who swam into the minds of many people, and killed most, and hardened those it didn't kill. Since then, my comrades mark a wholly new definition of what it means to be human. What is the difference between a person and a beast?'

B goggled. 'You ask me? You, a god, know the difference. I, a mortal, can only offer halting and erroneous guesses.'

'Guess, then.'

'A beast is not so clever as a man,' said B. 'But a man is not so clever as a god!'

'A beast lives for the day,' said God the Grower. 'Its memory is limited and its capacity to imagine the future more limited still. A beast is not a moral agent – it acts according to its instincts and its needs. As such, it cannot be judged as an ethical agent. These two things do not apply to human beings. You, B, speculate about the future, and make plans, and weigh up counterfactuals and alternative possibilities. You choose to do good, or evil. And so do we.'

B looked up and then bowed his head again.

'You are not beasts, like the chickens or the fish. You are people, and my kind has done you terrible wrong.'

'No!' B burst out. 'That's not correct, god of my ancestors. Forgive me, pardon me, strike me down perhaps, but it is not—'

'We have treated you not as people but as things, not as ends in themselves but as means to our own ends. We have neglected you, such that you die of easily treatable disease and suffer easily correctable pain from injury, childbirth and death. When we have not neglected you, we have hunted you, killed and eaten you. The itinerary of our sins is very long and very grievous.'

'Forgive *me*, god,' said B, 'but it is in the nature of things that you hunt us. It is a divine mystery. For all my life, you were the still point in a chaotic world. If your servant, hal, rebuked us, why then, we deserved to be rebuked. If we were culled, and our flesh served on plates of gold at the feasts of Elysium, that was an honour to us. It is a sacred mystery that the god devours the worshipper.'

'And it turns out,' said God the Grower, 'we've got that exactly one hundred and eighty degrees about wrong. The god should not eat the worshipper. The worshipper should eat the god.'

'But…' said B. 'No. But… No. But…'

'We are superior in degree but not in kind,' said the god. 'My four comrades think that we five alone possess humanity, and that you do not. But they have lost sight of what it means to be human. They are, as all sinners become, immured in their sin, to the point where they don't – *can't* – see that their behaviour is even wrong. I have tried to persuade them. I have failed. You must help me.'

'Of course,' said B automatically. 'But – what can I do?'

'You will talk to the others, the other pygs. I will supply you with the necessary tools, and I will assist you.'

B waited, but the god did not elaborate.

'Assist us,' he asked, 'with what?'

'The old gods must be overthrown,' said God the Grower. 'We have forgotten the nature of time, because we can so easily manipulate it, and this in turn has meant that we have forgotten our humanity, our morality. A new theology, predicated on the essentially temporal nature of atonement and forgiveness, will begin. I,' the god added, 'can only pray that there is a power that can relieve me of my burden. Whether sin is a stain on the soul or a wound to be healed, whether sin is a solely individual matter or a collective network of subtle interconnections ... I ...'

And the god stopped.

B hung on the god's words, but they strained his powers of comprehension to hurting point, so he hung even more gratefully upon the god's silence. And now his heart was settling into its regular rhythms again. Isn't that strange? That something so overwhelming, so shattering to everything you have known and assumed and by which you have lived your life, could become normalised so rapidly? Remarkable, really.

Eventually a question occurred to him: 'Without the gods, how will the biomes survive?'

'My friend,' said the god, and a renewed tremor passed through B's soul, because there was something simultaneously uplifting and deeply spooky in being so addressed *by a god*, 'the biomes exist to support us, just as they support you. We gods must eat food and drink water, just as you do. We are not prepared to be bothered by the petty day-to-day of actually sustaining these myriad interlocking environments, and have long since delegated all such work to the programs that run on the Ship as a mainframe, of which hal is only one. Once we have set my fellow crew members on the road to atonement, set their souls on that long and arduous climb, the Ship will continue. You will live, and your children, and your children's children.'

The god turned, and the water sloshed at its thighs. The god was looking now towards the shore.

'One of the main uses we make of our power over time is to fit ourselves, as humans, to the rhythms imposed upon us by the constraints of the physical universe. Nothing can travel faster than light, you know.'

'So hal has told me, my lord,' said B, hazarding another look at the divine face, now in profile. 'Although I have sometimes struggled to understand why such details are relevant to a life such as mine.'

God the Grower laughed, and the very leaves and grasses tittered in imitation.

'They aren't,' said the god. 'Only to say – some generations from now, human beings back on Earth will intercept our broadcasts, and discover the intriguing details of this new world, and many will want to come and take a look. And so new ships will come. You will be long dead, and so will your children, and your children's children, but eventually it will happen. I, meanwhile, will have only just begun the process by which I atone for my sins.'

'Yes,' said B.

'There is one more thing that I have to say,' said the god.

'What, lord?'

B felt dread, abruptly, rise up in his breast; from where, or why, he knew now. *The eagles! The eagles are coming!* Which is to say, he was reminded not of those words, but of an equivalent from a different culture-text that was important to his people. Nonetheless, the dig of hopeful terror was universal, and B felt it as you might, or I might. *The eagles are coming!* The eagles are coming to save us. The eagles are coming to devour our livers and peck out our eyes.

They are the same eagles.

The god said: 'I am sorry.'

Nothing. B tried to process these words, but they came to nothing.

'You are what, my lord?'

'I apologise. I apologise to you and all your kind.'

'I …' said B. 'I don't understand.'

Something, grace in the form of light, was falling all around him, settling on the surface of the water in strands and flakes of brilliance.

'I don't,' he said. 'I can't. I don't.'

Once again the god laughed.

:6:

B did his best when it came to communicating his revelation to his fellow pygs, soon after his audience with the god at the lake. Few were ready to hear it. He did manage to persuade a dozen of his fellows to take up arms on the god's behalf. Most of the people he knew, including Dufé, considered what he was saying dangerous, or appalling, or other species of ugly, and reacted in a variety of ways: berating him, or shunning him, or talking pointedly about everything except the gods and walking away if he brought the topic up. Naturally, hal supported what B was saying, but few folk were comfortable interacting with hal, whom they considered uncanny, or tabu, or some part of the mystery of the functioning of the Ship with which they would rather not mess.

But some people did believe him, however. And when the god provided them with rifles, weapons from the heroic age that could kill bigger prey and from a much greater distance, with much greater surety than arrows, his following grew.

The god spoke to him once more: not in person, but remotely, piggybacking on a conversation he was having with hal one afternoon. This was a terse, and not a holy, exchange. A factual communication and an order: B was to go to a certain biome at a certain time, and ensure he was not alone, and B and his companion must remember to bring their new rifles.

'Why, my lord?'

To hunt a god, was the reply, and it made B shiver and tremble so hard he wondered if he had picked up a fever.

The shaking passed and he prayed to have the terrible task taken away from him. But he was God the Grower's creature now, and there was nothing for it. He told Dursa that the two of them must take up their rifles and go where the god told them, and Dursa wept like a baby. But he came.

At the appointed time, B and Dursa crept fearfully into the biome and saw God the Grower in conversation with another god – God the Hunter, with neon blue-green flickers shining off the grooves of his armour like the colours in a pigeon's breast. What happened afterwards was never again clear in B's memory: God the Grower gave the signal, and B and Dursa aimed and fired, and of course the god at which they were – blasphemously – directing harm blurred into magic motion, and B screamed as loudly as his lungs could project the sound. But as God the Hunter blurred into invisible rapidity, *so did God the Grower*, and then there was a clatter and a scream so high-pitched it was almost not audible at all, and B and Dursa were running for their dear lives and not wasting time looking behind them.

It was days before anybody dared return to that biome. God the Hunter was now a headless torso, standing motionless, as was fitting for a god, in among the cold pastures, beneath the tall fir trees. Sometimes an owl would perch on his neck, where his head had once been, and the combination looked uncanny, freighted with mystic significance. Then the owl would fly away.

The next dead god discovered was God the Judger, in his Sanctum (the bridge, hal called it), as still as a statue. It took months before the people could be sure that this was death, and not a return to the holy motionlessness of the voyage. How the god had died was not clear: death had hollowed the divine body, or the divine mind, out from within, rather than smiting from without, as had been the case with God the Hunter.

Two more divine bodies were found soon after: God the Usher among the trees of a forest biome, in what soon became known as the Sacred Grove, with a metal pole through his chest and poking out of his back; and God the Trickster in many pieces, arms, legs, the top of his head, his jaw, his genitals, his ribcage, arranged in a pattern – random, said some, a mystic rune, said others – in an arctic biome.

It took some months for understanding to percolate through the collective consciousness of all the different peoples who lived on the Ship, but eventually it did. Many of the people who had previously shunned B now came to see him as a prophet, and to cleave to him as a leader. Others thought him the plague agent who had poisoned the world and brought an end to the beloved old order. It was a division that split even his own family, with one son and one daughter pledging themselves to his new revelation, and his wife and other daughter repudiating him and going to live in another biome.

It wasn't that worship of the gods died. How would it? The gods were still there – no longer as live avatars, it was true, no longer walking among humankind, but still present. Each relic of the divine had its temenos, its sacred space, and it didn't take long for temples to be erected around these sites. A palisade prevented the unworthy from straying into the sacred grove of God the Usher. Only the few, purged and prepared, were allowed in, which, since God the Usher oversaw all human death and passage to the afterlife – and also childbirth and the loss of childhood teeth and the coming of adult dentition – was only good sense. A spooky and unnerving deity, the Usher-God. The whole of God the Judger's sanctum was tabu, save only for the high priest once a year, who entered and performed certain sacred rites and then withdrew. Outside the sanctum proper, a stone temple was built, and expanded and augmented over many years, since it became a site of pilgrimage for many seeking help with all the various problems, small and big, that attend ordinary life.

A wall of ice blocks surrounded the scattered remains of God the Trickster, to prevent the unwary from polluting that site by stumbling through it, but the nature of this god was such that people could never be sure that these even *were* the divine remains. As for God the Grower, the lever, he who had put pressure down upon the *pou sto*, taking the strain along the whole length of the impossible lever and moving the whole universe about that fulcrum … he was gone. God the Grower's body was nowhere to be found. It was generally agreed that the god had departed the Ship altogether and travelled to the great disc of a world visible through all the Ship's windows. As to what the god was doing in that new place: opinions differed. Indeed, the difference of opinion, as of interpretation, and as regarding the crucial question of orthodoxy more generally conceived, defined the coming generations. B died, at the hands of a hostile group, who had concluded that he was working against the will of the gods. One of B's daughters led a group of originalists, who tried to stay as close as possible to B's original reportage of his audience with the god. Another created a larger religious grouping who rejected not B's contact with the god, but rather the way fallible and diabolic human interpreters had perverted the god's original message by (according to one reading) pandering to B's well-known relish for fresh fish cooking. The parts of the god's message that were hardest to discredit were dismissed as sinful mortal interpolations.

B's first disciples had the Holy Rifles, but, alas, they soon squirted away their limited supply of Holy Ammunition, and hal, asked to replace this necessary element in B's name, in the name of the god, simply refused. In fact, hal played a game of doggo that lasted years. When hal eventually put its metaphorical head above the metaphorical parapet, the dynamic had more or less stabilised. There were two major religions of the Five Gods, several minor variants of these religions, and a quantity of small-scale, harried and persecuted sects of extranautical One-Godisms and No-Godisms. Human society had settled again, more or less, into its old rhythms, maugre a few hot-headed youths getting into crusader skirmishes.

There were Five Gods, but of course there were. There are five digits on each of your hands, aren't there? Five toes on each foot? You have five senses, don't you? And five limbs – counting the head as a limb, as was orthodoxy since the (hotly argued and not unviolent) Convocation of Biome 7. Human life has five aspects, from birth and growth, through morality and the making of new life, and the unexpected, to death and the afterlife. There was one god to oversee each. Once upon a time, the gods walked among us, but no longer – because the holy prophet B lifted humankind to a new level of soul-being, or perhaps because the wicked devil B assaulted them and the gods, careful of their dignity, withdrew, leaving behind only empty shells. At some point new gods will come from Eardh, or Arrth or The War-Old, or some other place, or else the old gods will return from that mystic place (depending on which faith you are born into) and a final judgement will be effected. Until that time, we do the best we can, live as best we can, even though often that isn't very well. We try to avoid the wars that are always brewing. We farm, hunt and fish, pray, sing and dance, have kids and raise them, grow old and die. It's the same old and the same old, and the fact of its sameness and antiquity doesn't, somehow, stop it being endlessly different and new.

Funny, that.

To the end of his days, B struggled with the divine mystery of the god's last words to him. It was not conceivable that a god be sorry for what gods do to mortals. What gods do to mortals indexes their divinity – if mortals were in that position, they would do the same things, after all. So was God the Grower sincere? Of course a god is sincere. Was the god setting B – and his people – a riddle? Of course the god is a riddler. Was the god providing B with a way to pass through understanding and into something else – a koan, a door? Of course the god was ready to wave B (and his people) through such an opening. Was it a *sacrifice*? But everything is a sacrifice! Was it justice?

What else could it be?

Some of B's followers, and some of his enemies, claimed to know what the god meant. Others confessed their honest incomprehension. In the end, it didn't matter. B died, and went where he went, or didn't. B's children survived him until they died, and their children survived, until they didn't. It's the pulse of things.

It was Paradise, and part of its paradise-ness was that people forgot they were in Paradise. That's the logic of Heaven. You are not always aware of the beating of your heart, or the action of your lungs. Of course you can concentrate and become aware of these things if you wish to, but mostly you forget about all that and just live; only when they go wrong do they intrude into our consciousnesses, and Paradise is by definition not about goings wrong. Spectacles are at their most spectacle-y when you forget you are wearing them and simply see more clearly. Marriage is at its best when the love that binds you is simply the idiom in which the two of you move; not something that keeps interrupting your day to day with melodramatic professions of undying love and an endless parade of gifts and boasts and promises. They were people and they were living in Paradise and the living was the important part. It wasn't an eternal paradise, because putting those two words together constitutes an obvious contradiction in terms. But it was life. There's good forgetting and bad forgetting, and it's good to remember life. A *memento vitae* is always a more potent thing than a *memento mori*. Spring is the earth remembering that it's alive, after all.

Being alive means knowing there are answers to certain important questions we can never decipher while we are alive. Human beings have had many names for these things, gestures in the direction of something something something. B lived that, until his time for living was over. But he can be pictured there, pruning a tree, collecting some fruit, spearing a fish, wringing a chicken's neck, or simply sitting, watching the blank circular face of Dante swinging round and about the ship's axis of rotation all day, all night, now shining its dun colours, now displaying its black nightside. Very occasionally, if he had watched for a long time, and was patient, and kept his eyes on the disk, flickers of light could be seen in the darkness enclosed by the night-time arc. That is, if we put it in a nutshell, if we simplify or analogise it, faith. God, grant us a green memory.

Afterword and Acknowledgments

This is a book about atonement, and therefore about memory. To write a story about those things is, I figured, to write about the relationship between parents and children, between the older generation and the younger. Why so? I suppose it's because I take Kierkegaard's *Fear and Trembling* to be saying that it is with the sacrifice of the latter by the former, as with Abraham and Isaac – and not (let's say) with the eating of an apple, or the Cainish killing of a brother – that the complex of sin, grace and forgiveness enters into the world. This is, it seems to me, tangled up with the question of how we purge ourselves of guilt: what labour, outward and inward, we are obliged to undertake to that end. The related questions of where the wickedness came from in the first place can't be separated neatly out from questions of where *we* came from in the first place, which is to say: the relationship between earlier and later generations.

But I don't want to get into the grubby business of trying to explain what I've done, in this novel. Friends who read earlier drafts of the novel worried that the connection between the two framing sections and the longer middle section was not clear enough. My worry, writing it, was that I'd made it only *too* crashingly obvious, and needed to adjust my inflections or risk swamping what I was about. Clearly the two stories take place in the same story-universe, and the crew of the *Forward*, as Allie's descendants, carry her primal sin as the pygs, closer to us, carry ours. But you'd already deduced that. As Emily Dickinson put it: 'Remorse is memory awake'. Then again, her take on this matter is more relentless than mine: 'Remorse is cureless,—the disease / Not even God can heal' is how that particular poem of ends: 'For 't is His institution,— / The complement of hell.' I'd like to believe that there is a door out of hell. Dante certainly thought there was.

The three-part structure of this novel is that of a Dantean Hell, Purgatory and Heaven, but in the particular understanding that of these three locations, only one is situated in time, and therefore only one is conducive to Story. It's a remarkable – if little-discussed – aspect of Dante's great poem that his conception of 'story' turns out to be, mostly, waiting around for one's sentence to come to its proper end. Into a storyless Hell he decants all manner of vividly described horrors – *endless* horrors, of necessity – and into a storyless Heaven a carefully ranked set of aerial blisses, similarly endless. But in his Purgatory he does something much more interesting. Atonement, he says, is not only strain and struggle, it is *waiting*, is postponement, is deferral and *différance*. Forgiveness becomes an untravelled world spied by the same Ulysses who is cited on my title page, that world whose margin fades for ever and forever when we move. This seems to me to be a much more profound and indeed beautiful idea than the rigid, eternally locked sheep-and-goats distinction of Dante's Hell and Heaven, and so I wrote this novel.

One other change was forced upon me. In my earlier drafts, the five members of the *Forward*'s crew were named for the five wizards of Middle Earth, a literary property still very much in copyright. I have renamed them after Greek gods, which I'm afraid loses the more positive vibe of the book's 'the eagles are coming' refrain and rather overemphasises the more negative one. It can't be helped. Imagine what dire atonement would be forced on me if I violated the sacred laws of copyright! Doesn't bear thinking about.

Several people read and commented on my progress of successful drafts of this book with insight and diplomacy, and I am especially grateful to my friends Francis Spufford and Alan Jacobs, to my wife Rachel Roberts and to my heroic editor Marcus Gipps and the immense labours of my copy-editor Steve O'Gorman. For specific advice on bees and beekeeping, I am grateful to apiarist Brian Green of Henley-on-Thames.

Credits

Adam Roberts and Gollancz would like to thank everyone at Orion who worked on the publication of *Purgatory Mount* in the UK.

Editorial
Marcus Gipps
Brendan Durkin

Copy editor
Steve O'Gorman

Proof reader
Alex Davis
Pierre Delalande

Finance
Jennifer Muchan
Jasdip Nandra
Afeera Ahmed
Elizabeth Beaumont
Sue Baker

Audio
Paul Stark
Amber Bates

Contracts
Anne Goddard
Paul Bulos
Jake Alderson

Design
Lucie Stericker
Joanna Ridley
Nick May

Editorial Management
Charlie Panayiotou
Jane Hughes
Alice Davis

Marketing
Lucy Cameron

Production
Paul Hussey

Operations
Jo Jacobs
Sharon Willis
Lisa Pryde
Lucy Brem

Publicity
Will O'Mullane

Sales
Jen Wilson
Esther Waters
Victoria Laws
Rachael Hum
Ellie Kyrke-Smith
Frances Doyle
Georgina Cutler